to Emily
from Lauren

I love you so much!

to Emily
from Lauren,

I love you so much!

BOOKS BY BETH BROWER

The Books of Imirillia

The Queen's Gambit
The Ruby Prince
The Wanderer's Mark

The Q

The Beast of Ten

THE QUEEN'S GAMBIT

Rhysdon Press

THE QUEEN'S

BOOK ONE OF IMIRILLIA

GAMBIT

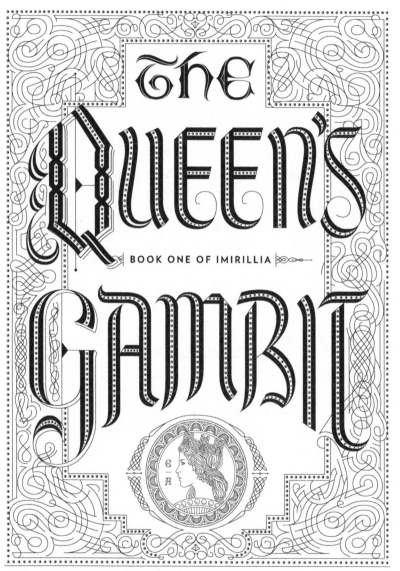

BETH BROWER

Published by Rhysdon Press

Printed in the United States of America

Publisher's Cataloging-in-Publication data Brower, Beth. The Queen's Gambit : Book One of Imirillia / Beth Brower ; p. cm. ISBN 978-0692665930. Fantasy. 2. Adventure and Adventurers —Fiction. I. Title.

Third Edition 2017
10 9 8 7 6 5 4 3

ISBN-13: 978-0692665930
ISBN-10: 0692665935
Text was set in Adobe Garamond

Cover by Kevin Cantrell Design
www.kevincantrell.com

To my parents,
who taught their children what is most important.

And who also gave us the book closet.
We often stayed awake reading after you had put us to bed.

But I think you already knew that...

Nation will war against nation, burdening the innocent; their battles birth death, and the midwives of the Illuminating God cover their ears for the cry of it.

—*Seventh Mark of the Second Scroll*

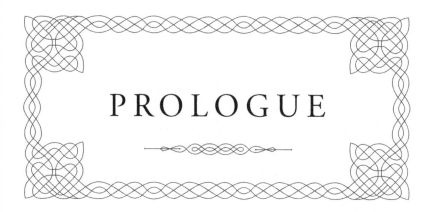

PROLOGUE

He crossed the courtyard in silent agitation. The darkness was thick, and sounds rose from the city beyond the walls. The stones of the lower courtyard, pressed and smooth, seemed to bend down beneath the heavy night that had fallen. He entered the stables to find Dantib and Annan waiting. Without looking at either, he approached his white horse. Hegleh had been saddled and was impatient for their journey. In the next stall over, Refigh, his favored stallion, pouted. He called to Refigh, touching his hand to the horse's face with brusque affection.

"I won't be gone long," he said to the horse, defending his leave-taking.

He watched as Dantib, the old stable master, continued preparing Hegleh, then he turned ruefully towards Annan, his comrade-in-arms and, consequently, his closest friend.

"You must ride quick to catch the company gone ahead," Annan said.

He offered Annan the hint of a grimace, lined with challenge.

"What is it?" Annan asked. "You have words waiting on the edge of your tongue."

He raised an eyebrow and gave a dangerous smile. "No words, my friend," he answered, "only obedience to my sovereign."

"Do you ride for your emperor unwillingly?"

"The emperor of Imirillia, and his sons"—he grimaced as he spoke—"demand a high price of this continent."

"And you believe your payment for the service you offer to be—?" Annan asked.

"Glory and honor," he replied sardonically.

Dantib now opened Hegleh's stall, leading the white mare out and handing the reins to Annan. Then, Dantib took his young master by the arm and walked him to the door of the stable. With his ancient voice quavering, he asked, "What name will you go by?"

The young man shrugged with irritation against the concern in Dantib's voice. After a halting pause, he spoke the name aloud.

"Wil. I'll go by Wil," he said.

"A name of your own." Dantib nodded, approving.

"A name of my own," he repeated, more to himself than to the old man.

"Is that all you travel with?" Annan asked.

Swinging his meticulously arranged saddlebags off his shoulder and onto his horse, he glanced down at himself: black clothing in the manner of the Southerners, cloak, straight sword, various smaller weapons, and a satchel strung across his back.

"What else should I want?" he asked.

"This, dear boy." Dantib held out a thin, black leather band, braided simply together, as knotted and worn as the old man's hands. "Hold out your right arm, and I will seal it upon you, if you accept it."

He did as Dantib asked, humility fighting a sour wish to be gone.

"I see you've removed all your other Safeeraah," the stable master stated in patient disapproval.

"Clearly," he said. "How could I possibly wear them on this journey? I bind myself to the covenants, nonetheless." He looked towards Annan. "They're in my armor trunk. Bring them with you."

Annan gave a quick nod.

"Well," Dantib said, clicking his tongue as he secured the humble leather band around his young master's wrist. "You must not forget the Safeeraah I give you now. Listen carefully." Dantib closed his eyes. *"Though I wander, I am the deep well; I seek transcendence by honor, as the seven stars."*

He waited for the old man to open his eyes, then he repeated the words earnestly, staring at the braided and knotted band around his right wrist: *"Though I wander, I am the deep well; I seek transcendence by honor, as the seven stars."* He lifted his wrist to his brow, then to his lips, kissing the band, then to his heart, sealing the Safeeraah and his covenant to it.

Dantib offered a thoughtful expression before speaking again. "I also see you have hidden the mark of your house," he said. "But do not think you can hide who you are; your honor is evident in your face. For that, I am glad."

"For that, I might lose my head," he said, giving the stable master a glance before taking Hegleh's reins from Annan and leading her from the stable into the heavy darkness beyond. Catching the saddle with a light hand, he pulled himself gracefully astride. Hegleh tossed her head in anticipation. Dantib and Annan waited, watching him.

Closing his eyes, he spoke a prayer of journey. The words felt weighted and significant on his tongue. When his prayer was complete, he exhaled, his fingers tugging at the swath of black cloth that he'd tied securely around his left forearm, covering what his skin revealed.

"Is he watching?" he asked in a low voice.

Dantib nodded, his eyes flickering toward a balcony above the courtyard. "Do not let him be your mind. Remember, transcendence by honor, and you have chosen honor."

Hegleh snorted and pawed the ground, and so he gave in to her impatience. Looking away from his friends, he cried out, sending his horse flying through the hastily opened gates. Not once did his eyes stray towards the high balcony where his father stood watching him. Not once did his heart question his leave-taking of this place.

CHAPTER

ONE

The rules of war had been changed. Queen Eleanor wanted to know why.

She sat atop a dusty table in the potting shed on the far back stretches of the castle grounds, surrounded by clay pots and plant starts, leaning towards the morning light coming through the diamond-paned windows. In her hands were the latest papers of state needing to be reviewed: reports sent from every fen in Aemogen, as well as the amended Marion constitution, having arrived from her ambassador in Marion City the night before.

The fen reports had been dutifully read first, but it was the Marion papers that had kept Eleanor awake. Marion was their strongest ally—as Aemogen was seabound to the east and south, and mountainbound to the north and west. There was only one entrance into her country, and it was through a mountain pass that connected Marion to Aemogen.

It was not uncommon practice for Marion to alter their amendments of state to suit their own advantage. King Staven had changed the rhetoric of his trade agreements, in an effort to glean the advantage for his country, many times over the years. This was never a surprise. But the amendments on allies and war had not been altered these past one hundred years, since the warring rulers of Aemogen and Marion had brokered a hard-won peace. And now the rules had been changed.

Having woken from a sleep she had never truly given herself to, for the strange dreams of the night, Eleanor had brought the papers of state with her, leaving them in the potting shed as she'd worked in the predawn gardens, fussing in the cold, sticky soil to ease the questions of her mind. Eleanor sorted her thoughts as she cleared away the winter debris, the forgotten, hollowed stocks of plants from the autumn previous, careful around the shoots of green fighting their way out of the earth. She needed this solitude. She needed to set her mind in place before the crown was once again placed on her head.

When the weak sunlight had fallen over the walls and into the castle grounds, Eleanor had returned to the potting shed and read through the Marion constitution once more. It made no sense. Frowning, she set the papers aside. It was foolish to worry. It was also foolish, Eleanor knew, not to question. Placing her head in her hands for the space of a long breath, she then slipped off the table and set a pottery shard to keep the papers of state safe from the breeze before returning to the garden. Only another hour more and she must prepare for the morning audience.

Digging in the soil, she worked until her cheeks were flush, until her body was warm despite the brisk wind coming down from the north river. Eleanor didn't mind the wind.

"When the wind comes," her father had told her, "you don't shrink from it, you breathe deeper."

This is what Eleanor did now. Brushing her hands, she looked up, the skirts of her dress whipping about, and watched the snowbells tracing the patterns of the wind with their own light movements. They were the only flowers brave enough to bloom in the forlorn beds this soon after the snow had melted. Swaths and patches of the delicate flowers danced in the wind around Ainsley Castle. As Eleanor watched, she ran her fingers along the edge of her trowel, removing the excess mud, and brushed a loose strand of copper hair away from her face with the back of her hand.

A movement from the corner of her eye caused her to turn, twisting to the left, lifting her knees slightly off the ground as she rocked back on the balls of her feet. There, coming down the gravel path in the shadow of Ainsley Castle, was a young man Eleanor had never seen before. Brushing her hands on her skirt, she wondered who had opened the gates so early.

Pressing her lips together, she appraised the stranger. His clothing—black, all of it, with worn boots and an old cloak—betrayed him as a traveler rather than an Aemogen farmer or tradesman. His pace was easy, but his eyes were watchful as they surveyed the ancient exterior of the castle, dropped into the garden, and then settled on Eleanor's figure.

He considered her—as she considered him—and as he neared where she worked, he gave her a nod.

"Good morning," he said.

"Pleasant day," Eleanor responded, her eyebrows drawn together. It was far too early for visitors.

He was younger than she had first thought, and when he moved, it was in the loose way of a confident young man. His eyes canvassed her face a moment too long for Eleanor's personal comfort, before he looked past her toward the outer boundaries of the castle grounds.

"I could understand being a gardener on so wild a day," he said.

Eleanor straightened her back, frowning. His accent was similar to that of a Marion, yet was unfamiliar all the same, trimmed with Northern intonations. His face betrayed the features and cornflower blue eyes of the Marion people, yet his complexion caught Eleanor's curiosity: his skin was an exotic olive, sun gold and rich, like that of the men of the far North. And his hair was as dark as the ink in her inkwell, cropped shorter than she was accustomed to. The stranger took a step back from her, lifting his hands to his hips, as if comparing the grounds to some internal measure.

"I heard once," he said, interrupting her thoughts, "as a small child, that the gardens of Aemogen were incomparable. And, I admit, I always imagined them to be larger." As he adjusted his cloak, Eleanor could see a sheathed sword about his waist.

She stood.

"This garden belongs to the royal family," she said. "There are more community gardens beyond the walls, which would meet your expectations." Eleanor brushed the dirt from her fingers. "By late spring," she added, "all of Ainsley is in bloom."

"With any luck, I'll see it." He turned to face Eleanor again. "I'm hoping to remain in Aemogen for some time."

Eleanor's internal bulwark pulsed. "I admit to feeling surprise, as you appear to have come from very far." She gathered her basket and trowel as she spoke, and stepped out onto the path, lifting her chin and constructing a careful assessment of the stranger.

"I might find something worth staying for," he replied with a disarming shrug. "Travelers ofttimes do."

"Hmmm."

The young man fell into step with her as she moved towards

the garden sheds against the north wall. Eleanor looked sideways at his face.

"Excuse me for pressing," she said. "But where are you from exactly? You've a strange mix of accents. I—I'm rather curious."

"My mother came from Marion, and my father—" he said, hesitating a moment before answering tightly, "—my father came from the devil." The tension in his voice seemed to catch even him off guard, and he grimaced. "I tend to be blown by every wind myself these days." She opened her mouth to ask him how one's father could come from the devil, but he interrupted her, an unreadable expression on his face.

"I hear there is to be a spring festival," he said. "That's what has been said in the streets of Ainsley this morning."

"Yes, it is true."

"I thought I might enjoy to see it for myself," he said. "I've also heard there is a tradition of Aemogen royals harboring travelers?"

"It is an old tradition," Eleanor granted, curious how he would have heard of such a thing. The expression on the stranger's face opened up, as if he were anxious to hear more, so Eleanor continued. "You attend morning audience with the monarch, and they grant you hospitality in exchange for useful work, skill sharing, or news. Only a few have requested it in many years," she added.

They had reached the back sheds, and Eleanor set the basket beside the door, not wishing to invite this stranger in farther. His eyes wandered through the doorway, and Eleanor stepped into the threshold, brushing her hands on her skirts again, keeping his eyes from seeing the reports lying on the table.

"As I said, it is an old custom not much practiced anymore," Eleanor repeated.

The young man shrugged and returned his blue eyes to her face. They were striking at this close distance, sudden, crisp blue against his olive skin. "My mother spoke fondly enough of the custom," he continued. "I dare say I shall try." His face practically tumbled into a smile as he spoke again. "I can't imagine them saying no for the sheer possibility of a diversion. There must be little to no variance from the day-after-day life in a place like this. It's such a quaint country."

By the way he had said it, Eleanor was certain he did not consider this an advantage. She looked away from his face for a brief moment and then returned his casual manner with an icier glare than she had intended.

"You would do well," she said, "not to mention your opinions while petitioning the queen, I am sure."

He laughed and took a step away from her. "You are right. I shall remember your advice." He rubbed the back of his neck, as if remembering he had just passed a sore night.

The breeze caught the wanderer's cloak just then, lifting a strange, exotic scent into the air. It was a familiar spice, though not one native to Aemogen. Eleanor couldn't recall the name, but her pulse rose unexpectedly.

"Pardon, for being so direct," she stated bluntly, feeling done with playing castle gardener. "But how did you get in? The gardens are closed to visitors at present, and the gates should all be shut."

He fought back a grin. "Yes, but the walls were so easy to breach. You can't blame me for trying." His eyes traveled her face, and he held out his hand towards Eleanor as if to take hers. "You may call me Wil," he said.

Eleanor declined the gesture. She knew her face did not hold the friendliest of expressions. He dropped his hand, untouched.

"A great pleasure, Wil, to have met you," Eleanor offered instead. "It might be a good idea to *wait* for the gates to open the next time you wish to visit these gardens."

He acquiesced with a nod of his head, saying nothing.

"Good luck in your petition," she continued, "and in your journeys." Eleanor offered this pleasantry, feeling only a tinge of remorse for her sharpness but no more. After all, Aemogen was not a place for wanderers to entertain themselves, and she had work to be about.

As if an understanding had crossed the young man's mind, he considered Eleanor again, his left hand playing with a black leather string on his right wrist for a moment before his bearing changed. Bowing slightly, stiffly, he offered Eleanor a weighted smile.

"May you have the same," he said. He turned away, back toward the far western gate.

Eleanor watched his departure. Wil was taller than most Aemogen men, and he was clearly no farm laborer, merchant or miner. The movements of his body were strong, controlled. They were trained.

After reclaiming her papers from the potting shed, Eleanor signaled to her Queen's Own, the soldier Hastian, who stood, waiting in a blind spot, behind a pillar near a back door of the castle. He stepped quickly towards her, his face ashen, probably from watching his sovereign converse with a stranger he knew nothing about.

"Had I felt worried I would have signaled you, Hastian," Eleanor said, as he met her along the path. Hastian did not respond, which was no matter. Eleanor knew how to read his silence. "I can see that you intend to speak with Crispin about this breach in protocol," she said, as he fell into step beside her. "I intend to speak with him as well. I don't wish to see that happen again."

Then Eleanor surprised herself by looking again towards the west pathway, now empty.

"Did you shake his hand?" Edythe asked.

Edythe was setting Eleanor's hair in place for the morning audiences. Eleanor had bathed, dressed in a gown of soft green, and sought Edythe out in the records hall to ask for her help. Hastian was stationed outside the tall, arched doors, ensuring the sisters' privacy.

"Here I am, attempting to study the changes in the Marion constitution, and you keep on about this morning."

"So, you did take his hand?" Edythe said, ignoring the deflection.

"No." Eleanor shook her head.

"Don't move your head."

"I simply said it was a pleasure to make his acquaintance and wished him luck," Eleanor said. "Or something of the sort."

"Hmm." Edythe was twisting Eleanor's long braids around each other and pinning them into place. "You do realize you have a maid to do this for you?"

"I like how you do it better."

Whenever Eleanor particularly cared about her appearance, she asked for Edythe's help, as her sister had always been graced at anything requiring artistry of the hands. Edythe was, Eleanor thought—feeling the slight tug and pull on her scalp as Edythe bound her copper hair—quick at everything she tried: dancing, recital, riding, calligraphy, music. Her disposition was sun-filled and sweet, and, for good reason, Edythe was the favorite acquaintance of many.

Where Edythe excelled, Eleanor was merely proficient, but she didn't mind: she had worked for her proficiency. Persistence had taught Eleanor to become a sufficient musician, a sufficient horsewoman, and a sufficient gardener. And *f* while she was not so outwardly gifted as Edythe, her true talents were manifest in the three things she cared for most: the well-governance of her people, the well-governance of herself, and a determination for knowledge. She gave the same passion to her studies that Edythe threw into life.

"Tell me what he looks like," Edythe said, "so I'll know him if he does seek an audience." Edythe's voice broke through Eleanor's thoughts, and she looked up.

"Don't move!" Edythe said. "I'm almost finished. You didn't bring me nearly enough pins." Edythe retrieved a pin that had fallen to the ground and cleaned it with her fingers. "Well?" she said.

"You'll know the traveler immediately," Eleanor replied, fussing with a strand of stray hair while looking at a faint version of herself in the long window they used for a looking glass. Meeting the reflection of her sister's eyes, Eleanor allowed herself a quick smile. "He carries Northern blood in him: a deep olive complexion and dark hair. Yet, his eyes, his expressions, are those of a Marion. He's quite handsome for all of it."

"More so than Aedon?" Edythe asked, setting a pin too sharply against Eleanor's scalp. Grimacing, Eleanor considered what she thought to be a silly question.

"Just different," she said.

"For all his good looks"—Edythe made a subtle face—"Aedon's endless discussions of fen policy can run a touch dry."

"He's good at what he does," Eleanor defended. "And if you showed more interest in the workings of the monarchy, you might realize how intelligent his observations are." Eleanor looked down at the papers before her while Edythe finished her hair.

"Would you consider Aedon for a match?" Edythe asked slowly, as if she had been waiting to ask this question.

"I see you're determined to distract me this morning," Eleanor said, setting her work aside. "You ask if I would consider Aedon? Possibly." Eleanor leaned forward towards the window. "He has the makings of a good monarch."

"Yet?" Edythe prodded.

"Edythe, Aedon is just Aedon," Eleanor answered. "And I don't want to discuss him in this way."

"But?" Edythe's face dimpled.

"He is fair, intelligent, considerate, and balanced, despite being a little marinated in his own certainty of opinion," Eleanor said. "I honestly can't say what I think about the idea other than it's very practical. The only thing I want for certain is the company of someone who could challenge not only my thoughts but his own, while realizing he is there to support, not to manage—" Eleanor left off, thinking of her parents instead. They had done this very well, in most things, at least.

"And someone who looks like your stranger?" Edythe added, making Eleanor laugh. "Beauty is no crime," Edythe quoted, the words coming from an old Aemogen ballad. "And some beauty you never want to forget," Edythe finished, almost absentmindedly. "Now, tell me, his face? His figure?"

Giving up entirely on the Marion constitution, Eleanor

answered briskly, trying to be sport about Edythe's penchant for nonsense. "Masculine, yet graceful," she said.

"Was he confident?"

"What does it matter? I'll never see him again, beyond these few days that he passes through Ainsley."

"It may well be he has set a mark," Edythe said. "I can tell from the way you're trying to pinch disinterest into your face. It's not working; I know you too well. At least someone has caught your attention."

"I'm sure there are many young men worth noting in Aemogen, if I ever bothered leaving my desk to consider them," Eleanor defended, growing impatient. "Enough. Let me simply say he trespassed in my gardens, appeared on the edge of arrogance, and, at one point, called Ainsley and all of Aemogen *quaint.*"

"It is quaint."

"But the *way* that he said it, Edythe. As you see, none of his conversation was very impressive by any rate." Eleanor turned to face Edythe, her eyebrows knit as she mused aloud. "You do realize though, it was the first time I've ever not been known as queen." Replaying his easy conversation in her head, Eleanor pressed her lips together. Standing and shaking out her skirts, she admitted rather openly, "I may never know what that's like again."

The council had already gathered in the throne room, waiting for Eleanor's arrival. She entered through her private doors, set behind some large tapestries behind the throne. Upon her appearance, some of the council began to move towards their seats, lined perpendicularly along the west wall.

"Not many requests and grievances today, I trust," Eleanor said as she greeted Gaulter Alden, the war leader, who not only served her but had also served her father, the position more honorary than practiced.

"No more than a handful, I should hope." The old man looked tired, yet he smiled at Eleanor. "I slept fitfully last night and could use a quiet day." Foreboding pricked at Eleanor's thoughts, and she looked at Gaulter Alden. "I didn't settle well either," she said. "Dreams, echoes of images—" She waved her hand. "It was a rather long night."

"You dreamed that the audience line was infinite, I'd imagine," Gaulter Alden said and then cleared his throat. "That would cause anyone to feel melancholy when they awoke."

Eleanor raised one eyebrow in amused agreement.

"Your Majesty, Gaulter Alden," Aedon, Eleanor's head councillor, said as he came up beside her. He bowed respectfully, first to Eleanor, then to the older man. "I hope your morning has been well," he added. She knew Aedon's words were genuine. They always were.

"I've been wanting to speak with you," Eleanor said.

Gaulter Alden now faded away in a particular attitude Eleanor knew well. He was as fond of Aedon as he was of Eleanor. So, he left them alone at every possible opportunity. The chief councillor caught the meaning of the old man's disappearance, and he and Eleanor shared a glance.

"Every time," Aedon said, pulling his mouth into a resigned line.

Eleanor gave a wry smile. "As the sun rises."

"You must shock the nation and announce your engagement to someone else," he said.

Eleanor ran her finger across her bottom lip in distracted

thought. "A distant intention," she said. "How's your morning been?"

"Fine. And yours?"

Eleanor shifted the weighted sentiments of the morning inside of her. "Puzzling."

She had Aedon's attention now. His eyes moved to hers, giving her his singular focus.

"Why?" he asked.

"Have you finished reading Marion's constitution?"

Aedon shook his head. "Forgive me. I'd just begun, but the weather was so distracting, after such a long winter, that I left my work and spent more time riding than I should have." He considered her expression. "What is it? Is King Staven altering Marion trade law again?"

Aedon's expression was so dismissive that Eleanor thought King Staven could probably feel the challenge from across the mountains.

"There are some changes to their trade policies that are certainly meant to affect Aemogen," she said. "But that isn't what's kept me worried."

"If King Staven wants to bandy trading terms, it's at his own peril. We, by far, have the advantage."

"That's true," Eleanor replied, not really thinking of trade law.

"What are you worried about?"

"Finish your reading," she said. "We'll discuss it this afternoon."

"I will," Aedon said, seriously, as was most often the tone anytime he said anything. "Then I'll find you in your private chambers."

Eleanor nodded, feeling her mind relax. Aedon and Eleanor had relied on one another since her father's death, which not only had left Eleanor on the throne younger than anyone anticipated but also had abandoned a young chief councillor without the years of tutelage the king had planned to offer. Despite it all, they'd proven a formidable pair.

The noise in the room had again increased, and it was almost time for the audience to begin. Aedon walked with Eleanor to the throne.

"Now that the weather has broken," he said offhand, "I was going to ask you to consider riding with me in the next day or so. When the seed bringers start to arrive, we'll have no freedom for weeks."

"The last time we rode out, you insulted my mount," Eleanor answered.

"Thrift is the most ill-favored beast I've ever seen," Aedon replied, unapologetic. "As sovereign, you should consider one of the finer horses in the stables." He then gave Eleanor a smile that he knew would make her angry. "At least dignify yourself with a horse worth looking at."

With a tilt of her head, Eleanor ignored him and stepped onto the dais, taking her place on the throne, as Aedon, still smiling, walked to his seat and began shaking hands with the representatives of each fen. Once the councillors were seated, the observers along the eastern wall quieted as well. Edythe took her place with the rest of the council, from curiosity, Eleanor supposed, rather than political interest. Behind them stood a court representative for each of Ainsley's fifteen fens.

"Your Majesty," the councillor of petitions called from his place beside the large entry doors. "This morning's assembly."

A small group entered and stood in a line before the doors. And although Eleanor did not look directly at him, she saw the stranger among them. Aedon, as she knew he would, measured the stranger, then looked at her to see if she was surprised. When he could see that she wasn't, he raised an eyebrow. Eleanor gave no signal in return as the first petitioner, an old woman, was called forward.

She walked slowly towards the throne, her stiff movements reminders of her age. When she stopped, Eleanor studied her face, knowing she'd seen the woman before, but not remembering at which fen.

"You may speak," Eleanor said.

"Your Majesty," the woman said as she bowed. "It's late spring, see, and I've about run out of flour. I do my own work, harvesting and threshing and all, but it's become difficult to do by myself. Could the royal stores grant me a small supply? I've got a grandson to feed."

"Do you have any other family?" Eleanor asked.

"None to speak of," the woman said as she looked up. "Just the grandson of six years. We live far outside Small Wood fen and don't have neighbors, either."

That was where Eleanor had seen her: Small Wood. "Do you have a skill to contribute towards fen or country for this flour?" Eleanor asked. Eleanor shifted, watching as the old woman squinted her eyes for a moment, thinking.

"I do know the old lace quite well," the woman said. "But without the finer lowland wool, it's hard to create. I can only afford the mountain worn."

"I'm sure your grandson will grow to be a great help with the planting and harvesting of your own land," Eleanor said. "But until then, let us supply you with some lowland wool that you might sell your lace at the fen lord's market and trade for what supplies you need. We can grant you a small start. If you plan well, you should be able to continue from there on your own."

The old woman looked away for a moment, her shoulders catching as if her bones had been worn too close together. When she looked again at Eleanor, her face displayed the emotion she felt. "Lowland wool is hard to come by," she said. "I'd be ever so grateful."

"Catton," Eleanor said and signaled for the councillor of Small Wood fen. He stood in place and waited. "See to our friend, assess her needs, and address them as I've outlined. Also, see that she is well rested before her journey home."

"Your Majesty." Catton bowed and showed the old woman out of the throne room.

Then the councillor of petitions spoke again, saying, "A request for hospitality from the crown."

Wil walked towards the throne, and although his expression was even, Eleanor detected slight amusement in his eyes.

"Good day," Eleanor said as if they had not met earlier. "You may speak."

"Your Majesty." He bowed respectively, watching her face. "An honor, truly."

"I understand you wish to ask hospitality of the crown, an old tradition, not much practiced anymore," Eleanor said, repeating the words she had spoken that morning.

"I do seek hospitality," he said. "I am a traveler far from home and desire some rest. Hearing tales of Aemogen's generosity, I now seek such a privilege as I travel through Ainsley."

"You do realize that by receiving my hospitality, you promise to share a skill, work, or substantial news?"

Wil shook his head slightly. "I was not aware until this morning, when one of your gardeners," he said, emphasizing the word, "mentioned it was expected. I can oblige anything Your Majesty would desire."

Eleanor did not respond immediately to the stranger before her. Instead, she took time to observe his figure, the attitude of his bearing, and any other hints his clothing might offer. She knew that he saw through her pause, knew she was scrutinizing him, and he stared back, perhaps gleaning what he could from her as well. Eleanor thought he exhibited a fierce independence of self. And although he was young, he did not seem to be foolhardy or inexperienced.

"Where is it you call home, stranger?" she questioned after a moment.

"My mother was a Marion," Wil replied confidently, again repeating what he had told Eleanor earlier in the garden. "I have traveled many lands in my time—the North countries, the West countries—to find myself, at last, in Aemogen."

Leaning forward slightly, Eleanor moved her finger along the patterns in the wood grain of the arm of her throne. He had not answered her question.

"And what is your name?" she asked.

"Wil Traveler," he said, lifting his chin.

"A traveler," she said, repeating the common title wanderers often declared for themselves. Eleanor did not press him for more. She was still curious, yet circumspect. They received so few foreigners in Aemogen that were not Marions. Why this young man had a desire to travel here she was not sure. "Our tradition requires a sponsor," she continued. "Be that the monarch or another member of my house. Since I cannot guess as to your character, I ask my council if any will speak for you and your request?"

Wil glanced towards the council, his bearing not quite arrogant, but sure. Eleanor's eyes flickered quickly towards Edythe, whose expression hinted approval.

"Council, what is your opinion of offering hospitality to this traveler?" Eleanor asked.

No one moved. Aedon cleared his throat and leaned back in his chair, looking at the stranger intently. Gaulter Alden frowned. At last, Edythe stood.

"I speak for our guest," she said. "It has been a long while without a request for hospitality, and as the spring festival is all but here, there is merriment to share. I speak to sponsor Wil Traveler." Edythe then sat down, turning slightly pink at her public bravery. Gaulter Alden grunted.

Eleanor schooled any hesitance she felt behind an even expression. "We welcome you to our kingdom," she said to Wil. "And we begin by offering you food and lodging, as is customary, for a fortnight." Eleanor kept her tone gracious. "After which, you shall be expected to know your own way. You may either be shown to the travelers' quarters now or enjoy the remainder of the morning audiences."

"I will stay, if it pleases you," he said.

Wil bowed respectfully and looked up at Eleanor, his eyes lingering a moment longer than she would have expected. Eleanor could not help but feel his expression was weighted with something other than authenticity. She felt a twinge of caution as he took his seat along the eastern wall.

Wil settled himself on a smooth bench, away from the other observers, and scrutinized the proceedings before him with interest.

She had surprised him, this precocious queen, who wore her unembellished crown so practically about that flame-colored hair. Placing his elbows on his knees, Wil leaned forward, caught more in constructing the character of this Queen Eleanor than in the lackluster affairs of the Aemogen state. She was poised, but sincere, guileless.

There were only a small handful of petitioners, who carried before their queen what Wil thought were simple requests. Yet, the Aemogen queen listened attentively and gave fair, thoughtful responses. Once, she asked a man to stay as a guest in the travelers' house until she could convene with her council and discuss his problem in depth. The words were polished, albeit, against Wil's own experiences, a bit staid.

His eyes wandered the throne room. Thin, high windows lined the eastern and western walls. Squared gray stones held muted tapestries, subdued, steady, and unsophisticated. Wil pulled on the inside of his mouth as he scanned the people present. A small country with an unaffected people, he thought. Perhaps he had not been such a fool; he may yet find a way to make the Aemogens listen to him.

A piercing look drew Wil's attention toward the line of councillors across the room. There, sitting among the queen's council, was a man a handful of years older than Wil, watching him with unapologetic distrust. Wil responded with an even look of his own, lifting his chin slightly, before turning his attention back to the queen. The audience had ended. She stood, as did the rest of the court. Wil brought himself to his feet and waited respectfully as she disappeared through a set of doors behind the tapestries on the northern wall. A single guard followed close behind.

———

"I'll be disappointed not to have your company," Edythe admitted to Eleanor, who was busy working in her private apartments. "I don't see why this one meal, of many, should be missed." She was sitting across from Eleanor, in a chair on the other side of her desk. "You do remember that Wil Traveler will be dining in the traditional place at your left hand?"

"I had remembered," Eleanor said. "But that formality will have to wait for tomorrow." She fingered the papers on her desk, then looked up towards her sister, much more absorbed by the work before her than by the day's events. "Was this Wil Traveler comfortably settled?"

"Yes," Edythe replied. "Doughlas saw him to the travelers' house, upon my request. I spoke with Wil Traveler only a moment, but promised him a general tour of the entire Ainsley Rise tomorrow. Have you heard that he has quite the fine horse with him? It was brought up from an inn yard in Ainsley to stable here with the mounts of the castle-guard. Rumors are it is the most beautiful horse to have ever been seen in Aemogen."

"Hmmm," Eleanor said. She had turned back towards her work.

"I do wish you would just come."

"Hospitality can be extended by others as well as the queen," Eleanor replied. "In any form, you are his sponsor. It will be quite appropriate for you to welcome him this evening." Eleanor moved her forefinger along the wood grains of her desk, and she looked towards her window, the remaining light of day draping into evening. "You know how I am when I've not finished my work," she added. Resting her hand beneath her chin, her fingers stretching down her neck, Eleanor smiled at Edythe. "Besides, I am expecting to meet with Aedon about the modified Marion amendments."

"Does it really signify?" Edythe asked. "Enough to keep you both from dinner?"

"Yes," Eleanor said, the corners of her mouth turned down. "Politics are always a caution, even with your nearest ally."

Edythe left Eleanor to her work just as Aedon was entering the queen's chambers.

He greeted Edythe, then said, "I understand the seed bringers from Common Field fen will be arriving soon, and Blaike will be coming with them."

"He most certainly is coming," was Edythe's enthusiastic response.

Eleanor watched from the corner of her eye as Edythe beamed and gave Aedon the details of Blaike's arrival. They would marry, Blaike and Edythe. All of Ainsley knew it, though the amicable young man had not yet dared ask Eleanor if he might marry the princess. Eleanor would say yes when he did, but she'd done nothing to lessen his discomfort at figuring out how he would approach his sovereign. When Edythe left, ribbons of happiness trailing behind her, Aedon closed the door, shaking his head. He sat down across from Eleanor.

"You really should encourage Blaike," he said. "Or she'll be waiting forever."

"Did you finish reading?" Eleanor asked directly.

"I did," Aedon said, tossing the papers onto her desk. His face was now as serious as she knew it should be. "The Marion rules of war have been changed."

CHAPTER

TWO

Sitting on an old barrel, Wil watched the Ainsley marketplace hurry itself about. It was late morning now, and many of the wares had been sold, but people still milled around in groups, as if they needed someplace to be in anticipation of the festival still days away.

Chidings, mixed with conversation, were called forth as children, directly disobeying their parents' cries to sit quiet, were caught up in roving games of dirt and quick calls. A few girls stood nearby, laughing and pulling in close to share secrets. Wil couldn't help but notice that, more than once, they giggled in his direction. Men stood with their arms folded, frequently holding a hand out, as if testing the air, and prophesying their distant harvests. Occasionally, a man or a woman would glance at Wil and frown. He watched it all with interest, these measured, yet conversant interactions of the Aemogens, so different from what he was used to.

"Uooff!" A small boy, tripping over his own feet, hit the ground near Wil. A running gaggle of children continued on their way, paying the boy no mind. He lay there, stunned, momentarily dazed. Then, after looking about, he burst into tears. Wil quickly scooped the little boy up, bouncing him up and down in his arms.

"That was quite a tumble," Wil said. The little boy stopped crying at Wil's words, staring up at his face. A worried mother rushed towards Wil, suspicion in her steps.

"Is this your boy?" Wil asked the woman.

"Yes." She reclaimed her child and wiped his eyes. "He is too small to keep up with the others," she explained, "and always ends up running himself right off his feet." She turned her attention to Wil. "And you are?"

"Excuse me," he said. "Wil, Wil Traveler. I'm spending a fortnight as guest of the queen's hospitality."

"Ah." The woman's face relaxed into a smile. "I've heard about you. It's been a long while since hospitality has been offered." The woman took in his height and face. "I can see why they gave it to you—you've a handsome face. Do you offer work, or skill, or *news*?" She had said this last word with effect, indicating herself to be a connoisseur of local gossip.

Wil laughed out loud, which pleased the woman and called the attention of others nearby. The mother preened in her temporary status of conversing with the foreigner.

"Whatever the queen desires, I assure you," he answered. "Speaking of, I am set to meet the Princess Edythe. It would not do to arrive late. Forgive me." He hesitated, then said, "May I ask your name?"

"Aurrey. That's my name. And this is Haide." She nodded to the now quieted child in her arms.

"Pleasure, Aurrey," Wil said. "I hope to see you again." With one last glance, he left the marketplace and headed up the hill towards the castle.

———⊰⊱———

It was in the records hall that Wil was to meet Edythe, and his own solitary observation led him to a tall building with wide windows of stained glass, settled on the east side of Ainsley Castle. When Wil pushed open one of the doors, he found a single large room with several empty tables, a high ceiling, and shelves upon shelves lining the walls. In the back, up two steps, was a raised section of the floor, where he could see the Princess Edythe working. To each side of the platform were a set of twisting stairs, leading to an open hallway that ran the length and width of the walls above the common room. Wil's eyes scanned the contents of the shelves: manuscripts, scrolls, books, and boxes, sitting undisturbed in their places.

"Hello," Edythe waved and smiled at Wil. Leaving her work on the table, she stood and stepped down onto the level floor of the main room.

"What sort of work do you do in such a place?" Wil asked, his hands behind his back, his head tilted as he admired the windows. The artisanship of the hall pleased him, and Wil wondered why the throne room did not boast such accoutrements.

"The royal archivist does his work here," she said. "As do I—the designated member of the royal family charged with the history and traditions of our people. This winter, I began the rather arduous task of creating a new system to organize records." The princess's face revealed a satisfaction so complete that Wil wasn't surprised when she next said, "It's a good work."

"I accept your time with hesitation," he answered. "As I imagine you have as much to do as the queen and do not wish to be distracted from your tasks."

"But therein lies the difference between my sister and I." Edythe's tone was obliging. "Where I will put down my quill, Eleanor would thank you for your consideration and continue working. I'll enjoy showing you Ainsley Rise and getting to know you better."

He soon learned that Edythe referred to the Ainsley Castle, and all its outbuildings and gardens within the exterior walls of the castle as Ainsley Rise. He saw that his initial impression—that of artless buildings thrown in any place—was not correct. It was, Wil admitted, a beautiful complex: the castle, rising in the center, and the surrounding buildings, set at artistic angles, creating arches and pathways and gardens between the tall, gray stones. The south entrance to the castle led to a square where, Edythe said, many of Aemogen's ceremonies were performed. Behind them, large gates opened towards a wide stairway, leading down to the houses and businesses of Ainsley. In the center of the stairway was another square, which Edythe explained was for festivals and dancing.

"It's called Ceiliuradh in the old tongue," she said. "Not many call it that anymore."

"But you do," Wil observed.

"Yes, and Eleanor. She remembers everything."

The walls that surrounded the castle supported a high tower in each corner. The travelers' house, where Wil had been given lodging, stood straight beneath the southwest tower, near the southern gate, with an armory and several store buildings arching from its side.

They followed a small, cobbled path that led down, past the terraced gardens west of the castle, to the stables, which were positioned near the western gate. Here they stopped to admire

Hegleh, Wil's horse, before continuing into the extensive gardens north of the castle.

"And what does the queen do all day?" Wil asked as they walked the paths, paying little attention to the gardeners working there.

"She manages the affairs of Aemogen." Edythe smiled, covering her eyes from the bright sun with her hand as she looked into his face.

"Yes," Wil persisted, "but what is her schedule? Her duties? What demands consume her time?"

Edythe gave him a questioning look for his odd inquiry.

"It's just that she is so young in her position," Wil reasoned. "I'm curious how she sees it done."

"You ask what Eleanor does all day?" Edythe shrugged as they continued walking. "She wakes early, studies for several hours, and, perhaps, slips into the gardens ahead of arriving at mid-morning audience." She paused and glanced at his face before continuing. "Afterward, she takes her meal in her private apartments while answering the communications of state or researching a pressing issue. Mid-afternoon, her council convenes—I, thankfully, am excused from these meetings a majority of the time—and they discuss the needs of each fen and of Aemogen as a whole."

"How long do they meet?"

"It varies on the day." Edythe greeted a gardener, then continued, "She may walk or ride out on Thrift afterward, but usually, she returns to finish her business or continue her studies until evening meal."

"Which she does not attend for being too busy," Wil finished with a smile.

Edythe laughed.

The queen was again absent from dinner. Wil sat in his seat to the left of Eleanor's empty chair, which, Edythe had told him, was the traditional place of welcome. Edythe had greeted him warmly but settled at the far end of the table. Even Crispin, the young captain of the palace guard, had nodded a greeting in Wil's direction, only to turn again to the young lady he was entertaining with a story.

An older gentleman, who had been on the queen's council, and the younger councilman that Wil had seen during his first morning audience—people were calling him Aedon—were deep in conversation regarding fen trade. Wil leaned back in his chair, watching them all. They were strange, casual, sincere, yet not sophisticated, as Wil may have previously guessed for a gathering of Aemogen's elite.

He tapped his fingers along the table, fighting disappointment. Had he wished for more of a welcome, more acknowledgments? He shook his head. Were he honest, Wil would have admitted that he'd wanted to speak with Queen Eleanor, but he had not seen her since the audience the day before.

Silence filled the room.

Wil looked up. The queen had entered. Her hair was braided in the tradition of her people, ending with a copper twist down her neck, set off by her simple gray gown. Wil stood, as had everyone else.

Eleanor paused as she passed Aedon, placing her hand on his arm, exchanging a quiet word, and then walked to her seat. A nondescript guard, always a few feet behind the queen, stepped forward and pulled back her chair.

"Thank you, Hastian," the queen said as she settled onto her place. "Good evening, everyone."

Those assembled offered greeting, then sat down and continued comfortably in their conversation.

Wil felt out of place, unsure of the protocol a guest of the crown should follow. He sat against his chair, then straightened his back, and ended up leaning slightly forward, lifting his head just enough to watch those around him. Eleanor's eyes scanned those in attendance, offering what Wil thought to be a preoccupied smile, as the servers began filling plates.

Once Eleanor began to eat, the rest of the table followed. For someone who was supposed to be a guest of Ainsley's hospitality, Wil felt more alien and unwanted than he ever had in his life. It seemed that Eleanor meant to pay him no mind. She was thinking carefully about something, pushing the food around her plate, her face knit in concentration. Finally, Wil ceased being invisible to her, for Eleanor turned directly to him.

"Wil Traveler," Eleanor stated simply.

"Your Majesty," he said, feeling uncharacteristically nervous, and he cleared his throat.

"Have you settled into the travelers' house?"

"I have. There was plenty of time yesterday. I've since had opportunity to see a part of Ainsley, and the Princess Edythe showed me about Ainsley Rise."

Eleanor nodded, showing civil interest. "Now that you have seen a small part of Aemogen, do you suppose you will enjoy your stay?" It was a polite comment, a slight emphasis placed on *enjoy*.

"To be honest," Wil said as he settled back in his chair with folded arms and tilted his head to the side, watching the queen's face, "I'm not yet sure."

Eleanor, Wil gathered, was surprised, for she set down her fork and looked at him as if finally giving him her full attention. He fought a smile away from his face, pleased.

"For the sake of conversation," Eleanor proceeded, "have you found something lacking?"

"Just different," Wil said, taking another bite of his simple meal, a vegetable stew, no meat, no spice, only herbs. It tasted flat in comparison to the food of the North.

"You have no example for me then?" the queen said, speaking louder, and Wil noticed Aedon glancing in their direction. He decided to give this Aedon a show.

Using a napkin that had been provided, Wil shrugged, set his fork down, and leaned towards the queen.

"Oh, I have plenty of examples," Wil said matter-of-factly. "I'm not sure you have that much disposable time."

"If you remember the audience yesterday," she said, "you are supposed to offer something in return for my hospitality." The queen's tone was light.

"What would you like from me?" Wil offered.

"Since it's not apparent you have any skill," she answered with understated jest, "news and conversation should suffice, and I will make time for it. Please, tell me of our strange, secluded ways."

Wil took the slight in stride, as this was his element. "There are many indeed. But should we begin close to home, as it were?" He raised his glass to her. "Your interactions as a monarch, as queen, are so familiar with all of those around you. Does not that undermine your authority?"

The young queen seemed surprised by his question, not responding immediately. Finally, as if deciding she had sufficient curiosity to follow his line of questioning, she replied with her own question: "What is authority without friendship and trust?"

"Power," Wil said. His answer was swift, and she appeared struck with how sharp the word sounded in his mouth.

"Power?" Eleanor rose to the debate. "Answer me this, Traveler: Would you rather people follow for loyalty and love, or would you reign through fear to gain allegiance?"

"Clearly, loyalty is what any leader desires," Wil answered, quick and even, enjoying the prospect of a verbal spar. "Love is dispensable." He waved aside her objection and continued, "I propose a third way: not love, not fear, but awe. A leader of any sort, a monarch especially, should maintain a level of separation from the people. You are not a mere mortal. They must view you as something powerful, separate, and superior. Then," he added as an aside, "they will perhaps love you, but it is only because you are what they never will be."

"And what is that?" Eleanor asked.

"Immortal. Just below the gods."

Eleanor laughed, and the entire table looked their way. "Amusing, Wil Traveler," she said. "Perhaps I should keep you on for entertainment." Edythe stared down the table towards them with interest, but Wil avoided looking at the other diners. He did not want to draw anyone else into their conversation.

"And I am too casual then?" she challenged. "Too close to the people? 'A mortal' in your phrasing?" Her smile had not faded as she continued to eat. Wil took a drink from the cup before him, then responded in a quieter tone.

"They call you *Eleanor*." He had said her name carefully, like it was a delicate glass he was not supposed to touch, and the queen stiffened.

"Only those who work closely with me call me that, and the familiarity has not weakened my position," she said.

"Weaken is exactly what familiarity does."

"So, I ban those around me from using my name?" Eleanor

responded. "Even Edythe?" The thought made her laugh again, but it was softer this time.

"I assume Edythe is second in line for the throne," Wil said. "As long as you are certain that she doesn't want your power for herself, she should also foster the distinction of superiority. If she has given you any reason to doubt this, watch her closer than your most dreaded enemy."

The smile faded from Eleanor's face. "I don't believe myself guilty of naiveté, Traveler," she responded in earnest, "but neither does your level of jaded interpretation fall within my perception of life. Are you so faithless in those around you?"

Wil shifted in his chair and did not answer. The table had again grown quiet, and the queen, noticing their finished meals, stood abruptly. Everyone followed suit, including Wil, who was not satisfied with the way the conversation had ended.

Eleanor looked towards him, as if to speak, but thought better of it. "Pleasant evening," she said, addressing the assembly. Then her guard stepped forward and escorted her from the hall.

"The queen appeared engrossed in your conversation," Aedon said, having come up behind Wil. Giving a slight nod to Aedon, Wil lifted his cup from the table and took another drink.

"Do you mind me asking what it was about?" Aedon's query was calm.

"No," Wil said and shook his head. "I don't mind you asking, but I'll probably not answer."

Aedon waited, and Wil set the cup back down on the table, moving away so a serving maid could clear the plates. With no intention of answering the councillor, Wil started for the exit.

"The protection of the queen is a serious thing," Aedon persisted as he fell into step with Wil. "And you, a traveler, are welcome, but a stranger nonetheless. My question cannot appear to you as unreasonable."

It didn't appear unreasonable, Wil thought, but Aedon, who had watched Wil more closely than the rest, was the last person he wanted to engage in conversation.

"That is very good of you, sir, to concern yourself," he said. "But I am certain the queen values her privacy, as I do mine." Wil gave an apologetic smile. "And prying would hardly be hospitable." Then he excused himself.

Eleanor was descending rapidly, her bare feet touching the cold spiraled stone, the sounds of her steps loud inside her thoughts, beating against the echoes of the dreams she'd had. Despite Eleanor's candle, the hidden staircase that led from her private rooms to the dungeons was rather dark.

Eleanor almost stopped, her hand pressed flat against the stone. She couldn't explain why she was acting so irrationally. "Something in my mind, almost a dream—" Eleanor said, speaking as she continued, "—a warning against the spring."

Faster, Eleanor hurried around the twisting staircase, downward through the walls of Ainsley Castle. The white lace of her nightdress washed against the worn steps like the waves of a frigid ocean. As if she had been submerged, Eleanor could now feel herself below ground level, the earth close around, hugging the castle walls, the chill of the long frozen winter reaching for her bones through the thick stone. She shivered, pulling her blanket closer around her shoulders. In a sudden moment, which startled her from the residue of her dreams, Eleanor found herself at the door.

Old and thick, the door was stooped, tucked away in a small

arch of stone. Eleanor held her candle up towards the lock and pulled at the chain around her neck, drawing out the key. After some effort, the tired lock gave way and released the door. Eleanor pushed it open and entered the dungeons of Ainsley Castle.

The rooms rested uninhabited, quiet in the dark. There were, in fact, no prisoners in the ancient dungeons, the cells being filled only with seeds for the coming planting year or in the case of failed crops. The well-ordered seed rooms were the physical expression of Aemogen's well-being, so this was where Eleanor came to assure herself that nothing was amiss.

Walking through the corridors lined with rooms, small and large, filled with seed cases resting in the cold, Eleanor was silent. Despite the early hour, she now felt alert and watchful. Everything appeared undisturbed, despite her tight lungs and the dreams sticking to her usually collected mind.

The tall pillars of the largest room leaned in beautiful arches towards one another. It was a calm space that Eleanor often sought out when she wished to think. A long table of aged wood sat stubbornly in its place at the center of the room, and there lay the ledgers and the registers, just as Aedon had left them last fall. Without hesitation, Eleanor withdrew a small stool from beneath the table, turning one of the heavy registers towards her, and opened the familiar pages.

She lit a few more dusty candles, already on the table, for more light. Then Eleanor turned back towards the long lists of stock. Page after page, the numbers had settled comfortably for the winter on the clean paper, exactly as they should be. Nothing was out of place. Aedon's broad, neat writing assured that all was accounted for. Her fingers moved quickly, her eyes watching the numbers pass as she reviewed each page a second time. Yes, everything was as it should be.

Eleanor closed the large book. She drummed her fingers on the table and looked up into the darkness. Her mind fell back to the Marion amendments for only a moment. Then she blew out the candles and took herself up to her rooms.

Back in her bed, the early gray of morning hinting at day, Eleanor sat, tucked between cushions and blankets, occupied by her thoughts as she played with the tips of her copper-colored hair. She now felt more curious than shaken. Burrowing down, away from the frigid air, Eleanor tried to return to sleep, but her mind was awake, and the attempt proved fruitless.

Gathering a blanket over her shoulders, she slipped off her bed and walked to the ledge beneath the windows, where she sat down, pulling her knees up below her chin, looking out over the early spring gardens. The rain of the night before, heavy and deep, had pushed morning low against the earth. Eleanor shivered and pulled her blanket tighter about her shoulders.

Wil didn't see the queen again until evening the following day. He had taken Hegleh out on a substantial ride, working her through her paces a considerable distance from Ainsley Rise, with every intention of enjoying the scenery. But instead of admiring the domineering mountains that rose in the distant north, Wil ran through his conversation with Eleanor in his head over and over again. The queen's manner was like a sliver in his skin, her thoughts, vastly different from his, young and idealistic. Wil did not like to think her wrong, but she was.

Arriving back late, Wil made himself as presentable as the walk from the stables to the hall would allow. Bursting through the doors, he expected to be one of the last to arrive. He had not expected to arrive mid-meal. His own rudeness was embarrassing, and Wil felt foolish for having come at all. But he was here, so there was nothing to do but play it out.

The queen was talking with Crispin, who sat, laughing, to her right. Eleanor deliberately ignored Wil's entrance. Nevertheless, there were plenty who stared. Gaulter Alden cleared his throat, watching him to his seat to the left of the queen.

As Wil claimed his conspicuously empty chair, Eleanor looked up.

"Please forgive me," Wil said as he stood again, bowing to Eleanor in earnest. "I was taking my mare for a ride and went farther than I knew. I cannot convey my embarrassment at having entered so late."

Eleanor motioned for him to sit down. "You're forgiven," she said. "I myself have lost time when riding in the woods around Ainsley Rise."

Wil gave her a grateful expression as he took his seat. "The groom showed me your horse, Thrift, before I rode out," he said. "He's an unusual beast for a queen's mount, unsightly and ill favored, but his frame underneath that dismal coat looks to be graceful. He must be a joy to ride."

Eleanor stopped and with pleasure behind her eyes, turned fully towards him. "Finally, I have an ally. It's a hard-pressed battle in Ainsley, and I've never had anyone side with me on the matter." She lifted her glass. "You've made yourself a friend, Wil."

He raised his glass in return, shifting so a servant could set his food before him, relieved to have not offended his host. It was, he noticed, the first time she had left off the title *Traveler* and had just called him Wil.

After leaving a comment with Crispin, Queen Eleanor turned back towards Wil. "I wish I could have thrown statesmanship to the wind and joined you in riding. It was the perfect day for it."

Aedon looked up, as if the idea did not suit him. Eleanor noticed the expression, and Wil tried not to look pleased when she next spoke pointedly to Aedon.

"Wil Traveler has paid a compliment to my horse, Aedon," she said. "He has an eye for the exceptional, don't you agree?"

Aedon displayed a challenge on his face, but he refused to answer audibly. Wil focused on his food, pretending not to notice when Eleanor exchanged an amused look with Edythe, who sat farther down the table. Eleanor seemed almost merry.

"I would be honored to join you in riding," Wil replied when the conversation at the table had resumed its normal course.

"Perhaps tomorrow we can—" she began, but she was interrupted by a disturbance outside the hall.

There was yelling and then noise in the corridor. Wil started as the doors burst open. A young man in simple soldier's garb came running into the hall. Dazed, he looked around frantically, setting his sights on the queen. Eleanor stood. He began to move towards her, then collapsed onto one knee, dizzy and disoriented. He tried to steady himself, but looked as if he would fall.

Gaulter Alden called out for something that Wil could not understand. People shot towards the soldier, no one quicker than the queen. Wil followed behind her. She knelt down, lifting the soldier's face towards hers, struggling to gather him into her arms as his body began to sway. It appeared that he would lose all consciousness.

"Water!" Eleanor cried out, never looking away from the soldier. "Soldier, what happened?" She pulled him to her, forcing his helmet partially off. The simple gold band around Eleanor's hair fell back, ringing sharply as it clattered to the floor. Wil picked it up, carefully. Soon, Aedon was there with water.

Wil stood quietly, his arms folded, his hand wrapped around Eleanor's crown, watching the scene. The queen took the glass of water from Aedon and held the young man's face against her shoulder as she helped him to drink. She spoke softly, setting the half-emptied cup on the stone floor, and brushed his hair away from his forehead.

Wil watched Eleanor, fascinated. Her tender confidence, coupled with her personal presence, would have made anyone think her an experienced mother, rather than a girl a handful of years younger than the soldier.

It was a slow process, but, finally, the soldier could focus his vision on the queen and moved as if to speak.

"Mason," Crispin asked, "is there news from the guard at the pass?"

The young soldier still struggled in his breathing; it was hoarse and tight. His eyes went past Crispin's, to Gaulter Alden's, then to Eleanor's.

"Dead," he said. "All dead." He took another breath.

"More water," Eleanor said as she helped him finish the glass. "Speak only when you are able, soldier."

The court physician was soon present, and Eleanor released Mason so that Aedon and Crispin could take him to the table. The servants hastily cleared away the meal and withdrew with everyone who was not of the queen's council. Edythe went with them, keeping them moving as she looked back over her shoulder with concern. Gaulter Alden had motioned to Wil, but Wil, crown in hand, shook his head at the old man and continued to stand behind Eleanor, his arms still folded across his chest.

At long last, when the soldier could speak, he pulled from his tunic a long, tightly bound scroll. "I have ridden two days and nights from the Aemogen pass to deliver this."

Wil's heart beat faster. The scroll was beautiful, with black rollers and creamy parchment, a silk ribbon beneath the seal. Eleanor's slight, fair hand reached around the scroll, and she took it from the soldier. She first looked at Gaulter Alden, then calmly walked to the head of the table and, without sitting, broke the thick wax seal the color of dried blood. The wax snapped in her fingers, filling the quiet hall with a brief moment of sound, only accompanied by Mason's labored breathing.

Wil followed as the men of the council surrounded the table. No one sat down. Aedon gave Wil a black look, but Wil turned his attention back to the queen, who bravely opened the scroll and silently read the markings before her with a controlled air. The ghost of a blink crossed her eyes before Eleanor looked up at the men of her council.

"We have been issued a warning," she said. "Surrender our sovereignty or risk certain war."

Wil frowned, his eyes resting on Eleanor for one apologetic moment before canvassing the room. He had never seen men more stunned, more unprepared for such news. The queen's bearing remained outwardly calm.

"Who?" Gaulter Alden asked. His deep voice, though strong, could not hold up the silence of the entire room. It sounded small and insignificant.

"The Imirillian Empire," Eleanor answered. "The same who, less than a year ago, desolated the country of Aramesh, just north of the Arimel Mountains."

Wil felt himself become unsteady. He reached a hand out to the chair before him, feeling the blood drain from his face. Gaulter Alden opened his mouth but said nothing. Aedon began asking even questions, and murmurs commenced to fill the space around the table.

The young soldier, still weak, looked up at the queen. "They're all dead, Your Majesty, all of the guards at the pass. They said it was a warning if you choose to neglect their terms—" Mason broke off, emotion choking his words.

Wil grimaced and cursed aloud. Eleanor gave him a quick glance, then rolled the scroll back together. Someone stepped behind Wil, and he looked back to see Hastian, the guard who always followed Eleanor, watching him, his hand resting on the hilt of his sword.

"Now is not the time, nor the place, to discuss this in detail, Aedon," Eleanor said as her eyes sought her councillor. "Will you see that Mason gets to a comfortable bed? And that he is fed and attended to? When he is able, review thoroughly what happened at the pass. Gaulter Alden, meet me in my rooms in an hour's time. Doughlas," Eleanor said as she found her fen rider. "Send a rider to the pass with a company of soldiers." She motioned towards Crispin. "They will secure the pass and bring back the dead. The entire council will convene in the morning to discuss in detail the contents of the scroll. Tell no one of this."

Eleanor lifted her hand, faltering only when she looked down. "We must have time to understand this threat," she said, "before spreading its news through Aemogen."

"Your Majesty—"

"Yes, Your Majesty—"

Their responses sounded like specters in the quiet hall, and Wil shivered, despite his palm beginning to sweat where he clung to the chair. His other hand felt the weight of Eleanor's crown.

As the room began to clear, Aedon came to Eleanor. They clasped hands as he stepped closer, Aedon lifting his other hand to her shoulder. Nothing was said, though Wil couldn't help but hear an age's worth of words exchanged in that intimate silence. Eleanor nodded, and the corners of Aedon's mouth tried to pull up towards his eyes, to conceal his concern for his country, concern for his queen.

"If I need you—" she began.

"Yes, I'll be awake—"

Eleanor nodded, then she motioned Crispin to her side as Aedon left. Wil thought she'd forgotten him, but Eleanor turned to look at Wil with tight consternation. "Apologies, Wil Traveler," she said, "for the events of the evening and that you are still here to witness them. Please keep this news to yourself. I expect no less and thank you for it." She turned away from him slightly. "Given what we now face, you must graciously accept a pair of guards to accompany you at all times. I am afraid we do not know you well enough to do otherwise. Crispin will see you back to the travelers' house and make the necessary arrangements."

Wil gave a slight nod, his head bent. "Oh, Your Majesty—" he said, almost forgetting. Wil held the crown towards the queen, and she took it from his hands.

"Thank you," she said.

Then Eleanor lifted her small chin, gripping her crown in her hand, and exited the room, Hastian accompanying her through the arched doorway.

<hr />

When Eleanor arrived in her rooms, she left Hastian in the antechamber and, pausing only to light several candles, rolled the scroll open across the thick table. It was in Imirillian above and her language—the language Aemogen and the country of Marion shared—below.

She could read both.

Eleanor had studied hard and spoke many of the continental languages. Her father had provided excellent tutors, who were pleased with their dedicated student. So, now, her mind fought the anxiety by meticulously reading the Imirillian text.

"Unbelievable," Eleanor said as she brought her hand down on the table, reading the scroll through in both languages again.

The terms, Eleanor thought, were ludicrous: Aemogen would surrender its sovereignty to the Imirillian Empire, which would send an occupying force from Zarbadast, the capital of Imirillia, to oversee Aemogen's agriculture and its several prosperous mines. Aemogen would also release a map of their southern port at Calafort, which was filled with dangerously impassable reefs—knowledge Aemogen had been unwilling to share with anyone for seven hundred years, ensuring that only Aemogen ships came in and that all other ships stayed out. Shaamil, emperor of Imirillia, would negotiate open trade with his continental allies out of Aemogen's port. If Eleanor cooperated, she would continue to reign as a figurehead queen. The terms would leave her people poverty-stricken, slaves.

"If the queen of Aemogen chooses to reject this treaty," she read, "the Imirillian Empire will secure the country and its resources with no regard for the queen, nor her people, and all members of the royal house and the queen's council will be executed."

They were given six months. Eleanor frowned, pulled at the

corner of her lip, and read the line again. In six months' time, the Imirillian army would invade Aemogen through the mountain pass that separated Aemogen from their Marion neighbors. Six months. That set the invasion to the final month of summer, just before the harvest. Six months. It didn't make any sense. Why would she be given such a lengthy amount of time?

Eleanor sat and pressed her hands to her face. She must think. What lay before Aemogen, in the form of this scroll, was a threat greater than any her father or grandfather had ever encountered. Now that the shock was wearing into somber reality, she felt an undercurrent of intense dread. She must grasp in her mind what this meant for Aemogen. Exhaling, she stood, walked to her desk, and removed several sheets of paper from a smaller drawer. Grabbing an inkwell and a quill pen, Eleanor sat at the table and began to write down Aemogen's options and the ramifications of each choice.

"Gaulter Alden is waiting," Hastian said, his voice pulling Eleanor from her notes. His blue eyes waited on Eleanor's face for a confirmation.

"Tell him to come through, Hastian," she said. Gaulter Alden entered and sat down across from Eleanor.

"I have been over the scroll several times in our own language and in Imirillian," Eleanor said. "Ultimately, the terms are these: surrender our sovereignty while the Imirillian Empire takes a percentage of our produce, wares, and commodities, plus gains open access to our port for them and their allies. In such a case, I would remain queen of Aemogen as a figurehead only, taking orders from a foreign government. I don't need to tell you that the levies would be difficult for our people to sustain and not fall into poverty.

"Or," Eleanor continued matter-of-factly, "we can choose to resist. If we fail, Aemogen becomes another colony of the Imirillian Empire, and I, my sister, and my entire council will be killed and replaced by an Imirillian governor."

Gaulter Alden slumped in his chair. He was a war leader who had never seen combat, the last of Aemogen's wars being in the days of Eleanor's great-grandfather, who, after maintaining Aemogen as an independent nation, took precautions to ensure that it would never experience such a loss again. He had forged an alliance with Marion, the only country adjacent to Aemogen, which had held for over one hundred years. Aemogen had no other allies, having refused any other trade agreements. The indomitable mountain range that shielded Aemogen's border to the north was impassable, and both the east and the south were safeguarded by tall cliffs that fell straight to the sea. The entry into Aemogen's port remained a navigational secret, ensuring their isolation. And their isolation, Eleanor had been taught, was their protection.

"I have given my thoughts to domestic issues, rather than the threat of war," Gaulter Alden admitted, as if Eleanor didn't already know. He moved his fingers along his trimmed, gray beard, looking sober and insecure. "How in the shadow of Old Ainsley did we secure the attentions of the Imirillian Empire? It is far to the north." He waved his hand abstractly, and his voice almost dropped to an incredulous whisper. "We are small," he said. "We have fewer people in our entire country than they have in Zarbadast alone."

"Take the scroll with you tonight," Eleanor said, thinking through his question. "Read it for yourself. We'll meet come morning in council to discuss our options."

Gaulter Alden sat in his bewilderment a bit longer, then,

remembering it was late and that he could retreat into sleep, he lifted his stiff body out of the chair. "You are wise, Eleanor, to wait until morning to discuss this," he said. "I will think, as will you, and return the scroll early, before the council has a chance to assemble."

Eleanor also stood. "Send it to Aedon once you're done tonight. He won't sleep until he's looked at it."

Crispin was waiting impatiently in the antechamber with Hastian and invited himself in as Gaulter Alden left. "All right, Eleanor," he said, "let's have a look at this thing."

"I sent it with Gaulter Alden, but here are the notes I took down." She moved the papers towards Crispin with her hand. While he scanned the pages, Eleanor pressed her knuckles against her lips, waiting, watching the bleak transformation on Crispin's face. He looked up.

"How will we survive this?" he asked.

She didn't know how to answer.

CHAPTER

THREE

Eleanor's every intention was to sleep soundly and wake clear minded, prepared. It had always been her determination to prove herself, despite her age, and that responsibly focused her thoughts on handling this situation with whatever wisdom she could gather. But when she had blown out her candles and the fire had died down—the darkness sleeping around her in the bed—Eleanor found herself grappling with the reality of the dreamlike evening. She knew the tales of the Imirillian army. Stories had traveled south into Marion and then into Aemogen of what people had called the Desolation of Aramesh.

Shaamil, the Imirillian emperor, and his sons had led their armies into Aramesh, sweeping through the entire country, burning fields, towns, and cities. Any civilians found were slaughtered. As the rumors told, Shaamil—who had raised Imirillia from a poor, desperate state to its current empire—held a boyhood grudge against Aramesh, with its beautiful ports and fertile fields, the least desertlike of all the Northern countries. So, he had left it barren.

As the long night marched haltingly on, Eleanor envisioned

what an army of thousands could do to her country. One particular question was the most perplexing: Why had Shaamil given Aemogen a six months' warning? It was a mystery, for the mercy of it did not seem like the emperor. As Eleanor worried and wound her questions around her mind far into the night, she began to see what the army would look like, coming down the Aemogen Pass. She had heard that Imirillian soldiers were trained from boyhood in the art of war, wearing the marks of their emperor or of their prince, and that their officers rode fierce, black mounts, horses of great strength and breeding.

When she finally did come to the edge of her dreams, Eleanor swore she could hear the countless steps of an army walking towards Ainsley Castle, and imagined that, in the morning, she would look over the downs and see them there, waiting, torches lit, scimitars in hand.

———

Come morning, the council met briefly, the scroll laid across the table between them, discussing the threat with its untenable terms. In Aemogen, difficulties of any kind were met first with thorough discussion, followed by thoughtful consideration, before possible solutions were set forth. It was how they had always handled pressing concerns. Yet, this was no simple concern. This unfathomable threat could mean the annihilation of their country, of their culture.

"Keep the threat strictly to yourselves," Eleanor ordered. "Take what we know, and think through every possibility for Aemogen's defense. We will meet again tomorrow and decide what we will do."

Aedon stayed in his chair as his fellow councilmen, speaking with each other in low voices, emptied out into the hall.

"I have too many questions, unanswered and raw on my tongue, Eleanor," Aedon said.

"Yes," Eleanor agreed, tired from her long night. "What troubles you the most?"

"All of it," he said. His words were sharp. "What are Shaamil's true motivations for this strange delay? Will they really hold themselves to the time given? Why give any warning at all before an attack? And how do we discover how big their army is?" Aedon waved his hand in the air, an unspoken expression that meant there were more questions to be had.

Eleanor watched him silently.

"Regardless of the answers to these questions," Aedon persisted, "how can we defend ourselves against any military, let alone the largest on the continent?"

"I don't know."

"Is acceptance of their terms the only option we have?" he asked.

"I don't know," Eleanor said again as she stood and threw her hands in the air, revealing a personal frustration only Aedon or Edythe ever saw. "I don't know, and I've no notion of what to do." She looked at her chief councillor. "But we will open it up to the council tomorrow. Then, we will put forth all our carefully deliberated thoughts and begin to formulate a plan." Lowering her voice, she said, "There must be some way through this."

Aedon stood and gathered his notes. "If you need me," he said, the edges of his words shaking, "I'll be in my chambers, hunting every corner of my brain for any alternative we might have."

While Aedon cloistered himself in his chambers, Eleanor retreated to the garden. She needed air and space. It was a cold day, with a gray wind and spring clouds all in bluster. The garden, only hinting at the season to come, felt vast and lonely. The space suited Eleanor's need for a private tumble of emotions that had become too much for her own body, too sensitive to trust to anyone else just now. Thankfully, no one was about, and Eleanor could empty her mind. Ordering Hastian to stay at a distance, she disappeared through the gardens, out beyond the north wall, towards the meadows flanking the river.

The steel gray water lipped and curled against the stones, the last visage of late winter, soothing her tight, guarded emotions. The sight steadied Eleanor, something to rival the tumult in the center of her own heart. Few were privy to that inner space, where Eleanor battled questions, so she stayed over an hour, breathing deeply of the wind and ordering her thoughts as she walked the worn path at the water's edge. Between the water's crystalline voice and the accompanying sound of wind through the winter-weary grass, Eleanor was beginning to calm.

Feeling the tug of her desk and inkwell, she began to retrace her steps into the garden. It was in the rose garden that she noticed the stranger, Wil Traveler, sitting at the far end, reading. Two members of the palace guard stood at a distance, watching him. Wil looked up at the sound of her passing, rose to his feet and bowed. Eleanor paused, nodding in return. He appeared to be waiting to see if her greeting extended beyond a simple acknowledgment of his presence. And to Eleanor's own surprise, it did. She turned, walking to where he stood at the far end of the garden, where the skeletal rose shrubs were beginning to come into their green.

"Good morning, Traveler."

"Your Majesty," Wil said as he bowed again. "It's a blustery day to be in the gardens."

Eleanor was prepared to respond with a pleasantry or two, then be on her way, but she thought a moment about his words before giving a more sincere answer. "It's the best kind of bluster: better from wind than from men."

Wil tilted his head to the side. "And by that do you imply mankind or *men?*"

"Mankind," Eleanor said, allowing herself a smile as her fingers reclaimed the loose lock of her hair flying across her face. "Granting your question more thought," she added, "I'm not certain I don't mean the other as well."

Although Wil smiled in return, his expression was one of thoughtful consideration, not levity. "I've been reading some of the historical ballads of your country," Wil said as he held up the small, hand-bound volume.

"We are a small nation but an old one," Eleanor said, looking towards the castle. "We do have our tales."

"It's beautiful—what I can understand of it, that is," Wil acknowledged, and Eleanor was unsure if he meant the country or the history. He placed his hands behind his back just then, as if he were working through his own thoughts. "I was thinking of walking along the river," he said. "Would you join me?" Wil motioned towards the path that Eleanor had just come from.

She could see that he thought she'd decline, but some trace she saw in his expression caused Eleanor to wonder what information he might possess that could be useful in sifting through her own thoughts. She needed to know more about this stranger, and something—the graceful lift of his shoulders as he shifted, his eyes catching hers—stalled Eleanor long enough to find herself accepting. Hastian trailed nervously at a distance, Wil Traveler's guards watching from the gate, where Eleanor signaled they wait.

"You have traveled a great deal," Eleanor said, as she stood again by the water.

Wil nodded in response.

"So, you know the Imirillian Empire," she said.

"Ah." He squinted for a moment. "Yes. I do know it. Rather well, actually."

"Is it as powerful as the stories tell?" Eleanor queried.

The brief whisper of a frown appeared on his face. "The army is vast. In truth, there is no power on the continent to compare," Wil said. "Have you traveled North yourself?"

"No, not beyond Marion," Eleanor said. "I'm sure it would be educational, enlightening even, to travel extensively, as you have." She had intentionally laced this thought with subtle irony that had, perhaps, been missed by the stranger. For, after watching her a long moment, Wil glanced away and smiled.

"To be sure," he said.

What did she care if he thought her simple? Eleanor wondered. So, she persisted in asking her questions. "And the Desolation of Aramesh—are the tales true?" Eleanor stopped, the toe of her shoe turning in the mud as she looked earnestly at his face. "They say that the entire country was burned, that thousands were left for dead, who did not escape the Imirillian army. Did you hear like rumors?"

"I—well, yes," he said. "The country was desolated." Shaking his head, Wil ran his fingers through his short hair as he struggled to speak. "I saw what happened to Aramesh, Your Majesty. It was not by rumor that I came to know of their destruction—I passed through and witnessed the scorched earth for myself." Pausing, he pursed his lips and looked down over the river. "May I ask if you've found a solution for your problem?"

"Do you know," Eleanor countered, pointedly ignoring his inquiry, "that I have heard the most wonderful things about your horse—unequaled in proportion, beauty, and strength, or so they say. Would you show her to me? I wouldn't mind judging for myself."

With a careful eye on his confused face, Eleanor turned back towards the northern gate. When she glanced back over her shoulder, he looked almost regretful, standing in place, watching her walk beyond him. She motioned for him to hurry. Taking a few long steps, Wil caught up with Eleanor and offered her his arm.

"To the stables," he said.

The sounds of combat could be heard coming from the stable yard.

"Either your guards are bored," Wil speculated, "or your horses are."

"Doubtful it's either," Eleanor said, half ignoring his humor. "Crispin uses the combat games for training. It's not an uncommon sound this time of day."

Entering the yard, they saw the young captain standing over his fallen opponent.

"Eleanor! You missed a spectacular moment," Crispin said as he grinned and helped the soldier up. "Quite a shame, really. I've run through all the willing men and still have won every match."

"Are you too tired from your last opponent?" Wil asked.

"Too tired for what?" Crispin huffed as he caught his breath.

"For a challenger."

"You?" Crispin's tone was doubtful. "Do you have much

combat experience?"

"Some," Wil said as he pulled his cloak back, revealing his sword. "Isn't the very nature of life a combat?"

"Perhaps." Crispin shrugged and raised his eyebrows. "I've never thought of it in such terms." He smiled good-naturedly. "I'll give you a moment to ready yourself," Crispin said as he caught Eleanor's eyes, and then hastily added, "If the queen has no prior claim on your time?"

Wil bowed to Eleanor, acquiescing to her desire.

"I don't mind waiting," she replied. "Actually, I'm rather interested in the match myself."

Eleanor took up a bench near the stable entrance. Wil followed, untying his cloak and laying it beside her. The scent she remembered from their first meeting in the garden lifted off his cloak, and this time, she could place what it was—cinnamon. It was cinnamon, a new spice just recently brought into the Aemogen port. Eleanor watched as Wil rolled back the sleeves of his black shirt, then pulled tight on a cloth wrapped several times around his left forearm, making certain it was secured. The only other thing that caught her interest was a worn, knotted piece of black leather about his right wrist. Without acknowledging how her eyes followed him, he turned towards Crispin.

"Ready?" he asked.

"Fatal touch, no blood," Crispin said matter-of-factly as Wil drew his sword. The sword, like his clothing, was all black, hilt and blade. One of the nearby soldiers whistled, and even Eleanor could see that it was exquisitely made.

"Any other rules?" Wil asked confidently.

"Other than good-mannered sportsmanship?" Crispin asked. He shook his head and took his position. "May the best win."

Sean, Eleanor's councillor of husbandry, who had been in the stables, came out and sat beside her. "Should be interesting," he said.

"Yes," she replied.

Eleanor watched the two young men approach one another. Crispin circled slowly, and Wil followed suit. When Crispin lunged, Wil spun deftly to the side and engaged Crispin in a brief parry.

"You've a confident form," Crispin said, stepping back.

But Wil's response was to attack. He swung in with strength, forcing Crispin to block the harsh blow. Then Wil, instead of pulling back and striking again, as Eleanor would have expected, applied pressure on Crispin's blade with his own before spinning around behind Crispin in an impossible instant and kicking him in the back of his knees. Crispin collapsed, and Wil was up, pressing his blade against the soldier's throat.

"Fatal touch," Wil said.

Eleanor flushed for Crispin's swift defeat, but Crispin only smiled. "How did you do that?" he asked. "I've never seen such a move executed so well."

Laughing, Wil helped Crispin off the ground. "Would you like another go?" he asked.

"Believe me that I do," Crispin grinned. "Now, I'm going to watch for dirty tricks."

Wil bowed.

The castle guard gathered around, calling out, whistling, and goading the challengers on. This time, Crispin was careful how he defended Wil's blows, moving fast and not giving him time to anchor his weight and repeat the trick.

Eleanor watched the spar, amazed. Wil appeared to be a

different swordsman altogether, going at Crispin in quick blows, relentless and fast. He never let up. Not once, after Wil began his attack, did Crispin have a respite from the unrelenting strikes. The men watching began to murmur as Crispin was beginning to tire. Still, Wil, never out of breath, continued to assail his opponent. Then he swung his blade from the left up to the right with such ferocity that Eleanor stood.

Flying backwards, Crispin tried to keep his feet under him, and he fell against a post belonging to the stable. Sean jumped out of the way as Wil lunged, pressing Crispin against the post, his arm pinning Crispin's throat. In one swift movement, Wil hit Crispin's hand with the butt of his black sword, and Crispin's weapon clattered to the ground.

"Fatal touch," Wil said as he breathed heavily, just now showing the signs of fatigue.

"That was brilliant," Crispin said, smiling through his broken breath. "You must teach me."

"Whatever you want to know," Wil offered as he stepped back, stooped, and picked up Crispin's sword, handing it respectfully to its owner.

Eleanor, who had stepped back towards the stable door as the combat had finished, slipped noiselessly inside and went out the back entrance. Wil Traveler—attentive, confident, opinionated, yet educated in manners—was a master swordsman. Eleanor wanted to know if he was a master killer.

CHAPTER

FOUR

Evening meal was silent. The members of Eleanor's council found they had little to say. The remainder of the court was also hesitant to speak, knowing something was wrong and not daring to ask. Most Aemogens did not think highly of idle and unbidden gossip. For this, Eleanor was grateful.

Wil was seated to Eleanor's left. He had glanced her way more than once before securing her attention. "You disappeared this afternoon," he said. "Before I could introduce you to my horse, Hegleh."

Eleanor waited to answer until the general sounds of conversation began to fill the room. After a few moments, she looked in his direction, considering.

"You have showed me something of equal interest, I assure you." Eleanor took a sip from her glass and continued to eat.

"What was that?" Wil asked in a direct manner.

"You're the best swordsman I've ever seen," Eleanor answered, unabashed. "Your display was astonishing." She looked him square in the eye. "If I were to hazard a guess, I'd say your skills put you equal to a professional killer."

Wil shifted and lifted his chin with defiance. "I am no mercenary, Your Majesty."

"I didn't say you were," she replied. "Simply that you have the skill for it." She knit her eyebrows. "Pray tell, what is your profession, Traveler? A man does not learn the art of war by sleeping on stones and begging for bread. Surely, you can't have spent many days aimlessly wandering the continent."

"I was not aware that your hospitality required each and every detail of my life's story."

"It doesn't. But in Aemogen, we say that only those who don't live in truth keep their secrets close."

"With that, I can agree," Wil answered, an edge in his voice.

"A few nights ago, Wil Traveler," Eleanor said, "in jest, I accused you of having no skill worth sharing with me or my people. Perhaps I was wrong. I might find I've a very great need of you."

She stood and, with a signal for Gaulter Alden, Aedon, and Crispin to follow, left the hall, Hastian ever in her shadow.

Later, after Wil had drifted to sleep, a pounding on his door jarred him from his dreams. Before he was fully cognizant, Wil was kneeling, knife in hand.

"Who is it?" he called out, sleep still in his voice.

"They want you in the throne room," a voice said.

Wil's heart thumped loudly against his ribs, and he cursed as he jumped from his bed and grabbed his clothes. "In the middle of the night?" Wil answered back while pulling his shirt over his bare chest, covering the mark on his skin.

"The queen desires an audience," came the voice, hovering

in uncertainty. After Wil was clothed, he reached for his boots, propped where he'd left them against the wall.

"Just a moment," Wil said as he pulled on one boot then the other, grunting as he forced his feet through to the bottom. What could the Aemogen queen possibly want this time of night? Wil cleared his sleep-fogged thoughts, breathing in deep, wiping his forehead. His stomach began to twist, and he took another deep breath.

Washing his face with some water from the basin on a table beneath the window, he then hid his knife under his shirt, against his back, and moved towards the door, expecting Crispin to be there, waiting. He wasn't. Two guards that he recognized from sparing in the yard were before him, conversing with the two already assigned to watch Wil's room. They asked cordially if they could escort him to the throne room, as if Wil had any other options. Crispin joined them en route, falling into step with his men after giving Wil a tired smile.

When Wil entered the throne room, it was empty of all but two men and the queen. Few torches were lit, but he saw their faces clearly enough, recognizing Aedon and Gaulter Alden. A shadow in the dim chamber moved, and Wil could see Hastian a few steps behind the throne. Crispin took a seat next to Aedon and said something to the councillor.

"Wil Traveler," the queen addressed him from her throne. Wil shifted his weight, moving his hand instinctively close to his hilt, but it, of course, was not there.

"We both know you are more than what you initially shared with the Aemogen court," she said.

Wil's chest tightened. His heart jumped, and he felt the pulse of tension he had long grown accustomed to in his life. Uncertain whether the queen expected him to speak, he maintained his silence.

"You are obviously a man of the North," Eleanor continued, "with knowledge and skills that Gaulter Alden assures me could have only come from formal training. You have spoken little of your past. Regardless, we have given our hospitality as a long-standing tradition of honor among our people." Eleanor studied his face. "We haven't pressed you, but now, for reasons obvious, we need to know who you are and why you have come to Aemogen at this time."

Wil nodded once, returning Eleanor's direct gaze. Gaulter Alden frowned. Aedon was rubbing his hand across his chin and staring relentlessly. Crispin watched the floor.

"Well?" Eleanor said as she waited.

"I'm from a noble family of Imirillia," Wil said.

Crispin brought his chin up. Gaulter Alden exchanged a glance with Aedon. Although no one spoke, Wil could feel the tenor of the air change. Each person had questions, but they waited. For what? Wil wondered. He did not know, until he followed the movements of their eyes. They were waiting for the queen. Had she been angry, suspicious, or cold, Wil would have felt prepared to negotiate the situation. Instead, Eleanor remained placid, calm, almost serene.

"Are you part of the Imirillian army?" she asked in the same manner she might ask if he enjoyed dancing.

"I was pressed into service at a young age," Wil said, lowering his head, his eyes still trained on the queen's. "But, as you can see, I am not standing with them now."

Eleanor waved her hand. It was subtle, but all the men in the room sat up straighter in response to the gesture. She had effectually opened the room for questioning.

Gaulter Alden spoke first. "Then, are you a deserter of the Imirillian army?"

"I wouldn't go that far," Wil said as he raised his eyebrows, tilting his head at an angle. He was aware of every person in the room—aware of their movements, who was armed, who was not—and aware of the knife against the bare skin of his back beneath his shirt. "I was recently given a commission in the emperor's army," he added, "which I refused."

"Why?" Crispin asked, looking genuinely confused, the only one without suspicious hostility. Aedon said something under his breath to Gaulter Alden, who harrumphed. Wil decided to tell the truth.

"The Imirillian army is responsible for the death of my brother. I have become," Wil explained as he challenged Aedon with a grim smile, "disenchanted, as it were, with its aggression."

Eleanor narrowed her eyes at him.

"If you are not a deserter," Gaulter Alden said, then cleared his throat and sank farther into his seat, "then how is it you have time to *tour* the Southern nations?"

"As I said before, I am noble born," Wil answered. "That affords me certain privileges." Wil glanced upward, searching his Aemogen vocabulary. "It's comparable to an extended holiday."

The queen acknowledged his words by scarcely breaking the line of her mouth in smile. Her expression made him feel strangely exposed and discomfited. Simultaneously, the queen's stare gave Wil an intense desire to know what she was thinking, sending Wil's mood toward an unaccustomed swivet. But Eleanor sat back, listening, seeming to have no intention of revealing anything.

"You see," Wil continued, when no one spoke, "my father

knows of my struggles and has given me time to know my own mind. He has a certain amount of...*pull* with Emperor Shaamil. My desire for time was granted easily enough."

"You claimed your mother was a Marion, yet your father is an Imirillian noble?" Aedon asked.

"My father governs the lands that press against Marion's northern border, on the edge of the stone sea. It is common, since Marion's alliance with Imirillia," Wil explained, "to marry women out of Marion. There are many such alliances in the region."

"When do you return home?" Crispin asked.

Frowning, Wil ran the back of his knuckles across his chin. "I couldn't tell you as I've yet to decide where I stand."

"Are you for hire?" Crispin inquired earnestly.

Aedon scoffed and interjected, "It's a little premature to ask such a question, before knowing anything about the man."

Eleanor seemed to pay no mind to Aedon's words, but looked steadily at Wil, as if waiting for him to respond to the captain's question.

"Wil Traveler's training could be invaluable," Crispin said, defending his question, before he pointedly looked back at Wil. "Well?"

"No," Wil answered flatly. "I am not for hire."

Eleanor finally spoke. "Are you willing to aid Aemogen without pay?" His astonishment at her question must have been clear on his face, for she looked at him with, what Wil thought was, a trace of distant amusement. And in the seconds after she had spoken, Eleanor appeared strangely ageless, a prophetess, perhaps. Emotions rose in Wil's chest—the edges of pride and shame, of homesickness and freedom—pulsing outward against the inside of his skin and back into his bones.

"I could be convinced," he said, the words feeling dry in his mouth. He had not foreseen this request.

"Then, we will consider if it be worth convincing you," Eleanor said as she stood. "We are done for tonight. I apologize, Wil Traveler, for taking you from your sleep. I hope you do not object to your retaining the companionship of the palace guard."

"I don't object," Wil answered, almost disbelieving his interview was over. "It's very understandable, considering your position."

"Good." With that, the queen stood and then withdrew through the door behind the tapestries. Hastian followed. Then Wil was taken back to his room in the travelers' house.

As soon as he had shut the door behind him, Wil let out a long breath, closed his eyes, and smiled.

Eleanor's knees felt limp. She had almost run to her apartments, and, after leaving Hastian in the antechamber, she had dismissed her maid and fled to her own room, where she fell across the bed. Her heart was pounding; her breathing, quick in her throat. She had used all her energy in containing her emotions: measuring out equally each word, each movement, and shaping her face to appear entertained, as if it were a game. The council had already spoken at length before the interview with Wil, whom she now knew to be an Imirillian soldier.

Now, the deep night left her alone with the reality of what was before her, and she could not quiet her mind or her pulse. Eleanor's heart pounded out in double rhythm. And with each breath, she tried to fill her lungs but found she could not reach the bottom.

She looked around her, searching for an anchor, something to catch her thoughts and settle her mind. The windows were now dark shapes, arching to a point, rimmed with cut stone. She had studied those windows every day of her life, and now she ran her eyes along the familiar angles of each line, calming her heart with the steadiness that was the stone of Ainsley.

The candle near her bed was almost melted away. Eleanor turned, blew it out, and fell onto her back, giving herself over to the static darkness of her room.

⸺◦⊰⊱◦⸺

Early the next morning, Eleanor assembled her war council.

They met around the long table in her private apartments.

"There is no sense in the Imirillian army waiting until almost winter to invade," Aedon repeated again, even though the council had spoken of this several times.

Eleanor looked away from the window to her councillor. "Unless they suppose that, rather than a fight, this will be the simplest campaign," she said. "They march in, anticipate little resistance, considering the size of our country, and plan to winter comfortably. That means Aemogen needs to have a substantial harvest for them to live on."

Gaulter Alden nodded. "You may be right, Your Majesty," he said. "Though they must think very little of our abilities to give us six months to come up with a defense."

"Regardless, we supposedly have time," she said. "The question before this council is what should we do with it?" Eleanor leaned forward in her chair and looked at each member of her war council individually: Gaulter Alden; Crispin; Aedon; Sean, councillor of husbandry; Briant, to oversee the armory; and Doughlas, leader of Eleanor's fen riders.

Hayden, the aged historian and scribe, was also there, as

secretary. Usually content to listen, he made a motion with his hand. Eleanor turned her eyes on him.

"What have you to say, Hayden?" she asked.

"A full battle run must take place," he said, his voice paper-thin, his hands shaking with age, as he shuffled through the old sheets of vellum before him on the table. "Its benefits are clear; its tradition, important—but it would need to begin soon."

Eleanor motioned towards Gaulter Alden. "We discussed the battle run last night," she said. "For a decision to fight or surrender can only be made once we've assessed the numbers and abilities of Aemogen's men. My suggestion to the council is this: the spring festival is in a matter of days. We will inform the people of the threat the day after, then encourage them to plant their fields, prepare their gardens, whatever needs be, within the month."

"Following that," she continued, "we begin the battle run, which can take two or three months' time." Eleanor moved her finger along the wood of the table before continuing. "We can't trust the Imirillian army to keep its word on timing, but we have been so long away from war as a country that our men need this training. I am willing to make the gamble that we will at least have three or four months, if not the full six months promised."

"And, if we have no time at all?" Aedon asked. "If they are mere weeks away from attacking Aemogen?"

"You know I ordered fifty men to the guard tower in the pass," she said. "They should be arriving today and sending word on what they find. I've also dispatched our fastest fen rider—"

Doughlas cleared his throat.

"Pardon, Doughlas," Eleanor said wryly. "I have dispatched our *second* fastest fen rider to the court of King Staven, asking if he will stand with us, since the Imirillian army will have to cross through

Marion to reach us. Our harbors, as we all know, are inaccessible to outside ships, so the only possible threat will come through the pass."

"If Staven will stand with us?" Sean asked. "Marion has been our closest ally for almost one hundred years. Surely, King Staven stands with us."

"If," Eleanor repeated firmly. "The Marion constitution has been modified, which includes the rules of war. It does not appear to be a significant change," she said, "but the implications are significant."

She picked up one of the papers before her and began to read. "The country of Marion retains the right to act, in times of war, in any manner best serving Marion's interests." Eleanor paused. "It used to say 'and the interests of Marion's allies.' That has now been erased. There are other subtle changes, which allow Marion to move forward with no obligations to honor past allegiances."

Eleanor looked up. "I'm certain you all remember King Staven's younger sister, the Princess Edith, who became the third wife of Shaamil, the emperor of Imirillia. Marion has since entertained cautious treaties with the Imirillian Empire. And now, a sudden change is made to the constitution, removing all barriers of previous allegiance? I suspect Marion will not be of any help," Eleanor said as she frowned. "In all actuality, I fear what damage King Staven may inflict."

"The arrogant fool," Aedon muttered with consternation, his arms crossed. "One cannot court a viper without being bit oneself."

After a somber moment where nobody spoke, Eleanor cleared her throat, and the council commenced with plans for the battle run. They were just finishing, when Crispin asked to speak. Eleanor gave him the floor, and he stood.

"I propose we enlist the help of Wil Traveler to—" Crispin said.

"He is an Imirillian soldier," Aedon interrupted.

"Yes," Crispin responded to Aedon, "and the best swordsman I have ever seen in my life." Crispin paused. "With due respect to Gaulter Alden, and all our men, we are no fighting nation. We have shunned war, so we do not know the art nearly well enough to defend ourselves from this threat."

"And how has he learned his art?" Gaulter Alden asked, raising his eyebrows, leaning forward against the table. "I have watched him sparring. He is a devil with a sword and, obviously, a young man with status and prominence. I want to know why he came into Aemogen mere days before the Imirillian Empire sent us their ultimatum. It is too much a coincidence."

Eleanor watched the faces of the men gathered around the table, listening to the questions she had already spent the night before asking herself.

Sean, in his thick dialect of the Aemogen hills, followed Gaulter Alden's comment with his own thoughts. "He rides the finest horse I've ever seen, and I'd like to know where I could get such a beast. I know for a fact," he said, "that the Imirillian Army uses only black horses. It's widely known to any man wanting to sell or breed a horse, even in Aemogen. We sell our black horses to Marion and know they trade them with Zarbadast."

"So he rides a white horse as a symbol of what he told us last night: that he has cast off the Imirillian army," Crispin posited.

"So," Aedon countered, "he rides a white horse to throw us off."

Crispin, still standing, spoke firmly. "We can't know his true motives in surety, but I do know that the palace guard are now better prepared for war than they were even a mere two days ago, thanks to his training. He is an asset. We should use him." Then,

Crispin turned towards Aedon. "It would be foolish," he said, "to make this decision based on suspicion or jealousy."

"Excuse me?" Aedon challenged.

"Please," Eleanor said as she stood, and Crispin took his seat. "I have given this a significant amount of thought. There is much we do not know about Wil Traveler. He may indeed be only passing through. Or," she said as she met Aedon's eyes, "his timing, what we know of him, all may be tied in with the Imirillian invasion."

Crispin moved to speak, but Eleanor held up her hand. "I have also seen him fight," she said. "Crispin is right: Wil's prowess is… astonishing. If he will stand with us, I want to utilize his skills."

"And if he is against us, as almost all the odds grant he is?" Gaulter Alden asked.

"If he is against us," Eleanor spoke quickly, "I want to use his knowledge in our favor, and I want to keep him as close as possible, watching his every move. The battle run must begin soon if we are to be ready in time to face the Imirillian army. I would like to appoint Wil Traveler as an assistant commander of the battle run. We will bring him with us and make certain he can entertain no mischief."

"Eleanor," Aedon said as he stood, "isn't it folly to let him see all our strengths and weaknesses before knowing his allegiance?"

"The queen is right, young man," Gaulter Alden said, motioning for Aedon to sit. "She realizes what, perhaps, you do not see. In war, you must balance what will be of greater service, even if that means apparent compromise."

"Clearly we are much smaller than the Imirillian army," Eleanor continued. "So, their knowledge of our numbers is a price worth paying if it means we can increase our ability to fight. Six months' time is not much, but it is enough to improve our chances," she said. "We won't know until after the battle run, but if we decide to fight, his training may prove to be our only recourse for survival as an independent nation."

Crispin nodded and thumped the table with his hands.

"I ask for a vote of confidence in my decision," Eleanor said as she sat down.

"Aye," Gaulter Alden said.

"Aye," Crispin echoed.

"Aye," Sean and Doughlas said at once. But Aedon sat stubbornly, then he looked directly at Eleanor. She raised an eyebrow, waiting for his answer.

"I will support you until the end, Eleanor," he said, "but, I do not cast my confidence behind this decision."

She studied Aedon's expression.

"I trust that, although you don't agree, you will back my decision?"

"If it is what you decide," he replied. "Yes."

"Well," Eleanor said, looking at the men around the table. "I can't understand a way through this. Yet, I feel it can't be impossible, despite our fears. We'll prepare for the battle run and, if Wil Traveler accepts, initiate him into our councils and gain whatever we can from his experience. If he will not offer his assistance," she added, "we will ask him to leave Aemogen, or we will finally make use of the dungeon. It has not seen a political prisoner in all the years I can remember."

Briant, the arms expert, was the only person who seemed pleased with this notion.

Then the council broke, the voices of the men engaged in immediate conversation as they rose from the table. Eleanor watched them as she deliberately kept her own thoughts from her face. Crispin approached."You've made the right decision, Eleanor," he said.

"I've seen him fight, Crispin," Eleanor said sharply. "And so, I want to know where he is at all times while in Aemogen. You will see that he is watched."

Crispin nodded. "He will be," he promised. "Should I ask if he will join us?"

Eleanor pursed her lips. "I will extend the invitation myself," she said.

"Certainly," Crispin replied, turning to leave.

"Crispin?"

"Yes?"

"We need to be ready for anything—" Eleanor began.

Crispin waited for Eleanor to finish her thought. It took almost a full minute, for Eleanor was unaccustomed to these words in her mouth.

"That means," she said, "you need to be ready to eliminate him if things go badly."

CHAPTER

FIVE

"What is the battle run?" Wil asked, not looking at Eleanor, who stood outside the stall where he worked. He had spent the last hour in the stable, brushing Hegleh's coat and seeing to her care. Waiting at a distance, by the door, were his guards.

"The tradition of our people is for the reigning monarch and the war council to ride out to all the fens. A call to arms is made, a count of soldiers is taken, and training begins. It is an old tradition," Eleanor said, and paused. "After the battle run, when we know our numbers and skill, we convene for a war council here, in Ainsley, with the fen lords, to decide if we surrender or prepare for battle."

Wil did not respond immediately, but he knelt down, moving his fingers gently along Hegleh's swollen fetlock. When he did answer her, he spoke from the ground, where Eleanor could not see his face. "It's lucky that you've such advance warning. You wouldn't have been ready for an immediate attack of any kind."

Wil pretended to be busier than he was, waiting for the queen to speak.

"We value deliberation here in Aemogen," she replied. "War is certainly nothing to rush into, but, when necessary, we have ways to organize more quickly."

Wil rubbed some of the grit from the stable floor between his fingers, sighed, and stood, facing Eleanor as he leaned forward against the stable gate.

She wore a beautiful riding dress of pale gold, the color of wheat in the fall. Her lips, pink against the cold spring wind, offset her fair skin, and her copper hair looked like fire, pulled away from her face in a dance of loose braids. He lingered a moment on the lines of her face before speaking.

"And you offer me, an Imirillian soldier, a post on your war council?"

"Yes."

He shook his head but bit off the edge of a laugh. "May I ask why?"

"We would benefit greatly from your expertise," was Eleanor's response. "I'm certain, after the few days you have spent sparing in the yard, you understand that for yourself."

Wil looked down at his boots and kicked the gate softly. "What I don't understand," his eyes returned to Eleanor, "is why you would trust a complete stranger, part of the empire that is invading you, into your inner confidences."

"I'm not a fool, Wil Traveler." Eleanor's words were barbed. "I know my country is underprepared. Crispin says your guidance would be advantageous. I agree with him. It's true; for all I really know, you could be a spy. Even so, whatever you could gain from us is far less than what we would gain from you. It is a risk I am willing to take."

She took some leather riding gloves in her hand and slid them over her fingers. "We would pay you well, and obviously offer permanent hospitality, if you should choose to accept it."

"I don't need payment from you," Wil countered the queen with a laugh. She looked annoyed, as if she had sensed what he was thinking: that all her wealth was a fraction, compared to his own.

"Why do you laugh?"

"You wear gloves to ride a horse but not to dig in the dirt," he deflected. "I find it a bit odd."

"Add it to your list, Traveler," Eleanor said, tossing the words over her shoulder as she walked down towards the far end of the stable, exhibiting a different persona from the one she'd shown in his midnight interview a dozen hours earlier. Thrift had been saddled and was waiting with a groom. Wil followed her out, not speaking until after the groom had helped her mount. "When do you need an answer?" Wil asked, leaning against the post as he looked up at the queen.

"The spring festival is in three days," Eleanor replied, her eyes on the western gates rather than him. "The morning after, I would expect you at a logistics meeting. The battle run begins in a month's time."

"Why so late?"

Her eyes came back to his own. "We are an agrarian society, Wil. What fools would we be to not get our crops in the ground." Thrift shifted anxiously beneath her, and she gave a light touch on the reins. "And to be clear, I never suggested taking you into my inner confidences."

She urged Thrift forward, riding from the yard through the west gate, into the fields beyond.

———◦◦◦◦◦◦———

Wil watched from the western battlement, near the travelers' house, as Thrift tried to run at the pace of a wild spring day across the downs of Ainsley. Eleanor, at length, gave the horse free rein, and they flew through the tumble of cloud and color. She rode proficiently, if not naturally, but the true grace was Thrift's, whose faultless form and sense of movement was far more spirited than Eleanor's methodical steadiness.

Wil wondered if Eleanor ever imagined all her thoughts and worries being pulled from her mind, getting caught in the waiting trees, blowing in all directions until nothing remained to trouble her, just the beat of her heart, pounding in rhythm with Thrift's hooves. That was how he often felt when he rode his own horses through the unsteady, wind-cursed sands of the Northern deserts.

Conscious of the guards at his back, Wil turned away from watching Eleanor and sat against the battlement. The stone was cold against his back. Pulling his cloak close around his shoulders, Wil looked up, following trails of cloud in the gray sky. The warm sands of Imirillia were so distant now, far from this hard-set place. And she had asked for his help.

Wil thought about the men he had seen in the Ainsley streets—farmers and day laborers. The miners that worked along the western mountains were sure to be strong, but a mine was no battle-field.

And Aemogen was no warring nation.

Wil ran his fingers through his hair and then pulled a knee up, resting his forearm against it. There, on his right wrist, was the thin and knotted Safeeraah given him by Dantib, his stable master and mentor. Wil scowled, pulling at the imperfectly woven band, so light that he had almost forgotten it was there. But the promise it symbolized weighed heavy in his heart. Before realizing what he was doing, Wil spoke the words out loud. "Though I wander, I am the deep well; I seek transcendence by honor, as the seven stars."

"I am the deep well," Wil repeated, letting his chin fall against his chest. He knew that if Aemogen chose to fight the Imirillian Empire, there would be an entire generation of men slaughtered, leaving the women and children in the hands of a foreign power. And Queen Eleanor, the young soul, would be killed for her refusal to surrender. The images were haunting as they invaded his mind; he brushed them violently away.

Wil had to convince the queen to surrender.

The bound collection of stories, which kept Wil sprawled out on his bed reading, secured his interest enough to ignore the noises echoing through the travelers' house. Every room was filling or full. Wil did not relish the idea of occupying the building with much of anyone. He was accustomed to his own space. So, he had closed the door and disappeared into the collection of tales, or, as Edythe had called them, Faeries.

In the middle of one tale, about a princess cursed to sleep for one hundred years, his door burst open. Someone his own age came through, carrying several bags and satchels. The young man, with light brown hair and eyes, smiled at Wil and disappeared, leaving his things strewn all about the floor. Almost annoyed, Wil had just turned back to his story when the door flew open again, and the same young man, with even more bags, came tumbling into the room. He stood, brushed himself off, and closed the door to the noisy hall.

"Hello," he beamed as he sat on the other empty bed nearby. "I'm Blaike, of Common Field fen." He extended his hand so exuberantly that Wil put down the tales and sat up, facing his fellow lodger and shaking hands.

"Wil is my name."

"Pleased to meet you, indeed. You must be the traveler that everyone's been speaking of." Blaike stood again and began placing his several bags and satchels against the wall. He bumped Wil's scabbard and sword, which were resting in the corner, knocking them to the floor, and scrambled to apologize while setting them right. Wil waved it off.

"What have they been saying?" he asked Blaike casually.

"Handsome as the devil and double that with a sword," Blaike answered, still placing his things in order and, unintentionally, setting Wil's effects in disarray. "Edythe wrote me all about it."

"Are you Edythe's man?" Wil hid his smile beneath a hand.

"Yes," the young man said proudly before his face fell. "And no. To make it official, engaged and all that, I have to speak with the queen."

"And?"

"She terrifies me."

Wil laughed, loud and hard, until he lay on his bed, wiping tears from his eyes. Looking up at the ceiling, he responded. "She terrifies me too, Blaike, although I have no idea why." Wil lifted himself up on one elbow. "How long have you and Edythe been a pair?"

"Three years, more or less."

The young man was obviously in love. He began to speak of Edythe's wit and humor and sweetness; how her blue eyes sparkled when she danced; and how, when she was upset, Blaike felt as if the world had ended. His affection was young and sincere, untouched by personal motives. Wil found himself grinning as he listened, enjoying Blaike's exultations. It was not often someone could disarm him so. Wil decided he didn't mind sharing quarters with the young man, however smitten.

"But you will ask for her hand while in Ainsley?" Wil goaded his new friend.

Blaike turned solemn. "So I told myself the entire journey here, but I don't think I can find the courage to ask the queen."

"How long are you here?" Wil asked, surprised he hoped Blaike's stay would be long.

"Tomorrow and the following day, the seed bringers will spend all day registering their seeds and receiving any needed stock from the palace, and all that. The Spring Festival is the day after. I am the second seed bringer from Common Field, so I'll be busy helping, but Brannan, the first seed bringer, has given me permission to stay a few days longer." He smiled, then added shyly, "They are all rooting for me back home, you know."

"Why don't we come to an arrangement?" Wil lay down on his back, arms folded beneath his head. "You answer any questions I may have about Aemogen, the royal family, and so forth, and I will set up a meeting between yourself and Eleanor."

Blaike's face turned ashen, and he pulled at his collar. "I'll have to think about that."

Wil began to laugh, giving Blaike an encouraging smile. "She'll say yes, you know."

⟡

The next morning, Wil stood in line with his fellow petitioners, waiting for the doors of the throne room to open. He hoped

Eleanor would be present, knowing she was involved personally in whatever work these seed bringers did. Blaike had left at dawn and had been occupied ever since. Wil waited behind a few men and a surly boy of twelve, who seemed displeased to be there. The boy started to speak and was cuffed soundly on the ear by one of his companions. Yelping, he stepped back and threw dangerous glances at all who passed. Only Wil remained exempt: the boy offered him curious admiration.

Finally the doors opened, and Wil followed the men into the throne room. The councillors were all in their places, including Edythe, who gave Wil a slight wave. Behind them, a representative from each fen waited.

Wil looked towards the throne. It was empty. He frowned. Perhaps the queen would not oversee the audience today. Then, the sound of a door, and Eleanor appeared from behind the tapestries, wearing a stiff, deep green gown. Hastian followed, standing behind her as she took her seat.

The councillor of petitions stepped forward. "A matter of justice to be decided."

"Which fen?" Eleanor asked.

"Faenan fen."

Eleanor motioned the Faenan fen councillor to stand. "You may come forward," she said, and the boy was ushered before the throne. Wil noticed that all the bravado had left his face; he now looked sick. Eleanor eyed the companions with curiosity. "What could possibly be the crime?"

The man who'd cuffed the boy in the hall stepped forward and bowed. "Your Majesty, Godric is my sister's child. He's caused enough trouble in Faenan, but lately, he's taken to shirking work and disappearing with the property of others. It's a small matter, yes, but he has gone before the Faenan council five times, received retribution, and it's done no good on the matter."

"What were the retributions given?" Eleanor asked.

"We've added work to his day, removed privileges, ordered apologies, and demanded an oath, all to no avail."

Eleanor leaned her elbow against the arm of her throne. "And yet, Godric, you have continued to fleece others for their belongings."

To Wil's ears, she sounded tired when she spoke. The boy, so startled the queen addressed him directly, began to shake, too frightened to answer.

Eleanor looked at his uncle. "What were the items he stole?"

"Uh," the farmer scratched the back of his neck. "If I can remember, a shovel, a small knife, some kitchenware. He'd take them out into the woods and right ruin them for proper use before they were found." Then, probably feeling he had been too casual, he dropped his hand and bowed while adding, "Your Majesty."

Eleanor surveyed the subjects before her. "What were you using the tools for, Godric?"

Godric did not answer until his uncle nudged him forward. Finally, a small sound came from his throat.

"I am sorry," Eleanor said as she smiled. "Will you answer once more? I couldn't hear, for my councillors were talking." She glared at Sean, who had been whispering with Aedon. Wil grinned openly at the rebuke.

"Hunting," the boy said, his small voice breaking against itself, causing the word to come out sounding very young.

"Well," Eleanor said, and motioned for Crispin to approach the throne. As they spoke quietly, the sound of her voice could be heard, but the words were indiscernible. Crispin disappeared, and

Eleanor sat motionless, waiting.

Everyone watched as Eleanor moved her fingers along the wood grain of her throne, her mind apparently miles away from Ainsley. When Crispin returned, he handed Eleanor what looked like a small knife with a belt and a leather case.

She inspected the piece, before saying, "Would you please approach the throne, Godric?"

The boy, eyeing the small knife with envy, walked to Eleanor. When she held the belt and knife out towards the boy, his young hands reached out eagerly, shaking as he took them from his queen. Wil pursed his lips and looked down, touched, certain that to Godric she must appear incomprehensibly wonderful.

"Godric, we do not steal in Aemogen, as you well know," Eleanor said. "I do not suppose you would like it if your uncle or, perhaps, a cousin came and took this knife from you, without asking permission to borrow it?"

The boy wrapped his fingers around the leather sheath, shaking his head.

"I will give this to you, Godric, as a gift from me, with the understanding that if you thieve in the future, I will have this sent back to Ainsley Castle. Do you understand what I propose?"

"Yes," Godric said.

"Good," Eleanor responded. "I also desire that you approach every member of Faenan fen from whom you have taken property and offer your services for the afternoon, whatever their needs be." Eleanor looked up around the room. "Do I have an officer to see it done?"

One of the Faenan men—not the uncle, but a shorter, older man—stepped forward.

"I offer myself as officer," he said. "I'll see it done and teach him how to use his knife properly."

"Good." Eleanor dismissed them.

As the men bowed and turned towards the door, Godric looked back as if he would throw his arms around the queen, giving her an impish smile instead—which Eleanor returned—before running after the men from Faenan.

The petitioner stood again. "A request for—" he hesitated, looking towards Wil, his eyes going wide. "A request for—" the man flushed. "A request, Your Majesty."

"Yes, Wil Traveler?" Eleanor was curt.

"I have a—" he began.

"A request," Eleanor interrupted. "Yes, I heard."

"I come on behalf of Blaike, second seed bringer of Common Field fen, who desires a private audience with," Wil paused as he bowed with a flourish, "Your Grace."

Eleanor looked stunned only a moment before a slow smile spread across her mouth. Crispin was laughing and saying something to an embarrassed Edythe. Even the corners of Aedon's mouth turned upward.

"You may tell Blaike that his request will be granted after the festival and that it would be my pleasure were he to remain in Ainsley as my special guest for several days after."

Wil nodded. "Thank you, Your Majesty. The third floor of the travelers' house is greatly indebted to you, as we will be spared any future moaning—"

Crispin laughed harder as Eleanor cut Wil off, inviting him to leave the throne room before all decorum was lost.

CHAPTER

SIX

Preparations for the spring festival could be heard all over Ainsley. People from different fens poured into the city, guests of friends, or family. They lifted colorful banners, ribbons, and spring flowers across the streets and above their thresholds. Craftsmen brought their wares, setting up in squares around Ainsley. Wild spring berries, breads, meats, hand-crafted cheeses, wood crafts, and stone crafts— all wrapped and prepared for the events of the following day.

Ainsley Castle made its own preparations, for Eleanor would host a grand midday meal for the fen lords, seed bringers, councillors, and their families. There would be games and dancing far into the night on Ceiliuradh, the main square. All was noise and energy. But, inside her apartments, Eleanor sat in somber discussion with Aedon.

"Those are the numbers," Aedon said as he presented Eleanor with a piece of paper. "I have made rough estimates of each fen."

Eleanor studied the figures Aedon had made. "So, you think we have little chance of pulling together more than twenty-seven hundred men?"

"Not necessarily," Aedon said. "I admit to being cautious. I didn't include those over sixty or those younger than fourteen in my estimates. Frankly, it's all guesswork, until we visit the fens themselves."

His honey colored hair was pushed away from his eyes, cut short by Aemogen standards. It had a slight curl that Eleanor had always liked. Aedon was working out another set of figures, his light blue eyes engaged in his work, when he noticed her watching him.

"What?" he asked.

"Nothing," Eleanor said as she waved his question away. "I was feeling envious of your hair, that's all."

Giving her a crooked smile, Aedon was about to reply, when the door opened. Crispin entered, followed by Wil Traveler. Eleanor looked down at the papers on her desk and gathered as much patience as she could muster. Of course Crispin, in his casual trust, would not think Eleanor would object to having Wil in her personal audience chamber.

"Eleanor!" Crispin said, apparently oblivious to Eleanor's displeasure. Wil, however, was shifting his feet nervously. He had not mistaken the weight of her mood. "Wil has made his decision," Crispin said eagerly. "He's to join with us in training."

What had felt like a weight, a stone, resting in Eleanor's chest shifted and dropped, getting caught in a new place, and she hesitated to respond. Whether it was relief she felt at the unexpected aid or a substantial fear at the gamble she was taking, Eleanor did not know. The emotions were difficult to decipher.

Aedon had not turned to face Crispin or Wil, but his expression exhibited the same balancing act Eleanor felt in the pit of her stomach. She met his eyes, taking courage from the discernible matching of their emotions.

"And will you pledge your allegiance and honor to the fidelity of your aid?" she questioned.

Wil's own struggle was evident. Eleanor watched his right hand tug at the black fabric covering his left forearm. With his voice catching on itself, he spoke.

"I offer my faithful allegiance to you and Aemogen for the duration of this battle run. I will help prepare your men for war, hoping you make the best decision for your people." Wil shifted and lifted his chin. "I will not hide from you that I do not believe you can defeat any part of the Imirillian army. I would be loath to counsel you try."

Eleanor sat, unmoving. She was aware of the afternoon sun burning through her windows, how it claimed patterns and shapes on the rugs of her apartment. She was aware of Wil's arrow-sharp expression. She was aware that she didn't want to believe him. Crispin stood silent, and Aedon sat tight as stone. Nothing was spoken, as if the day had fallen asleep around them and forgotten. Eleanor, unsure if she should regret her choice, watched the dust arching gracefully through the air before she spread her palms flat against her desk and looked back at the Imirillian soldier.

"I accept your pledge," she said. "And I will weigh the value of your counsel only after we know more about our own capabilities and the threat against us." Eleanor stood. "Thank you, Crispin, Wil. You may go."

Wil's guards were dismissed. He retreated to his room in the travelers' house and was relieved when Blaike announced that the evening meal had been canceled in preparation for the festival.

"Would you like anything from the kitchens?" Blaike asked.

Wil did not. He wasn't hungry, nor did he desire to join Blaike and his friends in their merriment. He lay down on his bed, pulling his arms tight across his chest, watching the light fade from the window before him. Never had he made a decision he felt so strongly to be right; never had he felt such a desire to question the sanity of what he had just done.

Morning came, and Wil woke to find himself still in his clothes, lying on the bed. He had slept soundly. Blaike was already awake and greeted him warmly.

"Edythe sent a fresh change of clothing for you," he said, pointing to some black garments, hastily thrown over a chair. "She said they will fit well enough and that, after the festival, you shall have more made to your liking. She is thoughtful, Edythe is."

Wil stood, stretching through the stiffness of the night, and inspected the garments, feeling the knit of the cloth between his fingers. They were similar in style and taste to what he wore already.

"Give Edythe my thanks." Wil yawned, noticing Blaike had already filled his basin with fresh water. He cleaned himself, shaving with a flat razor, before slipping into the new clothes. They fit well. Wil threw the windows open to let the fresh morning air into the stuffy chamber. It was chilled, cold even, having come down from the northern mountains. As he sat on his bed, pulling his boots on, Wil began to feel the day move in him.

"I assume you're guiding me through the festival?" Wil asked. He reclined on his bed while Blaike finished his own preparations.

Blaike, who seemed content enough to have spent half his morning whistling, obliged. "It'd be a pleasure. I dare say you will have never seen a spectacle more grand in all your days."

Wil released a slow smile and looked casually towards the

ceiling. Ainsley must be the seed bringer's height of a sophisticated setting. Wil knew it to be small, provincial, an out-of-the-way life.

As they left the travelers' house, Wil asked, "Will we stop in the meal hall for breakfast?"

"No," Blaike said as he shook his head. "Didn't anyone tell you? We all go without food to be ready for the ceremony."

"No breakfast?" Wil balked.

"Shh!" Blaike put his finger to his lips, motioning for Wil to be silent. "Everyone is gathered already."

Wil muttered, following Blaike through the square, believing his decision to miss dinner had been almost as foolish as his coming to this silly pocket of the world in the first place.

The entire Ainsley Rise was filled with people, standing as close as they could, waiting in silence. Even the children were hushed, none speaking or whispering. Before Wil could say that their celebration appeared more funeral than festival, he recognized the quality of the stillness: it was like a prayer. Wil bowed his head. Prayer he understood.

Fifteen men stepped forward into the empty space before the doors of Ainsley Castle. Most of them were old, with drawn eyes and loose skin around their jaws. A few were younger, taller, and less comfortable in their positions. One, looking more boy than sage, was wide-eyed, frightened. Their attire was simple but clean, their heads bent as they stood in a half circle in the center of the square.

"The seed bringers of each fen," Blaike whispered.

The doors opened and Eleanor's governing council, also consisting of fifteen men, filed out, forming a semicircle opposite the seed bringers. Wil scanned the familiar faces, then allowed his eyes to wander. He saw Crispin and several of his soldiers, standing at attention, spaced evenly about the square. Eleanor came through the doorway, followed by Edythe, who carried a graceful pitcher in her hands. The queen wore a gown the color of a spring storm, a garland of white blossoms woven through her copper hair. She moved to the center of the square, facing the seed bringers before her.

As Eleanor bowed her head, each person in the square did the same. Wil lowered his chin, keeping his eyes on her face. They came from her throat slowly, words he did not know and had never heard, full and rich, as if tilted sideways compared to the sounds of the Aemogen language now. It reminded Wil of the affection he felt for the antiquity of Imirillia's language and verse.

When the queen stopped speaking, she moved towards the seed bringer to her far left. He was the oldest of the fifteen, white-haired, his face given to wrinkles and time. Edythe followed her sister, standing at her left, holding the pitcher towards the queen. Eleanor placed her fingers into the pitcher. Then the seed bringer lifted his hands up before him, a humble expression resting on his face.

As Eleanor pulled her fingers from the pitcher, drops of water caught the morning sun and glistened as they fell to the ground. Eleanor placed her wet fingers in the palms of the old man's hands, speaking a line Wil couldn't hear. The man closed his hands around hers and knelt on the ground. She moved on to the next man, repeating the ritual.

As Eleanor moved closer, Wil began to understand her words. She was blessing these men to lead their fens to abundant harvests. As each knelt, the queen moved on. When Eleanor reached the youngest seed bringer, close to her in age, she smiled, performing the ritual with a clear measure of joy. When it came time for him to kneel, he grasped onto her hand for courage.

"The queen's cousin," Blaike whispered.

Eleanor returned to the center, the seed bringers still kneeling before her, and spoke another solemn line before approaching again the first seed bringer. Hayden, the historian, carried out a silver tray with fifteen bags made of soft green velvet, the finest fabric Wil had seen in Aemogen.

"They're seeds," Blaike explained.

As Eleanor approached each man, she handed him a bag and kissed him on the forehead, lifting him back to his feet. It was so intimate, this ceremony. The people stood in a strict reverence, watching their queen. Wil knew then that he should not be there, that this public moment had a private sanctity, undeserved by the casual outside spectator: thousands belonged to this closeness— one did not.

When Eleanor lifted the final seed bringer—her young cousin—to his feet, the crowd erupted into roaring cheers. Wil covered his ears, grinning at Blaike. Trumpets sounded, and Edythe ran to Eleanor's side. Shouts flooded out the southern gates and down the steps. Somewhere, musicians began to play as booths sprang into being, and the entire Rise lifted in colorful streamers. As he watched, Wil lost Blaike in the crowd.

Then someone clapped Wil on the shoulder. He turned to see Crispin at his side. Amid the press, Crispin shouted in Wil's ear. "And now the fun begins. There are more girls in Ainsley right now than I'll ever have time to flirt with."

"What's the day's schedule?" Wil asked as they pushed through the crowd spilling out of Ainsley Rise onto the stair towards the rest of the city.

"Enjoyment is the day's schedule!" Crispin waved to a few

young ladies, who called back in return. "But if you want to be more formal about it, the queen has a very grand midday meal, inviting the council, the seed bringers, and any fen lords to be found in the city. Did you receive an invitation?

"While all that formality goes on inside," Crispin continued, without waiting for a response, "which is not half bad if that's where you're stuck, people outside are playing games, having contests, and handing out rewards, prizes, sweet treats, and the occasional kiss." Crispin raised his eyebrows and smirked. "The games continue until late afternoon, when Eleanor and her party come to observe, participate, enjoy the spectacle. She takes petitions, mingles with the people, and makes an attempt to win some festival game. When evening falls, everyone is cleared to the edges of the large square," he said as he pointed down towards the Ceiliuradh on Ainsley stair, "and the dancing begins. It goes hours and hours, with plenty of pretty girls to go around. You'll not be disappointed."

"And you are free to enjoy the festival instead of serving at your post?"

"Of course," Crispin grinned. "My duties of the day were strictly ceremonial."

"But, will the queen be safe?" Wil asked in surprise.

"She has all of Aemogen watching over her—and Hastian. Of course she'll be safe," Crispin said, actually taking his eyes away from the displays of the festival to look at Wil while speaking, a rare touch of seriousness in his manner. "The queen is never safer than with her people."

"Does she ever dance?" Wil asked as he fought for space in the crowd.

"She used to dance more," was all Crispin responded, distracted by a wrestling competition.

Not relishing the thought of rolling through the dirt of the square, Wil returned upstream, as it were, to the castle grounds. The Rise was still bursting with people, as he knew the travelers' house would also be, and everybody was cheerful, friendly, which Wil, remembering he was hungry, was beginning to find suffocating.

He ducked behind the travelers' house and started up the stairs, taking them two at a time, towards the western battlements that overlooked the Ainsley downs. Perhaps there he could find space enough to breathe above the clatter.

Passing through a string of arches, he emerged onto the open battlements, taking the panorama into his lungs with the tight air. The general current of festival-goers drifted into the streets, leaving the Rise more subdued.

As Wil walked the west wall, its view and wind to himself, he thought about the rituals of the ceremony and Eleanor's part in it. He felt the need to cleanse himself somehow: to bathe, to pray, to receive pardon for his presence there. Wil's fingers searched his right forearm, still strangely disappointed to find nothing except the small, knotted braid of black leather.

Touching it with the ridges of his fingertips, he closed his eyes. "Though I wander, I am the deep well; I seek transcendence by honor, as the seven stars."

These words flew into the indifferent wind, and Wil exhaled, his anxiety eased but not answered for. A gust at his back pushed him towards the stone battlement, and he opened his eyes, seeing a flash of copper. Wil looked towards the northwest tower. Eleanor had walked out onto the battlements, still in her blue cloud gown, the wind whipping the fabric around her like ribbons of sand in the storm-ridden desert.

Wil straightened himself, wondering if he should turn to go, or greet the queen. She lifted her hand in acknowledgment, and he, unsure what protocol would dictate, moved towards her.

"Queen Eleanor," he said. She smiled briefly, but did not turn towards him. Rather, she looked away towards the north. "I'm sorry for the intrusion," Wil said, assuming that she wished he would leave.

Laughing at his worried tone, she met his eyes, the trace of tears on her cheeks. "If you want to make a brave man fearful, just cry," she said. She brushed her fingers, turned red from the lingering cold, across her face. When she spoke, it was with a cryptic relief. "All is well, Wil, no need for alarm. I've been hiding out in my secret sanctuary inside the northwest tower, an old room no longer in use that I've transformed into a study of sorts. No one can hear you through the walls, so it's a grand place for a good cry."

"I'd imagine," Wil said before he could check himself. "If I'm ever in need of a good cry—"

Eleanor laughed again and brushed the loose hair away from her face. "It's been such a beautiful day," she said. But her eyes were burdened.

"And tomorrow, you have to tell the people of the threat," Wil finished.

"Yes."

Wil turned around, leaning against the battlements, gazing toward Ainsley castle. "The ceremony of the seed bringers..." he began. "I was honored to have witnessed it." Then, braving a direct glance, he continued. "Quite touched, actually. And the rituals remain the same, then, year after year?"

"Yes." Eleanor took a deep breath. "And no. Each monarch

gives the seed bringers their bags and offers some gesture unique to their reign. My father shook their hand. My grandfather offered them a salute."

"And you," Wil said, looking at the queen, "a kiss."

"I was thirteen when I came to the throne," Eleanor began, laughing again, "and petrified. I didn't know what to do. Everyone promised I would, that it would be a natural show of the affection between the people and myself. But I was trembling. The first seed bringer was from Common Field, an old man whom I had known since childhood. He was so encouraging, so sweet that, after I gave him his seed bag, I forgot what I had intended to do and spontaneously kissed him on the forehead. And that was that." Eleanor's words were wrapped in such sincerity that it aggravated Wil's own unease.

"What did you give them?" he asked in an effort to deal with his discomfort. "What were the seeds?"

"A flower, revealed when it blooms." Eleanor drew her lips together, squinting her eyes against the coming emotion, but she continued to speak. "It happens every spring, you see. The people try to guess what flower it might be—it becomes a game among the fens. The monarch chooses a flower as a symbol for the coming year, a gift to the people."

"You love them."

"Yes." She had control over her voice now, and it was strong and quiet. "You should be down in the streets, Wil." Eleanor waved her hands at nothing, apparently finished with the discussion.

"My mother," Wil said, "used to say 'Never leave a soul who cries, until you have seen them smile seven times.'"

"If you follow that rule, you may never leave." Eleanor laughed again as she used the back of her hand to wipe her eyes. Wil turned back towards the downs, offering another phrase with a casual tone.

"My father often says, 'Sing today, tomorrow you die in glory.'"

"Such an outlook." Eleanor squinted, looking directly at him. "What else does he say?"

"That I am his greatest love and his greatest disappointment," Wil said. This time there was no amusement in his voice. Wil offered Eleanor a pained smile, regretting having shared anything at all.

"I am sorry." Eleanor's sympathy was apparent, but Wil shook his head.

"No, you must be glad of it," he said. "My father is not always a good man."

"And yet," the queen said, moving her hand to a string of white blossoms coming loose in her hair, "you love him. I can hear it in your voice, even as it sounds like you are disappointed in yourself that you do."

"Yes," Wil admitted as he crossed his arms and studied the stone beneath his feet. "I do love him, despite it all."

"Eleanor!"

They both turned their heads towards the stairs. Aedon stood there, paused near the tower. After expressing silent disapproval at Wil's presence, he walked to Eleanor's side.

"It's time to begin," Aedon stated after a worried scan of her face. "Are you well?"

"Yes." Eleanor nodded. "Wil and I have only been discussing parental wisdom." Eleanor's words did not appear to make Aedon feel any better as she linked arms with him in a familiar fashion. "Let's go down," she appeased. "There are all the festivities to be had—you're invited, Wil—and, after we eat, a full evening of revelry, games, and, once night falls, we dance."

Come evening, Ceiliuradh was awash and aglow with lights and occupied by dancers, vendors, and fairgoers. Crispin found Wil and took him under his wing, introducing him around the square.

"How many girls do you keep company with?" Wil asked, after Crispin led him away from a group of young ladies enjoying the festival.

"As many as I can." Crispin stopped at a booth and bought himself and Wil a drink. "Until it's time to settle down, why not be friends with all?"

After an hour of wandering through the vendors' booths and street games—including an agility contest Wil had won with ease—they found themselves watching the dancing. Dozens of couples were swinging to the musicians' lively tunes. Edythe and Blaike were among them, looking ready for the next dance to begin as soon as the last had ended. Spotting Wil over the crowd, Blaike waved.

Eleanor sat on a throne, surrounded by councillors, speaking in small snatches when she wasn't watching the dancing with what appeared to be a serene composure, celebrating the festival as if the next morning nothing in Aemogen life would be changed.

Crispin was saying something. "What?" Wil asked as he turned towards his friend.

"Do you have a girl in Imirillia?"

Wil shook his head. "No."

"No one ever caught your eye?"

Wil shot a glance towards Eleanor, only to find Crispin's elbow in his ribs.

Holding his hands up in surrender, Wil laughed. "I don't have any intentions towards your precious queen."

A shout went up and more laughter. The musicians began playing a quick piece, drawing couples from the crowd into the dance. It was lively, fast, as if the feet of those dancing would be burned by the music of the violins if they loitered too long on the ground. A young lady begged Crispin's company in the dance, and Wil soon found himself alone. He retreated through the crowd to Ainsley stair. There were a few of the fairgoers—couples, old women gossiping and tending children, men hiding from their wives—also enjoying the solitude and privacy of the steps. Wil sat down behind them all, stretched his legs before him, and watched the queen from his aloof vantage point.

Eleanor was watching the dancers as she clapped along and conversed with those around her. Aedon was her companion more often than not. Edythe and Blaike, still dancing except for the occasional break for refreshment, paused a moment longer to speak with the queen. Blaike was so obviously smitten with the princess, Wil shook his head partly in affectionate disgust, partly in envy.

The festival continued well into the night. Uncomfortable, tired, and intent on slipping back to the travelers' house, Wil pulled his body onto the soles of his feet and turned his back on the color and spin below him.

He was almost to the top of the stairs, when a rowdy chanting began. Turning with the corner of his shoulder, Wil glanced back to see about the noise. The people were all facing the queen, calling something he could not make out.

She smiled, brushing them aside, even as they shouted louder. This continued until a musician walked to the throne and handed

Eleanor a simple flute. She took it, running her fingers along the holes. After one last motion of protest, she lifted it to her lips.

Eleanor charmed a patient string of notes from the instrument, then, as if fire had been poured into her fingers, a rippling tune flew from the flute. And then, drums pounding, the dancers disintegrated and reformed in a dizzying pattern, violins matching the queen's melody, gaining and gaining through several variations, until, after several minutes, the dance broke like a wave on the shoals and dissolved.

Eleanor herself then melted into the crowd, and Wil lost sight of her, save for the occasional glimpse of copper hair in the torchlight. Once her face again became visible, Eleanor looked up, right at him, right into him, like she was touching his concealed intentions with her fingertips and spreading thin his soul.

Wil opened his mouth, as if to speak, to say that what she saw was not what *was*. That he disagreed with many of her opinions and admired her nonetheless. Standing outside the claim of Aemogen's lights, his fingers forming fists, Wil discovered that his admiration was followed by anger—anger at what she did not see, anger that she still believed the world to be the place Wil had long abandoned.

"The fool," Wil muttered, twisting away. He took himself to the travelers' house and threw himself over the bed. An hour later, when Blaike came into the room, Wil pretended to be asleep.

It was deep into the night before he actually was.

Music always made Eleanor less afraid. And the previous night's entertainment had been good, loosening her caution, challenging her despair, leaving her determined. Her council, when they assembled early the next morning, appeared to have felt the same. Around the table sat Gaulter Alden, Crispin, Aedon, Sean, Briant, and Doughlas.

"Is Wil not going to join us?" Crispin asked as he leaned in towards Eleanor.

As if on cue, the doors flew open and Wil stalked in. He did not seem pleased to be there, his face looking tired and dark.

"Thank you for joining us, Wil Traveler," Eleanor said, leveling her own voice against his apparent temper.

"I pledged my fidelity, didn't I?" Wil took the only empty seat, which was next to Aedon. This didn't improve his mood. His energy seemed sharp, and Eleanor met his confrontational expression with one of her own, irritated with his petulance.

"Gentleman," she began. "This morning I sent fen riders to all of Aemogen. Within three days, the entire country will know what we face. I myself will speak to Ainsley this afternoon. Each fen lord is instructed to take extra care. Every field must be prepared and planted, if possible, within a month. The battle run begins in three weeks time, starting with Common Field fen, working down the eastern coast to the Calafort port, then up through the western hills."

Wil stiffened and shifted, looking past Eleanor. "Did you hear that?"

Hearing nothing, Eleanor continued. "The traditional map of the battle run shows the timing—"

Wil stood, his chair scraping against the stone. Aedon scowled.

"Yes, Wil. What do you have to say?" Eleanor breathed out, impatiently.

"There's someone else in this library."

Eleanor listened. Nothing.

"There it is again," Wil insisted, walking behind Eleanor, disappearing into several rows of shelves holding a maze of manuscripts, books, and scrolls.

"Someone had too much punch last night," Aedon said coolly. Eleanor gave Aedon a warning look, just as there was a yelp and the sound of a slight scuffle. Eleanor heard Wil curse then tramp out from behind the shelves, dragging a young palace messenger by the hair.

"Ow! Let go! Let go!"

"I'll let go," Wil said, "as soon as you've learned not to listen in on what isn't yours to hear." Wil gave the boy's hair an extra tug, sending off another wave of cries. Marching him over to the library door, Wil threw the boy into the hall, slammed the door, and returned to the table, slumping into his chair.

Eleanor watched this display with some amazement.

"Of all the foolish things—" Wil sputtered, "you hold a war council and don't even clear the room?"

"It—" Eleanor caught herself mid-word. Clearly, his seriousness was warranted. And although this was Ainsley and the intruder was a small boy—with not the ear of a cook, let alone anyone of influence—Wil was right. Yet. Eleanor felt the smile rise on her face just before she broke into a tired laugh. She wasn't the only one amused. Gaulter Alden actually chuckled, and Crispin grinned. Doughlas made a smart comment of sorts, and they all laughed again as Wil glowered.

"Perhaps," Eleanor said, trying to tempt him out of his peevishness, "you should have spent your time dancing rather than sulking on the stairs the entire night. You might have woken in a lighter mood."

In response to her comment, Wil did not lighten his mood the entire council meeting. And as soon as it was over—the logistics discussed, the timing laid out, the training coordinated for the men of Ainsley over the weeks ahead—he took himself away from the library with no additional word.

Eleanor leaned towards Crispin. "That was an exhibition. You'd think it were his country being invaded."

"Yes," Crispin said, giving Eleanor a smile. "Remind me to steer clear of him in a black mood."

CHAPTER
SEVEN

"Have you nothing better to do, then?" Edythe asked. "You don't have to sit with me."

"It's a distraction I need," Eleanor admitted, watching her sister transcribe a worn document into beautiful calligraphy.

Edythe had listened with patience as Eleanor outlined the Imirillian threat. Having been there the night Mason had arrived, Edythe knew significant meetings were taking place, but she refrained from asking, knowing she would be told soon enough. The suspicion in Eleanor's mind was that Edythe did not want the weight of knowing.

"Are you frightened?" Edythe asked.

"What?" Eleanor broke away from her thoughts and found Edythe staring with her large blue eyes, her quill hovering above the page before her.

"I asked if you are frightened?"

"Yes," Eleanor said, stripping away all pretenses. "I am frightened. I fear I'll have decisions that I can't know how to make."

Edythe must have sensed how alone Eleanor was feeling, how

tight her heart beat as she breathed, how she was not sleeping. Setting her quill down, Edythe reached across the table, resting her hand on Eleanor's arm.

"What would you have me do for you?" Edythe asked.

"I would have you prepare yourself in matters of state," Eleanor replied, bluntly. "You are currently heir to the throne, and I can't ensure the outcome. I would also have you search the archives for any texts in Imirillian I've not already studied."

"I'll set the archivist on that now."

"And I would have you marry Blaike before the summer is out." Eleanor lifted her eyes to Edythe's. "I won't have you wait. You'll wed as soon as I've returned from the battle run. Uncertainty is coming. I will see you married before our fate is decided."

Eleanor was rereading a dispatch from the border—they had finished burying the dead, and the new guard was patrolling the pass—when an archivist delivered three scrolls. Setting the dispatch aside with a frown, Eleanor investigated the dust-covered documents.

Two of the scrolls appeared to be the First and Second of the Seven Holy Scrolls. That the Imirillian religion had seven texts of scripture was all Eleanor knew about it. She had never studied them. The third scroll the archivist had found in the archives was thicker than the religious texts for having several loose papers tucked inside. It appeared to be a compilation of philosophers' essays and poetry.

With an inkwell, several sheets of paper, and a handful of stones Eleanor had snagged from her desk, she encamped herself at the table. Dust lifted as Eleanor unrolled five feet of the First Scroll, then it settled like a silent spell across the stretch of parchment. Securing the stones on top to keep it in place, she then leaned over the antiquated Imirillian script.

"Now," Eleanor said, and she began to translate. It was slow, methodic, difficult work, words pressing against themselves, slanted and winding. She teased out the foreign shapes, writing what she thought was there, changing her mind, and beginning again. Pausing. Continuing.

Each paragraph of Imirillian scripture was known as a *mark*. And after the entire afternoon, Eleanor found it unlikely she would ever make it through the first mark, let alone an entire scroll. The Imirillian volume she'd studied as a child was a modern text, several centuries removed from this language. But Eleanor kept working, chasing away the specters of doubt that invaded her mind.

For several days, whenever Eleanor was not meeting with her council or preparing for the battle run, she translated the Imirillian scrolls, maintaining her dedication to unwind their meanings through sheer determination of will. The work remained tedious, and she was dissatisfied with herself.

One night, Eleanor sat staring at a mark she'd just translated from the philosophers' scroll. It was a graceful piece, several hundred years old, and Eleanor was doubtful she'd made an accurate translation. She leaned back in her chair, feeling her shoulder blades resting uncomfortably against the polished wood, listening to the sounds of flames coming from the hearth behind her.

Rubbing her finger along the wood of the table, she stared at nothing, her mind wandering from the translation to the days ahead. The battle run would begin in two weeks' time, and she was making so little progress. Eleanor's mind turned to a thought she'd had before and dismissed: should she enlist Wil Traveler?

They had not spoken in the week since the spring festival. Wil, now a full-fledged member of her war staff, had migrated down the table towards Crispin. After helping Gaulter Alden and Crispin organize an efficient training system and spending his days working with the castle guard, Wil and Crispin were now inseparable. Eleanor glanced at him occasionally at evening meal, and concealed how particularly she paid attention to his opinions during meetings, but she never singled him out individually. Now, before her cautious nature could pull her back, she called for Hastian.

The Queen's Own entered, his eyes intent on her face. "Your Majesty?"

"Is a messenger boy still at the door?"

"Yes."

"Have him bring Wil Traveler to me," she said. Hastian nodded, and Eleanor again bent her attention towards the scroll.

Wil made no attempt to hide his surprise when Hastian ushered him into Eleanor's chambers. He'd been in the room only once before, to pledge his fidelity for the length of the battle run. When the queen motioned twice for Hastian to withdraw, Wil found himself wishing he could also retreat. The room was dim, Eleanor's desk facing him from the left, the fireplace to the right, flanked by two settees and a chair. The fire offered the only light in the room save a collection of candles on a long table, running parallel to a wall of windows just before him. The table itself was cluttered with scattered scrolls, papers, and handwritten notes.

He realized that Eleanor was already speaking. "—so this is the mark I'm uncertain of. Would you be willing to read it for me?"

"Excuse me," Wil pulled his attention back from scrutinizing the space and looked at the queen. "What am I reading?"

Eleanor set her mouth in an effort, Wil thought, to hide her impatience, and began again. "I'm translating several sections from this Imirillian text," she said. "But a particular mark has given me trouble. Would you be willing to read it for me, aloud, that is?"

Intrigued, Wil stepped toward the table and ran his fingers over the scroll rolled out across it. This was the First of the Seven Scrolls, with several loose bits of parchment covered in Imirillian philosophy strewn about. Why did the queen of Aemogen have any copies of the Seven Scrolls? he wondered. After scanning the philosophical mark that Eleanor had indicated, Wil read aloud in smooth, articulate Imirillian, "*What has undone me is not the sweeping sands that would blow my soul across the earth, nor is it the endless heat and blinding desert; it is crashing against the high mountain, which will not bend to my will, but rather, break me on turrets no man can fight.*"

When he finished speaking, Wil looked towards Eleanor. She was leaning against the table, facing the fire, her arms crossed, her eyes closed, listening intently, the drumbeat of her pulse visible through the white skin of her neck.

"What did you wish to know?" Wil asked as he straightened his shoulders, looking away as her eyelids fluttered open.

"That was beautifully read," Eleanor said, turning towards the table, appearing flustered as she sorted through pages of notes, pulling one from the pile, and handing it to Wil. "Is this an accurate translation?"

Frowning, albeit with interest, Wil took the paper from her

hand and set it beside the mark. He reread the original Imirillian; he then read Eleanor's translation, three times. How had she managed such work? It was far beyond his own skill, to be sure.

"It's well done," he said. "I can't find a single fault with your translation." Wil rapped his knuckles on the table in an effort to appear more nonchalant than he felt. Looking at Eleanor, he spoke directly to her in his own language.

"I was not aware you had an Imirillian tutor in house at any time."

Eleanor waved off his statement with a brief response in Imirillian, "No Imirillian tutor."

Wil was incredulous, and he leaned against the table, waiting for an explanation.

"I learned the fundamentals of the Northern languages through my Marion tutor." Eleanor switched back to her Aemogen tongue. "Beyond that I've relied on my own study. My written Imirillian far surpasses my spoken, I assure you. Although, both are lacking."

The same sensation Wil had experienced on the practice field—that of an unexpected blow, causing one to stumble, unwittingly phased—was what he felt now, looking at Eleanor's mastery of Imirillian. The linguistic skill and the scope and intelligence of her mind were—well, unexpected.

Not wanting Eleanor to read his face, he turned his attention back to the papers before him.

Eleanor watched as Wil searched curiously through the translations before him. Regardless of how well she had prepared herself to ask for his help, it required an unexpected nudge of courage. Working through a weakness had always been a private endeavor, one she fiercely preferred to keep to herself.

"Would you help me?" she forced the words out. "Translating, I mean."

Wil did not appear amenable to the idea. Not answering, he continued to look at her work, strewn across the table, and Eleanor bit the inside of her cheek, waiting.

"I don't see why you need me at all, Your Majesty," he said. "This is pristine work. I couldn't do better."

Eleanor set her mouth and pointed to the last mark she'd translated. "If I thought I could translate quickly, I *would* see to it myself, but this paragraph has taken me several hours of very focused work." Lifting half a dozen sheets of paper, Eleanor let them fall to the table again. "This is all my progress of the last five days."

"So?"

"So, I don't have the convenience of time. Will you help me?"

Wil crossed his arms.

Breathing out through her nostrils, Eleanor was frustrated. She could translate his movements easily enough: helping her would be the last thing he'd want to undertake.

"You yourself have worried over the limited time Aemogen has to train an army," he said.

"And?" she replied.

"And you have enlisted my aid," Wil said. "I am giving it. Now, you're asking me to spend my time translating Imirillian scripture? Philosophy? It's not the best way to utilize what I have to offer. And I dare say, your time could be better spent as well." The hint in his voice was dipped in disapprobation.

"What do you know about how I should spend my time?" Eleanor rounded on his words. "What do you know of all my preparations and discussions and efforts? Is your desire that I dictate training as well? I think not, as my inexperience would be in the way of your experience."

She stared at Wil until he conceded with a shrug.

"I aim to be prepared in *every* way possible," Eleanor continued, speaking more to herself than to Wil. "I will know the mind of my enemy. No preparation is inconsequential. And for a scholar—which I am—that means studying Imirillian scripture and philosophy."

They stood in silence for a full two minutes before Wil replied. "Training keeps me occupied all day. You can't possibly feel it is more important that I be here—"

"And at night?" Eleanor parried. "After evening meal? Do you train the guard then?"

Wil laughed, exasperated now, and looked directly into Eleanor's eyes. "No. I retire to my room for rest, or enjoy the company of the guard."

"I'll provide a chair for your rest." Eleanor couldn't help but smile. "And the scrolls are company enough. Shall we begin tomorrow evening?"

Wil soon discovered that Eleanor was a dogged scholar. He joined her after every evening meal, to find she had worked far past where they had stopped the night before. These translations were difficult—it was an old form of Imirillian—and he did not have the ready equivalent in Aemogen's language on the tip of his tongue. This required that they work closely together, often for hours at a time.

Occasionally, they would exchange thoughts or observations

on other things. Eleanor showed keen interest in Wil's personal reports of training with the castle guard and the men of Ainsley. He, in turn, asked questions about her studies and Aemogen tradition. But translating absorbed most of their time together.

"You've such a quick mind," he stated one evening. Eleanor looked up, his words bringing her out of her work, before she registered what he'd said.

"Oh?" she said, her surprise genuine. "I think rather I'm just persistent."

Wil had seen persistence. She was bright. Her persistence only added to the intellectual force he struggled to keep stride with each evening. They had managed to translate the first scroll, in its entirety, in the two weeks before the battle run began because, early on in the process, Wil had taught Eleanor something she didn't know.

"Look," he'd said as he pointed to the text of the scroll on the table. "If you start with the first mark, it will give you a veiled outline of what will be spoken of in the next six."

"So, beginning with the first, every seventh mark is a summary of the text?" Eleanor knit her eyebrows.

"Yes," Wil said, leaning against the table. "I believe that scholars in Zarbadast first translate the Seven Marks, as they are called, and then return to fill in the remaining text as time allows. Many texts are found only in their Seven Mark form. And it makes the work of translating the remaining marks faster because you have an idea of what will come."

"Then, that is what we'll do," she said.

It was not long before they had developed a system. Wil would read a mark aloud once, and Eleanor would sit, ready, with a quill in hand. They would work out every line until the entire mark was translated; then they would review each word until Eleanor was satisfied that it represented the text authentically in her own language.

Some evenings, Wil would read a mark in Imirillian, and Eleanor would ask him to continue on, listening to his pronunciations.

One night, Wil read, "*All men are lost in their wandering, are lost in their sleep, lost to those they love, lost in their country, lost in their tongue, until they find in themselves honor. Then, no land is unknown, no sleep is but sweet, no stranger unloved, no language misunderstood, no love deemed unworthy. He who has honor has found himself forever and, as consequence, allows all others to be found.*"

Eleanor moved her finger across the tabletop, an idiosyncrasy he'd noticed before. "It's a beautiful thought," she said, "that freeing oneself allows others to be free."

Wil nodded, leaning back, away from the scroll. It was late, and the shadows in the room were reminding Wil of his exhaustion. He was having a hard time concentrating on, let alone appreciating, the nuances of holy scripture.

"From the text," Eleanor leaned towards him, "I assume that honor overshadows all other virtues."

"Yes," Wil said. "Honor is the ultimate way to transcendence."

Eleanor sat still, looking intent, as if expecting him to continue. Bringing his right hand to his eyes, Wil rubbed them a moment before obliging. "Honor of self, family, country, the seven stars—it creates expectations, codes, the way you are mandated to live your life. It's encouraged from a young age, this finding what honor means and what it will require of you in your life." Wil yawned as he leaned his head forward, resting his eyes and wishing for sleep.

"Did you leave the Imirillian army because of honor?" she

asked. "Or did you break your honor by desertion? Or both?"

Wil snapped his head up. "I did not desert."

"You left," Eleanor said as if she would not retreat.

Wil clenched his fist, causing a string of pops. He was agitated with Eleanor now.

"*There are not two directions, neither are there four; all direction is infinite*," Wil answered her with a line of text they had translated the night before. "Life is not so simple, Your Majesty. It's not just a matter of one way or the other."

"*Life may be unknowable, but self is not*," Eleanor replied with an Imirillian quote of her own.

"Seven stars, you are difficult!" Wil threw his hands up. "If you need an answer, then, no, I cannot fully reconcile honor to myself and honor to my country. It's a line I endeavor to understand."

"Are they not the same?"

"Are they?" Wil brought his hands down on the table with a slap and stood. "Forgive me, Your Majesty, I believe I am past being useful to you. May I retire?"

"Of course," Eleanor said, appearing surprised, yet polite. "Thank you for your work."

He shifted on his feet, but seeing that Eleanor had gone back to translation, Wil withdrew. Hastian was sitting by the door of the small antechamber. He stood sleepily and saluted as Wil let himself out.

CHAPTER

EIGHT

Wil had just removed his boots when a knock shook the door. He groaned as Crispin showed himself in. It had been a week since he had walked out of Queen Eleanor's chamber, tired and raw. They had continued their translations, but the conversation was now negligible. Wil was relieved, and unsettled.

"I've brought the stones, wood clamps, and polishing cloths," Crispin said. "Did you get the buckets?"

"Yes," Wil said as he closed his eyes and draped his arm across his face. "They're in the corner."

"Can't get lazy now, Wil. We leave tomorrow. Get up," Crispin added. "Your sword could use some attention." Crispin settled against the wall by Wil's bed and set his supplies next to him.

"I was hoping you wouldn't be back so soon," Wil answered. He forced himself into a sitting position and raised his eyebrows. "Doesn't anyone in Aemogen sleep?"

Crispin laughed. "Sure we do. And you'll be happy to know that Eleanor sent a message: there will be no translation tonight."

Wil raised his fist in triumph and reached for his sword. A rag hit him in the face.

"Let's get to it," Crispin said, motioning towards a stone and clamp he'd left at Wil's bedside. "Steady it with your feet there." The two soldiers set about sharpening and polishing their blades. Crispin taught Wil the Aemogen technique. It took longer than he was accustomed to, but left a beautiful edge. He soon moved on to his smaller pieces of weaponry.

"Tell me," Wil said as he looked up from his knife. "Hastian, the soldier who is always following the queen, why does he not share the detail with the other men of the castle guard?"

"Hastian is the Queen's Own," Crispin said. "He's not attached to the palace guard."

"You operate separately from him then?"

"No." Crispin offered a confused look. "We operate in tandem: he's the Queen's Own, and we're the castle guard."

"Do you envy him his position as Queen's Own?" Wil pressed.

Crispin tossed his rag away and looked at Wil with an expression near impatience that gave way to a smile. "What is it that you hope to hear, Wil?" he asked. "I have no envy of Hastian, and neither does he of me. We work together, with every soldier of Aemogen, to do our jobs. That is all. There's no malice among any of us here."

As he eyed Crispin skeptically, Wil knew that his expression lingered between admiration and incredulity. "I have seen more corruption in a country tavern than what appears to be in the court of Ainsley."

"Three cheers to that," was all Crispin responded. They continued their work in silence.

Wil finished before Crispin and set his weapons aside, lying on his back and thinking of the day. Tomorrow they would leave to tour the country, calling out the men, training them, and counting their numbers. Wil had unsuccessfully presented surrender as an option multiple times. But the entire council was against it, saying they would not make a decision until they had completed the battle run. Wil was sick to death of waiting and thinking. Another three months of it would be tiresome.

"Tell me of your family," Crispin said, breaking the silence. "They're noble, from what you've said. Is there much camaraderie, much love there?"

Wil cleared his throat and continued to look up towards the ceiling above him as he answered. "It depends on the day. We're like any other family: love, expectation, disappointment, misunderstanding, mistrust, brotherhood, commitment, independence, grief."

Crispin grinned. "It's little wonder the queen calls you jaded."

Releasing a short laugh, Will shifted so that he could see Crispin's face. "What about you?"

The young captain covered his thoughts with a smile and shrugged. "Not much to know," he said. "For almost as long as I can remember, I was an orphan down in Calafort, the port city of the south. It wasn't long before I struck out for adventure and ended up stealing from half the fens of Aemogen."

"Really?" Wil's interest piqued, and he propped himself higher against the pillow so he could see Crispin's face. "You're the first Aemogen criminal I've met—well, the first that wasn't a child—and you're a reformed one at that. How disappointing," he added. "But go on, let's hear the tale."

"They brought me before the king, Eleanor's father," Crispin said. "And when it came time for an officer, no one would step forward on my behalf, for I had neither kin nor sympathizer. In

Aemogen, we don't view those who break the law lightly."

"So I've seen," Wil granted.

"No one would stand for me," Crispin continued, his voice earnest. "After what felt like an age to my young mind, the king stood, looked at me for a long moment, then left his throne and came to stand at my side, his arm around my shoulders. Turning to the council, he pled on my behalf. The parole he offered? I would serve and work in the palace, and he would train me up to a profession. How could the council refuse?"

"How old were you at the time?" Wil asked.

"Twelve years," Crispin said. "The King was as good as his word, and I was accepted into his house. Eleanor and Edythe became as sisters, and the king, well, he educated me, cared for me, trained me in a profession, and treated me as dear as any son by a father."

"He sounds like he was a good king," Wil said.

"He was a good man." Crispin shrugged, trying to conceal his emotions. "When you're a good man, being a good king follows naturally."

Wil had to bite his tongue, tracing the lines of the ceiling instead. He didn't wish to disrespect Crispin by disagreeing, yet he knew that not every good king was a good man, neither was every good man a fair king. It was not such a simple balance.

Yet, later, far into the night, when Wil could not sleep, he replayed this conversation in his head.

The wind was relentless, cutting its teeth against the sandstone city, blowing it into dust. Wil covered his eyes, trying to see through the penetrating curtain of sand. His brother Emaad stood, serene and content, looking into the storm with an unaffected air. He turned toward Wil.

"You are fighting hard against the wind," Emaad said. His words were solid and stayed in place, as if he were speaking them on a calm spring morning.

"I can't look to you," Wil cried, but the wind ripped the words from his lips and sand filled his mouth.

"You must stop," Emaad said.

"I don't understand!" Wil yelled, leaning harder against the wind, the sound of it tearing at his ears. He covered his face with both arms, trying to escape the biting grains of sand.

"Stop!" Emaad commanded, and Wil lowered his arms. The wind was gone now. The blue folds of his brother's tunic moved in a pleasant breeze. His brother's eyes were gentle.

"How did you stop it?" Wil asked, but Emaad did not answer. "How did you stop it?" Wil tried again.

Emaad began to open his mouth, but his eyes went blank, and his head toppled to the sand. Wil stared in terror at his brother's headless corpse, and, when Emaad's head rolled against his boot, he began to scream.

"Wil!" someone called out, and he opened his eyes.

Crispin was shaking him. Wil jumped, throwing Crispin toward the door. The captain groaned as his head smashed against the wood.

"Ow! Come off it, Wil!" Crispin rubbed his head as he bit his lower lip. "I've come to wake you, not slit your throat."

Wil was standing, breathless, his hands shaking. He collapsed onto the bed and put his face in his hands. "You startled me."

"You were screaming," Crispin answered with concern. "Put on a shirt and come quickly."

"Where?"

"The battlements above the south gate."

Wil threw his black shirt over his chest and followed Crispin down the hallway of the travelers' house, the stones cold under his bare feet.

The night was not dark, but the shadows seemed fathomless. He saw his brother's face again and again and again. Wil shook his head, trying to loosen the images of his dreams. He took several deep breaths, and when they broke out into the open air, he gazed upward at the gibbous moon.

They left the travelers' house and walked up the tower stairs with quick steps. Wil could see other figures gathering along the south battlement. The men of Eleanor's council, the fen lords, their wives, staff, maids, gardeners, even the messenger boys—all gathered quietly, still in their nightclothes. Edythe and Blaike were among them, and Crispin pulled Wil through, to the inner circle beside the princess, and motioned for Wil to look down at Ainsley stair.

It was filled with ghosts.

Wil started, his brother's face still haunting his mind. He looked again—they were women, silent, still, phantomlike in their nightdresses. The crowd on the battlement parted, and Eleanor appeared, wearing a long, white nightgown, her hair loose down her back. Hastian, as always, was only a few steps behind her.

Eleanor took her place in the center of the observers and looked down over the battlements. Crispin lifted his hands briefly and put them together. A spark lit, only for a moment, and as if responding to his signal, lights began to appear among the people gathered on the stairs. Each woman held a candle. Wil, standing directly to Eleanor's right, watched, captivated. In the soft illumination, he could see that men were flanking the stairs with somber expressions.

Wil looked towards Eleanor just as the women began to sing. Their words were unrecognizable, but the sentiment was pure. It was a mournful tune, steeped in old beauty. The chorus of voices rang up all the stairs, for all of Ainsley had turned out to sing for their queen.

Wil's heart began to slow, the memory of his dream easing through the clear melody. He gave himself to the music. As if in response, the melody split into perfect harmony, continuing several minutes until, as they sang the final note, the candles went out.

The women descended the stairs, the moonlight almost tricking Wil into thinking they were a fountain of water, pouring down from the gates of Ainsley Castle and flooding the city below. He wanted to ask what the significance of the ritual was, but the mood was heavy, and people began to leave the battlements.

"We follow the queen," Crispin said at his back. As Eleanor passed, Edythe at her side, Wil followed, with the other members of the war council, in silence. Few torches were lit in the castle, casting strange patterns onto the walls.

When Wil saw that Gaulter Alden wore only his stocking feet, like the rest of them, he threw a grin at Crispin, who didn't acknowledge that he saw it. Eleanor led them up the stairs and through the large halls to her personal apartments. Edythe left her there, whispering something in her sister's ear before disappearing.

The queen invited her council in with a gesture, her eyes pausing on Wil with a flicker of consideration. A fire lit the room, and warm drinks were waiting. Eleanor sat in a beautiful chair of gold and soft blue, facing the hearth. The other men took their seats on the settees, or on other chairs, set about the fire as well. Aedon remained standing, passing warm mugs around the loose circle. Wil set himself on a soft rug before the flames, leaning against the arm of the settee.

"They sang with the spirit of Ainorra Breagha," Gaulter Alden said.

There was a brief murmur as the men nodded. Wil wanted to ask who Ainorra Breagha was, but he didn't. Aedon, looking rather rumpled and sleep-worn, sat near the queen, who was leaning against her elbow, massaging her temple with her fingers and staring at the fire.

It was as strange as it was beautiful, this intimate exchange of company with no words, everyone in—of all absurd things—their nightclothes. Wil watched Eleanor from the corner of his eye. Having never seen her in white, let alone in anything so subtle and timeless and, well—he didn't know. Her copper hair, always bound in braids, was now loose and long. The others paid no heed to her soft beauty, but Wil struggled to keep his eyes away. She did not appear to notice, watching the flames licking the firewood, snapping and rising. Wil told himself he should do the same, but he had little success.

After an hour, the men began to dismiss themselves, wordlessly, one by one. As each left, he paused before the queen and took her hand. She would smile and send him on without speaking. Wil turned towards the fire, though he knew it was time to go, and leaned his head back, sighing, preparing to get up and return to bed.

When Crispin roused himself a few moments afterward, pulling the dozing Wil along, Eleanor had already withdrawn to her bedchamber. They returned to the travelers' house to sleep the remaining hours of night.

Eleanor and Edythe sat together on the window seat in Eleanor's bedchamber, tucked in like a pair of wrens, watching day claim the gardens. Each was aware of the other's worries. There was no need to discuss the coming summer any further.

"It will be a quiet procession as you and the guard leave Ainsley this morning," Edythe said, leaning her face against the cold window.

"I imagine it will," Eleanor answered, lifting her finger as she spoke, tracing a map of Aemogen on the glass. They would leave Ainsley for the northwest, beginning with Common Field, then move east to the coast, following the cliffs along the sea southward, then go west, up through the western valleys, until they were home again. Fifteen fens, she thought. And how many days? Eighty? Ninety?

"You should wear your face like that as you ride out," Edythe said.

"Why?"

"Because you look brave."

Eleanor pulled her finger away from the window. "All right, then," she said.

It was cold as Eleanor's company filed through the streets of Ainsley, out the gates, past the fields and wide roads leading back towards the city. A flurry of wind riddled them the day through. Come evening, camp was set up without much conversation. But the following morning was warm with a bright sun, and the attitude of the company loosened. The breeze coming off the mountains was mellow, the tall meadow grasses full of early blue flax.

By late morning, Crispin and Wil dropped back to ride beside Eleanor. After informing her they would likely ride into Common Field fen before nightfall, Crispin added with a carefree grin, "I know several young men, including a few rather good friends, if you'd like an introduction."

Eleanor wrinkled her nose in distaste, but she laughed all the same. "Thank you for your consideration, Crispin, but, I believe my mind will be on more pressing concerns."

"Don't say I didn't try," Crispin said as he laughed in return. Just then, Gaulter Alden signaled him to the front of the column. "Maybe I should find another wife for Gaulter Alden," he said. "I daresay I'd have more free time on my hands if he were constantly being hounded himself. Excuse me, Eleanor." Crispin left them, while Eleanor ignored the smirk Wil was sporting on his face.

"You're looking for a match, Your Majesty?" Wil sounded amused.

"Not at the moment," Eleanor said as she looked ahead. "But that doesn't stop Crispin from introducing me to anyone he thinks might be eligible. His idea of a joke, I suppose."

"And what are you waiting for? Love?" Wil's tone carried an

acidic undercurrent, emphasized by a quick laugh as his eyes wandered the fertile fields they passed.

Eleanor turned in surprised. "You certainly don't seem to think highly of the idea."

"I don't," Wil acknowledged. "Not for a monarch."

"Oh?" Eleanor raised her eyebrows. "My father and my grandfather had successful marriages, equals in intellect and love."

Wil smiled. "How quaint," he said, then paused before choosing to continue. "But your country must have suffered as a result."

Eleanor laughed. "In what way, Wil?"

"Look at the riches of Aemogen—your mines, your fields, your climate—yet, you remain provincial, underdeveloped, and power-less," he said.

"You are a world-weary soul," Eleanor said. She took a deep breath and readjusted herself in her saddle.

"As a monarch, your country should be your lover," Wil continued, ignoring Eleanor's dismissive shake of her head. "That is where your passions should be spent."

"And what, pray tell, would my husband be?" Eleanor challenged. "A handsome figurehead?"

"A sire," Wil extolled. "Let him offer you sons. I see no reason beyond that."

"Really!" Eleanor laughed. "I'll hear no more of your bizarre ideas. Progression, only for the sake of power? A husband, only for the sake of children? No companionship? No support?"

"No successful monarch can love a person more than they love their country's best interests," Wil calmly continued. "You have to sacrifice all emotions to it, or you will prove unfaithful to your people."

"I disagree that the love of country and of spouse, or anyone else, must be mutually exclusive," Eleanor said, beginning to feel testy.

"You've not been on the throne long," Wil said. "You'll learn."

Eleanor reined up, causing Wil to pull Hegleh to a halt. "Are you such an expert on monarchy and matrimony?" she asked pointedly.

"I—" he began. Pausing, Wil's smile faded. "No, I am not."

Eleanor's glare gave way ever so slightly. "I curse you then," she said, "with a wife you will love above all, three daughters, and no sons. So many of your philosophies would be turned on their heads." Eleanor urged Thrift forward.

They rode in silence save the occasional call heard throughout the company. Eleanor began counting fens and villages in her head, as her thoughts strayed back to the stark reason for the battle run. Even the *threat* of war felt like a desecration of her land.

"My philosophies are still bothering you, I see," Wil said.

"Don't be a fool," Eleanor responded curtly. "There's an army at the threshold of my country, and my people are outnumbered and underprepared. The matrimonial observations of a jaded soldier don't plague my mind. I am thinking of the war."

"Point taken," Wil said. "What is your plan, then?"

"For defense?"

"No." Wil's mouth twitched. "For finding a husband."

Eleanor sighed. "Perhaps I should start by reconsidering my present company. It might open up opportunity to find what I am looking for."

Wil's laughter could be heard throughout the entire company, and Aedon glanced back to see what had caused it. "It's possible I am just the company you need," Wil said, trying to provoke her.

Eleanor gave no response.

Just before sunset, the company rode into Common Field fen. They had pressed hard for the last several miles, eager to arrive and greet the people there. Wil watched Eleanor as she dismounted and went straight to Adams, the fen lord, who bowed deeply before taking both her hands in his. They exchanged a few intimate words, with concerned expressions and obvious affection.

Those of the company were soon greeting friends, while boys led their mounts away to the fen stables. Wil was the last to dismount, handing Hegleh's reins to a young man who eyed her with wonder.

"See that she's rubbed down properly," he began. As Wil continued to give instructions, the young man turned the wonder he'd given the horse into admiration for Wil.

"Yes, my lord," the boy said, nodding respectfully as Wil finished his directions.

"Yes, well—see to it." Shaking his head, smiling to himself, Wil stepped into the crowd.

"Wil!" Blaike was at his side, giving him a hug.

"Whoa!" Wil said as he pulled away. "You are an affectionate group. Tell me"—Wil indicated the socializing between the queen's company and the people of the fen—"are you all that closely related?"

"To you, I will ever owe my gratitude," Blaike said in earnest, not answering what Wil had asked. "You have given me my life."

Almost scowling, Wil followed the moving company toward the fen hall. "I'm sure your mother would have something to say about that, Blaike," Wil said. "Away with you; love sick is not a disease I wish to catch."

Blaike laughed.

As soon as they'd entered the large fen hall, Crispin motioned for Wil to join him at the table. Eleanor was seated at the head, with Adams and the men from Common Field to her left, Gaulter Alden and the war council to her right.

After the initial greetings had taken place, Eleanor stood and called the meeting to order. She reviewed what they had already been told by the fen riders and answered any questions Adams had regarding the intentions of the Imirillian Empire.

"And we will fight," he stated simply.

"That is my intention, if all the fens will stand with me, and if we think it in any way possible," Eleanor affirmed. "As you know, the tradition of the battle run is to assess the strengths of our force. Gaulter Alden and the war council have organized the training. Wil Traveler," Eleanor said, motioning towards Wil, "is to oversee the combat training sessions, with Crispin, of course. Aedon will see to the archery. Sean will assess the mounts available for cavalry, while Briant, our weapons master, is working with the local blacksmiths. We plan to stay three days, possibly four."

The men of the fen, who had been eyeing Wil furtively, now openly stared. Blaike, sitting at the table, waved pleasantly as if they were planning a picnic. When all the questions had been answered, Eleanor turned the meeting over to Gaulter Alden to outline the days of training.

"We will appoint the best men from the fen to continue training their fellow soldiers," he explained. "When the fen lords convene at summers' end, if we've decided to fight, their men will be called to Ainsley, for a last camp, before marching to the pass. Are there any questions?"

Danth, Adams's oldest son, leaned forward in his chair and pointed in Wil's direction. "Why is he here?" Danth asked.

Wil could feel his pulse quicken. He stared back at the young man, but he didn't speak.

"To aid in the training," Gaulter Alden replied. "Wil's skill set is a particular asset to Aemogen."

"Aemogen doesn't need a dirty Northerner to teach her to fight," Danth stated.

"Have *you* ever seen the Imirillian army fight?" Eleanor asked. Danth's eyes looked down at this direct address from his queen, and he shook his head. "Until you have, keep your misinformed opinions to yourself. Apologize to Wil. He is on my council. An insult to him is an insult to the crown."

Danth flushed and gave an insincere, stumbling apology.

Although embarrassed for having Eleanor force this scene, Wil surprised himself by feeling a niggling sense of gratitude for the queen's defense. All the same, he avoided looking at anyone else the rest of the meeting, relieved when it was over and they were again outside.

Eleanor watched, feeling pensive, as Gaulter Alden spoke briefly to the men of Common Field, outlining what he had told their leaders the evening before. He then turned the training over to Crispin and Wil.

"We will divide out the archers later this afternoon," Crispin instructed the large group of waiting men. "You will work with Councillor Aedon. Until then, we will cover basic techniques of man-to-man combat, assess your skill levels, and specify your training from there."

The morning went simply, Wil and Crispin showing examples to the men of certain techniques in the art of fighting. They soon divided up into smaller groups, with a soldier from the Ainsley guard leading each, while Wil walked from group to group, observing, instructing, and, at most points, scowling.

Eleanor stood on a wagon at the edge of the training field. A blanket had been rigged up with rope and some poles for shade. She should have worn the heavy Battle Crown and ceremonial sword, as was the tradition of the battle run, showing the monarch to be ever battle ready. But Eleanor had left them inside. Gaulter Alden sat on a chair to her right, and Adams stood near the wagon on the ground, exchanging comments and observations with Eleanor. She thought he seemed most impressed with Wil's techniques and ability to instruct the men.

"Your Majesty," Adams said, glancing up at Eleanor. "Where did you say he came from?"

"Wil's mother is a Marion; his father, an Imirillian," she answered coolly. "He is traveling through Aemogen and has been a guest at the castle. When the threat came from Imirillia, he agreed to join our forces and help in our preparations. You will see that he's an invaluable asset to our training."

Adams appeared to be working several thoughts through his mind, but he did not ask more questions.

Eleanor was encouraging, complimentary, to the farm laborers and craftsmen turned soldiers. When the company stopped for a simple midday meal, she made herself available to the people. After eating, Wil gathered all the men to show them specific, advanced skills. Eleanor was back, standing on the wagon, silent as Wil worked with the men gathered around him. The women, who had steered clear of the training all morning, now began to wander into the crowd, watching with interest. Several of the younger ladies certainly found watching Wil Traveler worth their time. This amused Eleanor.

"If you can master these techniques, they will make you much more effective at hand-to-hand combat," Wil said, finishing his lecture. "Do I have a volunteer, who will challenge me in a mock fight, so I might illustrate?"

Danth stepped forward, his large frame confident and his expression hostile. "I don't mind a challenge," he said.

Wil bowed, but raised his eyebrows when Danth did not extend him the same courtesy. Danth instead lifted his chin and raised his arm to the crowd, saying, "Watch me master the arbast!"

Eleanor sucked in her breath at the term. It was a base insult, directed towards people of the North. But Wil did not acknowledge the slur.

"I assume you'll keep the rules of practice?" Wil said smoothly. "First touch, no blood."

Eleanor felt nervous as the two began to circle each other. Danth was solid and strong, his size a rarity among Aemogen men. Wil, also strong, was leaner, quicker, and more graceful. They began their initial sparing. Relying on his strength, Danth tried to overpower Wil with the sword, but Wil's quickness and agility allowed him to deflect Danth's robust blows without getting trapped. Then Wil cut under Danth's attack and rolled behind, kicking the back of Danth's knees without so much as a shout. Danth fell to the ground. It was, Eleanor remembered, the same tactic Wil had used his first time in combat with Crispin. Wil backed away, allowing Danth time to get himself up.

"Arbast," Danth muttered as he set himself in the ready position. A glint of anger touched Eleanor as Danth repeated the insult, but Wil ignored him and fought on, so she let it pass. Again, Danth seemed to gain the advantage, when Wil cut his sword up towards Danth with great force in one swift move, causing him to turn around and stumble backward.

Wil stood steady and verbally illustrated his defense move for the men watching as if he were bored. When he finished, he asked if there was another volunteer. Danth cursed and yelled that he was still fighting. He stepped back into the circle, egging Wil on for another go.

Wil relaxed his stance and stood up straight. This caught Danth off guard, so he straightened up as well. Eleanor looked toward Crispin, who also watched Wil with suspicion in his face. Placing his sword on the ground, Wil motioned for Danth to do the same.

"Are you ready for the next part of your training?" Wil asked.

Hesitating for a moment, Danth finally lowered his weapon to the ground and looked back up in question as Wil stepped towards him. Wil punched Danth in the face with a force Eleanor had never seen. Danth stumbled backward and fell. Adams frowned, but he didn't move save to glance toward Eleanor. Shouts went up, and Danth's sister rushed towards her brother, helping to staunch the bleeding from, what Eleanor thought, was a well-deserved bloody nose.

"The most important lesson is to remember this:" Wil said to the stunned crowd, "regardless of your training, you should hinder your opponent in any way you can." Wil picked up his sword, sliding it into its sheath, and walked towards Eleanor, Gaulter Alden, and Adams. "This portion of training has been most effective, Your Majesty," Wil reported. "I believe it's now time for Aedon to lead the archery, and Crispin can organize the final exercises of the evening. I'm finished for the day."

"I would have supposed you had more discipline than that, Wil," Eleanor responded.

"I do," Wil said, his face tense. "I just don't have the humility. If you'll excuse me now, Your Majesty, Sir, My Lord." Then Wil walked towards the road that led to the outlying fields.

Eleanor turned again towards the crowd, whom Crispin and Aedon were trying to quiet, a hint of sanction in her eyes.

Later that night, after a brief council meeting, Wil disappeared from the fen hall with a blanket to sleep in the fields. Eleanor had taken exception to this, remarking to Crispin that it seemed strange Wil would go off on his own, away from the entire company.

"Is he so determined to isolate himself?" she asked.

Crispin gave Eleanor a hesitant look and shrugged. "There were some nights, in the travelers' house, that I could hear him scream in his sleep. I don't think rest is peaceful for Wil, Eleanor. This might be a possible reason he seeks to be alone."

Eleanor did not respond. She turned away and entered the fen hall, where an upstairs room had been prepared for her use. Miya, Eleanor's long-suffering maid, helped ready Eleanor for bed. Once she withdrew, Eleanor retreated into the small bed in the corner and thought over the day.

It had been taxing to watch the men awkwardly handling their weapons, looking longingly into their newly planted fields. If the entire summer was to be this way, it would require everything Eleanor had. Her head burned and her muscles ached from sitting so tense. And then there was Wil. Opening her eyes in the darkness, Eleanor turned onto her back. What did Wil dream about to make him scream in his sleep? Was it terror? Was it pain? She couldn't guess.

The three days at Common Field ended with mixed results. The war council understood better how to organize the training, most of the ideas coming from Wil's experience, and the men had, in the end, responded well. They would continue to practice and train throughout the summer as Eleanor and her company moved on. The council had also met to discuss skills and deficiencies of the plowmen turned soldiers. Most of the criticism also came from Wil, whose opinions did not reassure Eleanor.

Now, on the final evening in the fen, they prepared a bonfire for the dance. This was another tradition of Aemogen: everything ended with dance. The entire fen seemed to find energy they did not know they still had for their preparations, and Eleanor watched them from the window as she and Aedon reviewed numbers.

The dancing began soon after dark. Food was had; refreshment, spread around. Danth, who had made a stubborn peace with Wil, even brought Wil a drink. Eleanor clapped with the music and smiled, relieved with their Aemogen ability to set aside concerns and be happy in each other's company.

—◦◦◦◦◦◦◦◦◦—

They moved on the next morning, the company stretching itself across the northern hills to the High Field fen, the smallest in Aemogen. There were fewer than one hundred and fifty people in total and far fewer men. Still, they did as they had done before, meeting with the leaders, organizing the training, and working for several days to teach techniques and drills.

Eleanor split her time between watching these proceedings and joining with the women in their work, hoping to hear their thoughts and opinions about the decision to fight. They were not so easily convinced as the men.

"It's just, Your Majesty," Claira, wife of the fen lord, said hesitantly to Eleanor when they were alone, "we understand the need to fight, of preservation. But we would rather be subservient than have our husbands and sons dead. It would be a high price for tradition, would it not?"

"So, you would not have us fight," Eleanor stated.

"Oh, I don't know—" Claira said, her head bent over her sewing as she spoke. "Won't the land be stripped and our culture changed, the Imirillian terms leaving us a nation destitute? I'm loath to send my son to war, and I'm loath to see him starve for not having enough food to pay tribute and feed my family."

The days were quick, for the men of High Field were willing to listen and learn, despite their quiet demeanor. Their determination, Eleanor observed to Aedon, seemed bred from generations of winters in the northern mountains. Even Wil seemed pleased with what he saw.

"Fifty," Crispin said to Eleanor, watching the dancers around the bonfire on their final night in High Field. "Aedon said there are possibly fifty men, if we take the youth who are thirteen and fourteen."

Eleanor closed her eyes. "Thirteen? How can we possibly decide to fight if it means our young men, boys really, must go to war? They won't make it out."

She and Crispin stood in conference, away from the gathering, their heads together. They had been discussing what they'd seen in the exercises that day.

The entire fen had come out to dance and had built a single, large bonfire for the small community. Wil was also standing back, watching and occasionally speaking with a member of the guard. He had not spoken to Eleanor, beyond in council meetings. But during the dancing, he glanced towards her several times. She was aware of his attention now, and it seemed that he began to move towards her, only to be accosted by a young lady, whose admiration he'd caught.

"Without Wil," Crispin conceded, following Eleanor's eyes, "we would be at a severe disadvantage."

"So it appears," Eleanor said, creasing her brow. "I don't love his art of war. It's so—"

"Lethal?" Crispin filled in.

"Ruthless," Eleanor said passionately. "I can hardly bear to watch."

"Ruthlessness, sadly, is a great asset in this game," Crispin answered.

Leaving High Field, the company set off towards Large Wood fen. Their journey would take two days if they kept a good pace. Eleanor repeated words of encouragement to Thrift, knowing they were really for herself. She disliked traveling by horse for great lengths of time. Fortunately, their journey took them through the northern fields of Aemogen, where woodlands spilled down from the imposing mountains, tripping into old fields marked with walls of stone.

The day was quiet, and Eleanor spent time discussing with Gaulter Alden, Crispin, and Aedon. Wil appeared content to keep to himself. Eleanor told herself that she welcomed this respite from the cutting aspects of his conversation, so available in their council meetings.

They stopped in a picturesque field on high ground. It was covered with rich, late-spring grass as it was used for grazing. Camp was set up, and dinner was had. Then, discussion and stories were shared over the fire. Eleanor spent a few hours studying in her tent by candlelight. When she finished, finally setting her volume down, she was tired yet restless. She left her tent, telling Hastian she would walk the perimeter of the camp and that he might remain at his position.

"I've a whole camp of my own men," she said. "No need to follow—or worry." She knew Hastian would worry.

The moon was full, and night accepted its light, draping the trees and fields in silver. The perimeter guards saluted as she passed, but they left Eleanor to her own thoughts. As Eleanor passed the southern line of camp, she noticed a figure sitting alone on the long stone wall of a lower field. She walked down through the grass towards the solitary watchman. As she came closer, he turned. It was Wil. He pulled himself off the wall and scrutinized Eleanor like he was unsure where to place her. After a moment, he bowed.

"Your Majesty."

"Wil."

"Join me," he motioned towards the wall, "if you wish."

Eleanor looked down at the moonlit valley, her heart responding to this quiet country. "I will, for a moment," she said. "Thank you." She accepted his hand—it was the first time she'd touched him—as she settled onto the stone. Wil sat a few feet away, his feet swinging without touching the ground.

"Did someone drag you into serving as a perimeter guard?" Eleanor asked.

Wil shook his head. "No. I've come to sit, think. Watch the moon."

"I'll not deny it's a beautiful moon," Eleanor said. Late spring blossoms were giving way to the full leaf of early summer, and the scent of leaves as they unfurled slowly was heavy in the night air. The grass stood still, moonlight sliding down the delicate stems towards the shadows and rustlings of the field mice.

"She captivates me," Wil said, as much to himself as to Eleanor. His speech had turned soft and young. "I have always felt a love for moonlight. The sun burns your eyes, but the moon allows you full wonder, full inclusion. The sun may be a mighty force, but she is a companion, a compass, a messenger."

"She?" Eleanor asked, looking earnestly upwards, feeling more child than queen.

"Ah." Wil looked at Eleanor somewhat pleased. "The consummate scholar has not read the Fifth of the Seven Scrolls."

"They are the holy cannon of *your* religion," Eleanor reminded him, in defense. "No, I have not studied it yet, as I only possess the First and the Second. But I plan to read them all, at some point," she explained. "What does the Fifth scroll say about the moon?"

"The text goes like this," Wil began slowly, reciting it from memory in a lyrical tone:

"Seraagh, the declaring angel of the Illuminating God, served in holiness and might before Him. She spent her days in the services required. But after a time, she forgot her obligations, for she began to love the sun, which was set up in the sky to guide the mortals in their journeys. The Illuminating God chastened Seraagh and set her again on her task. For many years, Seraagh pleased Him, but she could not forget the warmth and beauty of the sun. One evening, as the sun was setting in glorious flame, Seraagh cried out, 'O, that I might not be separated from what I love.' She followed the sun and left her work undone, diminishing her love for the Illuminating God. When He saw that she had neglected the charge which she had been given and that it had caused pain for His mortal children, He was displeased with Seraagh.

"The Illuminating God sent down judgment on Seraagh and banished her into the night, where she would become a constant guide for the mortals of the earth. Her post was then given to another. Seraagh lamented greatly, for she loved the Illuminating God even more than the sun of the day, and she wept bitterly. Her tears fell about her in the sky."

Wil broke his narration, briefly, a thought passing across his face as he stared at the stars. He then continued. "But the Illuminating God loved Seraagh, and, after a month's time of serving, He sanctified her repentance and made it holy. The tears she had wept were filled with light and cast about the darkness around her, and Seraagh was no longer alone. The Illuminating God spoke with Seraagh, calling her *choice* in her service unto Him and unto the mortals of the earth. He promised that once in every month's calling on the earth, she could leave the night sky and serve Him. This pleased Seraagh, and she was glad. The Illuminating God also promised Seraagh that, when the earth had given herself completely, and the mortals were taken home unto Him, she would be with the sun forever and never again be sent into the night."

In the silence that followed Wil's narration, the sounds of crickets and owls pressed against Eleanor's ears. She watched the moon and thought of Seraagh. Wil turned his eyes on Eleanor, and then looked away again into the sky.

"It seems a long time to wait," Eleanor finally said after some time.

"She has her work," Wil offered.

"Yes." Eleanor felt a small, worrisome feeling creep along the back of her neck. She shook it off. "Is there any more written in the Seven Scrolls about Seraagh?"

"Much is written," Wil said. "There are some lines, a mark in the Sixth Scroll, that state, 'And Seraagh, clothed in white, rode her fair horse above the earth to fulfill every command of the Illuminating God. And she reflected His glory: aflame and alight. And all were humbled by the beauty of her obedience before Him.'"

"My mother loved the tale of Seraagh," Wil continued. "She would teach it as a story of obedience before the Illuminating God, explaining that all rewards would be ours if we served Him first in our station. She would also point to the sky on the days when night mingled with day and the horizon was purple, the days when the moon was already in the sky long before dark. She would say to me, 'Seraagh has come to her post early, so she can glimpse the sun, setting across the ten thousand miles of the world, and be glad for the future.'"

"Oh, that is lovely," Eleanor said, looking at Wil. "And awful."

He seemed surprised. "Awful? How so?"

"To see the one you love across ten thousand miles of the world and not be able to go to them, not be with them? It is no wonder that, some nights, the moon is so melancholy in her beauty."

It was not long before Eleanor said good-night and returned to her tent, her mind full of Wil's story. Before sleeping, Eleanor sat with her writing board and copied down the tale. She would show it to Wil another day to be sure she had not forgotten anything.

Wil Traveler. Eleanor put the cork in her inkbottle and blew out her candles. She crawled to her bed and pulled herself under the blankets. His conversation with her had been sincere and straight: no sarcasm, no jaded edge. Eleanor's final thought, before falling asleep, was wondering how long it would be until he was across the ten thousand miles of the world from Aemogen.

CHAPTER

TEN

"Try again," Wil said, motioning to his opponent, who was struggling with one-on-one combat. They were at Midland fen. Training at Large Wood, Small Wood, and Faenan fens had gone well, encouraging Wil, but the people of Midland fen showed no predisposition for fighting. Crispin and Wil took far more time, instructing the men individually, on basic sword maneuvers.

His current student was pathetic. As Wil watched the old farmer lift the sword again into position, he hoped his expression did not betray his thoughts: these men were no match for a horse boy in the Imirillian army, let alone a soldier.

"Don't drop your shoulder like that, and don't lean back," he instructed as they began a slow conversation with their blades. "You give away the advantage of having your weight behind your movements."

The farmer nodded and tried again, paying painstaking attention to Wil's instructions. Finally, when the man had mastered at least two proper movements, Wil told him to keep practicing and moved on to a group Crispin was teaching.

"How did it go with old Rion?" Crispin asked pleasantly. Squinting against the afternoon sun, Wil chose not to answer; rather, he adjusted the strap of his quiver, which was biting into his neck. He wished he had his personal archery effects with him as his own quiver was sized to fit his frame perfectly. The day was getting warmer. He rolled his sleeves up to his elbows.

"That bad?" Crispin smiled. "That must have been a sore trial for you."

"Why do you say that?" Wil asked.

"Well," Crispin shrugged, "it's easy to see when you're displeased with an exercise versus when you have found a bit of challenge in it. Granted," Crispin added quickly, "very few actually challenge your skills."

"It's tedious work, teaching a plowman the art of war." Wil pulled at the black cloth around his left forearm, checking it to be secure. "We are finishing the sixth of fifteen fens, and it feels like getting my teeth pulled. Is your entire country lacking in physical coordination?"

Although usually good-natured, Crispin took exception to Wil's slight. "I think you may be going about it in the wrong way, if not looking at it backwards."

"Do you tell me I don't know my own craft?" Wil asked, honestly. "I've trained thousands of soldiers."

"No," Crispin said, drawing out the word. "Perhaps I am telling you that you don't know theirs. If we were to suspend training for a day and let the men go into the fields tomorrow, I think you would find yourself surprised with their abilities and, maybe, better understand how to incorporate their natural strengths to teach them weaponry."

Wil wiped his forehead and shrugged impatiently. "I'll try anything."

As good as his word, after discussing the plan with Gaulter Alden, Wil and all the soldiers spent the following day helping in the fields or working with the fen smiths. Wil volunteered for the fields and was assigned to a group of men who were removing rocks and stumps. The misery Wil felt during the work was palpable. He and a few others were working a large stump with difficult and extensive roots, and the farmer would allow no shortcuts.

"Remove all the tree now, or break your plow later," he repeated in a dialect singular to Midland fen. Wil's hands developed blisters as he loosened the ground with a pick, ripping the roots from the soil. More rocks than he could have imagined seemed to rise out of the earth, blocking his way. For each stone rooted out and cast to the side of the field, a multitude of others rose beneath it.

Crispin found Wil when they had stopped for a midday meal, and the two sat stiffly in the shade.

"Imirillia has no such rocks in its soil," Wil complained as he ate stale bread and cheese. "Demons, every one."

"Imirillia," Crispin said, his eyes glinting good-naturedly, "has no such harvests, either."

Two days later, as they left Small Wood fen, Wil admitted to Crispin that his torture hadn't been for naught. He had understood better how to describe maneuvers to the men, using descriptions they could recognize from their everyday work. Even old Rion had improved, however slightly.

The company left Midland fen, riding straight for the eastern cliffs that rose high above the South Sea. To Eleanor, this was the promise of a reprieve, for they would rest three days at the crumbling fortress of Anoir. Miya had ridden ahead with a small company of soldiers to open the old fortress and prepare rooms for the queen and her council. The palace guard would camp inside its dilapidated walls in the courtyard.

As they came closer to the cliffs, seabirds began to appear with their melancholy cries, and Eleanor began to forget the war and remember her childhood. Every summer they would come and spend time in the old fortress. She had not been back since her father's death, always telling Edythe they would return, always calculating the reasons not to. But she had delayed too long, and a freedom she had not felt inside her lungs for years returned and began to beat with her heart. Even Aedon noticed the change, saying it was good they had come.

When the company arrived, Eleanor, after telling Hastian he could ease his post in the safety of the isolated ruins, rushed to her room. Miya had tirelessly cleaned it before the queen's arrival, and it proved itself a sanctuary. Eleanor secured the door, removed her travel-worn clothes, and washed herself before lying down to enjoy the isolation. And, with the sound of the sea, she slept.

It was late afternoon when Eleanor stirred. She smiled carelessly, staring at the leaded window, stretching her arms above her head. Now fully awake, she slipped her shoes back onto her feet. Her hair had been bound up in braids, so she unbound and brushed it before weaving one simple braid down her back, loose and young. She left her room, intent on spending the remaining daylight walking the cliffs.

The moss-covered stone of Anoir created an enchanting scene, reminiscent of the old tales, and the entire company had settled into its beauty, seeming as contented as the queen herself. As she was leaving the arched entryway of the fortress, Eleanor almost ran straight into Wil. He was carrying firewood, from the few tangles of wind-bitten trees, into the courtyard.

"To the cliffs," Eleanor said, when he inquired where she was going.

"I've never seen the Southern sea," he said in response. "Is it much wilder than in the North, as I've heard?"

Eleanor tilted her head. "We may have finally found something in Aemogen you can call neither simple nor sedate," she said. "Would you like to come and see for yourself?"

Wil laughed, accepting her invitation good-naturedly, piling the firewood in the courtyard before coming to walk alongside Eleanor on an old, worn trail that led to the sea.

She walked free of the path as they came over the rise, the view of the ocean stretching endlessly before them, a spangle of silver and green under the heavy clouds. Eleanor hurried faster, consuming the view with a fierce desire to be as close to the sea as she could. Once they arrived, Wil leaned against the remains of a wall that ran along the cliff's edge. The sound of the birds rang off the stones, and Eleanor laughed out loud as the wind blew its saltwater smell against her face. What a wonderfully, overwhelming thing it was to return to the happiness of one's childhood. She fought the sudden emotion of it.

They kept quiet company, neither speaking nor feeling the need. Eleanor chased down the shoreline with her eyes, the vibrant greens of the grass shocking and bright above the petulant sea. The image of herself and Edythe passed her mind, as if she could see them playing along the cliffs, only children, barefoot and wild. "We came here every year," she said, breaking the silence, "to the fortress of Anoir." The words felt like home on Eleanor's tongue. "Edythe and I spent hours playing along the cliffs and climbing down to the sea."

"I'm sure your mother wasn't pleased with that," Wil said, eyeing the steep, sharp stone dropping down into the riotous water.

"She was never worried. It was my father who was cautious and staid." Eleanor considered the ocean before her, her mind working over an array of memories. "My father may have been too cautious. And, I suppose, the irony in all of this is that if my mother had had her wish, we would have created an alliance with Imirillia long ago."

Wil shifted and looked at Eleanor. "In truth?" he asked. "Tell me."

"Do you want to know?" Eleanor paused, a small smile on her face. "It will sound more like a tale of faerie than one of lost political advantage." Wil looked at Eleanor, studying her nostalgic demeanor with a strange expression.

"Please," he said.

"I suppose you may have heard bits of the tale," she began. "Seeing as how you are from Imirillia, but—" Eleanor bent to pick up a small rock, tossing it out towards the sea. It fell and fell, until the small gray stone disappeared soundlessly into the waves. "My mother was close with the Marion princess, Edith—friends enough to have named my sister after her, obviously.

"Now," Eleanor continued, "Edith of Marion was the youngest daughter of Edvard, King of Marion. He had five children—the oldest, Staven, is now their king. When the Imirillian Empire began to grow in strength, Edvard thought it wise to form an alliance, to keep Marion protected and in favor with the country that was coming into such great power."

"So, he sends his beautiful young daughter to the Emperor Shaamil for bargaining," Wil provided in answer.

Eleanor shook her head. "Actually—and I only know of the

details because of my mother—Edvard tried first to send his elder daughter, Anne, to be Shaamil's bride."

"Did he?" Wil asked, now fully engaged in the story. "So, what happened?"

"Anne did not please Shaamil. He sent her away within the hour of her arrival in Zarbadast, declaring that she had neither the beauty nor the spirit he demanded from a wife. You see, he had two already," Eleanor explained as she gave Wil a mischievous look. "I suppose he knew what he wanted."

Wil laughed. "Go on."

"Anne was sent home in quiet disgrace. My mother never cared for Anne, so she told the story with more harshness than do I." Eleanor laughed. "King Edvard now began to worry what might happen to Marion if he did not provide another alternative for this alliance.

"Edith was his youngest daughter, and, by all reports, the most beautiful woman anyone had ever seen. My mother used to tell me she was a most striking, delicate girl with eyes of so brilliant a blue that she could just look at the rain, and it would stop."

Wil smiled. "Hmmm."

"So, King Edvard, though he preferred Edith to all his other children, requested that Shaamil take his youngest daughter to wife. Shaamil accepted but on the penalty that if she did not please him, then the alliance would never come to pass, and she would be executed."

Eleanor crossed her arms, feeling the sea wind on her fingers as she looked over at Wil. "Edvard deliberated much, for it broke his heart to send his daughter so far away. Finally, he decided to send Edith north. She was a guest at Ainsley Castle when the news of her betrothal came. My mother said they cried and cried, but that in the end, they began to speak of the wonderful things that might come of this marriage: how their children would wed and how Edith would bring her family to Aemogen. So, Edith left Ainsley with courage and determination, and my mother waited anxiously for news.

"Months passed before she received correspondence from Edith. She had made the journey north to Zarbadast and was brought directly into the throne room, before Shaamil and his entire court. But she was blindfolded, so she could not see the emperor. And although frightened and weary from the journey, she stood straight with her chin raised."

"And he was won over by her beauty, made her his third wife, and she endured Zarbadast life," Wil guessed with an edge on the words.

Eleanor paused, almost hearing the words again from her own mother's lips. "Edith wrote that the emperor had stood without speaking until a long moment had passed. He then dismissed her from the court, commanding that the guards take her to his favorite garden. She was led to a beautiful enclosure where there were fountains and large basins, holding flowers and plants, above streams of clear water. A young maidservant helped Edith change and bathe and left her to await the Emperor Shaamil alone." A soft smile crossed Eleanor's face. "And then, the most unexpected thing of all. Shaamil came into the gardens. He was younger than she had supposed—well, relatively, considering she wasn't quite eighteen years old. She wrote to my mother that when she saw his face, every question in her life had answers, and she knew that the center of her heart would ever end in Shaamil."

Wil did not speak for a long time. He ran his hand through his hair and turned to take in the view of the sea. "How would your mother have formed an alliance with Imirillia through this Princess Edith?"

"She and my mother wrote for several years, before the letters stopped. Edith bore Shaamil a son," Eleanor explained. "Basaal, he was named. Edith wrote that Shaamil showed Basaal special favor, despite having many sons already. I was born only a few years after, and my mother wanted an alliance—a marriage.

"He was not the firstborn as I was, so Basaal would share my throne. Edith also hoped they might secure an alliance, placing Aemogen in an advantageous position. She even sent an Imirillian song for me to learn—" Eleanor paused at the memory. "A peculiar tune that I can't quite remember, but I loved it as a child."

"What happened?" Wil asked, watching Eleanor intently.

"I'm not altogether sure," she admitted. "My father didn't like the idea. The Imirillian Empire was growing in land and in power, and it was a warring nation. For every sweetness that Edith wrote of Shaamil, there were ten stories throughout the land of his conquests and dominance. My father wanted, as had his father before him, a quiet existence away from the eyes of other sovereigns, which meant my marrying an Aemogen. Perhaps he felt that the safer road for me."

"And what—" Wil paused. "What of the Princess Edith?"

"She died," Eleanor said, turning to face the ocean. "My mother had written to her for over a year with no reply. The boy would have been ten or eleven then. I remember when my mother heard the news that Edith had died of a fever," she said, stopping for a moment at the memory. "I had never seen my mother so despondent. She cried and mourned, begged my father to invite Edith's son to Ainsley. She wanted to know Basaal's face. But father would not make the invitation. He said it was for the best, yet I've always wondered if that was a mar on their marriage." This confession was difficult for Eleanor. "My mother died a few years later."

Eleanor was reluctant to recall her mother's sadness. It felt heavy on her chest as it had when, as a child, she could do nothing to make her mother stop crying.

Wil looked down, kicking his boots in the dirt. "That is a sad tale," he said.

"It is," Eleanor quietly agreed. "I have always thought of it as a beautiful ghost story: bitter and sweet."

Wil offered Eleanor a sincere glance. "Perhaps that is the hazard of loving too deeply." The wind had picked up, lifting itself off the sea and up the gray cliffs.

"Do you know him?" she finally took the courage to ask.

"Do I know who?" Wil asked.

"Edith's son, Prince Basaal. Have you met?"

Wil kicked the earth again and looked away from Eleanor. "We have met," he said, "several times, actually. Though, I cannot say I know him well."

"Sometimes," Eleanor confessed, "when going through my mother's letters, I wonder about him and if—" She shook her head and lifted a shoulder, "*If.*"

Wil cleared his throat. "To be honest," he said, "and, I mean no disrespect to either of you, I cannot see how he would have pleased you. He's as selfish and prideful as any of them, the princes of Zarbadast: spoiled, supercilious, arrogant."

Eleanor blushed, closing her eyes against the coming gale, feeling her hair work itself loose from her braid and fly across her cheeks. "I miss my mother," she said, filling the space with words to wash away her questions. *"Cha bhi fios aire math an tobair gus an tràigh e,"* Eleanor said softly in an old Aemogen tongue.

"Meaning?" Wil inquired.

"The value of the well is not known until it goes dry."

Wil's face absorbed the sadness of her statement.

They headed back towards camp as evening settled, keeping to their own thoughts, walking side by side on the windblown trail. Allowing herself a rare indulgence, Eleanor thought more of her mother than she had in years: the small movements, the way her eyes would wait for Eleanor to understand, the way she teased Eleanor out of unreason.

At one point, Wil spoke. "I feel as if you are conversing with your dead," he said. "Your sobriety is too weighty for this world." She didn't answer, but his comment made the silence between them comfortable.

They found the camp content—fires built, the men sitting in groups talking, the horses cared for, and the work of the day finished. Crispin was leading a conversation by one of the fires. Aedon was sitting quietly, reviewing the reports that Doughlas must have brought down from Ainsley. Eleanor watched the men for a moment and then turned to Wil, who was still standing at her side.

"Just wait until Old Ainsley fen," she said.

"What is at Old Ainsley fen?" Wil asked, curious.

"That is where Aemogen keeps all her ghosts."

The sea, Wil found, suited him.

Late that night, after the others had gone off to sleep, he took himself down towards the cliffs and wrapped himself inside his cloak on the lee edge of a stone. Sleep was kind, as if the wind coming off the sea had swept his dreams away before they could rattle him awake. Come morning, he was refreshed.

That had not happened for a long time.

———◦◦◦◦◦———

A few days later, the company set out in the delicate, gray morning. Since their conversation on the cliffs, Wil and Eleanor's days had twined together more than before, so it did not seem strange for Wil to be riding near Eleanor.

"Why is this fen called Old Ainsley?" he asked. Eleanor turned her face towards Wil, the air off the sea claiming the loose strands of her hair.

"The original capital of Aemogen was Old Ainsley fen," she explained. "The remains of the old fortress and castle are still there."

"Why did the capital move north?"

"Aemogen grew," she said. "The winters along the coast are harsh and cold. Up north has a far better climate all the year round. Ainsley, officially named New Ainsley, is a more central position: closer to the pass and easier to reach by all the fens."

"Ah," Wil said. "Admittedly, I was hoping for a tale less pedestrian."

"To be fair, there is more of a tale," Eleanor said as she smiled.

"We have a way yet," Wil shrugged. "Tell me the story."

"I think not," Eleanor replied. "It's a tale you should hear for the first time at the Barrows of Ainse, and probably at night."

"*The Barrows of Ainse,*" Wil said, mimicking Eleanor's accent.

"Laugh at me, Traveler," she warned, "and you'll get no tale."

Wil did laugh, pleasantly.

The days passed quickly, and Wil learned from Crispin the unique history of the Old Ainsley fen.

"There was no fen there twenty years ago," Crispin told Wil matter-of-factly. "Thayne, the current fen lord, was a Marion nobleman who grew disenchanted with his own country and the aristocracy there. He asked our king if he, and any willing tenants and friends, might establish a humble fen in Aemogen, an artisanal fen, where metalwork, woodwork, and the like could be produced for the benefit of the entire country. Some very skilled craftsmen came with Thayne," Crispin explained. "So, the King gave them the lands of Old Ainsley, which no one else had wanted to occupy."

"Can I ask why, or do I have to wait for the queen's story?" Wil asked.

"Ah," Crispin said and shook his head. "She wants to tell you at the Barrows of Ainse?"

"Yes. At night or something just as superstitious," Wil said.

Crispin smiled. "It's worth the wait."

<hr />

It was late the next night when the company arrived at Old Ainsley fen. Wil dismounted, passing Hegleh off to one of the men taking their horses to the stables, and scrutinized his surroundings.

The fen hall was quite large and different from any other he had yet seen. It was built after the traditions of Marion craftsmanship, with arches, careful stonework, and a wooden balustrade winding around a balcony on the second story. Eleanor had dismounted quickly and embraced a man Wil assumed to be Thayne. It was the most tender encounter he had yet seen between the queen and a fen lord. Their love for one another was evident.

The Marion aristocrat was simply but elegantly, dressed. His beautifully drawn face lent itself to his long gray hair, pulled back and tied with a ribbon. Thayne knew almost all the company by name and saw to it the soldiers were settled as he invited the council indoors.

Thayne and Aedon also exchanged a hearty embrace, greeting each other with familiarity and respect. Wil had never seen Aedon so animated, and he felt the intruder as he followed behind Crispin. After Thayne exchanged a greeting with the captain of the guard, he finally noticed Wil.

"Thayne of Allarstam," he introduced himself to Wil with a curious look on his face.

"Wil Traveler," Wil said as he shook the fen lord's hand.

"Yes, I had heard," Thayne responded, about to usher Wil in the door. Then he paused, his eyes narrowing in question. "Have we met?" he asked Wil. "You strike me as familiar." Thayne's tone was pleasant, but Wil stiffened.

"It's not likely we've ever met," Wil said. "I have spent most of my days in the Northern countries, far from Aemogen."

Thayne gave a peculiar smile but shrugged and motioned for Wil to join the company in the beautifully furnished fen hall.

"I have a warm dinner for every man," he said, once he had entered the room, pleased to be playing host. Then Thayne stepped up behind Eleanor and set his hands on her shoulders. "For you," he said, "I have two warm dinners."

As the company ate, they spoke with Thayne about the doings of the fen. The conversation surprised Wil, as it was much more personal and open than he had seen with the other fen lords. After they had eaten, Thayne spoke.

"I know you are all tired, and so I will not keep you discussing politics. I assume tomorrow you will begin your training?" he asked, looking expectantly at the faces before him.

"Yes," Gaulter Alden replied, outlining their visit.

"Good, good," Thayne said cooperatively. "You will find our men ready and efficient. If I have any questions, I will ask them come morning." Thayne turned towards Eleanor. "There is one item I would be most eager to speak with Your Majesty concerning, something the entire council should hear. Perhaps it can wait until tomorrow, after evening meal?"

"That would be fine," Eleanor answered. "We usually have a council meeting to start the day, but we never do things here at Old Ainsley like we do everywhere else, do we?"

"Indeed, no, My Lady," Thayne said. "No need to take us by the hand at Old Ainsley. Here, you must enjoy your stay."

Seeing as how they had rested well at the fortress of Anoir, Crispin spoke to Eleanor about hiking to the Barrows of Ainse that night.

"We could all do with a good story," Crispin said. "And Wil has been as impatient as a hornet to hear the tale."

Wil, who was sitting at a table nearby, talking to Gaulter Alden, guffawed in response. But when Eleanor appeared inclined to accept the idea, he grabbed his cloak, following the rest of them away from the Old Ainsley fen on the coast and up towards the barrows.

"These were the old burial mounds of the Aemogen royal families for hundreds of years," Crispin whispered to Wil as they climbed the strange landscape of hundreds if not thousands of mounds, piled around and atop one another. "The markers have long since been erased, so, there's no telling who is beneath you at any given moment."

"They say," Crispin continued in a low voice, "that you can see the ghosts of Aemogen on still nights, when all is unearthly and quiet. They also say Eleanor has seen them, but she's never spoken of it."

The prick of this supernatural thought caused Wil to shiver, and he socked Crispin in the arm as a way of dissipating the unsettling atmosphere. The captain hit him in return, stifling his laughter and receiving a "Shh!" from someone behind them.

"You're not going to convince me of shades and haunts," Wil whispered to his friend. "I don't believe in them."

"What, then, do you do with your dead?" Crispin asked in all seriousness. The image of his brother caught in Wil's mind, and even in the darkness, he could almost feel the sun against his back as he had when kneeling alone over his brother's open grave, having prepared Emaad's body for his journey into the afterworld.

"We send them on," he finally responded to Crispin's question. "They do not linger in this world."

Aedon and Eleanor, who had led the small company, stopped in the middle of the barrows and sat down. The soldiers waited, almost reverently. Aside from the spring ceremony and the singing before they'd left on the battle run, this was as close a moment to religious ritual as Wil had seen in Aemogen.

Wil settled himself at the edge of the company, wrapping his black cloak around his shoulders and pulling it tight. The evening felt surprisingly cold for summer, and his soul began to lean towards the melancholy of the place. Ahead, in the dark, they could hear the waves of the sea crashing against the cliffs and withdrawing. Then, as if crying in their defeat, they would rush once more, breaking into spray and air before they fell back again.

Wil could feel someone settle in behind him, and he turned, expecting Crispin. But no one was there, just the empty darkness over the rippled graves of Old Ainsley. Feeling the grip of the unknown, he turned slowly forward, training his eyes on the queen and his mind away from the barrows at his back. Eleanor waited until the noise of rustling stopped, and then, as if it were a ceremonial part of telling the tale, she unwound her braids until her hair hung long before her shoulders.

"Seven hundred years ago," she began softly, "when the Old Ainsley towers were tall above the cliffs of Taise, and the Aemogens had fought this wild and unknown land into a calmer place, Queen Ainorra Breagha ruled in confidence over her people. She knew the wealth of Aemogen: the depth of the land, the faithfulness of the seasons, and the strength of the mountains.

"When other countries sought to deal with Aemogen, to take her treasures, Ainorra Breagha was careful and wise. She weighed offers of trade and alliance with care, refusing many before she settled on the ancient country of Bylja Svain, making a treaty with Hildr Rogg, their king. They were far across the water, but they were sea-born and sea-bred, and they traveled far in their mighty ships."

Wil drew his eyebrows together. He'd heard but little of the Bylja Svain, and had not known Aemogen shared history with that ancient nation. "They brought gems and jewels, skins and gold," Eleanor continued. "Aemogen, in turn, sent metals, weapons, grains, silver, and seeds. But Ainorra Breagha would not tell the Bylja Svain's captains the way around the dangerous port of Calafort. Unless committed to perfect memory and touch, no man can navigate these waters safely. So, the Bylja Svain would anchor far from land and wait until Aemogen ships came for trade," Eleanor said, pausing briefly.

"At first, the Bylja Svain were amicable, but soon their king, who had sought Ainorra Breagha for his bride and been refused, pleaded the cause of his captains. 'They are weary from their long journey across the Darke Deyja Seas,' he said. 'Since we have been friends these many years, teach my captains how to navigate the Aemogen Sound.' Ainorra Breagha refused.

"But Hildr Rogg grew angry and sent a message, saying that if a show of friendship was not made, he would withdraw his trading. The councillors of Ainorra Breagha would be remiss if they lost such a powerful and wealthy ally. So, they pled with the queen. She finally sent word to Hildr Rogg that three of his captains would learn the Aemogen waterways and be allowed to harbor at Calafort."

"The Aemogen sailors spent many months teaching the Bylja Svain captains. They practiced until they could wend their ships past those unseen graves of many a man. All was well for five more years, and both countries thrived in wealth."

Wil shifted, and waited for Eleanor to continue. A fierce look had come into her eye.

"One evening, as the sun was setting far across the western mountains, shadows were seen on the sea. They were Bylja Svain ships. But rather than three coming for trade, there were twelve. Each wound its way, following signals and lights from the ships ahead," Eleanor said, gesturing with her hand.

"The people of Calafort were afraid as they heard the calls of war from the water. Soon, men with weapons and shields poured into the streets. A messenger was sent to ride hard for the towers of Old Ainsley, where Ainorra Breagha lay sleeping. He arrived in the night, calling out the news of the attack.

"Now, Aemogen had no national army, but rather a company of men assigned to each fen in the land," Eleanor explained, her eyes moving to Wil. "Ainorra Breagha knew that Hildr Rogg's men would march up the eastern coast and capture Old Ainsley. So, she called on the men of the castle and on the men of the nearby fens. Who were the fastest riders? Who were swift? Who could rally the men of the fens and call them to battle?

"Fifteen young men were chosen." She smiled as she continued. "They were true and virtuous. Ainorra Breagha blessed them each with a queen's blessing and called them her fen riders, sending them out as the early touches of the day lit the eastern sky.

"She now had only one hundred men around the castle. They prepared and waited as Ainorra Breagha walked from turret to turret along the high battlements, her red dress blowing in the morning wind. She walked and watched and waited, praying speed down on her riders and courage into the hearts of her men.

"More horsemen arrived from Calafort," she continued. "It had been ransacked; men, women, and children killed. The survivors fled to the towers, claiming four hundred assailants were at their heels. Old Ainsley took in the seafolk from Calafort, prepared the men for war, and waited for word from Ainorra Breagha. She continued to walk the battlements, watching the southern road for Hildr Rogg and his army, and the northern road for her own.

"When she reached the western turret, she looked out across the Barrows of Ainse. There, the graves of all her predecessors lay, mounds of soil to cover their bones from winter's chill, grass and flowers, as reminders of beauty, growing above them in spring. As numerous as the pebbles of the beach below the cliffs of Taise, their graves stretched west towards the woods. Then she remembered the legend of the first king and his son, Prince Coir. When the King lay dying, he pled with his son to bury him in the fields west of the humble walls beginning to form the towers of Old Ainsley.

"'Bury me close,' he had said, 'that when trouble arises, I am at hand.'

"'I will see it done,' the son had vowed.

The son did as his father asked and buried his mother the same. For hundreds of years, the men and women of Old Ainsley were buried in the Barrows of Ainse, uttering the same promise made by the first king: that they would offer aid to their children and their children's children.

"When Ainorra Breagha remembered the promise, she called her captain to her. 'Stand fifty men before the towers, facing the south road,' she told the captain. 'Then stand the remaining fifty to the west, the barrows behind their steps. When the men of Hildr Rogg come up the south road,' Ainorra Breagha explained, 'the men from the west must run them into the sea, and the men standing before Ainsley towers must hold their ground and see that the towers are kept.'

"The young captain argued with his queen, saying that she was a fool and that they would all die." Eleanor's voice broke as she told this part of the tale. Wil knew that he had thought her a fool many times for trying to defend with so few against so many. He bowed his head as she took a deep breath and continued. "Nevertheless, he set his men: fifty before the castle and fifty standing with their backs to the barrows on the west. Ainorra Breagha returned to the battlements, a single archer at her side, and watched the road. When Hildr Rogg and his men came into view, her soldiers stood, trembling. None had come to their aid save a few.

"The men of Hildr Rogg fanned out to face both flanks of the Aemogen forces. Hildr Rogg himself saw the queen on her tower and demanded her surrender. She called down to Hildr Rogg that he had broken his covenants to the people of Aemogen and that if he continued, his men would not see the light of another star.

"Hildr Rogg laughed. 'What are your men against my warriors?' he said. 'We are trained for war, and you are trained unto servitude.'

"'We are trained for triumph,' was the answer Ainorra Breagha gave." Eleanor lifted her chin higher and continued, "The men of the fens began to arrive. They came from the west and from the north, and fell into the line of the men at the edge of the barrows. Hildr Rogg called for his soldiers to advance and take the castle, so Ainorra Breagha told her archer to release a warning shot. But Hildr Rogg only laughed and swore he would sit on her throne before midday.

"The battle commenced. It was a dark day—the sun did not break the clouds—and many fell against the gates of Old Ainsley, their blood smeared on the gray stone. As the soldiers continued to defend their queen, men of the fens began to arrive in greater numbers. They joined in strength and fell upon the battle-weary Bilja Svain before the Ainsley gates. The young captain celebrated the fidelity of the fens and took courage, swearing until the day he died that an unseen hand had rested on his shoulder and urged him forward, and so, forward he went."

"As the battle continued, three of Hildr Rogg's men broke through the gates and entered the towers of Old Ainsley, hoping to burn it to the ground. The Aemogen men rallied, and as they came upon the men of Bylja Svain, their courage took hold, and they ran the army of Hildr Rogg over the cliffs of Taise, letting them fall to their deaths in the angry sea.

"With victory won, they turned towards the flaming castle. The eastern tower had fallen, and the queen was no longer seen on the battlement. The soldiers could not put out the fire, neither could they find Ainorra Breagha. But then, out of the smoke, came the single archer, carrying Ainorra Breagha to safety. She called him *her own,* and for the rest of her days, he served to protect his queen." Eleanor paused, her voice taken by the winds coming off the cliffs of Taise. No one spoke, and no one moved. All waited for her to finish the tale, listening as the sounds of the sea crashed in the distance.

"It has been said," she continued, "many times over the centuries that on nights when the wind lifts itself above the waves, it moves as if it is beating against the ancient towers of Old Ainsley, diverted, as it were, by invisible walls where the castle once stood. And if one is to look up towards the battlements, there can be seen a beautiful queen, walking the invisible turrets against the night sky, an arrow in her hand. And out from where the castle towers of Ainsley once stood, there can be heard the rushing of one hundred hoofbeats, riding from all directions across the Aemogen landscape, coming to the aid of the queen."

Eleanor sat still, Hastian silent behind her, his face sober. Her soldiers also remained unmoving. Wil bowed his head, telling himself that he did not want Eleanor to see his face. But he wondered if he, in truth, did not want to look up and risk seeing the beautiful ghost of Ainorra Breagha, walking along the shade of her long crumbled towers, looking straight into his heart.

CHAPTER

ELEVEN

"Training in Old Ainsley fen will be different," Crispin had promised.

And to Wil's pleasure, it was.

The tenants of Old Ainsley had brought with them from Marion a cultural love of swordplay. At last, Wil found himself engaging with men who offered him a more robust challenge. He relished the fights and, for the first time since his arrival in Ainsley, fought full and hard, sparing no thought for his opponents.

He needed to shake the ghosts of Ainsley away. And he needed to forget that Eleanor was preparing for an impossible war, hanging onto tales of impossible victories. Wil felt anger rise with each blow, and he gave himself over to the fight, forgetting all else.

The council gathered inside the fen hall after dusk. Eleanor watched each man as they waited for Thayne to come and join them. Gaulter Alden and Crispin were happy with the training; Sean was pleased with the mounts; and Briant, satisfied with the craft and weaponry of the Old Ainsley smiths, was whistling. Doughlas was absent, having been sent back to Ainsley Rise with a dispatch for Edythe. Aedon had admitted to Thayne and Eleanor, earlier in the day, that he feared the numbers of all Aemogen would not be sufficient to fight, and the worry of it rested still on his face. Wil sat looking sullen at the opposite end of the table from Eleanor, inside his own head. As for herself, Eleanor did not feel well: her eyes were sore, her neck aching, and she wished for sleep.

"Thistle Black is not friendly to your monarchy," Thayne began, once Eleanor had opened the meeting.

"I know," Eleanor said, looking down at her hands. "He criticized my father's rule in the past and, consequentially, my rule as well."

"Yes," Thayne nodded. "But it is more than that. I've heard him say that the mine of South Mountain fen belongs to his family, not the country of Aemogen."

"Ridiculous," Eleanor stated. "It was my grandfather who sent Black and his family south to open more mines, and who provided all the equipment and support for years. It is a national mine. His role, as fen lord, is a gift of the crown as well."

"Thistle Black, according to some of my men, does not agree with fighting the Imirillians," Thayne added. "He wants to join forces with Zarbadast and become a useful asset to the empire. He has already considered forging his own trades."

"That's treason," Aedon said flatly.

"Surely we can win his allegiance in some way," Eleanor said, looking around the council. "Make him see the foolishness of his aspirations and how it would affect the entire country," she suggested. "Is he so unreasonable?"

"Thistle Black has always wanted power," Gaulter Alden said

as he sat back in his chair. "He was like that as a young man. And power and reason are rarely the same thing."

"Humph," Wil disagreed, drawing Thayne's attention to him.

"What are my options for regaining his allegiance without removing him from his place?" Eleanor asked, as much to herself as to the others. She stood up and walked behind her chair, clutching it with her hands and drumming her fingers along the wood. "Any ideas?"

Thayne was about to speak, when Wil's voice cut across the room.

"It's clear what you have to do," he said. All eyes turned towards him.

"Is it?" Eleanor said.

Wil stood. "You and I have disagreed about how a monarch should relate to their people." His eyes were set directly on her, and she did not look away. "You favor loyalty born of love and friendship. I favor deification of a monarch to inspire submission."

Thayne was now watching Wil carefully. Every part of Eleanor was tired. She was not feeling up for a challenge, or a verbal spar, especially with Wil. They had gotten on so well the last several days.

"This entire battle run," Wil continued, "you have ridden up to the people in plain dress, greeting them as if they were all second cousins—talked, laughed, encouraged—and the fens have loved it," Wil admitted. "Clearly, they are affectionate towards you as their monarch. But," he added, "now you have this man, Thistle Black, who, although I have never met him, appears to have little respect for all of that."

"Get at a point, Wil," she said.

"You must ride into South Mountain fen in power," Wil stated.

"No laughter, no games, no disorganized guard calling hello to their aunt." Wil raised his voice and lifted his hands. "Make this man see you for the person you are, in the station you are in. What is a fen lord to a queen?" Wil demanded, hitting the table with his fist with unexpected force. "Nothing!"

No one spoke. It was as if the others present felt they were eavesdropping on a personal exchange. Eleanor opened her mouth to speak, but she knew she would not sound steady. Eleanor instead took another deep breath. Wil, appearing suddenly conscious of the others, began to sit down and then, as if still more had to be said and he was determined to do it, stood up straight again and pointed a finger at Eleanor.

"I'm not sure if you realize this yet, Your Majesty," he said, "but you are the supreme power of this country. What you say goes whether your council agrees with you or not."

Eleanor began to object, but Wil held up his hand. "They have power because you give it to them. Only when you fully know *that* will you become a threat to any dissenters—or any foreign power, for that matter."

Crossing her arms, Eleanor gave Wil a terrific glare. His own expression narrowed in response, and he continued.

"When you ride into South Mountain fen, let your guard be sharp. Let your call for aid be accompanied by a grueling day of training. Instead of being encouraging and complimentary, as you have been, criticize them, be exacting; make them earn any praise you have to offer." A hint of fervor passed through his features, something that both needled and comforted Eleanor: he wanted her to succeed, badly.

"Do not let your power stop there," he continued. "They run a national mine? Ask them about the workings of it. Ask them what their profit is. A disgruntled man with thoughts of his own ambition is often a thief, in my experience. Check their records. Chances are he is stealing from the crown. Let him know that you are onto him and that if he does not fall in line, there will be consequences. Make this Thistle Black fear he is of so little importance that he can be disposed of, easily, along with his entire family, if you so desire."

"That sounds a bit harsh," Eleanor heard herself reply.

"It is," Wil said curtly. "And that's exactly what you need to be if you are to earn the respect of a man like Thistle Black." Wil sat down again in his seat and leaned back, his arms folded, his eyes burning.

She stared back, challenging, agreeing and disagreeing in one long, visual exchange. Then someone cleared their throat, and Eleanor broke the connection. Thayne was looking from the queen to Wil and back again. He frowned as Eleanor sat down in her chair.

"I will not change who I am," she said. It was meant to be a personal thought, but the words had just spilled out.

The room was silent, everyone avoiding looking at Eleanor and Wil.

"Let's hear your thoughts, council," Eleanor snapped, when no one would speak.

"This young man may be right, Eleanor," Thayne said, braving the taut atmosphere between the queen and the traveler. "You have great maturity for your age, which causes you to shy away from using your power to force those around you. That is to be commended. But, there are times when, used wisely, rulers must show that they wield this weapon—"

"And for the sake of anything that is in heaven," Wil interrupted

Thayne, "take advantage of the impressive skills of this fen to get some decent clothing. Let them tailor you a wardrobe that no one could mistake as that of a plain country noble. You are a queen," Wil added, "so look the part, act the part. Be a monarch they dare not cross."

"Yes, thank you, Wil, for your observations on my wardrobe," Eleanor shot back with uncharacteristic acidity. "I believe, council, that the arguments have been clear. It is late, and I desire some time to think about the problem Thistle Black poses. I would appreciate if you would do the same. We will continue this conversation at a later time," she said. "Please have dinner sent up to my room."

Wil stood, as did everyone else, when Eleanor left the table and retreated up the back staircase. Her cheeks burned, but with an internal plea towards her more measured self, she refrained from slamming the door.

Only Aedon and Wil remained at the table after the room had emptied, the other councilmen seeking fresh air away from the tense exchange.

"Say it," Wil said, pushing his chair back from the table, although he did not get up.

"Say what?" Aedon looked away from the figures on a paper before him and candidly met Wil's glare.

"Whatever it is you disapprove of."

"To be quite honest," Aedon said, "I agree with you, as I am sure will Eleanor—if not in method, then in spirit. Thistle Black is a stubborn, self-important bully, and I would love to see him set in his place for the benefit of all. It was your delivery that was, on the one hand, inflamed, and on the other, quite—" Aedon hesitated, "personal."

Wil felt the memory of his exhibition pull at his chest, and he frowned, moving his fingers across his forehead, feeling uncomfortable beneath Aedon's calm scrutiny. "If you think that was inflamed," he finally said, "you should witness the arguments my family gets into."

Aedon stared. "Pass," was his only response when it came.

Wil smiled despite himself. The tension in the room cleared, and he disappeared out a back door of the fen hall, seeking whatever solitude he could find.

Eleanor sat on the edge of her bed in the upstairs chamber, staring intensely at the patterns in the floor. It had not occurred to her, until that evening, how wearing it was to always be in the presence of others, with little personal respite. Her emotions had gotten the better of her, her thin patience pushing back. She bit her lip, angry and embarrassed. Why had Wil's biting counsel antagonized her so? Why could she not have listened dispassionately, rationally thinking through his words, and stated her response with clarity? Why did his words feel like a threat? And why, of all the silly things, did she care so much for his opinion? He was only a foolish, tempestuous soldier from the borders of Imirillia.

"And what a temper he throws about," she hissed, still angry that she had buckled and exhibited the same lack of self-control. A knock sounded on the door, which she ignored. Eleanor remained on the edge of the bed, cursing her public reaction. To make a spectacle of oneself was the worst kind of torture. The knock came again a few minutes later, and then the door opened.

It was Thayne who entered, closing the door behind him and

sitting next to Eleanor. Putting his arm around her, he kissed her on the forehead and pulled her close. Eleanor sniffed, fighting her tear-rimmed eyes. Thayne was always whatever Eleanor needed him to be; he was her personified mainstay.

"You have done well," he said. "Your father would be proud."

Eleanor nodded numbly, but she didn't look up.

"Is all well with Edythe?"

"She is engaged."

"Well," Thayne said as he squeezed Eleanor's shoulder and rested his chin on the top of her head. "I thought he would never ask. You can be quite fierce to approach."

"Can I?" Eleanor gave a quick laugh and pulled back, interpreting Thayne's expression. "That's not what it sounded like this evening."

"Thistle Black is a fool," he said. "You have proven yourself to all of Aemogen time and time again. You need not change who you are for him."

"And yet—" Eleanor added dully.

"And yet?" Thayne asked and paused.

"And yet, you agreed with Wil." Eleanor took a deep breath, as if she were struggling for air. The sound of the nearby ocean pounded against her chest. "I am so tired tonight. Even the thought of waking in the morning for training is almost—" She broke off.

"It is late. A dark night is never the time to make a decision, for your emotions always get in the way. Let us deal with Thistle Black tomorrow." Thayne smiled and looked at her face. "The people of my fen love and respect you; they also don't require anything that you don't have to give. You can sleep tomorrow, if you do not wish to rise. But for now, come join me below. You will feel better once you have eaten. The others have already gone. After you eat, we will walk the cliffs, watch the stars, smell the ocean. Let the wind blow your sorrow from your bones."

"Father always said you were a bit of a poet." Eleanor smiled and leaned into Thayne's arms, her head resting on his chest.

"So I am, dear," Thayne said as he looked out the window. "So I am."

"Well, what else have you to say?" Eleanor pressed. "I know when you've got something catching on the tip of your tongue."

Thayne pulled back from her and looked at her honestly, moving the muscles in his cheeks, as if reforming a question several times in his mind. "I am rather curious," he finally said, "about the newest member of your war council, this Wil Traveler."

"Ah," Eleanor sniffed. "Wil." She rolled her eyes. "And you have already spoken with Gaulter Alden or Crispin, haven't you?" Eleanor asked as she turned on the bed and faced Thayne, her leg tucked beneath her.

"Aedon actually." Thayne crossed his arms and frowned.

"Aedon!" Eleanor sighed. "I do wonder how he tells such things."

"Succinctly, practically," Thayne said evenly. "He explained the benefits of using the traveler in preparations for war and all of that: what you are gaining from him is of far more use than whatever he could come to know, and so on. But I would like to hear the details, before you go, from you."

"I can answer whatever questions you may have, willingly enough," she responded with a worn earnestness. "But tell me this, Thayne: do you, in your heart, mistrust him?"

Thayne cleared his throat and sat up straighter. "The training this afternoon was efficient and very—" he paused, searching for a word, "admirably executed. The only other clear interaction I have had with the young man was in our meeting tonight."

"Where he called me out before the entire council," Eleanor said.

"Where he offered you some sound and strong advice," Thayne said, "delivered in a hard, but most intimate manner." Thayne left a place for her to reply, but Eleanor refused to acknowledge the observation, so he continued. "What does he say of his experiences previous to coming to Aemogen?"

"As Aedon told you, I am sure. He is from a noble family of Imirillia. It's clear he is a very skilled warrior who has held leadership capacities. His ability to organize training declares that much. The information he has volunteered about himself was that he refused a higher post in the Imirillian army on a matter of conscience, due to some events he has not spoken of involving the death of his brother," she explained. "We asked him directly if he was a deserter."

"What did he say?"

"His answer was odd. In public, he said, 'I wouldn't go that far,' but in private, he expressed to me that his honor has driven him from the army. Whether that be forever, I don't know. To Wil," she explained, "privacy is paramount, so he would speak no further. What are your own suspicions?"

"He is no stranger to statesmanship, Eleanor," Thayne said. "You have found yourself a man with mind and scope. In theory, there could be no one better to be assisting you in this battle run than he. Aedon mentioned the odd timing of his arrival in Ainsley, but his skill seems more significant than any harm he could do, were he indeed a spy." Thayne paused. "Aedon also said that Wil took a pledge for the duration of the battle run that, to my own eyes and Aedon's, he has fulfilled strictly. Your gamble appears to have been a wise one, on the whole. The men have gained much."

"You are rather complimentary." Eleanor frowned. "But something else worries you."

"I am complimentary to his skill," Thayne said. "What bothers me is, I swear I have seen him before, but I can't place his face."

"You have not traveled much in the North, have you?" Eleanor asked. "Perhaps you and he met in Marion?"

Thayne stood and walked towards the window, looking down on the soldiers gathering around fires in the courtyard below. "When I look at that young man, I can't help but feel I am staring into the eyes of a ghost."

CHAPTER

TWELVE

Wil woke early to the sound of the ocean. He was wet, his cloak covered in heavy dew. Standing, he shook it off, throwing it over a bramble to dry, and walked towards the predawn light along the cliffs. No one else stirred. The ocean rang with sound, deep and dark, but the silver clouds hinted at sunrise.

Wil walked the path parallel to the cliffs, stretching his legs, running his fingers through his hair, and enjoying the sharpness of sound that morning always seemed to bring. He continued on, out of sight of the fen hall, beyond many of the houses, towards the wilds that tumbled seaward. Wil had never seen anything like it before. In the dim of early morning, the hills and rocks rose and fell, settled into their places for years, yet not appearing restful. It was a wild corner of the world, and Wil could see why Thayne and his people had chosen to stay here. He could also see why others would choose to leave, for to his back were the southern edges of the barrows.

"Getting acquainted with our ghosts?" a voice behind Wil said. Wil turned, his hand instinctively moving to his sword. Thayne stood on the slope, watching the ocean. He was dressed in fine clothing but looked very much in place.

"I see I've startled you," Thayne continued. "I'll take that as a compliment, as I assume it's not an easy thing to do. Speaking of ghosts, Wil Traveler," Thayne said, stepping down beside him, "I've been racking my brain about you. I've no clear recollection of where I may have seen you before, yet you're as familiar as my own blood." Thayne moved his tongue along his bottom lip and looked out over the sea. "Then I realized," he glanced again to Wil, his eyes intent and strong, "you're a ghost."

Wil stared at the older man.

"You are a ghost," Thayne repeated. "I just can't figure out whose ghost."

Bending down, Thayne picked up a smooth rock, weighing it in his hand before tossing it over the cliff and into the water. "But I know your eyes," he continued. "They press into my soul, and I've not slept for it."

"I am certain we've never met before," Wil answered, wishing he had not come so far, wishing the tumbled hills and stones could disappear and take him away from this sacred, haunted place.

"Tell me of yourself, Traveler," Thayne said. "I admit that my curiosity has gotten the better of me. I've invented stories all night."

"It's dangerous to live in stories," Wil said, meeting Thayne's eyes briefly.

"Yes."

Thayne's stare would not let Wil rest. Wil took a few steps forward, towards the edge of the cliff, and crossed his arms, watching the sun begin to make its appearance.

"I know you have more questions for me," Wil said. "It would be easier for both of us if you simply asked them instead of hinting around."

"Yes. But would you answer them?"

"I'll give you answers," Wil hedged. "Though, I'm almost certain they will not satisfy you." The sun was lifting itself above the line of the sea, a soft golden tone pressing against the cliffs beneath Wil's worn boots.

"Who are you?" Thayne asked.

"A traveler, caught in the middle of another man's war."

"Where does your allegiance lie?"

"With my own individual honor," Wil said. Out of habit, he moved his right hand to his left forearm, which was still bound, concealed with the now filthy strip of black cloth.

Thayne's eyes followed the movement. "What is your true intent in all of this?" Thayne asked as he had asked all the other questions, with a subtle challenge in his voice.

"To cause as little blood to be shed as is possible," Wil replied.

The sun broke fully over the water, causing Wil to squint against the morning and lift his arm to block out the blinding light.

"Why do I know your face?" Thayne asked.

"I am not the one to answer that question for you," Wil said as he turned and walked away from the interrogation, back towards the fen hall.

<hr />

The following days of training went well. The tense feelings over Thistle Black were eased, and Eleanor's council thawed. Although she and Wil spoke little, Eleanor was polite and amicable. Wil returned these sentiments but spent his time almost exclusively with the soldiers. He did not eat with the council and avoided

Thayne entirely.

On the final evening, the fen prepared a great meal to precede the traditional music and dancing. Eleanor had spent many hours reviewing her translations of the Imirillian texts, so she was ready for the socializing. Thayne asked her, curious, why she studied the pages.

"I have crossed my mind for a way to defeat the Imirillians," she confided to the fen lord. "An idea, a thought, can come from anywhere. My tutor once said that to defeat an enemy, you must know his heart. Perhaps that is why I keep coming back to these passages." She tossed them across the table to Thayne. "They're beautiful yet yield little concrete direction, I admit."

By day's end, Eleanor's maid had packed the translations away in her saddlebags, and Eleanor prepared herself for the night, encouraged by Thayne to leave her worries and enjoy the good conversation and fine music.

"I know you favor our Marion tunes in your heart," Thayne said as she joined him.

"I won't deny my fondness, Thayne," she admitted. "But don't you dare say a word."

"I have heard a rumor," Thayne said as if mentioning the thought casually, "that you have not been dancing. Do prove me wrong."

The entire fen had gathered outside the hall. Musicians began to play in a jovial way, and those who had gathered were lively. Wil was not present for the first dances, and Eleanor didn't worry over him.

Once it was clear she had decided to dance, Eleanor never lacked for a partner. Even Gaulter Alden agreed to stand up, laughing all the while and saying he was too old. Wil soon appeared at the outskirts of the circle, hanging back with a mug of cider, paying especial note to the music.

Eleanor sat down and began talking with Thayne, when the musician announced that they would play the Marion Catch.

"A favorite of my mother's, I believe," Eleanor said.

"So it was," Thayne responded. "I haven't danced it in ages, but if you would like—?"

"I would," Eleanor said as she smiled. Just as she stood, Wil appeared at her elbow. But he must have realized Thayne had invited her to dance, for he stepped back.

"I see you already found a partner," Wil said. "I was going to brave the crowd and ask you myself," he explained. "It's one of the few Marion dances I know."

Thayne laughed. "I've never pitted myself against a younger, more handsome man," Thayne said. "And I'll not start now. Please, let me rest while you show Eleanor how to enjoy a dance."

Eleanor took Wil's arm. "I'm all amazement, Wil Traveler," she said. "I had supposed that you never danced."

Wil didn't reply until he led Eleanor into the circle. "Please accept this as an apology for the other evening," he said.

"You gave sound advice, Wil."

"Yes, but my delivery was unnecessarily abrasive." His gaze was direct. "I want you to succeed in this thing, Eleanor. I know you disagree with my views, but please consider in part what I have said, forgetting my rudeness."

He reached out and took Eleanor's hands. This gesture startled her, until she remembered that this was how the Marion Catch began.

"I don't care much for such happy dances," Wil admitted.

Eleanor surprised herself then—for she laughed.

The musicians set the rhythm, drums clipping at the pace of a fast horse. Their fellow dancers whooped and called out, but Wil's mouth remained stern. Then, as the violin began to carry a merry melody, the catch began. Wil led Eleanor around him—to the right, to the left, and facing each other again—before spinning into a circle. All the crowd joined in, clapping along with the beat as the dancers spun.

Wil's enthusiasm did not match that of their fellow dancers on the floor: he remained stiff, understating his own movements, maintaining a certain dignity that he seemed to think important. As he lifted Eleanor's hand above her head, sending her twirling in rhythm with the song, Eleanor laughed again. Wil did know this dance, and he knew it well.

Despite his stubborn decision to underplay the movements, his style was graceful and sure. Eleanor had never fancied herself a very good dancer, but she found following Wil easy. They traded partners throughout the reel, returning to each other often. The crowd cheered as the dancers put on quite an exhibition, and then, as suddenly as it had begun, it ended in a flourish of melody and sound, with Wil and Eleanor facing each other, out of breath, her hands in his. He even smiled.

"I'm impressed, Wil!" Eleanor pressed her fingertips into his palms for emphasis.

"You're always surprised when I do something well." His face was flushed, but there was a lightness in his eyes. "I'm not sure if I should be offended by that or not," he added.

"Not so," Eleanor opened her mouth in defense. "Sometimes you do something well and it irritates, rather than surprises."

His laugh in response was perhaps the most spontaneous expression she had ever heard, so unlike what he had been these last two months. This brief, authentic moment was significant to Eleanor: it pleased her, and drew her eyes to his face as they wound through the circle of dancers to a quiet spot on the edge of the circle, just down from where Thayne sat with Gaulter Alden.

"Your mood is obviously improved," she said.

Wil tilted his eyebrows up in what seemed some sort of internal concession as he looked over the crowd. "Blame that on Crispin," he said. "He talked me out of my bad mood. You'll hear no more from me tonight on politics."

"Good," Eleanor responded.

"Oh? Is it so bad, my pontificating?"

It took Eleanor a moment to grasp his self-deprecating humor. "What I meant," she explained, "was that I don't think I can talk about anything serious tonight. I am spent, and my impatience— born of exhaustion—and your complex temper—born of what, I can't say—are quite the pair when we are worn down. Let us not tempt them." Eleanor pulled in a deep breath, feeling the smoke from the bonfire in her lungs. "But do feel free to tell me anything of no significance," she added. "And I will promise to be attentive."

Wil had his arms crossed, his shoulders back, and, when he looked down at her, the edge of his mouth was turned up. The firelight played across his face, and Eleanor looked away, back towards the dancers. She'd had to. What had once been an unacknowledged, nuanced attraction was rather quickly becoming, Eleanor confessed to herself, overwhelming. He was difficult, layered, and stubborn, and she felt distracted by the memory of the weight of his hand on her waist as they had danced.

"I promised Crispin another dance," Eleanor said, sounding hesitant, though it had been intended to sound light. "Excuse me, Wil." She walked back toward Gaulter Alden and Thayne, forgetting to look for Crispin for the feeling of Wil's eyes on her back.

—◦◦◦◦◦◦◦◦◦—

The next day, the company left Old Ainsley, heading west to Rye Field fen. Their parting had been brief but heartfelt. Wil watched as Eleanor said good-bye to Thayne, understanding now that the fen lord was closer to a father than a friend for the queen.

Reluctant to make eye contact with Thayne, Wil mounted Hegleh and sat stiff and aloof. He wanted no conversation with the Marion nobleman, for he would not play a role in any man's ghost story. What he wanted was to speak with Eleanor again about things that had nothing to do with wars and politics.

Along the route, Aedon, Eleanor, and Wil rode side by side. They were halfway through the battle run, and they shared thoughts as to the strength of Aemogen's forces.

"I worry," Aedon questioned aloud, "if our unwillingness to trade has been a forerunner to this invasion."

"Has the Imirillian Empire offered you a treatise of trade before?" Wil asked, curious to hear their answer.

"Not the emperor but merchants, yes," Eleanor said. "We received requests from Imirillia, Capabolt, and Aramesh, among others."

"But you accepted none?" Wil asked.

"We accepted none," Eleanor answered frankly. "We do limited trade with Marion, and do not use our resources on the greater international market."

"Why?" Wil asked. "It could greatly profit Aemogen."

"You heard the tale of Ainorra Breagha," she said. "Our history bears it out for us. We only entered into treaties with Marion with the utmost caution."

"As you have noticed," Aedon said, his response to Wil almost sounding congenial, "we are fierce about Aemogen tradition and all we have fought to attain. This is a peaceful country with good laws, a working justice system, and endless resources. To enter into negotiations with another country puts all that in jeopardy."

Wil was dissatisfied. He felt a conflict rising in his chest.

"Say what is on your mind, Wil," Eleanor said. "You're frowning."

"It's only that I have seen all these countries who have sought trade with you," Wil answered. "They are filled with barren lands, where people suffer to sustain themselves. They have arts and skills to trade, knowledge of many things, but hardly any food to speak of. You are an abundantly blessed nation, which—from what I have seen and heard—has food and materials to spare after every harvest. Do you not feel it your duty to reach out and aid the hungry in return for valuables that could benefit your own people?"

Wil paused, choosing his next words. "I feel passionately that the strong must help the weak. And as much as you might criticize the Imirillian Empire, I think it would surprise you to know the earnest endeavors of some in the noble class on behalf of the poor. Imirillia's expanse has blessed many with abundance."

"Yes," Aedon replied, "but it is through taking the rights of other people. Even if something is done with the best intentions, it cannot be done through force."

"But you do not share when asked," Wil retorted.

Eleanor looked towards Wil. "My role as queen is to protect my people, to see them thrive," she said. "I commit myself first and foremost to this responsibility. If our isolation causes pain, I am sorry for it, but I can't risk the well-being of my people for another country."

"Then you are held captive by fear," Wil responded.

"It is reason," she said, "not fear."

"It is seeing to one's own stewardship," Aedon added.

"Well, I will enlighten you on one thing," Wil said, looking at Aedon, then at Eleanor. "Your isolation does not only cause pain—it causes death. People in the North starve. Remember that the next time you feed your pigs such fine slop."

CHAPTER
THIRTEEN

"Again!" Wil yelled. The young man lifted his sword, swinging at Wil with all his force. Wil defended the blow as he would flick a grasshopper. "Again!" Wil yelled with each swing. "Again! Again!"

Finally, the young man dropped to the ground, exhausted of his strength. He looked up at Wil with an almost fearful resignation.

"Up on your feet," Wil said. "Again."

But the young man bent his head, his hands shaking.

Wil slid his own sword into its sheath. He knew the men of Rye Field fen were all watching, waiting to see how he would respond to this young man, who had failed so miserably in his training. Wil knew he should berate the young man or encourage him on with visions of success. But instead, he motioned for Crispin to continue without him and crouched down before the youth.

"What is your name?" he asked.

"Tarit."

"What is it that you do, Tarit? Farmer? Thatcher?" Wil guessed.

"Potter, sir."

"You make pots? Clay vessels and the like?"

Tarit nodded.

"All right," Wil said as he stood. "Come, show me your work."

Tarit looked up, confused. "But it's the training day. All men must be present by order of the queen."

Wil shrugged. "I'm friends with the queen. She'll not mind." Wil helped the young man to his feet.

Rye Field was set up differently from the other fens Wil had seen. There were separate buildings for tradesmen to work in, directly surrounding the fen hall, so all commerce remained in the center of the fen. Then the houses sat in a loose circle, and the fields behind them, spreading out like the spokes of a wagon wheel. Tarit led Wil to a humble, but sturdy building that was full of well-proportioned pieces of pottery.

Wil whistled. "Are all of these yours, or are some of them your father's?"

"All mine," Tarit said, setting his shoulders back, like a man discussing his trade. "I've no father; mother and sisters is all."

"Is all?" Wil replied. "That must be quite the responsibility. How old are you? Fourteen?"

"Thirteen, sir."

Wil shook his head and looked about the small workroom. It was clean, but humble. The wheel was set in the corner so that Tarit could see anyone coming in or out of the door.

"Will you show me how it's done?" Wil asked, pointing to the empty wheel.

Tarit seemed incredulous. "You want to see me at the wheel? But why would such a thing interest you? You're a soldier."

"I'm curious," Wil said. "You've spent your morning learning some of my trade, so I would be pleased to learn some of yours."

Without needing any more encouragement, Tarit went to a stone bench of sorts and lifted off the lid. The aroma of wet earth filled Wil's nostrils. Tarit removed a large, round ball of clay and slammed it down on a smooth stone nearby. Wil watched as the young man expertly kneaded the clay.

"It's to get all the air pockets out," Tarit explained as he worked. Tarit's arms were strong, and his hands, quick. After working the clay into a soft, moldable consistency, he threw it onto the potter's wheel, dipping his fingers into a worn bucket of water—filthy and gritty.

Placing the clay soundly in the center, he proceeded to turn the wheel with one hand, while dipping his other in the water and bringing it back to the spinning mound before him. Once the wheel was going fast enough, Tarit used both hands, guiding the clay into shape. It looked effortless, even easy, an action of absolute grace.

Wil sat in the corner, somewhat envious of the obvious pleasure Tarit took in his work. The boy picked up a wooden stick leaning near the wheel, and, in a few quick movements, he left a beautiful design in the piece. Within moments, he presented Wil with a shallow bowl of perfect proportion.

"I don't have the kiln ready just yet," he said, "because I've been at training all morning. But if you would like, I could place a bowl just like this in the kiln for you tonight, and it would be ready before morning."

Touched, Wil nodded. "That would be an honor, Tarit. Thank you." Wil's eyes wandered around the shop, noticing how precise and uniform Tarit's many completed bowls were. Drying next to other finished pieces on a large shelf, the vessels were all natural shades—browns, creams, and reds—both dark and light.

"In my land," Wil began, "our potters use something called a glaze. It's a liquid paint of sorts that they put on a piece of pottery before it goes into the kiln. It comes out in beautiful colors, smooth, with a shiny surface."

Tarit's looked impressed. "I've heard rumors," he said. "But I've never seen anyone actually use such things. Do you know how to make them?"

"Not myself," Wil said as he shook his head. "But I may be able to find out, and someday, I'll share the secret with you. You'll be the most successful potter in all the fens."

Tarit grinned at the thought.

"You know," Wil looked the young man square in the eye. "I am sure that what you just showed me is more difficult than it seems. Am I right? Your friends have all tried it and failed."

Tarit nodded.

"Well, I've been fighting for a long time." Wil fought the sadness of his own smile. "For all intents and purposes, it's my trade. I think, for a first attempt, you did well today. I hope you won't have to become very good at fighting and that soon you will be back to your potter's wheel, learning how to use the glazes I will send down to you. But don't give up on trying to learn the sword just yet," Wil added. "You are stronger than you think. I saw that as you worked your clay. Just imagine that you are the wheel when you fight. Use your sword to create the shapes that you need to block the enemy's parry and to strike back. Also, spend some time with Aedon on archery," he added. "It might prove to fit you better than man-to-man combat."

Nodding, Tarit stood up and rinsed his hands in the dirty water, wiping them on his breeches. "I'll try again, if you promise to send me those glazes," Tarit stipulated.

"You have my word of honor," Wil said solemnly as they left the potter's shed, walking back to the training.

"I've never been so sore in my life," Wil said later to Crispin as the young captain joined him in the shade of the blacksmith's hut. Crispin nodded, wiping sweat from his forehead with his fingers. They were in the middle of their last day at Rye Field fen.

"We've been going long enough to feel it," Crispin said, "but not long enough to be tough against it."

"On days like these I ask myself why I ever left home, where servants drew me a daily bath, warm, with oils and soaps." Wil sighed. "Curse the freezing rivers of Aemogen."

"I can't draw you a warm bath," Crispin said, "but I could do you one better." A slow grin spread over Crispin's face. "There is a collection of warm mineral pools in the hills above Rye Field. A few of us are going up there tonight after the bonfire," he explained. "I saw Doughlas ride in an hour ago. He'll join us for certain, so it should be good company."

After the bonfire, Crispin called Wil to join him and a small party of soldiers, most of whom Wil had shared conversation with throughout the course of the battle run. Wil greeted Doughlas, inquiring after Ainsley, and found he had a letter from Edythe, a pleasant diversion as he waited for Crispin and the others. Aedon had also decided to join them.

They set out on a path through the woods that traveled into the hills. Wil conversed easily with the men about the day's training as Crispin threw in several humorous observations.

Even Aedon added to the conversation, responding to something Wil had said amicably. It was not long before they came to an outcropping of rock with several pools. A sequence of small waterfalls found their way down the mountain on the right, but, to the left, steam could be seen rising out of mineral-encrusted basins in the rocks.

"We are not exactly sure how they exist, but it's a jolly good bath," Crispin told Wil as the men stripped themselves of their clothing. "The locals come often, putting different plant oils in the water, or some such nonsense. A friend from the fen gave me this for my soreness." Crispin held up a small glass bottle. "If you can credit the idea."

After all the soldiers had settled themselves in the warm water, their conversation turned to home.

"I swear, Meg won't wait out the summer," Doughlas sighed. "The butcher's son on New Ainsley Road comes around every time I'm off on a ride, and wooing her back is a sure fight. She'll be wed before I get home."

"With your dashing looks?" someone called out, and Doughlas grinned. He was handsome and lithe, with a grin as mischievous as a cat's.

"You're too young to marry," Crispin added. "And how in the world are you supposed to decide which one you want to settle down with?"

"And chances are," Aedon said without a smile, "when you do find her, she'll have walked out with Crispin a time or two before she chooses you."

The men laughed, and Wil settled his sore body farther into the warmth of the mineral water, stretching his arms out along the edges of the pool. He enjoyed this company: their conversations, jokes, and personalities. Even Aedon was not as stiff to Wil these days. Although, Wil did notice Aedon studying the mark on Wil's chest with curiosity. When he knew that the councillor had looked away, Wil checked to ensure that the black fabric about his left forearm was still secure.

"And what about you, Wil?" Sean said. "Tell us about the girls you left back home. Any that you regret?"

"There are some women at home," Wil said, "who kept my mind occupied for a day here and there, but I've yet to meet one that's made me feel regret." Wil shrugged. "When I do," he added, "I'll send you a letter."

"Just don't send it by fen rider," Doughlas quipped. "I'll be busy courting Meg or fighting the butcher's son."

Wil grinned.

"So you don't plan on settling down anytime soon?" Crispin asked.

"Not in the future I see before me," Wil said.

"Then why, under the blue, blue sky," Crispin began, "does everybody give *me* a hard time for doing the same?" Crispin rounded on his friends. "All of you do. Even Eleanor prophesies me dying alone for the lack of choosing a wife."

Duncan, a soldier that Wil did not know as well, spoke up for the first time. "Tell the queen you will wed as soon as she does," he suggested. "And I'll bet she won't whisper a word for ten winters."

"Ah, get off it," Crispin said with a laugh. "Eleanor will marry soon enough."

"Are you privy to information we're not?" Doughlas asked in a rascal's tone. Wil watched as all the soldiers actually seemed very interested in hearing what Crispin would have to say.

"I know nothing," Crispin said, putting a cherubic look on his face. "Well, aside from a name and a date." The soldiers all laughed, and he waited for the laughter to die down before pointing to Aedon. "There is the man that may know something," Crispin said. "He is the queen's foremost councillor."

"The oldest and wisest amongst us all, for he is almost to the ripe old age of thirty," Duncan teased. "Oh, Aedon, what news from the council chamber. Will our queen wed anytime soon?"

"Why would I know?" Aedon responded to the curious soldiers. "And Sean is much older than I am."

Sean made some sort of show, and they all laughed.

"The real question is not when but who," Crispin said, elbowing Aedon, and then Doughlas said something smart.

Aedon smiled and flicked water at Crispin's face with his fingers. "You're elbowing the wrong man."

"Why?" Wil finally spoke up, drawing back the attention of the group. "You wouldn't want to marry the queen?"

"It's not if he would want her," Crispin answered for Aedon. "It's if she would want him."

"A man like Aedon, in his prime, not wanted by the queen?" Doughlas said, sounding tragic before breaking out a smile. "Well, we all knew she'd never have him. His dinner conversation is so dull."

Wil let out an amused breath.

"Come on, Aedon, out with it," Duncan persisted, as Aedon's expression turned long suffering. "We all want to know if you are sweet on the queen. It's not as if you're the ugliest man at Ainsley Rise."

Before they could get the now smiling Aedon to answer, a few more soldiers came up the path from the woods. Two of them were Crispin's men, and the third, to Wil's surprise, was Hastian, the Queen's Own. A general greeting went up from the group, and it was not long before the newcomers had shed their clothing and settled into the pools.

"Here is the man you should ask," Wil persisted, curious to see what he could find out. "Hastian, who holds the queen's heart? Does our friend Aedon have any chance?" The men went silent, and Hastian's eyes flicked to Wil's, filled with a defiance that Wil had never seen in the mild-mannered soldier.

"He can't answer you," Duncan said quickly. "He's the Queen's Own."

"Meaning?" Wil shrugged.

"Meaning that Hastian will never speak of the queen before anyone," Aedon responded diplomatically, but firmly. "He does not reveal her activities, her comments, or her interactions. He can't even tell you her favorite color if he knows it."

"Hastian's job," Crispin added, "is to ensure that, although the queen almost always has an armed guard at her side, she is given the respect of complete privacy. He can never repeat anything he sees or hears while serving the queen. He can't even discuss her as we are now," Crispin explained. "Technically, he is to never speak her name."

Hastian sat quietly in the pool, listening to Crispin with a self-conscious look on his face.

Wil ran his hand through his hair, laughing at an offhand comment Crispin then made about Duncan, but really thinking about Eleanor and her Queen's Own.

Not long after Hastian had arrived, Aedon excused himself, drying off as best he could before slipping back into his clothes and heading down the mountain. Wil was tired and pulled himself partway out of the water, so his chest and back could dry in the night air.

"You heading out Wil?" Crispin asked.

"Yes. I'm ready for sleep," he said. "We leave early."

Crispin nodded. "I'll go down with you."

The woods were still, and the crescent moon small, making the path difficult to see in the dark, but Crispin knew the way well enough. Wil was content to follow, enjoying his loose muscles and less tired bones.

A noise in the brush caused Crispin to pause a moment. "Just a deer, I suspect," he said.

Wil was remembering their conversations at the spring, and he finally spoke into the silence of the summer night. "Does Aedon truly fancy the queen?" he asked.

"I am not altogether certain if it's anything beyond the affection of a dear friend," Crispin answered. "They are very close and have relied on each other a great deal. But she is young," Crispin said, more to himself than to Wil. "And although Eleanor has only been on the throne for little more than five years, she is wise enough to know that much must be considered in her choice of husband: politics as well as love and respect."

"Who would she choose from?" Wil asked, curious.

"The fen lords have sons," Crispin said, his voice drifting through a yawn. "There are also councillors, wealthy merchants, and seed bringers who carry a certain weight. But most likely, it would be a titled man with an understanding of how leadership and politics work in Aemogen."

"So, Aedon would likely not be considered."

"Aedon is titled, he's just quiet about it," Crispin said as they broke out of the woods into the field near the fen hall. "He's a very eligible option, I would say. Frankly, I don't know if Eleanor could choose better."

When they reached the fen hall, Crispin excused himself to go ask a question of one of his men, and Wil entered the building alone. Gaulter Alden was still up, speaking with Aedon about trade. Wil was also surprised to see Eleanor, sitting on the opposite side of the room, writing with the light of several candles. Seeing her at work, oblivious to the conversation and jokes about her marriage, Wil felt guilt tinge his mind. He looked away and was about to join Gaulter Alden and Aedon, when Eleanor called his name.

"Do you have a moment?" she asked.

He nodded, noting that Aedon had looked up briefly before continuing his conversation with Gaulter Alden.

"Remember those loose pieces of paper I had saved to translate during the battle run?" she asked.

Wil admitted that he did not.

"Well, I have finally pulled them out," she said. "Come tell me what you think."

He sat down next to Eleanor, hesitantly.

"Forgive me, Wil, I didn't see how tired you were," Eleanor said sincerely as she looked at his reluctant expression. "This can wait. I know you've had a long day."

"No," Wil said, turning towards Eleanor, settling his shoulder against the wall. "My body is tired, but my mind is not."

Eleanor smiled appreciatively. "I was finding this text very challenging," she said. "It's a poem by the Northern philosopher Taimzaeed—"

They worked on Eleanor's translation together, far into the

night. Hastian had returned, standing silently on the far side of the room. Gaulter Alden and Aedon had retired soon after Hastian had come, leaving Eleanor and Wil alone with their translations. Just as one of them would tire, the other would figure out a difficult word or finish a particularly interesting line, urging the other to continue.

"Taimzaeed's philosophies are interesting because he was rejected quite forcefully by the scholars in Zarbadast until two centuries after he had died," Wil told Eleanor.

"Really?" Eleanor was surprised. "But his philosophy is so clearly in line with what I have read in the Second Scroll."

"Yes, but his other works advocated social reforms that were not trusted at the time," Wil replied. He then thought about what she had just said. "I didn't realize you had begun reading the Second Scroll."

"I brought it along and have read most nights." Eleanor smiled. "Especially after you teased me for not having read the Seven Scrolls." She paused and tapped her finger once on the table. "Are the archives of Zarbadast very great?"

Wil felt his heart miss a beat, but he shook his head. "I'm not the person to ask," he admitted. "My father's ambition has more to do with expanding Imirillia's borders than with digging through the scholarly archives of Zarbadast."

Eleanor nodded and turned back to a translated verse of Taimzaeed's poetry. Her penchant for study was—of all things—a bit endearing to Wil. She seemed taken with a particular poem, very famous, that Wil had even studied as a boy. The luminosity created by Eleanor's voice, as she read aloud, crowded out any shadows in Wil's chest, save those cast by her wonder.

I once believed the stars were old souls,
Passed away, yet scintillating in their rest,
Now, I see they are but the nursery
Of the Illuminating God.

And at the birth of each man
Therein is placed a star beside his heart,
And while the heart gives its beat to the body,
So the star gives its light to the soul.

"Hmm," he said and smiled, feeling he had experienced something fresh, something new, as if the tiredness of the late night were suspended by her articulation. "What about that verse do you love so much?" he asked.

"It's only—" Eleanor let a long, satisfied sound escape with a sigh. "The imagery is beautiful, and although I don't believe Taimzaeed means a *literal* interpretation—admittedly, I could be wrong—it's a wonderful idea: each human being endowed with a star to guide one's soul."

"So that each birth is an increase of light—" Wil said.

"And each death, a star extinguished."

When Wil did not answer Eleanor, she continued. "My father held the value of an individual as paramount in making decisions for the whole," she explained. "He believed in the influence of a man or a woman for good or ill: that one soul could make a great difference. I believe he would have liked this verse."

Wil picked up an unlit candle and set the wick alight in the candle that had almost burned its course. "You don't mention him often," Wil said.

"I think of him."

"What do you think he would say to you now?" Wil asked.

"He would counsel a clear mind. He would tell me that things work out." Eleanor set her mouth in a straight line. "He would say that I should keep pressing my mind to the problem until it gives way."

"For your sake," Wil said as he pressed his finger into a drop of melted wax, "I hope it does."

<hr />

When Eleanor went to her room, she lit a candle, changed into her nightdress, and lay on her bed, rereading the first translations she had done with Wil back in Ainsley. She read the words, remembering hearing Wil speak Imirillian for the first time—it was a language that moved her.

"What has undone me is not the sweeping sands that would blow my soul across the earth, nor is it the endless heat and blinding desert; it is crashing against the high mountain, which will not bend to my will, but rather, break me on turrets no man can fight."

Eleanor reread the words again. She sat up and spoke the line aloud. "It is crashing against the high mountain, which will not bend to my will, but rather, break me on turrets no man can fight."

Against turrets no man can fight.

Eleanor jumped up and ran to the door. Hastian, sleeping on a cot outside, sat up.

"I need Aedon," Eleanor whispered.

Hastian went.

Eleanor returned to her room. She took a breath and sat down, mapping out what she knew of the old mines, long abandoned now, that twisted inside the walls of the pass between Aemogen and Marion.

CHAPTER

FOURTEEN

When Wil woke, the clouds were heavy. He ate breakfast with the men—some form of porridge they had had most days—and prepared himself to leave. As he was entering the stable to prepare Hegleh, he encountered Doughlas, leading his own horse out in haste, a look of excitement on his face.

"Are you off?" Wil asked, moving to the side of the stable door to let Doughlas pass.

"I am."

"A letter for Edythe I presume?" Wil said.

"I ride not to Ainsley," Doughlas replied, looking hurried. His saddlebags secured, he mounted. Then, glancing at Wil briefly, Doughlas urged his horse forward, riding fast towards the west.

Later, as the company rode out, Aedon and Crispin separated themselves out, speaking in furtive conversation. Wil pulled his horse back, not wanting to overhear anything they had to say if it was not intended for his ears.

Gaulter Alden told the company he thought a storm would break before they could set up camp and that they should look for a place amongst the trees long before dark. In late afternoon, as the wind picked up and the clouds were petulant and suffocating, they came across a small cottage with a large shed, a barn, and a few other outbuildings.

The couple who lived there, an older man and his wife, were astonished at the request to host the queen and her company for the night. They hurried about, preparing space for the soldiers and making accommodations for the queen and her senior councillors inside the cottage. They even gave up their room in the garret for Eleanor's comfort.

Rain hit as predicted. It poured straight from the low-hanging clouds until just before dark, when the gales began to sweep over the hills, throwing it hard in every direction.

Most of the soldiers had settled comfortably in the sheds, and Eleanor, with her council, sat around the small hearth, eating a humble meal prepared by the farm wife. A warm fire served well the entire evening as they sat, gathered in conversation. Gaulter Alden reminisced about the storms of his youth along the south coast. Aedon spoke of High Forest fen to the northwest, his own home.

"The gales were not as wild and encompassing as they are in the South," Aedon explained. "But the lightning is what caused the most fear, for it crashed down on stone and pine and men. One of my boyhood friends was hit; he died instantly."

The tales continued. Eleanor listened to the stories, content to be silent.

"I'll not argue with all of you," Crispin said at some point. "But off the coast of Calafort, when the waves peak higher than Ainsley Castle, and there you are, strapped to a small ship, with wind, lightning, the force of all heaven tossing you towards the ocean. In that moment," he said and half laughed, "you knew whether you were a man or not."

"And if you never felt fear of the storm," Eleanor added, resting her chin on her knees, which were tucked up under her skirts, "but rather dreaded the mess come morning, you knew you were a woman."

They laughed, Gaulter Alden especially, who, as Eleanor looked at him, seemed to be entertaining reminiscences of his late wife, his face set in the wistful expression that he only had when he spoke of Elaine. And for a brief moment, Eleanor could see Gaulter Alden for the old man he really was: his cheekbones, having lost their flesh, protruded, and firelight accentuated the angles and wrinkles of his age. Yet, uncomplaining, he was preparing for war. She did not want to ask herself the question of whether he could survive it.

No one spoke for some time, each traveling in their own thoughts. Aedon had looked across the room to where Wil sat, in the corner on a small stool, his back against the wall, his cloak pulled around him, looking as comfortable as the shadows of the fallen night.

"What are your tales, Wil?" he asked, a tone of camaraderie underpinning Aedon's question.

With the back of his head against the stone of the cottage, Wil shifted his eyes across the small company. "Wind and rain sound like a welcome relief compared to what I dread most on this earth: sand. You sit on a clear day, the merciless sun beating down on your caravan crossing the desert. And as much as the heat seems unbearable, you press on against the blinding light. Then, sudden and fierce, a wind sent from hell begins to blow in from across the desert, a dark shadow, rolling in on its own evil intent.

"It grows fast," he continued. "You try to find shelter, but there is none. Your fingers struggle with the lines of a tent, but it hits you faster than you ever thought possible. The grains cover your skin as sand soaks into every crevice and orifice, until you know your eyes have been replaced by filth, your ears stopped up, your tongue coated. You can't breath—even under a cloth, the sand blows into your throat.

"The wind rages for what seems to be hours, and you find the dunes you stood above shifting underneath your feet until they are around your legs, then around your waist, and you know that no one will find you, until some year in the future, when your bones will be revealed by a happenstance storm, and a merchant's caravan will look down at your twisted frame and never know your name."

The company was silent. Wil's imagery moved across Eleanor's mind, with the sound of the relentless wind outside for accompaniment. The old farm couple that owned the cottage and had settled down quietly beside their guests, stared, wide-eyed and terrified by Wil's tale.

"It's the cheer of your disposition we value most amongst us, Wil," Aedon remarked. The company laughed, and Wil's spell was broken. Smiling, Wil accepted Crispin's invitation to come closer to the fire, sitting in the only open place, which was next to Eleanor.

The tales and stories now leaned toward warm remembrances of holidays and mirth. Although the storm persisted, it was no longer heavy and urgent but rather a beautiful sound against the strong, stone house. Eleanor listened more than she spoke, enjoying the cadence of each voice, the quips, and jokes.

Finally, after listening for most of the night, she said, "The perfect culmination of all these tales would be a winter storm in Ainsley Castle."

"Yes," Aedon agreed.

Crispin nodded.

"What is it like?" Wil asked, his eyes on her face, so close; she could feel his breath on her cheek.

Eleanor looked at him then back at the fire. "It's hard to describe," she said. "The pantries are well stocked, the lights lit full, and through the windows, layer after layer of perfect white snow falls. It can grow so deep that we don't leave for days. There are games and entertainments and plays. The windows frost over, the large fireplaces are filled with wood that has been cut and stored for such days. There is a patience about the place, and you are unaffected by worry." Eleanor could feel brightness in her eyes as she looked again at Wil. "You know every trouble will work itself out."

The memories stretched in her heart, and Eleanor wished for the peace of it more than for anything else in the world.

"You'll have to come see it for yourself, Wil," Crispin offered. "Spend a winter with us in Ainsley. You may get restless," he added. "But you'd have all winter to learn our secrets—by the time spring comes around, we've all blackmailed each other at least once."

Wil laughed, but Eleanor noticed he did not accept Crispin's invitation.

Later, Gaulter Alden asked if she would play some Aemogen songs on her flute. Eleanor agreed, playing late into the night. Wil listened to her music intently.

Calafort, the port city of Aemogen, was not as large as Wil had imagined, but it was as beautiful: terraced, with buildings and houses easing down towards the substantial port. As a result of having the largest population in all Aemogen, there was more energy there than in all the sleepy fens combined. To Wil, who was long accustomed to the largest cities on the continent, it was a welcome change.

They stayed in a well-appointed house, belonging to a cousin of Eleanor's father, where the queen's entire war council was treated with the utmost courtesy. Wil was given his own private room, where he bathed and rested, pleased to have been given a day away from the rigors of training or travel.

Crispin was happy to be home and forced Wil to spend the entire afternoon seeing his native city, where he had scavenged for port jobs, signed up to sail, and ran into bits of trouble, before leaving to explore the rest of Aemogen at age twelve. Sunset found Crispin and Wil at the Calafort docks, standing in the shadows of the silhouetted ships, talking as the water of the port burned orange and red from the setting sun.

"It's a good community, the sea community," Crispin said, his expression almost blissful as he sat casually on a barrel. "And I'm glad for the lot that gave me my boyhood here."

"It seems just the place for it," Wil agreed as a band of dock boys slipped by, laughing, eyeing Wil's and Crispin's weapons as they passed.

"What of your boyhood?" Crispin asked, looking towards Wil, blocking the final, aggressive rays of the day from his eyes. "Did it offer you like adventures?"

Scratching the back of his neck, Wil shrugged. "It was a different place, a different culture," he said. "But I managed to get into my own worthy troubles, now and again."

"I figured as much," Crispin said and laughed. "But you never speak of it, so I've only to guess."

"I can't say I wish to think on it, let alone speak of it right now."

Crispin let it pass good-naturedly as the sun disappeared to the west and the port sank into a purple cast.

The training was far more extensive in Calafort as there were several hundred men to organize into companies, and weapons— even practice weapons—proved scarce. The company planned to stay in Calafort a full two weeks. Training took place in the fields above the city, and the queen only attended a few hours each day, choosing to spend her time with her father's cousin and the people of Calafort, who were eager to have an audience with the queen.

One evening, as Wil was seated beside Eleanor at dinner, she leaned towards him. "You'll be vindicated to hear I visited one of the Calafort dressmakers."

Meeting her eyes at a close glance, Wil reached for his glass. "Vindicated?" he asked. "How so?"

"You thought I should look the part," she replied, "when I ride into South Mountain fen and confront Thistle Black."

Taking a long sip, he moved his glass between his fingers and smiled. "I had assumed the whole of my advice was to go unheeded." Wil took another sip. Then he continued, his tone having intentional humor. "I'm glad that you've seen my enlightened reasoning."

"Don't take such credit," Eleanor replied with an open expression. "I've needed new formal gowns for six months, and our best tailors live in Calafort," she explained. "Edythe mandated the visit long before you did."

Wil guffawed.

"I admit," she added, "I've considered your advice and am willing to approach Thistle Black head on, as they say." Eleanor leaned back in her chair. "My cousin has provided me with proof of the mischief he's been about in Calafort. Thistle Black has been asking around to find a ship's captain willing to open a smuggling ring with the countries of the North, the main cargo being silver from my mines."

"I assumed that he would have done that already." Wil took another drink and settled back into his chair, his shoulder touching hers. Holding his breath a moment, Wil waited to see if Eleanor would shift her position. When she did not, neither did he. "So, were any captains willing?" Wil asked.

Eleanor shook her head. "No. You see," she said so that no other dinner guests could hear, "there are three groups with extreme loyalty to the crown: the fen riders, the seed bringers, and the maritime men of Calafort. They alone are entrusted with the secrets of how to navigate the port, and the monarchy has always seen that they are well taken care of for their loyalty. Once a year, I am invited to Calafort for a special dinner, and they travel to Ainsley as my guests each fall, when the seas turn wild."

Wil half laughed, shifting so he could look directly at her. "There is a saying they use in the streets of Zarbadast that would have served Thistle Black: Never bribe a bride-to-be. In your scheming, you should always know whom best to corrupt."

"Quite," Eleanor agreed, a line of humor in her face. "Not that I plan on using that advice anytime soon. But, I will keep it in mind."

"Then, the only question left is what colors did you choose?"

"What colors?" she asked blankly.

"For the dresses."

"Oh," Eleanor said, giving him a rare, shy smile. "I decided to beat him at his own game. One gown will be black, trimmed in an abundance of gold."

"To top his silver, of course," Wil replied.

"Of course. I also commissioned a similar gown in deep red, which will make my hair look rather bright," Eleanor added sartorially. "But I indulged nonetheless. There is a third gown that is to be pale gray, studded in silver."

Wil grinned and lifted his glass. "I toast to your choices. And for not allowing me to think I had any influence on such an extravagant purchase."

Eleanor raised her glass, and as she touched it to his, it gave a subtle ring.

"I have one more suggestion to make," Wil said, clearing his throat with apprehension. "I know that Thayne sent you with several pieces of his wife's jewelry."

"Yes. Aedon has them, I believe."

"I think you should utilize them," Wil said, meeting her eye. "Nothing says 'I am queen' more than jewels."

"I'm sure you've noticed, Wil, that I don't often wear any jewelry beyond my crown," she said evenly.

"But why on earth not?"

Suddenly, the openness previously gracing Eleanor's face was gone, and Wil couldn't quite understand why. Somehow he'd irritated her, and he opened his mouth to ask her why she should take exception. But thinking better of it, he changed the subject.

As Eleanor had hoped, Doughlas returned during their stay at

Calafort, and the news he brought her bolstered her spirits and played with her hope. She shared it discreetly with Aedon, Gaulter Alden, and Crispin, and none else. She shared with Doughlas her thoughts on Thistle Black as the two of them met privately.

"You'll be sent to South Mountain fen the day before we ride out," she explained. "From the time you arrive, you are to keep your eyes and ears open for any hint of insubordination. I have plenty of proof," she added. "But you never know what additional information can do."

Eleanor then spent the morning discussing trade and the politics of Calafort with Aedon, who, as chief councillor of all the fens, maintained direct contact with the Lord of Calafort.

"We have suspected Thistle Black of minor treason, but had little or no evidence," Aedon said, repeating what both already knew.

"I was never as worried as I should have been," Eleanor conceded. "Wil was right on that count: some men need to feel your power to keep themselves in line."

"He seems to be right about a lot of things," Aedon answered.

"Hardly," Eleanor replied with a sharp laugh. "But he does know the game of power and intimidation or, at least, how to play it." She moved her finger along the table and looked up at Aedon. "In this circumstance, it follows he may be right."

Aedon nodded. "I agree. You're a good and capable queen, Eleanor. And if Thistle Black can't get that through his head, you have to get him to understand it another way. A man should need no reminders of where his loyalties lie."

<hr>

Wil and Aedon came in late on the last day in Calafort, having seen the taking down of all training areas completed before they returned into the city. The walk back was quiet, occasionally interrupted by an observation or comment from one or the other. Certain that they'd missed dinner, Wil followed Aedon down a stairway of the great house and into the kitchens, where the staff was busy cleaning up and putting away food.

"Did you miss evening meal?" asked a serving girl, who had been making eyes at the men all week.

"Yes," Aedon replied. "Is there possibly anything left over?"

The cook, who had not been making eyes at anybody, harrumphed.

Before long, they were settled in the corner of the kitchen, sampling a hastily thrown together abbreviation of what the other guests had already eaten.

"Is Eleanor prepared to ride out tomorrow?" Wil asked Aedon as they ate. She had been short with Wil for the last week—he figured he'd said something else which had raised her ire—and they'd avoided speaking as much as possible.

"I believe so," Aedon replied matter-of-factly.

"Miya said her gowns were finished a few days ago."

Aedon gave Wil a tilted smile. "You've been reconnoitering with her maid?"

"For the sole reason," Wil defended, "that for the last seven days, Eleanor has been as likely to singe my eyebrows off as to speak civilly with me. I've found that information at a distance serves just as well."

"Eleanor? Singeing?" Aedon asked. "She's never like that—at least, not for long."

"Not with *you* maybe."

Aedon laughed, loud enough that a few of the kitchen staff

looked in their direction. "You do bring something out in her that no one else does," Aedon admitted.

"Hmmm." Wil chewed on his bread thoughtfully. "Do you have any idea why?" he asked. "Aside from all the major faults she sees in my character, of course."

"Clearly," Aedon conceded good-naturedly. Then his eyes rested on Wil, and his aspect turned thoughtful. "Would you honestly like me to answer that question?" What Wil saw behind Aedon's composed face frightened him, and he backed away from that truth.

"No, I don't," he replied.

Aedon did not press.

"Eleanor said that she'd left Thayne's jewelry in your safekeeping," Wil said to Aedon, shifting the conversation.

Aedon nodded.

"Has she asked for them?" Wil asked.

"No, I don't believe she intends to use the jewelry," Aedon replied. "Does it really matter?"

Wil slumped back in his chair and pushed his empty plate away. "If there is one thing that I have learned as a son of Imirillia, Aedon, it is the art of intimidation. It may sound like a small thing, but I wish Eleanor would consider it."

"Then quit hiding behind her maid and tell Eleanor again, straight out, why you think it's a good idea," Aedon counseled. "Eleanor has never once let her temper trump her reason. She will think through your words, even if she finds you annoying in the process."

Laughing, Wil gave Aedon a double take. "I don't hide."

"You don't hide," Aedon said thoughtfully, "except from Eleanor. She seems to have *that* effect on you. Something is said, and you disappear, distancing yourself for a few days."

Wil almost responded by asking, *Do you want to know why?*

And Aedon, as if he could read the question in Wil's face, shook his head. No, he did not.

"Come to my rooms in the morning," Aedon said. "And you can take the jewelry to Eleanor yourself. If you feel it's important enough to discuss again, you can trust she won't take your head in the process," Aedon added, then he stood. "Good night, Wil."

Wil watched the councillor leave the kitchen and then grimaced, pressing his own fingers firmly against the table. It was not his head he was worried about losing.

The company rode out early, making their way west. In a few days, they would break journey at a royal hunting lodge in the forest near South Mountain fen. And then they would deal with Thistle Black. Eleanor, not as accustomed to the amount of noise and movement Calafort had provided, was, for now, relieved to find herself alone with her thoughts with two days' ride stretched out before her. The council did well to give her space, and whenever they stopped, she would disappear, Second Scroll in hand, taking a few moments to read—and think.

Wil Traveler she ignored altogether. It was trying enough, to always have his voice inside her head, and alluring enough to seek him out in conversation, which nearly always turned to a frustrating challenge of differing opinion. So, she kept her own company and counsel. And two days later, when they rode into the stable yard of the hunting lodge, she dismounted, informing Gaulter Alden and Aedon that they would leave for South Mountain fen come morning, and disappeared into the privacy of her rooms.

Eleanor slept early, and before dawn she awoke, making preparations for the ride into South Mountain fen. Miya braided Eleanor's hair, causing it to fall down to the side of her neck, tucked in a graceful knot, before helping Eleanor step into the black dress of Marion velvet. It was elegant and full, more abundant than the gowns Eleanor usually wore. Calafort, being a port city, often kept abreast of the styles in Marion. As a result, changes in Calafort fashion moved faster than in the rest of Aemogen, and to Edythe's dismay, that included Ainsley.

Miya pulled tight as she laced up the gown, grunting and asking Eleanor to breathe in.

"I do have to be able to inhale, Miya, if I am to ride a horse for several hours. You do understand this?"

Her maid, who had apparently had enough of the battle run, pulled harder. As the form of the gown wrapped around her body, Eleanor stared at her reflection. The neck of the gown was cut square, lower than usual, with black lace trim around the bodice that ran up the neckline to her shoulders. The lace then turned, resting up the back of her neck, creating a high collar. Eleanor raised her fingers to touch it, feeling self-conscious. The sleeves came to her elbows, trimmed out in black lace and gold beads, as was the hemline. The velvet around Eleanor's waist was pulled and wrapped towards her left hip, sewn into place and embellished with a gold broach. The skirt, made from yards of velvet, entertained many folds and full tucks. As Eleanor moved, the folds opened, revealing scatterings of gold beads and embroidery, cascading like fountains of stars when they caught the light. Her skin, set dramatically against the black, had never appeared fairer.

"Can you see yourself properly?" Miya asked, adjusting the large standing mirror.

"The opulence of this gown is rather embarrassing," Eleanor replied. Her waist looked diminutive, compared to the voluminous skirts, and Eleanor felt she could not breathe, it having had been laced so tight. Miya kept wondering aloud about the fine material, the sewing, and the unusual detailing.

"It makes you look—" the maid tried to explain as Eleanor stared at the dress before the mirror. "You almost don't look like yourself," Miya faltered. "Like you are a woman I don't know. In such a gown, you're very compelling, but—"

"But what?" Eleanor asked, her cheeks turning pink.

"Oh, I don't really know, Your Majesty," Miya said. "It's just different."

They heard a knock, and Eleanor sent Miya to see who was there. As soon as she was alone, Eleanor pressed her palms against the waist of the dress, embarrassed, despite being alone. She moved her fingers to the lace neckline again. Her collarbones were exposed, the whiteness of her skin striking.

"You look very nice," Wil said from the doorway. "With a few adjustments, it could be perfect. Would you mind stepping away from the mirror a moment?" When Eleanor spun around, challenge wreathing her expression, Wil paused before he added, "Please?"

"Since when have you been given the right to burst into my private rooms?" Eleanor said, indignant.

"Miya said I should come in," Wil explained, pointing towards the outer chamber. "She's speaking with Hastian, if you want to ask her."

Eleanor knew that her cheeks were red with embarrassment, and she passed over his words, responding with her own foremost thought. "You accuse me of lacking formality, yet you break all rules of propriety," she said, adding, "You are not welcome here."

"I am here to help you finish your ensemble," he said, quite serious. When her expression did not ease, he held up a small bag in his hand and attempted, what Eleanor supposed, was humor, "I come bearing gifts."

Eleanor's sense of privacy felt acutely invaded, but she forced herself to take as much of a slow breath as the gown would allow before she spoke. "Show me what you have and then get out."

"Your new persona is working already," Wil quipped bluntly as he walked toward her, discomfort finally appearing in his own expression. Eleanor itched under her self-consciousness as Wil gave a detached study of her dress. "They've done a beautiful job," he finally said. "It's an improvement on the current styles of the Marion court and a definite improvement on the dresses you have worn throughout the battle run."

"Old Ainsley forbid I spend two months in comfortable clothing," Eleanor shot back. Wil raised his hands against the attack, looking as aggravated as Eleanor felt.

"Truce!" he said. "I didn't say that you haven't looked nice."

Eleanor wanted to throw him out on his ear. She wanted to be home. She wanted the immense pressure of the unknown to disappear, to evaporate. She wanted reassurance. With a stony expression, Eleanor faced Wil.

"I was not angling for a compliment," she said.

"I didn't think you were," Wil said, lifting one of his hands in an effort to respond without escalating the conversation. "Now, I know it is a traditional stance in Aemogen to wear little jewelry," he began. "But—and please consider what I tell you now—in a situation that could lead to treason, however small, it's worth using every painstaking detail for leverage. Better wit and power, rather than violence. Isn't that how you feel?" he asked. "So, while details like jewelry may seem unnecessary to you, a man like Thistle Black will take note and mark it as a symbol of power."

Lips tightly pressed, Eleanor ordered her interior frustrations to be silent and thought about his words before responding. "The advantage offered would be so slight—"

Wil took a step towards her. "Slight advantages are what win contests, Eleanor."

She creased her eyebrows together. It was the first time he had used her name. Wil must have had the same thought, for a flush spread up from his neck.

"Will you please try them on?" he asked.

"Fine."

"Right," Wil said as he stepped away, opening the bag onto the top of a nearby bureau. He picked something up between his fingers and turned back towards Eleanor. A small unripe apple was in his hand. "I don't think you are going to like this very much. Miya?" he called out, looking away from Eleanor's questioning eyes as the maid entered the room.

"Are the awls heated in the fire?" he asked.

"Yes," Miya said, looking from Eleanor to Wil and back to Eleanor again. She looked terrified.

"Awls?" Eleanor's mouth dropped open, and she grabbed her earlobes. "Are you mad?"

"It's hard to wear earrings with no holes in your ears," Wil reasoned.

"You *are* mad," she said. "I'm not doing that."

Wil groaned and clenched his left fist to his eyes, muttering something. But, Eleanor was distracted by the motion. For, under his sleeve, the band he'd kept so meticulously bound about his forearm was coming loose. And there was a mark on his skin. He dropped his hand to his side as he continued to speak, and it disappeared beneath his sleeve.

"—I have not come to kill you," Wil was saying as Eleanor's focus returned to his words. Then Hastian came running into the chamber, a look of alarm on his face.

"My queen?" he said.

"It's all right, Hastian," Eleanor said, her mind on what she'd seen. "Miya and Wil have conspired against me, but I've not let them impale me yet." The soldier, seeming cautious, looked at Wil before stepping back. He did not withdraw from the chamber.

"The earrings are the finest pieces in the set," Wil said.

In a motion, one of the earrings was dangling between his fingers. Eleanor's mouth formed a line. It was a tear-shaped diamond, perhaps the most beautiful gem she had ever seen.

"Thayne sent these earrings from his personal collection," Wil explained. "Aedon said they had belonged to his late wife, who was the granddaughter of a king. They were a gift from him to her. I wasn't expecting him to have sent anything of this caliber," Wil admitted as he wrapped his fingers around the diamond and set it back down. "Now, I understand if you don't want to do this, but just to satisfy my curiosity," he put his hand on his chest, "do you have some philosophical or religious objection to the act of piercing your ears?"

"No," Eleanor said. "Edythe wears earrings."

"Then consider it a happy surprise for her wedding," he suggested. "Now, do we proceed?"

Eleanor looked back to Wil's arm, willing to leverage pain for knowledge. "Under one condition," she said.

Uncertain whether it was wise, Eleanor sent both the maid

and her guard out of the room. Hastian's mouth twitched, but he reluctantly followed Miya, pulling the door shut behind him.

"Your left arm," Eleanor said when they were alone. "I want to see why you keep it wrapped."

Wil shook his head. "No."

"I've sent them out," Eleanor stated, gesturing towards the door. "You can trust in my discretion."

Wil stepped away from her and leaned against the bureau, setting the apple down before he folded his arms across his chest. Eleanor couldn't read his thoughts, but her hope was that he was considering her offer. He didn't look away from her face, but Eleanor knew that his mind was weighing the risks of her condition, and he wasn't really seeing her.

"Why is this important to you?" Wil asked at length.

"Because it is obviously of value to you," Eleanor said.

"Why do you care what I value?" Wil gave a slight lift of his chin, and his eyes caught her face in sharp focus. The palms of Eleanor's hands felt warm, and her mouth went dry as she looked at a vein pulsing in Wil's neck.

"Are we not friends?" she asked.

"Are we?" he said.

"Are we?" she asked him in return.

At first, Wil seemed far away, an observer of the conversation rather than a participant. But as Eleanor watched, something about Wil's stance, some attitude of his bearing, shifted, like a flag changing colors, and behind his eyes, she saw a trace of something he had previously withheld: trust.

"Yes, we are friends," he conceded.

"Yes." Eleanor lifted the corners of her mouth, feeling grateful, willing to accept this unspoken gift he offered. "Now, don't tell me that I should let you impale me *twice* without anything in return."

Wil pushed himself forward and stood before Eleanor. He looked her in the eye as he rolled up his left sleeve and undid the knots with his right hand. Eleanor held his stare, not looking until the fabric had fallen away. Then Wil held out his arm.

"It is the symbol of where I belong in the Imirillian army." Wil cleared his throat. "More or less."

Eleanor took his arm in her hands, and because Wil's skin was lighter where the fabric had covered it for months, the mark almost seemed to jump off his skin. It was in the shape of a shield and beautifully done, deep blood red in color, almost black. Inside the shield, a bird of prey rose elegantly, surrounded by intricate patterns and symbols. She had never seen such artistry, and she had never seen such a thing set in the skin before.

Eleanor moved her fingers across the mark. It was smooth and large enough that her hand could not cover it completely. When she tried, he breathed in, jerking his arm ever so slightly and clenching his fingers. Eleanor knew she had trespassed somehow, and pulled her fingers back.

"I'm sorry," she said.

Wil withdrew his arm from her hands, carefully wrapping the black fabric over the strange mark again, fumbling with the knot and then pulling it tight with his teeth. Then he rolled his sleeve down.

"Shall we proceed?" he asked.

As Eleanor called Miya back into the room, Hastian's footsteps could be heard pacing in the audience chamber.

Wil took the awl from Miya and handed her the two earrings. Then he picked the apple up off the bureau and came back, standing close, directly in front of Eleanor. Lifting the apple behind Eleanor's earlobe, he placed the awl against her skin—the pin-sized tip was still warm from the fire—and leaned in closer, careful and focused.

"Keep the earring ready, Miya," Wil said. "We'll slide it in immediately after I remove the awl."

Eleanor's stomach began to protest. She tilted her head, lifting her chin, watching Wil's hands nervously from the corner of her eye. She was extremely aware of his knuckles brushing against her skin.

"Now," Wil said quietly, "You will hardly feel—"

Eleanor bit her lip as the awl went through her ear and into the apple. Wil pulled it out and moved so that Miya could slide the earring into the bleeding hole. But Miya was clumsy and almost missed, sending the earring hook into Eleanor's ear rather than through it—the pain was acute. Eleanor bit her tongue, tears coming to her eyes. Miya corrected the hook's direction and slid it through the hole, her hands shaking.

Eleanor's eyes watered, but she made no sound, despite the heaviness of the earring.

"Now, let's finish the other," Wil said, sounding apologetic. He lifted his hand to her chin, tilting her face to the side.

"Why did we not do this sooner?" Eleanor asked, readying herself as Wil positioned the awl on her second earlobe. "Riding a horse just now will be miserable. It'll rip out of my ears."

"You wouldn't have done it sooner," Wil speculated, giving most of his attention to the second hole he was about to pierce. "It won't be unbearable. I've an oil that will make it so you can't feel a thing. And," he added, "you can take all your anger out on Thistle Black."

The awl flashed through her earlobe, and Eleanor bit her

cheek against the rush of pain. Wil grabbed the earring from the unprepared Miya, slipping it into place.

"Done," he said.

Miya handed him a clean cloth, and he placed it over Eleanor's bleeding ear. Tilting her head back, Eleanor cursed herself for agreeing to such a foolish vanity.

"I am not sure we are friends any longer," Eleanor said stiffly. "This feels awful."

Wil laughed—genuinely laughed—and stepped back. In that moment, the atmosphere began to thaw between them.

"This will help," he said, picking up a small vial from the top of the bureau. After dabbing it on the cloth in his hand, Wil handed it to Miya. "Wipe this on both of her ears carefully."

"He said *carefully*!" Eleanor flinched, for the maid was none too gentle.

"Oh, Your Majesty!" Miya seemed shaken by the entire ordeal. She fretted, trembling as she finished, which only increased Eleanor's discomfort.

Wil, in the meantime, had lifted an elaborate necklace up to the light. It was a beautiful companion piece to the earrings, a web of diamonds which, once Wil had handed it to Miya to secure about Eleanor's neck, fell across her collarbones.

It felt heavy and cold, taking Eleanor's mind off her throbbing ears as she looked into the mirror. She leaned forward, scrutinizing the reflection of the necklace.

"Miya," she said. "Fetch the Battle Crown."

After the maid left, Eleanor looked towards Wil. "I don't think I'll wear the necklace," she explained. "The crown and earrings will be enough."

"It must be quite the crown," Wil said.

"It is," Eleanor replied, relieved as the oil began to take effect. "You've surprised me again, Wil Traveler," she added. "Instead of recruiting you for training, I should have appointed you as wardrobe mistress."

"I am no lady's maid," he said, and Wil's smile had an edge on it.

—⋙⋘—

"Here it is," the maid said, lifting a silk-bound object as she came back through the door.

Wil looked over his shoulder with curiosity, and turned to watch the maid reveal the Battle Crown. It was not like the simple circlet that Eleanor had worn in Ainsley, but rather a remarkable piece. When placed on the queen's head, it appeared to catch every ounce of command from her body, holding her in place.

A distant observer might have only seen a crown fashioned of gold, but Wil's closer view revealed a pattern of carved stones and battlements: ten squared turrets rose around the band, the strong stone towers bound by vines. It was a show of strength. It made Eleanor look older. Or rather, Wil thought, timeless.

She was right. The crown, the earrings, the way her hair fell, curved against the nape of her neck—it was enough.

"What's wrong now?" Eleanor asked, turning her steady eyes on him. Wil pulled his face out of a frown.

"I had not even thought to ask," Wil said, raising his eyebrows. "But do you know how to draw your sword properly?"

"Not to your standards, I'm sure," Eleanor replied. "Miya?"

The maid scrambled to retrieve Eleanor's ceremonial sword and scabbard. The silver and gold weapon had been polished thoroughly throughout the battle run, although Eleanor had declined to wear it.

"I don't really know how to do this well," Miya said as she held the weapon gingerly, and she looked towards Wil for help. After asking Eleanor wordlessly for permission, Wil took the weapon from the maid and stepped towards Eleanor.

"Pardon," he said, and he secured the sheath to Eleanor while trying to maintain a respectful distance, pulling it tight against Eleanor's waist. From the corner of his eye, Wil could see Eleanor's face tighten and was unsure if it was in response to the scabbard or to his proximity.

"See how the scabbard falls down below the hip?" Wil stepped away, speaking briskly. "Now, try to draw your sword."

"I've drawn a sword," Eleanor said.

"Indulge me," Wil said, motioning for her to try. "This dress is more inhibiting than your usual wardrobe. If the need arises, you do not want to appear a novice."

Eleanor's mouth twitched, but she pulled the sword from its sheath, struggling against the confines of the dress. The movement caused her earrings to swing, and Eleanor tightened her jaw.

"Try it again," Wil motioned. "Lead with your elbow instead of your shoulder."

Eleanor drew it out again, leading with her elbow. It was easier.

"Good," Wil said, sounding deliberately professorial. "If I were you, I would practice that same movement a dozen times. The sheer act of drawing one's sword can be intimidating."

Hastian entered the room. "Your Majesty," he said, "the men are assembled and ready to ride out."

Eleanor nodded. "I need a few moments alone," she said. "Then I will be down."

Hastian watched as Wil left Eleanor's room, his eyes sweeping Wil with an unreadable expression.

Wil was talking with Aedon and Crispin when Eleanor stepped out onto the steps of the hunting lodge. Crispin stopped in the middle of a word and stared, and Aedon turned, the edges of his eyes creasing when he saw Eleanor. Wil took note, scanning each face in the company as they saw their queen.

Eleanor took a few more steps, then came to a stop. The sun reflected off the gold beads embroidered into her gown, off the Battle Crown, refracting through the earrings that shimmered as she paused at the top of the stairs. She looked like the blackest night, illuminated only by points of brilliant starlight; the white of her skin was crisp, her copper hair, bold. She reminded Wil of the night sky over the Imirillian desert.

Hastian stepped forward and offered her his arm. Then they descended the steps to where Thrift was saddled. But it was Hegleh, not Thrift, which was brought forward.

"I forgot to mention this before," Eleanor said, turning towards Wil, the folds of her gown complementing the movement, "but I'm commandeering your horse. It was your idea, was it not, to present an image of complete power? And as Hegleh is the most impressive mount—" she added. "You may ride Thrift until I am finished with Hegleh."

"An honor," Wil said, and he bowed. He was pleased more than surprised. Once Hastian had helped Eleanor to mount the war-horse, Hegleh's white coat provided a sharp contrast to Eleanor's attire. The queen sat higher now than any of the men in the company, for Hegleh was a good two hands taller than their mounts. The sheath of Eleanor's sword caught bright slices of sunlight, completing her already striking visage.

A soldier handed Wil Thrift's reins, and he mounted, falling in line beside Gaulter Alden.

"And now, you look ready to meet Thistle Black," Crispin called from behind.

Eleanor turned and smiled at him with a capricious confidence incongruous with her image.

"I've been practicing before the mirror," she said.

Crispin laughed, and some of her council smiled to one another, though, Wil thought, not as freely as they usually would have.

CHAPTER

FIFTEEN

As the company began their march across the valley, they were greeted by a sun-drenched morning. Wil removed his cloak and thrust it into his saddlebag. A few hours into the ride, the clear sky gave way to gray clouds coming in off the sea, which only added to the pleasure of the day.

Eleanor rode Hegleh carefully, lifting her hand to her ears occasionally, but the oil's effect appeared to hold. The company continued in near silence, the soldiers remembering the instructions given of how Eleanor wanted them to act.

As they came closer to the mountains, Wil could see stone buildings rising up among the trees. Tall pines stood, dense and strong, mingling with homes and outbuildings. According to the map Wil had seen, this was the farthest fen from Ainsley. So, it was little wonder that Thistle Black felt the freedom to set himself against the queen. A large sound, like the rumble of thunder, came echoing off the mountain, and Wil looked sharply to the sky, but the clouds were calm.

Aedon rode near Wil and saw his expression.

"The mines," Aedon said over the noise and jangle of the company. "They're opening mines farther up the mountains."

"But what caused the noise?" Wil asked. "A rockslide?"

"No." Aedon shook his head. "It's our powder. It ignites and causes a reaction of sorts, a fire strong enough to blow away rock," Aedon explained. "Aemogen's large mining industry is due to our use of it. I wouldn't think that you have this in Imirillia. Marion has been after our formula for years."

"We have powders that, when ignited, send bursts of color into the night sky," Wil said. "But I don't know if they can break stone. Imirillia traffics in sand, remember."

"What I cannot reconcile," Aedon said, setting his face, "is why men are working up on the mountain when, by the queen's order, they should all be awaiting training this afternoon?"

When the company rode into South Mountain fen, Eleanor did not slow her pace. The company rode through the town, directly to the fen hall. People, mainly women, stood about, looking uncertain. A few raised their hands to the queen, but many remained quiet.

Eleanor held her head high. She reined Hegleh to a stop before the fen hall. Wil and his companions did the same. Then they waited in silence, breathing heavily from the ride into the fen. The door opened, and a large man with a gray beard stepped forward. He looked at Eleanor before his eyes moved over the rest of the militant company. He offered a bow, but he did not lower his head.

"Queen Eleanor," he said.

Eleanor was poised as she looked impassively at Thistle Black. "Why are the men of South Mountain fen not assembled and awaiting training?" she questioned evenly.

Doughlas was coming down the street on foot towards the company. He bowed before the queen, out of breath.

"Your Majesty," Doughlas said. "I gave Thistle Black strict instructions to have the men present and ready upon your arrival. This morning, he sent the miners back up the mountain in direct defiance. And the farmers were ordered into their fields."

Black glared at Doughlas. "I know how to run my own fen," he said defiantly.

"No," Eleanor corrected. "You know how to run *my* fen. Doughlas, retrieve the men from the mountain and gather the laborers in from their fields." She looked back to Thistle Black. "I will be glad to have a few hours' conversation with you, Thistle Black. Shall we start with a full review of all mining records for the last three years?"

Thistle Black hesitated before his face opened into a smile. "It has been such a long time, Queen Eleanor. I had rather hoped that we would have time to discuss more pressing matters, and for you to meet my children, before we begin our work."

Crispin rolled his eyes and gave Wil an expression of impatience. Wil shifted in his seat, seeing right through the fen lord. So had Eleanor. She snapped her fingers, and Hastian dismounted, then, in turn, helped Eleanor to the ground. Thistle Black eyed the stature of Wil's horse, then looked back down at the queen. The war council dismounted as well, handing their reins to the few nervous men nearby.

Eleanor stood before Thistle Black, looking uninterested in his proposal. "Would you rather discuss your plans for treason?" Eleanor asked as she removed her riding gloves.

Black did not answer.

"Let us compromise, then, and go straight to the mine records."

She walked past him into the fen hall.

Wil watched as Thistle Black pumped his hands into fists nervously and shouted at a young man, who was in the doorway of a nearby home. The war council walked past Black, one by one, with little acknowledgment. Wil paused and leveled his eyes at the man. He guessed Thistle Black to be more bluster than anything.

Eleanor began speaking in angry tones, and as Wil's eyes adjusted to the dark room, he could see why. Thistle Black had turned the fen hall into his private residence. His wife stood in the corner, nervous, wringing her hands.

Eleanor walked to the hearth and turned as Thistle Black entered. "I am waiting for the records, Black," she said.

"I've just sent my messenger to retrieve them," he said gruffly.

Eleanor raised her eyebrows. "All records are to be kept in the fen hall. Why are they not here?" she demanded. "Was it, perhaps, because you found there was not room, once you had decided to move in for more space to raise your family?"

"As I am sure you understand that with six children—" he began.

"I understand," Eleanor interrupted, "that with six children, you should be worried about building a larger house rather than spending your time in Calafort, instigating an illegal smugglers' ring."

Black's wife covered her mouth and made an uncomfortable noise as if she would cry. Wil almost felt sorry for the woman.

"You've not proof of anything," Black said. "I am as loyal as the next man."

"*That* you are most assuredly not," Eleanor snapped.

A young man arrived at the door, holding a bundle of papers in his arms. He was tired from running and looked from Thistle

Black to the queen. Black motioned for the boy to drop the papers on a table in the center of the room.

"Black, please remove all your belongings immediately to your own home," Eleanor said. "The fen hall is for the use of all, not the comfort of one."

Wil leaned against the wall and crossed his arms, watching everyone in the room. Aedon stood calmly, as did Gaulter Alden. Crispin bounced nervously, clearly upset by the whole event. Thistle Black narrowed his eyes and yelled at the boy to begin moving furniture.

"Is this your son?" Eleanor asked. "He does not appear familiar."

"No, he is—"

"If he is not your son," Eleanor interrupted, "he need not do your work. You may remove any furniture belonging to your own family yourself, with the help of your wife, of course, while my councillors and I review the records." She shifted her eyes to the young man. "Are there any other records in the fen you are aware of? Answer honestly, and it will save us the search."

The boy began to shake his head, but he was nervous, scratching his neck and mumbling to himself. He finally nodded. "I could not carry them all," he said, glancing anxiously at Thistle Black.

"Crispin, this young man will need help," Eleanor said. "See to it and invite your soldiers to stable their horses and stand ready for training this evening, when the men have returned from the mountains."

Crispin bowed and exited the building, taking the shaking young man with him. Wil could see through the window that Crispin had put his arm around the poor fellow and appeared to be lightening the mood.

Aedon pulled a chair out from the table, offering it to Eleanor.

She sat, and Wil followed suit as the council began to organize the papers before them. Thistle Black's wife had now begun to weep silently, picking up small trinkets and placing them in a basket. The fen lord was red faced, still standing by the open door.

"You need not wait for us," Aedon said simply. "We can do without you just fine while you remove your belongings. You may begin now, as I assume you have possessions to remove from upstairs before we settle ourselves in for the evening."

Black stormed out of the fen hall, his wife following at his heels, her head bowed.

Wil took his gaze from the empty doorway and returned to the work at hand. But the mood was heavy and uncomfortable. Eleanor did not look at her friends, but rather focused on the papers before her. Her hands were shaking.

<hr>

By evening, three things had taken place: Thistle Black and his family had removed themselves from the fen hall; the records had been studied, all initial accounts showing inaccuracies; and the miners had come down from the mine, their eyes downcast as they stood, discomfited, before their queen.

A large field, west of the fen hall, served as training grounds. Many of the men were raw from a day in the mine and were not eager to begin training so late in the day. Eleanor sat astride Hegleh, towering over those gathered, not speaking. Gaulter Alden was mounted as well and rode before the group, asking directly why they had gone to the mountains when their queen had requested that they await their training? No one answered, but several men glanced at Thistle Black, who stood nearby in silent fury. Gaulter Alden said a brief word about loyalty and turned the men over to Wil.

"We usually begin by assessing your individual skills," Wil said. "But since the men of this fen seem to struggle with knowing whom to follow, strength training would be more appropriate." Wil paced before them. "And so, we begin. I want all you men to line up in twenty even rows, a man's width apart in all directions." He clapped his hands. "Hurry to it!"

Wil ran the men through drill after exhausting drill. By the time they began fighting maneuvers, the sun had long set. Several bonfires had been built by the battle run guard, and Eleanor remained astride the white horse, looking impassive, still not speaking.

They began training early the next morning and continued relentlessly through the day. Midday meal was cut short, and little socializing was had. Eleanor and Aedon retreated to the fen hall to study the records, and when they returned to wordlessly watch the training, Wil could see that she was not pleased.

Day three was little different. As the training came to a close, the people of the fen walked with bent heads, beaten. The women prepared for the traditional festivities of the evening with a joyless effort. At the very end of the day, Eleanor asked Wil and Crispin to call the men to attention. She dismounted from Hegleh, sending her to the stables, and stood in the field, Hastian a shadow behind her.

Each man, Eleanor instructed, was to come before her, one by one, and declare his fidelity to the crown. Wil sent the first man to the queen. She stood forty feet away, and as Wil watched, he knew two things: first, he had a splitting headache from the rigors of the training at South Mountain, and second, Eleanor was miserable.

When the first man arrived, instead of having him kneel directly, the queen spoke to him for a moment, her words unheard by those who waited. The man returned a reply before kneeling and swearing his fidelity to the queen. She offered him her hand, lifted him off the grass, and smiled.

The next man came forward, and a similar exchange followed.

Women and children began to gather. The children, more willing to cast off the weight in the air around them, began to cheer as each man swore his fidelity to the queen. The noise grew louder and louder, and Wil looked around him. The people had begun to relax and smile with one another for the first time since the battle guard had arrived in the fen three days before.

It took over two hours, but Eleanor gave each man a personal greeting and enough time to hear his words in return, before he offered his pledge.

When the seed bringer came forth, he fell to pledge immediately, which brought a cheer from the crowd. Wil looked at Aedon, who had his arms crossed, a hand covering the smile on his face. They exchanged a triumphant nod.

After the final man had given his pledge to the queen and walked the distance back to the crowd, all eyes turned towards Thistle Black. He stood silent, an expression part resentment, part fear, in his eyes. Eleanor waited—the outline of her black dress disappearing in the deepening shadows behind her, the Battle Crown glinting in the firelight.

Thistle Black lifted his head and crossed his arms, rocking back on his feet obstinately. Wil watched the struggle of the two wills, his own emotions taut. The crowd grew quiet again. For several minutes, they faced each other: Eleanor staring directly at Thistle

Black, unwavering, unmoving, emotionless.

Black cleared his throat and looked down, placing his hands on his hips. He toed the earth with his boot, then looked back up, beneath his heavy brows, towards the queen. His lips moved as if he were about to speak. Finally, the large man dropped his arms and lifted his head up. He took a step towards the queen. The entire fen erupted in a loud cheer as Thistle Black made his way across the field.

"Stay where you are. Stay where you are," Wil whispered to himself. He was worried that Eleanor, in a show of solidarity, would walk to meet Thistle Black and weaken her position as this man's sovereign. But she did not move. Eleanor waited firmly in her place.

When Thistle Black arrived before the queen, he said something to which she responded, and then he dropped to one knee, his head bent in submission. After he pledged, Eleanor offered her hand and helped Black to his feet. She smiled.

The crowd cheered again, and music began to play as the people gathered around the bonfires. Crispin clapped his hand on Wil's shoulder, a smile of relief on his face. When Wil looked back towards the fen lord and the queen, Thistle Black was coming towards the celebration, but Eleanor had disappeared.

───◦─◦◎◎◎◎◦─◦───

After the company left South Mountain fen, Eleanor did not speak to anyone for two days. She had changed back into her usual clothing, replaced the earrings with a smaller, unobtrusive set of green stones, and she'd reclaimed Thrift. Wil did think it interesting, however, that Eleanor did not remove the Battle Crown. She now wore it every day. Wil was satisfied with the victory at South Mountain, and when he had a chance to come upon Eleanor alone, he said so. Had she, he had asked, gained a better sense of what she could become?

Eleanor had given him a veiled smile, responding that she had understood a clearer picture of what she hoped never to become.

CHAPTER
SIXTEEN

Eleanor could not quite remember how it had begun—perhaps she and Crispin had just finished a game and Wil had joined in— but for the last several weeks of the battle run, Eleanor and Wil had sat together in the evenings, playing chess.

Having already been familiar with the Imirillian variation of the game, Wil was astute in picking up the Aemogen rules. He, in turn, tutored Eleanor in the Imirillian style. Crispin, who Eleanor knew had played only to charm her from her somber mood, happily relinquished his position to Wil, leaving them to work at besting each other in the late evenings, after the traveling or training had ended.

"Check," Wil said as he moved his rook. Eleanor repositioned her king, and Wil moved a pawn.

"Check," he said again.

Eleanor studied the board and sighed. Aedon looked up from where he sat reading by the fire of the Irgead fen hall. He watched the pair, then turned back towards his letters.

"You might as well surrender now," Wil said, interrupting her thoughts.

Barely acknowledging his words, Eleanor scrutinized each piece on the board. They looked heavy in their place, as if resigned to their failure. Frowning, Eleanor looked harder, her eyes moving from piece to piece. Then, a possibility revealed itself in an instant, the glimmer of hope she had been looking for. With the ghost of a smile on her lips, she moved her queen to protect her king.

"Sacrificing your most valuable piece?" Wil asked, leaning back, putting his hands behind his head on the chair. "Desperate, Eleanor."

Wil had now taken to comfortably calling her Eleanor. She hadn't objected, although her feelings towards Wil had grown more complex since Old Ainsley fen. There were certain views he had, ways of seeing the world, which she could not condone, let alone reconcile.

Wil captured her queen.

Eleanor put her plan into motion; it was only three moves away. Back and forth they moved and she thought she had lost her chance, but then he placed his rook exactly where she needed him to, and she moved her pawn into place.

"Checkmate," she said.

"What?" Wil scrutinized the board. When he saw the game had, indeed, ended, he hit the table. Aedon looked up again.

"How did that happen?" Wil asked.

Feeling pleasure with her victory, Eleanor met his eyes. "It was a queen's gambit."

Wil shook his head, leaning forward across the board. "A what?"

"A queen's gambit," Eleanor answered. "You sacrifice your queen to win the game."

"A queen's gambit," Wil repeated as he moved the pieces back into place. "I wasn't expecting that. You win." He rapped his fingers on the table, looking resolved to not be outmaneuvered again. "Another game?"

Eleanor shook her head and leaned forward on her elbows. "I should sleep," she said. "We'll be riding all day tomorrow."

But she did not leave.

The imminence of the invasion had hung around Eleanor's neck like a stone ever since leaving South Mountain fen. She felt that if she put the weight down, even for a moment, picking it back up would be impossible. And so a pressing soberness stayed close, just as the threat did.

Eleanor lifted her fingers to the crown on her head. "Do you think—" she began quietly. Wil pulled himself out of his own thoughts and lifted his head towards hers.

"Yes?" he asked.

"Is war ever worth it?" Her question was quiet off her lips. "And, Wil, I'm not asking you in terms of logistics or practicality. I'm asking about the principle, the soul of the thing."

Time passed, their heads bent close over the chessboard.

Eleanor gave him space, for she could almost feel his thoughts, moving through her question, sorting out a response.

"I think—" he said, sounding distant. "I think that the principle of what you are fighting for, the soul of it, is right. But I cannot answer if it's ever worth it."

They continued north, now with only two fens remaining before they would return to Ainsley for the final vote and for whatever preparations they must then make. The fen lords and most of the men expressed their desires to fight rather than become a servant class in their own country. Wil still voiced his opinion that they should work with the Imirillians, arguing, as often as anyone would listen, that they simply did not have the men for such a fight. Nobody ever responded, and he suspected that there was something happening of which he was not privy.

Wil watched the landscape change and alter. The grasses were now studded with protruding stones, and the forests surrounding the narrow valleys were thick. They also passed several lakes. Wil could not claim that the company became more jovial the closer they were to Ainsley, but he had noticed a change in temperament, a fresh calmness beneath their final push to finish the battle run and return home. It had been a long summer, and Will found that he was also thinking more of home.

Doughlas came and went almost daily, and Eleanor became more excited each time he brought her a new message.

"How is Ainsley?" Wil asked him one evening, after Doughlas had just returned.

The fen rider shrugged. "I haven't been to Ainsley in almost a month," he said as he pushed past Wil and entered the fen hall, where Wil could then hear Eleanor's anxious greeting. Her hope in Aemogen's possible victory seemed to be rising, a mystery to Wil, who only saw its impossibility. After a dismal afternoon of training with the men of Quickly fen, Wil had no such optimism. He felt the entire council had become delusional regarding the abilities of their people, for he knew that they couldn't win.

"I would say we have two hundred good men here," Aedon remarked to Wil as they stood under the shade of an outbuilding in the late afternoon.

"I say fifty," Wil answered.

"Is that all the faith that you have in the men of Quickly?" Aedon asked, looking surprised. "And I thought I was the overcautious mathematician in the council."

"Put your two hundred down on the charts," Wil responded, irritated. "Heaven knows you need every last man. But don't count on more than one of every ten returning from this war." A soft look entered Aedon's eyes, and Wil balked. "Oh no," he said, "I've seen that expression on your face before: it's Councillor Aedon, determined to fix the disgruntled masses."

Aedon did not smile, but neither did his expression harden at Wil's jab. "You appear very upset," he said, "for someone who, on multiple occasions, has insisted that he is only here for a limited time and limited investment."

Wil shook his head, walking a few steps away from Aedon. It had been a dismal day of training, and Wil wanted to believe that the men had been asleep rather than actually trying.

"You still think we have no chance then?" Aedon persisted.

"I think that Eleanor actually believes that you do!" Wil replied in frustration. He kicked a nearby swill bucket, and it clanged against an outcropping of rocks as it rolled down the hill by the outbuilding. Turning to face Aedon, Wil struggled to control his emotions. "She actually thinks that you can win and that you can defend Aemogen against the largest empire on the continent with shovels and rakes held by farmers!"

"And you do not think it is possible," Aedon said, his tone steady and pragmatic.

"We have been through almost all the fens of Aemogen, Aedon," Wil said. "And unless your High Forest fen is full of professional soldiers waiting for a fight, this will only end in misery." Wil's voice quavered in frustration. "And she is going to be racked with guilt for having sent all of her country's men to their deaths," he added. "What an ugly scene that will be."

"Do you care how she will feel?" Aedon asked.

"Do you not?" Wil replied instantly. "Does not every man here follow her leadership gladly? Eleanor is good all through." Wil spat these words from his mouth as if he hated them. "I have never seen a ruler so good and pure and determined. She has claimed the allegiance of all of us through her own strength of character. Yes, I care how she will feel. And I can't bear the thought of her destroying herself when she sees that this war has doomed her people."

Aedon looked at Wil regretfully.

"What?" Wil demanded. His anger was subsiding, but his sharpness of temper was not. "Don't look at me with that expression." He stooped and picked up a few rocks from the ground, tossing them into the heavy fields beyond, bracing for Aedon's response.

"I have misjudged you, Wil," Aedon said, and he moved as if to leave, but Wil laughed, causing him to pause. It was an ugly laugh, heavy with irony.

"Perhaps, Aedon," he said. "But not in the way you suppose."

Aedon knew the woods well, and his satisfaction from being in them was evident. Wil followed, tired yet relieved to escape the fen. Things at High Forest fen had gone well, better than Wil's own expectations, but he was at an end. When Aedon suggested that he and Wil should leave the training early to hike his favorite trail, Wil accepted gladly. A brotherhood had formed between them: Aedon appeared far more willing now to listen when Wil made a comment about a technique or strategy, and Wil, in turn, began to seek out Aedon's company in between obligations, allowing that the councillor did have a scope and knowledge that would appeal to him in a friend.

Aedon seemed at home in the woods, content and introspective.

"I'd have never thought you much of a woodsman, or a poet," Wil said when they had stopped to rest. "If you truly want to know a man, see him in his home."

"Is that an old Imirillian saying?" Aedon asked, being used to Eleanor and Wil sending them back and forth between each other. Wil reclined against a large stone, accepting the bread and cheese Aedon offered.

"No," Wil said, "simply my own observation."

Northwest Aemogen rolled out before them, fresh and vast. Wil searched for the landmarks he knew they'd passed down in the valleys. As his eyes wandered the forests and fields, he almost believed what Eleanor had told him several nights back: that Aemogen had been part of heaven before it fell to the earth, crashing against Marion and forming the impassable Arimel mountains on the west and the north. High Forest fen itself was a sight that leaned towards the picturesque, with a wide river easing between the houses.

"Do you miss spending your days here?" Wil asked.

Aedon stretched his arms behind his neck and did not answer for a long while. "High Forest fen will always have my heart," he said. "But my work is in Ainsley. I'm not content with the smallness of my home fen. I desire to do something in this world while I have time in it," he explained. "I'm the youngest head councillor ever in the history of Aemogen, you know."

He looked towards Wil. "I try to be fair, engaged, meticulous, and conscientious. I value my service to the queen and would not have it any other way. That being said," Aedon's speech drifted, yielding to the air around them, "there are days when my heart pushes on my mind to settle in this forest, along the river—keeping a garden, breeding horses—have a family with whatever woman would have me."

Tempted as Wil was to make sport of Aedon's humility, he let the moment pass for the sincerity of this exchange.

"Does a man leave his home or return unto it?" Wil posited.

"Have you made your decision?" Aedon asked in response, seeming curious. "Will you return home?"

"I do have some obligations that must be met," Wil replied. "After that, it's difficult to say."

Ainsley. Eleanor could just see Ainsley rising above the plains. Men of the company began to call out to one another, pleased to be on the threshold of home. The day was early yet, and a few wagered that they could arrive by nightfall if they kept good speed.

"Not likely," Aedon told Crispin. "It's a deceiving view, and our animals are tired. It wouldn't be wise to push them."

Eleanor's stockpile of strength was dwindling quickly. She needed to return home. She needed some quiet days to prepare for what was ahead. She needed positive reports from Doughlas, who had been working tirelessly with the miners of High Forest fen. Most of all, she needed her plan, known only to a few, to work without injury.

The wind had picked up, blowing north, and Eleanor brushed the loose strands of her hair away from her face. Then a call caught Eleanor's attention, and she followed the motions of a soldier that was riding the flank. Smoke was rising from the direction of Common Field fen.

"Burning a field," Sean replied to Wil's inquiry. "It's a bit early for that yet, except they may need to utilize the space."

Two riders were coming across the plain from the north, heading east towards Ainsley. Then one of them changed his course, turning instead towards the Queen's company.

"He must have seen our banner," Gaulter Alden said to no one in particular.

Eleanor felt the hairs rise on the back of her neck, and she motioned the company to a halt as the rider drew near. He began yelling, but they could not hear his words over the wind.

"Your Majesty! Your Majesty!" the rider said as he reined up, dismounted, and ran toward Eleanor.

"Your Majesty," he repeated, fighting for breath. "Common Field has been attacked."

⸺❦⸺

They heard the sounds first: women calling to one another, children crying. When Eleanor came into full view of Common Field, her lungs caught in pain, not from the smoke but from the sight. It was burned to the ground. A line of bodies, bloodied and run through, had been gathered onto the road.

The people were scared, scattered. Eleanor searched their faces as she dismounted. The men of her company were soon around her, flooding into the scene of misery to see what they might do. Eleanor couldn't block out the sounds of crying, and she needed to find Adams. The smell of charred wood rose with the smell of charred flesh. Danth, Adam's son, found Eleanor after the initial confusion of her arrival.

"What happened?" Eleanor asked, grabbing his arm.

"They came at dawn," he said. "Before any of us knew what

was where, buildings were on fire and people were shouting. We tried to fight," Danth said, looking away and wiping his forehead with an ash-ridden arm. "Tried to fight as we've been training all summer. They just killed us, right through, no stopping." He was dazed as he pointed towards the bodies on the road. "They're all over the fen."

"How many?" Wil asked. He had come up behind Eleanor, reaching for Danth's other arm. "How many were killed?"

"There's no way to tell yet." Danth shook his head numbly. "We've not found all the dead, let alone counted them. The children—" he added, his chin shaking. "We've begun taking the bodies of the children down the hill to the burial grounds. They're easier to carry, and our horses were almost all killed."

"Damn them!" Wil shouted, covering his face and disappearing through the crowd. A murmur rippled through the stunned villagers, and someone began to cry. Eleanor pressed her palms against her eyes, took a breath, and dropped her hands, shaking herself awake.

"Danth, where can I find your father?"

Danth looked away for a moment, then motioned towards the bodies in the road.

"No," Eleanor said as she shook her head. The stink rose in her nostrils, and everything was moving too fast and too slow around her. Then Crispin was beside her, saying something.

"The wounded?" Eleanor asked Danth, ignoring what Crispin was saying, not because she wished to but because she couldn't stop in all this confusion to think about anything besides the plan forming in her own mind. "We must help in any way possible," she said. "Do any buildings stand?"

"The granary," a woman standing nearby said as she pointed to a building beyond the charred remains of the fen hall. "We saved the large barn, too." She wiped her hands on her already soiled apron. "After the raiders left, we were able to put the fire out."

Eleanor grabbed Crispin's arm. "Gather the war council to the granary," she said and then sent half the soldiers to search for survivors and carry the wounded to the barn. The others soldiers were sent to set up a perimeter.

Gaulter Alden, Aedon, and Crispin, as well as Danth and a few men of the fen, followed Eleanor past the smoldering fen hall into the granary.

It was a small storage shed, used only at harvest time, but they crowded in. Gaulter Alden sat down on a crate and covered his eyes. Danth had entered, upon Eleanor's request, but he kept looking anxiously towards the door. The rest of the men crowded in, leaning against walls or standing quietly near the center.

Eleanor couldn't think. Pacing back and forth, she put all her efforts towards quieting her mind, towards dealing with the sick weight inside her chest. When she finally spoke, her hands were shaking.

"The soldiers are searching the fen," she said, "for the remaining dead and wounded. Those still alive are being taken to the only barn still standing. We must be calm as we—" As if on a cue, Wil pushed himself through the door into the crowded room. His clothes were wet with blood, his face ashen, and he looked anything but calm.

"As I said," she continued, despite her own tremendous panic, "we must remain calm." She looked directly at Wil. "For the people of Common Field fen desperately need our strength."

Wil cursed under his breath.

"We need to find anything we can to care for the wounded."

Eleanor's voice grew solid. "Are there any medicines or salves that can be found? Danth, you would know the experienced healers. Let us find which are still alive. The second rider should be in Ainsley soon," she added. "And supplies will come tomorrow or, perhaps, the day after. Briant, could you see what can be found of blankets, buckets, pots for water? What of food? A perimeter around the fen has been set. Those not standing watch or seeing to the wounded should begin to dig the graves."

"You're going to need someone to—" Wil interrupted.

"Wait," Eleanor said and held up a hand. "Everyone go about your work. If there is anything Danth needs, see to it immediately. He is now fen lord of Common Field." The men emptied out of the granary—Danth as shaken as he could be. Wil did not leave with the rest. He stood in the center, angry, his jaw working back and forth.

"Will you listen to me now, Eleanor!"

"You, Wil, are to go into the woods and cool your head." She emphasized these last three words.

He almost gave her a belligerent expression but checked himself before speaking. "There is something I must tell you—" he began.

"Your anger," Eleanor interrupted, "when we first arrived: you stalking off through the crowd—" Eleanor stopped speaking. She was drowning in the images that now crowded before her eyes. Common Field was destroyed—how many people were dead? They didn't know. And Danth had mentioned something about children?

"These people," Eleanor heard herself continue, though her voice sounded one hundred miles away, "they need calm and order; a firebrand reaction is of no use."

He opened his mouth to speak but shut it again, pressing his lips tight as he exhaled before speaking. "We don't know how many men came into your country last night," he explained. "We don't know if they retreated back through to the pass or if they lie in wait near another fen."

Eleanor lifted her hands to her face. "You're right, just let me think—"

"The time for thinking is done!" Wil practically shouted. "You have to respond now. This is the reality of war, of you choosing war."

"Give me one moment!" Eleanor yelled back, pulling her face up.

"A real leader," Wil said, "uses the momentum of moments like this—"

"You are out of line!" Eleanor said. "You swore your services to me. Now be still, and let me think." She turned away from him, taking three steps and lifting her fingers to her eyes before looking back at him.

"You're right that we need to send a scouting party after the invaders," she said. "But it will not be you. Is that clear?"

Wil clenched his jaw, shaking. Tears threatened his eyes, and he fought them back, angrily. When he finally spoke, it was a fierce whisper. "I have to do something." His voice rose as he pointed his finger towards the door. "Other than carry Blaike's body down the hill!"

"What?" Eleanor blinked. She stumbled back against an old crate along the back wall. She reached her hand towards it and sat. "Blaike?"

It was then Eleanor understood the blood on Wil's clothing.

The only sound in the small shed was her forced breathing. She moved to speak but couldn't.

"I am so sorry, Eleanor," Wil said.

"You are sure he's dead?" she whispered.

Wil didn't answer.

The news felt like a thick fog, and Eleanor couldn't think past what it meant. "I must go and—I must see to—" she said.

"Yes," Wil agreed.

She stood, unwilling to meet his eyes. "You're right," she said. "We must scout their retreat—immediately."

"I can go," he said. "And it would be safer alone. Let me do this for you."

Eleanor brushed the tears from her face, fighting to maintain some semblance of composure. "Very well," she managed. "What do you need?"

"Nothing."

"You should take someone with you. Duncan, perhaps."

"No."

"But—"

"You never need to worry over me, Eleanor." He shook his head, lifting his hand to the back of his neck. "If I leave now, I'll find their camp before dawn," he explained. "Though, it might be a few days before I return. I'll look for you first here, and then I will come to Ainsley."

"I'll not be here." Eleanor spoke the words without thinking, but she knew them to be true. "Find me at Ainsley," she said as she brushed her fingertips across her cheeks, not looking at him. "Don't do anything rash," she added. "We need information, not another death."

"I'll be fine," he said, his voice turning almost tender. "Will you?"

The corners of Eleanor's mouth pulled down as her eyes closed, and tears came, warm on her face. She turned away. "You should go," Eleanor said, but she could hardly make out the words. "Take Thrift. You need concealment, and scouting in the woods on a white horse is—"

Wil waited, perhaps to see if Eleanor would say anything more. Then he pushed open the door to the granary when she didn't.

"The fools," she heard him mutter as he left, unsure if he had meant the Imirillians or the Aemogens—or both.

CHAPTER

SEVENTEEN

Wil moved unimpeded through the woods. Tracking was easy, for the Imirillian company hadn't bothered to cover their tracks. Neither had they bothered to conceal their camp. When he came across it, later that night he could hear their laughter and arguments through the trees. The anger in his chest was pulsing stronger than his heart, and he knew if he let himself slip, if he gave the anger space, it would result in a fierce exhibition.

"Control yourself," he warned himself aloud as he twisted his hand in Thrift's mane. After uttering an Imirillian battle prayer, he mounted and rode Thrift towards the camp. As he approached, instead of slowing down, he urged the horse forward, breaking through the trees and into the center of the Imirillian war party.

There were shouts as men turned, grabbing their weapons. When the men saw his face, they dropped their swords and backed away from his glare.

"Your Excellency!"

"The prince!" Shouts went up.

"Who leads this band?" he demanded as he dismounted Thrift.

From the other side of camp, Drakta came into view. The prince walked towards his father's war leader, drawing out his blade.

"Prince Basaal!" Drakta said, sounding surprised. "This is a rather unexpected—"

Prince Basaal grabbed Drakta by his collar. "What have you done, Drakta?" he said as he tightened his grip, slamming him against a large tree. "I gave you strict instructions!" He slammed Drakta again. No one moved. The entire camp stood frozen.

"Prince Basaal," Drakta tried to explain, "we were following orders."

"Whose?" Prince Basaal yelled. "You were following whose orders? If I remember, the last time we spoke, I made it quite clear that I would call every move. And you—" he said as he threw the man against the tree again and then tossed him to the ground, pointing his sword into Drakta's neck. "And you would do as I said."

"Your father the emperor—" Drakta began.

"My father?" Prince Basaal raged. "My father understood that I would lead this conquest on my own terms and that you, Drakta, were not to play nursemaid." He kicked the man, then spat on the ground near him in insult. "You and your men will pack up and leave Aemogen."

Drakta climbed back onto his feet. "We have been marching the last four days. We had to go high up the mountain to get around their soldiers in the pass. The men deserve a rest, Your Grace." He said this with malice and fear.

"Do they?" Basaal asked, dropping the point of his sword as he looked around the group. Few were his own soldiers, to his utter relief. Most belonged in the small company of his father's men that Drakta had brought with him.

"Do you all feel that you have been working too hard?" he asked them.

None dared answer.

"I've seen what you have done to that village," Basaal said, walking slowly in a circle, eyeing the still company. "Dishonor. Dishonor on all of you!" He spat at the ground again. "I gave strict instructions that you were to remain outside the pass until near the time of attack, which is still thirty days away!"

A large man in the group, a man the prince did not recognize, whispered something to his neighbor and smirked. Prince Basaal glowered, walked towards the man, and threw a fist at the soldier's nose. It gave way under this assault, and the large man stumbled backward to the ground, blood running between his fingers.

"Would any other man like to share an opinion contrary to my command?" Basaal asked.

Silence. Drakta's expression was dark, but subservient.

"Good. Now move out," Basaal said. "I will be down the pass in thirty days time, and I expect you all to stay in Marion, doing absolutely *nothing*!" He turned to Drakta. "Have I made myself quite clear?"

"Yes, Your Grace," Drakta said, kneeling before the prince.

"Good. Get up." Once Drakta was on his feet, Basaal took him roughly by the arm and pulled the man close, so he could whisper. "And Drakta, if you ever disobey my orders again, I will hang you immediately. I don't care if you are my father's war leader," he added. "You will swing for it. Do you understand me?" The prince did not wait for an answer. Instead, he turned back towards the silent soldiers.

"I have been working towards a surrender," Basaal said to them, "so that you men could return home to your families instead of dying on a foreign field. Do you realize how disobeying my orders has put not only my life in peril but also your own and the welfare of your families?" He was shaking as he spoke, but the passion of his voice carried the message.

"Pack up," he said as he turned again to Drakta and motioned for the other captains to come forward. Basaal took a deep breath. "Is all well with Annan?" he asked. "Has the army arrived in Marion?"

Drakta's eyes burned with hatred, but he answered the prince's question. "Yes, the Marion king grows impatient, but the camp will be set up just as you have instructed, in thirty days time."

"And the number of men who will be in camp?" Basaal asked.

"All seven thousand of your troops plus an additional company of your father's officers."

The prince nodded, unwilling to show any more emotion. "You'll leave within the hour, Drakta. I'll not be pleased to hear otherwise," Basaal warned. He turned from Drakta and walked back across the camp. There, one of his own soldiers held Thrift's bridle. Prince Basaal knew the man.

"Thank you for holding my horse, soldier," he said.

"An honor, my prince."

Pausing, Basaal considered the man before him. "They call you Kavi, don't they?"

Kavi nodded, pleased that his prince knew his name.

"Are you loyal unto life or loyal unto death?" Basaal asked.

"Unto death," Kavi said, pulling his sleeve back, revealing Basaal's crest on his left forearm.

"Please tell Annan I am well and still yet hope for a surrender," the prince said, his voice quiet. "He must in no circumstances bring any men into this country without me."

"I will do as you have asked." Kavi made a quick signal with his hand, showing his promise.

The prince spoke even lower. "Did Drakta bring any Vestan with him?"

Kavi nodded. "Two of them ride with us," Kavi said. "I heard rumors that there may also be more assassins on the road."

"Thank you," Prince Basaal said, and he mounted Thrift, meeting the eyes of those who were still watching. Disgusted with their butchery, he rode away from the clearing.

CHAPTER

EIGHTEEN

There were no words to describe the way Edythe collapsed into herself when she heard the news of Blaike's death. At first, she did not believe Eleanor.

"It could not be, could it Eleanor?" Edythe said again and again. But the ghost of the life that would not be, the only life she had ever considered, settled behind Edythe's numb eyes.

"The grief will leave no part of her untouched," Eleanor tearfully told Aedon, who had come with her to Ainsley. "When she wakes from her numbness, she won't be able to bear it. I can't bear it myself."

It had been raining for three days, and the gardens were content to drown in the late summer showers. But it was cold in the palace. Ridiculously cold, Eleanor thought as she stood at the window, watching the wet afternoon. She was in her private audience chamber, trying to focus on the numbers before her in the report that Aedon had prepared, but she found little success in these efforts.

It was well over a week past now, and Eleanor knew that it

was time for her to decide what the massacre at Common Field meant, politically. The Imirillian raid had come as a warning, so it seemed, a show of their strength. And now, every aspect of their threat was met with utter distrust. Eleanor could not know if their army would wait to invade until their promised date or if, when Eleanor surrendered, Emperor Shaamil would honor his terms. And her scheme, the brazen idea that she'd had in Rye Field fen, confiding it only to the members of her war council and a few miners from High Forest fen, depended on having time—as much time as the High Forest miners could get. She had not told Wil her plans.

Wil.

Eleanor was also plagued with guilt over his disappearance. He should have returned by now, but they had heard nothing.

"Wil should have been here days ago," Eleanor had told Aedon.

"You don't suppose he had a run in with the Imirillians before they left Aemogen?" he'd asked.

Eleanor hadn't answered, rubbing her finger against the wood grains of her desk, her breathing shallow for the hurt around her heart. A fen rider had arrived from the pass three days before, saying that the Imirillians—a small raiding party thirty or forty strong—had left the country but had first encountered the Aemogen guards in the pass. Of all the men killed in the skirmish, fifteen were Eleanor's soldiers, and five were Imirillian.

The rain came harder now, beating against the glass, sending loud echoes through the tall room. Eleanor set her hand against the cold of the window, the sleeve of her mourning gown sliding down to her elbow. She wore black for Edythe, for Blaike, and for all the dead: one hundred and thirty-four souls. Eleanor left the window, passing the table where her papers and figures lay, and sat down on the soft rugs before the fire, trying to believe the words her father had often spoken, that things would work out.

—◦◦◦◦◦◦◦—

"Eleanor, wake up."

Eleanor felt a hand on her shoulder. It was dark except for the light of the low fire. Wil was crouched next to her, resting on the balls of his feet. "You've slept away the afternoon," he said. "And I thought you might prefer to wake up sooner than later."

"What hour is it?" she asked.

"It's past sundown, but only just."

"How long have you been here?" Eleanor asked as she sat up and rubbed her eyes. Then, as her memory caught up with her, she cried, "You're here!" Eleanor flung her arms around Wil and took a deep breath. "I was so worried you had—" she began. "But when did you return to Ainsley?"

His fingers were pressed against the back of her neck, tangled in her loose hair. "A few hours ago," he said softly.

Eleanor pulled away and studied his face. He looked terrible.

"Crispin said you would want to see me," Wil said, as if to explain his presence. His hand was still on the back of her neck. "But you were asleep when I came in. It was so quiet that, I admit, I stayed for the solitude."

"What took you so long to return?" Eleanor asked.

He paused a moment. "To be honest, I could have been here sooner, but I couldn't face it—not any of it."

"Sit with me," Eleanor said as she shifted, moving to the side. Wil settled himself beside her, leaning into the heat of the fire and holding his hands towards the flames.

"Crispin said you'd already heard about the fighting in the

pass," he said. "I didn't see it, but I did manage to come close to the Imirillian encampment. From what I could gather, this attack was not sanctioned by those leading the conquest," he explained. "The Imirillians intend to keep their word, or so it seems."

Eleanor made a dubious sound.

"How have things been here?" Wil asked.

"Awful."

"And Edythe?"

Eleanor shrugged her shoulders and shook her head.

"Would that the Illuminating God should see me cast into the ocean and damn me forever for the events of these days," Wil said.

At first, Eleanor thought his desperate words to be an Imirillian expression. But the pain on his face was cast in such sincerity that she knew they were his own. "Are you faithful to the Imirillian God?" she asked. "I had not thought…"

Wil looked at Eleanor almost blankly, dark circles under his blue eyes. "I'm very devout," he said. "It's all the more reason why—" He shook his head once, but did not finish his thought. Turning his palms away from the fire, Wil stared at them. "I cannot remove the blood from these hands."

Eleanor could see no blood, but his tone was layered, inaccessible. Eleanor lifted her fingers to the side of his face, relieved to ignore her own pain in favor of his. At her touch, he looked towards her, and Eleanor spoke aloud a line from the second scroll: "I am sorrow born, and my days sorrow bound, but I will rise with the Illuminating God and be made holy."

Wil closed his eyes and covered her fingers with his. "But can I ever be made holy?" he asked. "You don't know, Eleanor. You know so little of my life."

Eleanor did not have an answer. When Wil opened his eyes, all she could see was a mirror of her own grief.

"I had forgotten," he said. "There was something that I'd determined to give you." He released Eleanor's fingers and pulled a small red cloth from his black tunic. "A gift, something I've carried with me and would like you to have." It was with obvious effort that Wil shook past the sadness in his voice.

Eleanor accepted the small item wrapped in a bit of scarlet velvet. "It's rare to receive a gift like this in Aemogen," she said.

Wil forced a confused smile. "Are you never given presents?"

"Not often," Eleanor said as she shook her head. "We offer songs, poems, and remembrances." The corners of her mouth tugged downward, weighted by sadness. "Or, if you desire to give something very special, you offer a new dance, a bit of music, or, perhaps, the seeds of a flower to plant in a garden."

"You and your people baffle me." Wil actually laughed, tired and tight. "I've thought your customs odd and strange, but this—" He shrugged. "My people love gifts," he said. "For every occasion there is something given, something exchanged."

Eleanor's fingers pulled at the string that held the folds of velvet together, and, as the knot came loose, she pulled the fabric back. There, set off by the scarlet, lay a golden pendant, a circle the size of a large coin with a beautiful bird of gold rising through a delicate pattern of red stones.

"It's beautiful," Eleanor said as she held it up before the firelight. "The intricacy is—" she began, then she realized that she recognized the design, and she raised her eyes to his. "It matches the mark on your arm."

Wil did not answer.

"I don't think this is mine to have," Eleanor said, holding the pendant out to Wil.

He didn't take it but leaned back against his hands and half shrugged. "It's meant to be a symbol of my friendship to you, and your people," he said. "This time in Aemogen has been important to me, and I hope, regardless of the future, to remain your friend."

Eleanor moved her thumb over the pendant, the stones breaking the smoothness beneath her skin. She closed her hand around the gift. "And so you shall always be."

Her words seemed to add pain to his face, and Will appeared haunted as he turned to stare at the fire.

The sound of rain had faded, and the room was still. He was sitting so close that she could feel each breath.

"I should go to Edythe now," Eleanor said, touching her fingers to his arm. "She'll be glad to know you're safe."

Edythe was lying on her bed. It was cold, for her window had been left ajar. The call of crickets, come out after the rain, filtered up into her room, and the sweet smell of the rose garden accompanied the sound. Instead of speaking—asking Edythe if she was all right, if she was well—Eleanor lay down behind her sister, putting her arm around Edythe and moving closer. Edythe responded, putting her hand on Eleanor's. Sighing, Eleanor kissed Edythe's hair.

It felt unwise to Eleanor, but she let her mind wander, thinking of the impending Imirillian army waiting to attack, growing larger each day, and suffering the images of death from Common Field fen. Eleanor closed her eyes and pulled Edythe closer.

"Wil has come back," Eleanor whispered. The words strung out in the darkness, but then Edythe swallowed.

"I am happy for you," Edythe said.

Eleanor's cheeks burned, and she didn't answer.

"Have you found a way to save us?" Edythe said. "Crispin said that you had found a way to save us."

"There is one way," Eleanor said. "It's not a certainty, but it might work." Night hung close to Eleanor, and she felt tired. "I will tell you more come morning." Several more minutes passed.

"Edythe," Eleanor finally said, feeling hesitant to probe her sister's emotions. "I wanted to tell you that the last time I saw Blaike, he was ever so happy. And I know Wil spent some time with Blaike while on the battle run. Would you like—" she added, pausing briefly. "Would it do you well if I asked Wil to come and speak with you about him?"

It took a while for Edythe to answer. "I would like that very much," she finally said.

"I'll ask him," Eleanor promised.

Edythe did not respond. Pulling away from her sister, Eleanor lay on her back and stared at the ceiling, wondering if a person could ever carry all they were called to bear in this life. Some pain was so acute that it would cut you, twist you from the inside, until you finally gave into it. And some aches were so overwhelming in nature, that you seemed doomed to drown.

Eleanor kissed her sister on the cheek and quietly left the dark room.

———

The fen lords had arrived in Ainsley to begin their meetings. Wil had not been invited. Left alone, tired of the small, restrictive walls of the travelers' house, he took his thoughts to the streets of Ainsley. Paved in cobblestones, the streets ran and bent around one other, garnished with houses, tall and thin, intermingled with alleyways and gardens. As Wil studied the city, he thought of the people here and of the slaughter of Common Field, wishing the Aemogens would not choose to fight. But his arguments for surrender had still gone unheeded, and Eleanor did not wish to discuss it with him.

"Hey, you! Traveler!"

Wil looked over his shoulder. Back where the cobble-covered road twisted up to the market square, a woman was walking with a bucket in hand, its water splashing onto the ground. She greeted him with a smile.

"Do you remember me? We met several months back?" she said, coming to a stop, breathless from her heavy load. Wil thought her face seemed familiar.

"My name's Aurrey," she said. "You helped my son, Haide, after his tumble in the market on one of your first days here—months ago now." She waved her free hand in the air.

The memory crossed Wil's mind, and he offered a polite smile. "I do remember. How are you?"

"I'll be better once the little ones are fed, but all is well with us," Aurrey said. "And you? Why are you wandering Ainsley instead of sitting at supper?"

"The fen lords are meeting into the evening," he explained. "I will take a meal in my room later."

"And the battle run," Aurrey said, stating the words as if he would know her full meaning behind them. "We've heard tales of you."

"Have you now?"

Aurrey flushed. "You'll have to straighten them out before us, so we know what's true," she said. "Come on then."

"Pardon?"

She blew out of her lips impatiently. "Come on then. You

must supper with us. My husband is home, and he enjoys good company."

"I don't—" Wil began.

"You do," Aurrey interrupted. "They say that war is coming. Let's get some food in you before it does." She motioned down the street. "Come on then."

Aurrey continued walking, and Wil followed obediently, offering to carry the water for her. Several streets down, they stopped at a drooping home made of stone with a strong thatch, tucked in between two taller houses.

Aurrey opened the door and welcomed Wil inside as a burst of wails assaulted his ears. Two children were poking and fighting each other, Haide and a girl who was older than he.

"No supper for noise makers!" Aurrey said, rushing to a small hearth, pulling a pot of boiling soup off the flame. The children quieted down, but not before Haide had jabbed his elbow at his sister and then looked away, innocently, when she began to cry. The children, bored with their petty fights, turned their eyes on Wil, who stood in the center of the small room, still holding the bucket of water, feeling out of place in this domestic scene. The girl stared, wide-eyed, at Wil's sword.

"Where's your father?" Aurrey asked the child.

"In the shop." The girl pointed towards an open door in the back.

"I'm here," a man said as he passed through, wiping his hands clean on a rag. He was a solid man, neither short nor tall, with a wave of light brown hair and an intelligent face that had not been shaved in several days. He looked from Wil to Aurrey and back again.

"This is Wil," Aurrey said, nodding towards Wil as she added a dried herb to the soup. "He's the one I told you about, who helped on the battle run. Wil, this is my husband, Haide."

Haide stepped forward and extended a hand. "Pleasure," he said.

"Your wife found me wandering Ainsley and kindly invited me to have your meal with you."

"She's always bringing in the strays," Haide said and gave a half smile. "Sit then, and make yourself well in my house. The day is long, and good company will be pleasant."

Wil sat. There was only a small table in the corner, where Aurrey worked as she finished her preparations, but there were chairs enough for all. The girl, after being chided several times by Aurrey, gathered a stack of clean bowls and spoons from a cupboard, carrying them precariously to the table.

The simple meal was served, and the conversation remained light. The young girl, whose name Wil discovered was Anna, sat next to him and stared at his face while he ate. Wil swallowed a bite of soup and smiled in return. Instead of looking away shyly, she was encouraged by his attention.

"Why is your skin almost burned?" she asked.

"Anna!" Aurrey chided.

But Wil laughed, lifting his olive-skinned arm. "Burned?" he asked. "My brothers mock me for how fair my skin is."

This did not appear to satisfy Anna.

"I am from the North," Wil answered, "where little girls like you have sun-filled skin and black eyes, bright as the night sky. I might ask you why your skin is so pale. Are you a ghost?"

Anna shook her head.

"Strange," Wil said. "I could almost see right through you."

"Your eyes are blue, not black," she informed Wil, as if worried that he may not know.

"Yes, as were my mother's."

"Leave the poor man to eat," Haide said, leaning back in his chair with an empty bowl in his hand. "Take your brother, and you can play in the street until dark."

The children scurried outside, and Aurrey began to clean up.

"What news of the meetings between the queen and the fen lords? Is it war we're marching for?" Haide asked, as if the question had been waiting only for him to finish eating his meal.

"I don't know," Wil said, thanking Aurrey as she refilled his empty bowl. "They are still in discussion, and I am not privy."

"I've heard tell of your role on the battle run: the man experienced with combat, the Imirillian soldier who pledged himself to help the queen." Haide paused over these words before continuing. "What are your thoughts?"

"Surrender is your only option," Wil said.

Haide harrumphed. "It would have to be desperate indeed for Aemogen to surrender its sovereignty."

"It is," Wil replied. "The odds are impossible."

A hard look settled in Haide's face.

"What?" Wil asked between spoonfuls of soup.

"I would be interested to know how the queen feels, is all," Haide said. "Despite the impossible odds."

"I don't know her mind for certain," Wil said. "But she seems bent on fighting. She most certainly will not listen to my advice that she surrender."

Haide smiled and scratched his chin. "I'm ready to fight," he said. "And I would follow my queen to war."

Wil waited for Haide to say more.

"A foreign invasion would destroy Aemogen," Haide explained.

"We are a unique country, tucked away, quiet and all. But we fight hard to live such a life in such a place, and our heritage is deep. I would rather die, trying to save Aemogen for my children, than live and see it change. But I can see by your face that you don't agree."

Wil looked down into his soup, then up again, tilting his head and considering Haide. "Surely, it is better that you live and provide for your children," Wil began, "than that you die for a battle that cannot be won?"

"Here, here," Aurrey said from the table, her back to the conversation.

"Like I said," Haide replied, "I would know the queen's mind before deciding what is impossible and what isn't." Haide settled back in his chair and remained quiet for some time before speaking. "Have you heard of the heart of Ainorra Breagha?"

Aurrey took Wil's empty bowl, and he thanked her. "Queen Eleanor told me one legend at the Barrows of Ainse," he said, leaning forward in his chair, towards the fire. The evening air tasted strangely cool for late summer.

Haide nodded. "The stories say that her heart knew things," he explained. "A few years after she had come to New Ainsley, our Ainsley, Ainorra Breagha felt a warning against the spring and asked all of Ainsley not to plant their crops. Now," Haide said, scratching his arm and looking Wil in the eyes, "to tell an Aemogen man not to plant is to tell him not to breathe. We come from this earth, and we will go into it—it's our nature. The planting season was ripe and ready, and you must plant on time," he explained. "For when winter comes, it comes sharp. We've no time for an extended harvest. But Ainorra Breagha asked the men not to plant."

"Did they listen?" Wil asked.

"Most did, but some did not. Time passed," Haide continued. "And after a month, the rumors flew that the queen was crazy. Never had a fairer season been seen, and the few planted crops did well. Weeks passed, but then, a storm came in from the South Sea. It was a vile thing, hard and cold. Blossoms froze right on the trees as it beat upon the land, all snow and hail," he explained. "The crops planted were lost, every one. After the storm passed, Ainorra Breagha told her people to plant."

"And those who lost their crops learned their lesson and went without," Wil guessed.

"Their neighbors shared, of course, but learn a lesson they did." Haide shrugged. "It may be only a story to you, but we Aemogen's know better. And Queen Eleanor reminds us all of Ainorra Breagha. They are the only reigning queens in the history of Aemogen, which is why Eleanor is named after her."

The evening was settling around them. Aurrey had gone to the door to speak with some women in the street, leaving the men to their conversation.

"I hadn't realized that she was," Wil said.

"A daughter, born first, after seven hundred years?" Haide said. "You better believe she was."

"And so if Eleanor felt, despite all the impossibility, that Aemogen's best interests were to fight, you should follow—"

"I would, proudly," Haide insisted. "She is a good monarch, and I love her for it."

Wil creased his forehead. "You almost speak as if she were your daughter."

"She is," Haide said. "The queen is daughter, mother, and sister to us all. We honor her, and she us. I remember the morning of her coronation—she was a young start," Haide laughed. "They all were. Councillor Aedon, too, was just barely a man: intelligent, but young. The king had intended to train him up a good ten, fifteen years, if not more. But when he died unexpectedly—" Haide said, lifting his hands.

"So, there we were," he continued. "With a slip of a queen and the head councillor just more than a boy himself—children, really. After the ceremony, Queen Eleanor stood and said, in a small voice, 'I will give all my heart to you. Will you do the same for me?' That crowd cheered longer than any I'd ever heard. She was smart and good and had spent her life preparing. The queen was ready."

"Surely, she has made mistakes in her youth," Wil said.

"And I make mistakes as a man," Haide answered practically. "The people do not hold her mistakes against her, and she does not hold ours against us. It's a contract, you see. She reigns by contract: we give our best to her, and she gives her best to us," he explained. "That is what we speak of. If one party falls short today, well, we know to rise up and better ourselves for tomorrow."

Wil rubbed his hand across his face and leaned back in his chair. "So, you do not believe that she reigns with divine right?" he asked.

Haide laughed and shrugged. "I personally don't think God cares," Haide said. "If I were a king, I might think differently though. Be it gods or ghosts who put her there, if she stays true to us, I will follow her, for I have seen what other countries are."

"Have you traveled?" Wil asked, surprised. He ran his eyes over Haide again. "Most don't leave their fen, let alone Aemogen."

Haide raised his eyebrows in agreement. "I'm a cobbler, a shoemaker," he said. "To you, it sounds simple, I see. But I am good at what I do. You might even say that my wares are popular. I travel the fens every year, twice going into Marion. As a younger man, unmarried with the world before me, I traveled all the countries of the West before settling home again."

"And you chose Aemogen?"

Haide grinned. "I chose Aurrey. Aemogen came with her."

Wil laughed. As if on cue, Aurrey came in through the doorway. "The children are off down playing games," she said. "They'll be a fright come bedtime. What are you both grinning at?" she asked, glaring at Haide.

"My reason for staying," Haide replied.

"I'll be your reason for going if you don't stay in line." She gathered some mending from a basket and settled down near her husband. "Tell us of the battle run, Wil. I've collected all the stories to be found in Ainsley," she explained. "But my, is what they say of South Mountain fen true? Tell us from your own eyes."

Wil told the tale, and as he spoke of Thistle Black finally giving his allegiance, she laughed.

"Never met the man," she said, "but he seems to be filled with his own self, now doesn't he?"

"Queen Eleanor did well," Haide approved. "And it's wise she does not treat the other fens so."

"Why ever not?" Wil asked as he glanced out the open doorway. It was full dark, and the sounds of children could be heard down the street.

"I'll say it this way," Haide said, gesturing with his hands. "My mother—"

"Oh!" Aurrey rolled her eyes. "Why we have to talk about your mother, I'll never know."

Haide chuckled. "When my mother comes by the house, she

calls Aurrey out on things fast, and Aurrey bristles. But sometimes when she comes and praises Aurrey for what she's done, my wife is suddenly glad that I've a mother, and before the day's out, is asking her for advice."

"True enough," Aurrey conceded.

"That is the nature of the Aemogen people," Haide continued. "It always has been. We don't do well with forced criticism, or by having someone impose themselves on us. But if given the space, we will choose loyalty and be grateful too. Our monarchs have done well because they understand our temperament."

"What is she like?" Aurrey asked, interrupting Haide.

"Who? The queen?" Wil frowned.

Aurrey blushed. "It's only that people are saying the two of you are familiar," she said. "And I've never spoken with her myself."

It was uncomfortable for Wil to answer this question. Or, perhaps, it was the implication of the question. He looked again towards the door, then back at the floor.

"The man doesn't want to answer the question, Aurrey," Haide said. "Let him be."

"I don't mind telling what I think the queen to be like." Wil pulled his mouth to the side for just a moment before continuing. "I find her very thoughtful, determined, patient, and more intense than one would think, but she controls it so well that one would hardly know. Though, I believe I have learned something of her here, tonight, I had not understood previously."

To Wil's relief, Haide picked up the question. "Last year, I was traveling between fens and found myself on the same road with Councillor Aedon. I asked him about the queen and what she was like. He thought awhile and said, 'She carries ten thoughts in her head at all times but will only give you two of them. The rest you must discover.'"

Wil smiled.

The evening soon ended, with Aurrey gathering her children in for bed and Haide offering to make Wil a new pair of boots.

"The front of my shop lets out on the street behind," Haide explained. "Come by anytime you can. I don't know how long I will keep it open if it's come to war."

They parted with a handshake and friendly words before Wil stepped into the darkness. He thought about what Haide had said, about the people and their relationship with Eleanor. Wil liked Haide: a sound man, articulate in his opinion whether Wil agreed with him or not.

For a moment, as Wil walked up towards Ainsley Rise in the dark, he envisioned Haide, sword in hand, being swallowed up by the Imirillian army that waited at the pass and left for dead. The young prince leaned in the shadows against a wall, wiping his forehead on his sleeve, his hands shaking. I must distance myself from these people, he thought. All of them.

Torches lit the south Ainsley stairs, and Wil took them two at a time, slipping into the castle gates, just before they were to close for the night. He was turning left, towards the travelers' house, when one of Crispin's soldiers grabbed his arm.

"Have you heard, Wil?" the soldier said.

Wil flinched. "What?" he asked as he took a step back.

"The meetings between the queen and the fen lords are over," he said. "It's come to an end."

"And what have they decided?" Wil asked.

"Aemogen fights."

Wil swore and, without taking his leave, changed the course of his direction and went straight into the castle. Fen lords were walking down the corridors, greeting Wil, discussing amongst themselves, but they weren't coming from the direction of the throne room.

"Miya!" Wil grabbed the maid's arm as she passed him in the crowded hall. "The queen and the others, did they not meet in the throne room?"

"No," she said as she shook her head. "This evening, they met in the library."

"Thank you," he said. Wil took the flight of stairs that led to the east wing of the second floor, passing Thayne with scarcely more than a nod as he hurried by. The door was ajar, so Wil pushed it open.

"Wil!" Crispin said. He and Aedon were standing just inside the door, talking, and Wil had almost knocked them over.

"Crispin," Wil nodded, just out of breath. "Aedon, is Eleanor here?"

"Yes," Aedon answered.

They stepped aside, and Wil saw Eleanor, sitting at the end of the long table, speaking in low tones with Gaulter Alden and Sean. Doughlas and Briant were talking with one another at the other end of the table. Eleanor looked towards the door, and her eyes locked on Wil's.

"They said you're going to fight," he said, his voice loud enough that all sound in the room stopped.

Eleanor continued to stare at Wil, unblinking.

He took a step towards her, his hands spread out, baffled. "Your *only* chance of survival is immediate surrender," he said. "You know there aren't enough men in Aemogen to battle! What did you tell them, the fen lords, to make them think this was possible? Eleanor?"

There was no audible response from anyone; quiet filled the room. Aedon closed the door behind Wil and followed Crispin back to the table, where they sat down with the rest of the war council. Doughlas and Crispin exchanged a look, seeming uncomfortable, but Eleanor remained still, a thought lingering behind her eyes that Wil couldn't decipher.

"You don't have enough men to sustain a position of any kind against the Imirillian army," he said. "There will be thousands of soldiers down that mountain pass. Aedon is right when he estimates that Aemogen has, perhaps, three thousand men. And what, with only two hundred of them trained soldiers? Your *best* chance is one man against two, and each of those Imirillians will be a battle-hardened professional. They are neither farmers nor merchants nor miners. Accept the terms of surrender and save your people!" Wil pled with the council.

"We will not surrender our sovereignty," Eleanor replied. "I am afraid that I cannot give on that point. So, we must find ways to increase our chances of fending off the Imirillian forces."

"Eleanor, it's impossible," Wil said desperately. "Don't you see?"

"We will not surrender," Gaulter Alden said, sounding steady and sure. "We will work with the resources we have. Our men are far more ready than they ever have been and will be even more so after they have spent a few more weeks in Ainsley before marching to the pass."

"Aemogen can still exist as an independent nation, Wil," Aedon said next. "We simply have to make that happen."

Wil wanted to pull his hair out. He settled, instead, for pacing, crossing his arms over his chest, biting nervously at his thumbnail, and muttering. "This is madness," he said as he turned, almost laughing from frustration. "Do you hear yourselves? You're delusional, all of you! You cannot win! Every man that you send to war will die, and then, so will you, Eleanor." Wil turned towards her, his voice growing strained. "They will kill you as an example to the people," he explained. "You will die. Is there nothing that I can say to make you understand? I have seen wars all over the North. What waits at your door is like nothing you in Aemogen have ever imagined.

"The Imirillian army will march up the pass in a month's time," Wil continued, walking forward and leaning against the table, his hands spread out. He stared at the face of every person sitting silently at the table, before pleading again with Eleanor. "And, unless you can bring down the very mountains to block the pass, nothing will stop them!" Wil hit the table with his fist and stepped back, perspiring.

Eleanor looked to Gaulter Alden and then to Aedon. Crispin cleared his throat and drummed his fingers on the table. Sean scratched the scruff on his chin and whispered something to Doughlas.

"What?" Wil said, his question sounding flat as he stood with his hands on his hips. "I can see that all of you have something that you're not telling me." Suddenly, Wil registered a thought, an impossibly wild and improbable thought. He looked at Eleanor, who stared at him evenly, looking unapologetic.

"You are going to bring down the mountain," he said.

Eleanor watched Wil as he almost stumbled back, stunned. His eyes traveled around the war council, all of who knew of Eleanor's plan—all but Wil. Eleanor rubbed her finger against the wood of the table as he continued speaking.

"You're going to bring down the mountain," he said again. "That is your plan? You have a way to close off the pass so that the damned could not enter, let alone the Imirillians." Wil laughed, but it did not sound entirely sane, and his voice broke. "The battle run was more of a ruse than anything. I have been agonizing all summer, almost sick, to think of your people slain—" He laughed again, harsher. "And you have been planning on bringing down the mountain all along."

"The battle run was not a ruse, Wil," Eleanor said quietly. "We needed to know how many men we had, to train them, and to prepare them for any eventuality. It may not work, despite our careful planning. And the idea only came to me when we were in Rye Field fen," she explained. "From one of the texts we had translated, actually, the one about being unable to fight against the mountains."

Wil laughed again as Eleanor continued. "There are old mines, riddling the mountains above the pass," she said. "But significant repair work has been needed—"

"Please." Wil held up his hands. "Don't tell me any more." He seemed shaken, but his eyes were less haunted when he finally looked at Eleanor again. "I'm greatly relieved that you have a means of defending yourself. But please, spare me talk of any details. It's something that I do not desire to know. Please, excuse me, Eleanor." Wil took another step back before turning on his heel and leaving the room.

CHAPTER

NINETEEN

Wil spent the following morning training with Hastian. The Queen's Own had sought Wil out, asking for individual training, and Wil was happy to oblige the quiet soldier.

Frustrated and relieved from the evening before, Wil was relentless in his aggression. Hastian tried his best, but he could not fend off Wil's attacks. Only after Hastian held up his hand, begging for breath, did Wil allow the soldier time to regroup.

"You are the last defense between any threat and the queen," Wil said, sounding impatient even to his own ears. "I cannot be soft with you."

Hastian breathed in deeply, kneeling on one knee, looking at the ground. Wil's thoughts turned to the meeting of the night before, wondering if their scheme was truly even possible.

"I'm ready, Wil," he said.

"All right, then." Wil did not come at Hastian again in straight combat. Rather, he took time to work with the soldier on small details that would improve his efficacy. "Hold your sword like this if someone is coming straight at you," Wil said, demonstrating.

"It will allow you to cut both under and above as needed. Here, like this."

Wil stopped their spar to arrange Hastian's hands. "I know it doesn't feel like much, but it will make a difference when using this particular attack. Ready?" Wil swung his sword in a steady rhythm, counting out loud, reminding Hastian of the best ways to defend his skilled blows. They worked through the exercise several times before Wil began to build up speed and let himself fight more forcefully. To his surprise, Hastian not only kept up but also improvised, which showed he had been practicing what he had observed during the battle run.

A brief flicker of Eleanor's determined words from the night before split Wil's attention, and suddenly he found himself on the ground, dazed, looking up at a triumphant Hastian.

Cheers and good-natured insults came from the men watching nearby. It was the first time that he had been knocked down in Aemogen. As Wil sucked the air back into his lungs, Hastian offered him his hand and pulled Wil up from the ground. Wil took another breath and clapped Hastian on the shoulder.

"You caught me completely unaware," he admitted. "Bravo."

"To be honest with you," Hastian said, indulging in a modest smile, "I could see that your mind was elsewhere and figured that I would take advantage of the only time I could get you to the ground."

"Quite right. As you should have." Wil brushed the dust from his clothes. "Enough for today, I think, Hastian. We'll do more training tomorrow." Wil sheathed his sword. "No doubt, I'll be a bit stiff."

Hastian met Wil's eyes, the modest, self-congratulatory satisfaction still in his face, before he turned away, accepting the praise of the castle guard. A messenger boy came running to Wil as he was leaving the training ground, a note in his hands. Wil took the folded paper, rubbing it almost absentmindedly between his fingers. Once he was alone, leaning against the wall of a supply shed, he opened it between two of his fingers, staring at the words before him.

She had written in Imirillian.

"All the sands of Imirillia—" he breathed out. It was not in the formal Imirillian, used for philosophical and scholarly texts, with its stiff articles and rules, but rather the personal form, which is only used between friends or family or in a few conversations inside the Seven Scrolls. It moved him in that cursed way, where someone touches the center of your heart, not even knowing quite what they have done.

The note said that Eleanor wanted him to speak with Edythe, and her request was accompanied by a brief explanation and then by these words: "I realize you would prefer that I did not ask this of you, but I believe it would be of help. Thank you, Wil. Ever, Eleanor."

He disappeared into the travelers' house, where he washed, changed his clothing, and reread Eleanor's note, moving his thumb over her name before leaving the note lying on the bedside table.

"My sister said that you were the one who found Blaike's body," Edythe said pleasantly, as if she were asking about something Wil had found at a fair.

Wil sat on a chair, facing Edythe. He held both her hands in his, her knuckles white for how hard she held onto him. He had found her in the records hall, as he knew he would. Sunlight streamed throughout the hall, playing off the colors of the stained glass. The smells of paper and leather permeated the air. And her hands reminded him of Eleanor's.

"Yes." Wil gave an empty nod. "I did find his body."

Hesitating only a moment, Edythe responded. "Tell me what you saw, all the details. I want to know what I can of his death."

The image of Blaike's ghost-like face, stilled and frozen, crowded into Wil's mind. He looked reluctantly at Edythe.

"Are you quite certain?" Wil asked.

She nodded.

"I found his body near the seed hold in the far field," he said, continuing to hold Edythe's hands between his, focusing on them and not looking at her face. "It appeared he had been run down by a horseman who'd had a sword or a scimitar," he explained, pausing before continuing. "His stomach had been cut open, and then he had been stabbed through the ribs. I found him laying on his back, his hand covering his wounds, staring at the sky."

Edythe did not move for a long time, clasping Wil's hands, her head bent. Enough time passed for the shadows to rearrange themselves in the room. When Edythe did finally speak, her voice was soft.

"What was the look on his face?" she asked. "Was it only agony or was there any hope of peace?"

"I don't think he had much time for either," Wil admitted. "The second strike would have made his a relatively quick death." Then Wil changed the tone of his voice. "He spoke of you often, during the first time we arrived in Common Field. There was nothing he said that did not commend you in some respect, for your charm, your constancy, or your beauty. It was all I could do to not hear him continually say how much he wanted you to be his wife."

It was now that Edythe pulled back, as if her hands were stung by these words.

"Thank you, Wil," she said, "but I do not wish to speak of what will never be."

Eleanor called all men to Ainsley, and the fen companies arrived within the week. They came somber and uncertain, thinking, she assumed, of their lands and families back home. Rumors of her plan had circulated, but only those directly involved were privy to the details.

"They come with the hope they will never have to lift their swords, that Eleanor can save them," she'd heard Aedon say to Wil as they watched the men of Aemogen arrive.

If Wil had shown admirable leadership on the battle run, it was with even greater skill and direction that he now organized the camp. Eleanor received reports about Wil's efforts. Spreading the camp across the Ainsley downs, he had guided Gaulter Alden and Crispin in the placement of arms, tents, and training grounds. The blacksmiths continued to work day and night, making weapons and armor and whatever horseshoes that Sean needed, to prepare the cavalry.

In between giving attention to Crispin's exercises, Wil had worked with Aedon, training archers and overseeing the last of their arrow and bow production. She had noticed that their bond had solidified even stronger than Wil's easy friendship with Crispin. As the days passed, Wil and Aedon were seldom without each other's company, discussing, planning, and talking about life far beyond the threat of war. One night, a week before the march to the pass would begin, Eleanor called Aedon to her private quarters, and he sat next to her on the settee near the fire.

"You and Wil have been much together these last weeks," she said.

"Yes." Aedon played with a loose piece of braiding on the arm of the settee. "We have moved past our grudging friendship. In truth, I admire him immensely, and we've grown in confidence with each other."

Curious, Eleanor quizzed Aedon. "What is it you speak of?"

Aedon lifted one shoulder and looked at Eleanor. "I suppose we speak mostly of our different experiences and of our views on life, philosophy, and the like," he said. "He's a good man, underneath all those edges and flares."

"Does he ever ask about our plan to bring down the pass?" she asked.

"No," Aedon said, sounding almost defensive on Wil's behalf. "Quite the opposite. He eagerly avoids hearing anything of our plans. When a fen rider returns from the mines along the pass with a report, he disappears into camp."

Eleanor stood and began pacing the room. "I'm worried there's something we haven't considered in regards to bringing down the pass," she said.

"We've walked through our plan one hundred times over," Aedon answered practically.

"Then, indulge me once more," Eleanor said, gesturing with her hand. "First, the old mines that run through the cliff walls above the pass are almost finished being cleared and prepared. And ninety percent of all Aemogen's powder has been moved to High Forest fen—"

"Where it will be placed in the empty mines," Aedon continued for her. "Within nine days, they will have finished placing the powder throughout the shafts."

"If everything goes well," Eleanor nodded, "when we ignite the powder, it will cause the entire pass to crumble in on itself. It will be a full day before the Imirillians are set to invade."

"If everything goes well," was all Aedon replied.

"And Doughlas," she added. "In his last report, he has assured me that the tunnel of Colun Tir is cleared and safe."

"Yes."

"Good."

The Colun Tir was an ancient Aemogen fortress on the west side of the mountain range that separated Aemogen and Marion. It was forgotten by most, for it had only been used to house supplies for the Aemogen guard, stationed at the pass a handful of miles away. What was not known by most was that during the last wars between Marion and Aemogen, one hundred years before, a tunnel had been constructed through the narrowest point of the mountain, leading from the Maragaide Valley in Aemogen to the other side of the mountain, near the Colun Tir fortress, which looked over Marion.

This tunnel had served to smuggle men, weapons, and supplies between Aemogen and Marion without being detected. Its creation had been a long and arduous endeavor, claiming the lives of many who had worked to build the structure. But it had held firm and strong. Eleanor, like the monarchs before her, had kept its existence and location a secret, except from the few who were assigned to its maintenance, her most trusted councillors, and the fen riders.

"We will go through the tunnel," she reviewed aloud, "so that when the pass crumbles onto itself, we will be watching any movement of the Imirillian forces below the mountain, on the plain. Once we know that the Imirillians cannot come through, those of us at Colun Tir will return through the mountain tunnel, which will then be sealed off."

"*If* the tunnel should be sealed," Aedon ventured.

"Why would we keep it open?"

"Our contacts in Marion," he said.

"I know, but—" she said, deciding to change the subject. "Your man supervising the preparations in the mines—Tomas is his name, I believe—should we review his report for the day?"

Aedon looked at Eleanor with a funny expression. "We went over all of these details earlier today, Eleanor."

Taking exception to that comment, Eleanor responded tersely. "Are you accusing me of being too thorough? It's a bit rich coming from you."

Aedon raised an eyebrow and crossed his arms.

"I'm sorry," Eleanor said, sitting down. "I'm sorry, Aedon. It's just that—well, why couldn't I have thought of it sooner? The pass could be down by now, with our men back at home, readying themselves for the harvest, and the Imirillians stuck on the other side of the mountains."

"It's well you had the idea as early as you did," he said. "Come." He stood, catching Eleanor's hand and leading her towards the door. "Enough with the din inside your head," he added. "Our plan is well thought out. Lay your stress down for one hour while we go for a ride. You can see the encampment and fawn over Wil's wartime brilliance."

"I have never *fawned*," Eleanor disputed as he pushed her out the door.

Their last week in Ainsley went by fast. The men claimed they were ready to fight, but Eleanor knew that all their hopes were for the success of her plan. As Aemogen's tradition begged, they planned a large celebration—a dance—the night before the army would ride out to the pass. The thought of dancing did not bring Eleanor pleasure, but plans to gather marched forward regardless; her people believed in joy with their sorrow. Aside from the meetings of the council, where they did not discuss her plan, Eleanor had spoken with Wil only once during the week. She had come upon him in the Ainsley Gardens, now full of late summer color that only just hinted at an early fall.

"The gardens are closed to visitors at present," she said. She moved a basket full of cut flowers from one hand to the other as she stopped before him.

Wil greeted her and then added, "I'd like to think the queen would offer me hospitality."

"Perhaps," Eleanor said, looking up at his face. "I have not yet had a chance to thank you for speaking with Edythe. I don't know what you said, but I believe it was helpful."

Wil didn't look at Eleanor's face. "It was an honor to help Edythe," he responded. "And a pleasure to serve you while I still can." When he looked back at her, his eyes seemed distant. "I must confess, I'll miss Ainsley Rise. It's a place that does have a sense of home about it, doesn't it?"

"As a small child, I was afraid of it," Eleanor replied.

"You supposed it was haunted with one of your Aemogen ghosts?" he guessed.

"No." Eleanor shook her head. "When I was younger I had nightmares the walls would fall and I would never be able to find my way back to my parents."

As if what she had said was curious, Wil stared a moment at Eleanor, looking like he wanted to speak but then thought better of the idea.

"That was years ago," Eleanor said, brushing it off lightly. "I've not had dreams of anything crumbling for some time. Now it is the dearest place in the world to me. I miss it terribly when I'm away." She set her mouth in a line, then asked, "And what of your home?"

Wil's eyes froze, his hand moving toward his heart before it turned into a fist and dropped back to his side. "My relationships there are complicated, but"—Wil swallowed—"its beauty haunts nearly all my dreams, and waking is almost always a disappointment."

"Then, I hope you return again," Eleanor said, after a pause.

Wil would not look at her. "I should be getting back to the encampment."

"Yes."

He turned on his heel and left the garden. It was difficult for Eleanor to watch him, wondering if, when he left Aemogen altogether, he would be found in her dreams. Wondering if waking would be a disappointment.

"Have you spoken much with Wil?" Edythe asked later.

The question pulled Eleanor from her private thoughts, and she looked into the mirror, back at Edythe.

"No," Eleanor said. "We are both endlessly occupied in separate directions." Edythe watched Eleanor with obvious concern.

"What?" Eleanor asked.

"Nothing," Edythe said as she returned to the tuck she was altering in Eleanor's gown for the dance. "The two of you have been so remote with each other, I was just wondering if you had quarreled."

Eleanor opened her mouth, but no words came out. She brought her hand up to her chest, where, beneath her dress, the golden pendant hung. "Of course we haven't quarreled," she said.

"He watches you," Edythe explained. "At every evening meal, when you're busy speaking with those around you, he watches you."

"I, we—he doesn't watch me," Eleanor said, turning around in her chair to face Edythe. "He spends the entire time speaking with Aedon or you or Sean or whoever else is sitting beside him at the far end of the table."

"Just because you don't see it, doesn't mean—" Edythe began, but stopped herself. "He looks at you," she insisted. Then she added more hesitantly, "The way Blaike watched me."

Eleanor felt struck. "Nobody has ever looked at anyone the way Blaike looked at you."

Her sister's face paled, and Eleanor cursed herself for responding in such a way. Edythe pressed her pallid lips together and turned her attention back to Eleanor's dress.

In the silence, Eleanor looked at the ethereal white gown spread over her sisters lap.

"I read," Edythe had said a week ago, "that in the last battles, over one hundred years ago, the king rode out in all white as a symbol of his pure intent. And," she had added, "so must you." She had also insisted that Eleanor wear it at the dance.

So here they sat, in silence, while Edythe made a small adjustment, helping Eleanor dress for the night ahead.

"I'm sorry, Edythe," Eleanor said, moving her fingers along the chain that held Wil's pendant.

"No," Edythe replied, pulling hard on the thread. "I only think at least one of us should have happiness." She looked up. "Don't you?"

"And you think my happiness would be found with Wil?" Eleanor asked, not disbelieving her own words.

"You would tell me that it's a premature thought," Edythe admitted as she gathered the dress in her hands and stood. "But, Eleanor, I know you as well as anyone, and he suits you so perfectly that I hardly thought it possible. Now turn around so I can help you into your dress."

Eleanor did as she was told, her cheeks so pink from embarrassment that Edythe actually laughed for the first time in weeks. Slipping her dress off, Edythe then helped Eleanor step into the white gown. If she noticed the chain Eleanor wore, she didn't mention it. "You have complementary passions and humors," Edythe continued, "different enough to balance one another—"

"Or throttle one another."

"With—" Edythe continued, "enough similarities to understand where the other person is coming from."

"I don't understand where he comes from at all," Eleanor disagreed. "I know nothing of him. Well, that is not quite true, but your thought certainly is premature. And I, for one," Eleanor added, taking a gold belt from Edythe and cinching it around the waist of the white gown, "have never entertained the idea—seriously. More importantly, he only committed himself for the battle run. He is not planning to stay in Aemogen."

"When is he leaving?" Edythe asked.

Eleanor sat down, leaning her elbows against the dressing table before her, avoiding looking at herself in the mirror. "I haven't asked," she admitted as Edythe began to pin Eleanor's hair. "You think I should ask him to stay?" Eleanor looked at her sister's reflection, not certain she wanted to hear the answer.

Edythe sat down beside Eleanor. "Do what you will," she said. "But ask yourself if, when he is gone, you'll wish you had."

"I don't know him, Edythe," Eleanor said, voicing what she had thought multiple times. "Not who he really is. You can't think I would ever put a foreigner on the throne without gaining the utmost confidence in his character and in his regard for Aemogen."

"Then begin tonight."

It was a warm, almost humid late summer night, and Eleanor's dress clung to her. She moved a strand of stray hair, which was stuck against her neck, back into place. Thayne appeared at her side. In just a few minutes, they would descend into the square.

"It's a heartbreak to see Edythe in black," was all Thayne said.

They'd all gathered: the people of Ainsley, the people of the northernmost fens, and even many from the south. Thayne had returned again from Old Ainsley and would ride out with them in the morning. Eleanor asked if he would remain with her during the course of the evening. She amused him by claiming it was to keep her in line; she knew it was to underpin her courage.

"I saw Wil Traveler today," Thayne said, dropping his voice as he spoke, standing close to Eleanor. "He greeted me but appeared extremely agitated."

"Did he?" Eleanor straightened the Battle Crown on her head, shifting it slightly for more comfort. "We're all anxious for the coming days," she said, giving a possible explanation.

"Well," Thayne said, looking up as the doors opened. "You look lovely, in any case."

Several layers of the ethereal fabric rested just above Eleanor's feet, and the only adornments aside from the Battle Crown were the gold belt, tight about her waist, and Thayne's diamond earrings, bright in the torchlight.

The people were packed into Ceiliuradh. Night was hovering just outside the light of the square, and only a sliver of moon graced the dark sky. Musicians were tuning their instruments, torches were lit, banners lifted up. Sounding somber and hopeful, a cheer rushed towards Eleanor as they saw her on the stairs. She leaned on Thayne, her arm through his, and searched the faces below as they descended. Crispin stood, waiting at the bottom, ready to escort Eleanor to her makeshift throne, flanked with chairs for her council and the fen lords.

He cleared the way before her. "They've all come, Eleanor, thousands of them," Crispin yelled over the noise as he accompanied her to her throne. "Spilling down into the square in every direction," he added. Eleanor stepped up and half turned, looking out at the endless mill of people before her. Crispin, when he saw Eleanor's expression, rather unceremoniously kissed her on the cheek.

"You know you've just started a legion of rumors." Eleanor kissed Crispin in return before sending him out into the crowd. Thayne settled himself at Eleanor's right, while Edythe sat still in the chair to her left.

"Are you certain you want to lead out?" Eleanor asked her sister again.

"Yes," Edythe said. "I have my role to play, just as you have yours."

Eleanor swallowed and looked at the men and women taking their seats on the platform beside them—Gaulter Alden, Sean,

Briant, and the fen lords—gathering and discussing. She caught Thistle Black's eyes and gave him a somber nod.

Aedon had just come down the stairs, documents in hand, of course, reviewing something and paying little attention to the scene around him. Eleanor smiled, and then her eyes rested on Danth, Adams' son, the new fen lord of Common Field. He was sweating and seemed nervous, pulling at his formal coat with uncertainty. Perhaps feeling her gaze, Danth glanced at Eleanor. She nodded, and he raised his eyebrows in return, shrugging and forcing an unhappy, half-hearted smile. Then Danth looked away as if someone had called his name. A figure settled into the seat beside him, putting an arm around the young fen lord and bending in close to say something. It was Wil.

He was wearing clothing Eleanor had not seen before, perhaps brought along in his saddlebags and never worn: black—always black—but it was a jacket with a high, stiff collar and buttons running up the front, perfectly tailored to his form. His breeches matched, and the boots he wore were also black, well treated, and crafted better than any leather Eleanor had seen before. He was beautiful. As Wil moved, responding to something Danth had said, Eleanor saw that the high collar was trimmed in patterns of gold.

The music stopped, and the musicians, their instruments held at ready, turned to face Eleanor, waiting. Grabbing Edythe's hand for just a moment, Eleanor stood, and the night was stripped of any noise.

"A good evening to you all," Eleanor said, speaking loudly, brushing her fingers along the wood of her chair's arm for support. "As you know, tomorrow we will march down the pass in the hope our plan will succeed. We have prepared well, but I have also feared that we will not be enough on our own." A ripple of voices went through the crowd.

"I, as your queen, would call upon those ancestors who have lived in Aemogen to be with us," she continued. "I can only hope that they are aware. We also remember our fallen countrymen, our border guards, our friends from Common Field," Eleanor added, looking towards Danth. "And we dedicate our gathering this night to them."

She felt Thayne take her shaking hand in his as she looked out across the crowd of people. "I cannot say what the coming days will bring, but I can tell you this: I have loved my service to you as your queen, and I continue to pledge my life to your well being. May we all return home to the safety of those we love. May we secure Aemogen."

Their voices called out with approbation, and Eleanor motioned towards the musicians.

"You are certain you can do this?" Eleanor asked again after she sat down, leaning towards Edythe, whose wide blue eyes looked frozen. A small, nervous series of nods was all Edythe gave before stepping down from the platform onto the square.

People cleared a way, and Edythe walked to the center. Eleanor watched, her heart constricted, wishing she could have convinced her sister not to lead the traditional dance. Edythe paused in place, and the square went silent. Then a flute began to play the delicate Aemogen melody. Drums joined in, and, as another flute now rose with the first, Edythe began the lithe motions of Aemogen's most common ceremonial dance. She was delicate, graceful, as perfect in her motions as were the stars in the sky.

Eleanor had watched Edythe dance before but never in the shadow of such sorrow. It was a relief when, one by one, young women joined Edythe in the square, following her lead, until hundreds of them filled the square. On a signal from the musicians, the women paused, mid-motion, waiting with anticipation on their faces.

The drums beat louder and faster until, with a whoop, all the young men ran onto the square and stood before a partner. Edythe was easy to spot, the only girl in black, and Eleanor sat straight and stiff until she saw that Crispin had found Edythe. The violins began to carry a merry tune, and the couples began to dance in perfect synchronicity, their laughter and calls spilling over the square, until finally, as the drums beat even louder, the women ran from the dance floor.

The men, left alone, began to dance in strong and decisive movements, calling out several times in unison. The intensity of their movements matched the music, the drums building as the young women again found their partners on the floor. Then the melody broke above the drums, full and clear, and all the dancers turned their last and stopped.

The crowd of thousands cheered. The evening had officially begun.

"This is something you Aemogens do well," Thayne told Eleanor after several dances had passed.

"What is that?" Eleanor asked over the noise.

"You dance, you gather, despite sorrow, despite what is ahead." He waved a hand towards the festivities, and then added apropos of nothing, "I should have given them to you long ago, the earrings. They become you. To be honest, I'm not sure if you would have accepted them. I underestimated Wil's ability to convince you."

Eleanor moved her fingers along the edge of one of the earrings and looked back towards Danth, who was now sitting alone. A dance had just ended, and conversation filled the air as the square cleared, the people waiting to hear what the musicians would call out next.

It was then that she saw him, standing beside the lead musician, pointing to a sheet of music. With a nod from the violinist, Wil turned away from the musicians and walked in Eleanor's direction. His bearing was stiff, even distant, as he came towards her, having perfect posture and a sense of presence and dignity. When he stopped before Eleanor, bowed, and extended his hand, it was as if Eleanor were meeting a person she had never before seen.

"I offer the gift, Your Majesty, of a new dance," Wil said.

Eleanor almost recoiled—his manner felt so strange, and she was uncertain if he even saw her, or if he was looking past her— but Eleanor stood and stretched her fingers towards his, accepting his invitation. Wil's hand slipped around hers, and he led her to the center of the square in silence. She pressed his palm with her fingers: her way of asking what was wrong. He did not acknowledge the movement but brought Eleanor formally to a stop and turned to face her, standing quite close, waiting.

That Wil was not pleased was clear, but there seemed to be something else. Worry? Apprehension? She almost took a step back as she identified it. Disdain. He flicked his eyes towards the musicians, and they began to play. A paced and deliberate drum was soon joined by muted bells, ringing against a young musician's palm, and a violin, stretching over four haunting notes. All the while, Wil remained unmoving, his chin tilted high. Eleanor shivered involuntarily and looked away from his face. He held her right hand in his as if it were a foreign thing. Only as a low, clear flute began to play did Wil lift her hand towards him.

It was a haunting melody, striking Eleanor as a story she'd once heard and then forgotten. She knew the notes before they played yet was surprised with how they came together. Wil's movements were deliberate and slow, half-paced, so that she might follow. He stepped to the right, and Eleanor followed suit, stepping to his left. He moved towards Eleanor's left, and she to his right. In pattern with the drums, he released her hand, lifted his own, and clapped sharply to the side of his face. Eleanor mimicked his movements.

He repeated the steps, this time to her left, and she, in turn, stepped to his right. After repeating this twice, he raised her arm high above her head and led her in a circle: Wil remaining in the center with Eleanor revolving around him. They repeated these steps and increased in speed, now following the melody at the intended pace.

Wil led confidently, his movements controlled, watching her face all the while with a look she couldn't understand. A few times she had seen Wil dance and had thought him formal then, but it was nothing like the manner he now exhibited: stiff, straight, his eyes watching her, his chin tight, almost defiant. He released her hand and lifted his fingers to his palm in a clap, before stepping around her and clapping again. Eleanor followed. Then Wil lifted her right hand with his, leading her around again, and she spun beneath it. The music increased in speed and volume, and he dropped his hand to her waist, as they repeated the steps of the dance.

Other couples soon joined in, mimicking Wil and Eleanor, until the whole floor was filled. The melody still carried the dance, strong and strange, but familiar. Spell-like, Eleanor thought.

Each time the dancers lifted their arms to clap, it was like a whip, cutting through the music, beautiful, arched, harsh. All the strings had now joined in, building the flair of the melody, and the dancers responded. Eleanor was certain that the dance must be beautiful to watch, the movements being so intimate and strong between the women and the men, between her and Wil. She was so close to him, but he still kept her out.

As she turned, Eleanor saw Thayne, watching from the platform, standing with his eyes narrowed. She lost her view of him as other dancers moved before her, and then Wil lifted Eleanor's arm, spinning her around.

The instruments were reaching with great exertion, and Wil spun Eleanor faster and faster in the motion of the music. All the dancers, now confident in the steps, wove around one another. Eleanor felt her body follow Wil's. This dance was not like the native fluidity of her people, and Eleanor felt herself being carried away. But by what? The waves of the sea? A constant wind? Or, a desert in storm. Eleanor blinked and tried to pull her hand away, but Wil held on. The music increased, heading towards a finish, and she stared at Wil, wide-eyed. She did know this music, she realized, and the memory of it flooded her mind. She had played it as a child, when her mother had desired her to learn the Imirillian song sent down by her friend Edith from the court of Emperor Shaamil. The musicians played the final note, and the dancers spun to a perfect stop, their hands clasped above their heads, faces close together, breathing hard.

Eleanor caught her breath as she suddenly understood everything: the music, the questions, the careful narration of his past. Eleanor knew that she stared into the eyes of an Imirillian prince.

"Who are you?" she demanded, breathing hard, her face close to his. "Tell me!"

"Maydan dabyen veratym," he said. The words were soft, but

Eleanor had understood. In perfect Imirillian, Wil had said, "I have to go."

He was still holding her hand above her head. Eleanor slipped her fingers away from his and gripped his wrist.

"Guards!" she cried out.

Thayne was shouting as Wil gave Eleanor a last look, the corner of his mouth twitching as if in pain. Then, with a sharp twist of his wrist, he was gone. She could not hold him.

Hastian was at Eleanor's side in an instant, as was Aedon. The crowd on the dance floor disintegrated into confusion.

"Eleanor, what happened?" Aedon asked.

"Find him," she called. "Find Wil! He's a traitor."

"What happened, Eleanor?" Aedon asked again. "What did he say?"

Shouts of the search could be heard spreading down the stairs as guards raced into the torch-lit city. Eleanor stood, feeling stunned, listening to their calls, while the haunting melody of Imirillia played itself over and over in her head.

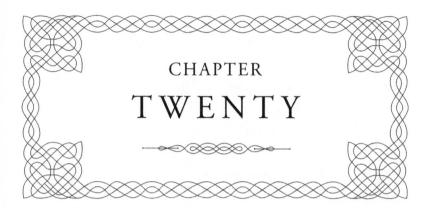

CHAPTER

TWENTY

The war council convened soon after Wil's disappearance. No one knew what to say. It had been a risk to trust him, something they had coolly calculated up front, and now, none of them believed it to be true. None of them had bothered, after the first few months, to check their attachment, Eleanor realized as she stared at the empty chair at the table.

"Why are you so insistent he's an Imirillian prince?" Aedon asked. "There is no sense in that. Surely, he was simply a soldier or a spy."

"I know who he is," Eleanor replied sharply. She was furious. "He is Prince Basaal, the seventh son of the emperor of Imirillia." The words choked in her throat.

Thayne joined Eleanor and her council, sitting pensively and listening.

After hearing Eleanor's suspicions, he lifted his hand to his chin. "You're right," he said. "I knew he was familiar to me—his eyes, that face—he is the son of my cousin, the Marion princess, Edith, third wife of Emperor Shaamil."

Thayne's confirmation cemented Eleanor's self-conscious rage. The afternoon that she had spent in his company, at the fortress of Anoir, where she had spoken so openly about Edith and her mother, flitted across her mind, and she blanched.

"It still makes no difference," Aedon answered pragmatically. "We took every precaution to keep any essential information from his knowledge, and he did not press it. He is a traitor," Aedon said, tilting his head and raising his eyebrows. "And if the queen's instincts prove correct, the possible leader of this entire invasion," he added. "It was a gamble that we took because, in one fashion or another, we would gain more than we lost. And we did. He prepared his enemy's army for war and prepared them well."

Eleanor knew what Aedon said was true. It made all rational sense, being the very argument she had presented six months previous. But the thought of Wil's intimate associations with her, with all of them, stung severely. She pulled at the chain around her neck.

"But he knows we are planning to bring down the mountain," Gaulter Alden pressed. "If the soldiers we dispatched cannot catch him—"

"They won't," Eleanor interrupted.

"Then he will move his army one day sooner," Gaulter Alden continued, "and we are finished."

"He won't," Eleanor said. "If there is anything that I do know about this *prince*, it is that his honor would not allow himself to use any information he might have gained to his unfair advantage." She stood then, taking a few steps back, gripping the back of her chair. "I could strangle him."

Late into the night, long after she should have been asleep, even long after a storm had rolled into Ainsley and began to pelt the windowpanes with rain, she finally allowed herself to admit what she had felt for Wil. But Eleanor refused to stay on this thought, moving past what it confirmed, back into her anger. She had used him, she decided, as he had used her.

It was all so very politick, she thought.

The soft, dismal rain greeted Eleanor's army the next morning as they prepared to move west. She was dressed in her white gown but wore a deep green cloak to keep dry. To the chagrin of the stable master—and the rage of Eleanor—Thrift was discovered to be missing from the stables. Wil, or rather, the Imirillian prince, had made use of Thrift's speed and nondescript coloring, leaving his own horse, Hegleh, eating contentedly in the stables. Eleanor decided to ride the white horse to war, in part practicality and in part revenge.

Now, as her army moved out of Ainsley, Eleanor focused only on what was ahead. They would bring down the mountains, and her people would be protected from the invading force that threatened her country. They would then go to whatever lengths necessary to ensure that Aemogen was insulated from the hungry powers of the continent. She determined to do the same for her heart.

As the soldiers of Aemogen continued to march, Eleanor's resolve on behalf of her people grew. It was late when they stopped for the day. The rains continued on, but the men settled themselves in as best they could. As Eleanor lay alone in her tent that night, she again found herself awake, fighting the misery that plagued her in the darkness. When she did sleep, she dreamed he was next to her, and she had dismissed something that he said with a shake of her head but had smiled at him all the same. His company had felt sure, and she had turned towards him with a question.

Then Eleanor woke with a start. A lightning flash filled the tent, and she saw the silhouette of a man standing before her. She cried out, jumping to her knees, but the flash came again, and no one was there. Eleanor knelt, frozen on her cushions, wide-eyed and gasping for breath. No one had heard her scream, for the storm was too loud, but her heart pounded fiercely.

She cursed herself and fought back the warm tears, angry at herself for wishing she had Wil at her side as they were marching into war. Angry at herself that she still wore his pendant around her neck. As she lay back down and covered herself with blankets, she cursed him; with all the pain in her heart she cursed his path.

"How can it be?" Eleanor cried to Aedon in dismay, disbelieving what he had said. "How could the rain have damaged the powder to such a degree?"

After three days of marching, they had arrived, and the cliffs of Aemogen pass stood tall before Eleanor and her men. The news, when they had arrived, had rattled Eleanor's already damaged spirits.

"The rain these three days has been relentless," Aedon answered, after conferring with the High Forest miners, who were responsible for orchestrating the powder lines through the abandoned mines. "It has waterlogged the mountains, causing parts of several tunnels to collapse. We are lucky that it did not ignite a spark and send half of the mountain down on itself already, without enough powder to finish the job," he explained. "The miners have been working tirelessly, but it is a dangerous proposition. Almost all the powder we have is trapped up there in those mines."

"We must close off the pass," she said, her voice sounding frayed. "To fight is impossible!"

"Steady, Eleanor," Aedon said, grabbing her shoulder. "You are speaking from fear. We'll go back to camp and think—this is your strength. Let us use it."

Eleanor closed her eyes. "I will speak with Tomas and the other miners directly, Aedon, to know the extent of the damage. Perhaps it will only take a few hours to resolve, and we will be ready to bring this mountain down tomorrow, as planned."

They rode back towards the miners' camp, which was set up a safe distance from the pass. They gathered together in council with the men of each mine. Thistle Black was there, displeased and none too quiet regarding his disapproval of how High Forest had operated things. Then Tomas stepped forward, mud beneath his boots, brushing the rain from his face as he addressed Eleanor, her council, and the miners.

"We all know that some of the tunnels have been damaged—a sheer miracle that the mountain has not already blown," Tomas said, looking harried. "Which could also indicate significant water damage to the powder. There are only a few barrels left that have not already been placed in the mines, and we need to use them in the most effective way possible. The Imirillian army is set to attack tomorrow," he said. "So, we'll need to be quick about what we try to do. Who has an idea?"

They all stood silent. It had been such a brazen plan, dangerous, almost mad, Eleanor realized. One spark and half the mountain could have come down on itself.

"Can we clear the tunnels?" a man asked.

"Not enough time," Tomas replied, "and using a shovel with all that powder underneath would be a death wish."

"Is there no way to connect the tunnel around the rubble with the powder that remains?" another miner asked.

"It may have once been possible," Tomas conceded. "But now, there isn't time."

"Exactly how many barrels can still be placed?" a man from Quickly fen asked.

"Ten," Thomas said. "We packed the tunnels with almost everything we had."

"Then, let's try and connect the lines with the remaining powder," came the shout.

"Don't be idiots," Thistle Black said. He had finally stopped grumbling quietly to speak aloud. "We could use those ten barrels to better advantage if we increased our area of impact."

"What do you mean?" Aedon asked.

"Don't just blow up the cliffs from the inside," Thistle Black explained. "There is ample powder there already. We need to place the remaining barrels at the base of the cliffs for additional impact."

"But we have to be able to light the powder without killing a dozen miners," Tomas replied. "And there are pockets of powder that are now isolated inside the mines because of the internal rock slides. The only openings are too small for a man. We need a way to ignite them."

"Well, if I didn't have a way to do both, I wouldn't have spoken up now, would I?" Thistle Black shouted, leaving the group and walking towards his own supply wagons. Eleanor waited with the other men for him to return. When he did, he carried a long spool of what appeared to be rope.

"We've been using this technique at South Mountain fen," he explained. "It's a rope that we run from the powder towards a safer location, where we can light it on fire."

"We've experimented with that before," Tomas said. "The flame doesn't always make it to the powder, and we have such long distances to cover that it'd be impossible. I still can't see how we're going to light the powder without men willing to do it themselves."

"You've tried it before, yes," Thistle Black said. "But not with rope steeped in South Mountain pitch." He looked around the circle. "We can string this rope far, and it will catch fire, running all the way up the damaged tunnels if we're careful how we thread it through. We have a way to finish this job, we just need the time."

"We have the rest of the day," Aedon said, "then first light to-morrow morning, to use the daylight pouring naturally into the shafts."

"Is there no way to work through the night?" Crispin asked, who had sat silent with Eleanor and the other councillors.

The miners all laughed darkly.

"Only if you want to blow yourself up," Thistle Black replied.

"Then let's get this job done," Tomas said, with a confident nod. "We'll need all the willing men experienced with handling the powder," he said, then turned to Thistle Black. "We will follow your lead."

The war council left Tomas and the miners to their long day of work and rode back to the army camp between the pass and the Maragaide valley. The camp consisted of just over three thousand soldiers. Crispin apprised them of the situation, of their

race against time, warning the men to be ready for battle if needs
be. The atmosphere was heavy and sober, and the rain, although
reduced to a drizzle, did not help the morale.

Doughlas was waiting there for Eleanor with three of her
riders. "I've pulled together the fen riders," he reported seriously,
"and given them posts. Some are at the head of the pass; others,
throughout the valley. We four will come with you through the
tunnel to Colun Tir, so you'll be able to get a message through the
mountain as fast as humanly possible."

"Good," Eleanor said, and she put her hand on his shoulder.

Gaulter Alden, Aedon, and Eleanor prepared to leave for
the tunnel of Colun Tir, along with fifty mounted cavalry that
Crispin had handpicked. Crispin would wait in the valley with the
Aemogen army, ready to lead the soldiers should Eleanor's plan
fail. When Eleanor said good-bye to Crispin, they gripped one
another like siblings, not daring to make promises that all would
be well.

———◦◦◦◦◦◦◦———

Eleanor and her company left just after midday. The entrance was
in the high woods beyond the Maragaide valley, several miles from
the encampment. The ride was uncomfortable and hot now that
the rain had stopped, the clouds breaking to let the late summer
sun through. Eleanor's Battle Crown bit into her head, pinned
securely in place. They were all quiet, especially Aedon, and only
the steady beats of hooves against the earth and the clanging of
metal against itself could be heard.

Doughlas led the company to the tunnel's entrance, hidden
behind a large outcropping of rock and the dense foliage of the
foothills. There, Gaulter Alden set up several guards and one fen

———◦◦◦◦ 318 ◦◦◦◦———

rider to wait for their return or be ready for any messages from the Colun Tir.

After resting their horses and giving them a long drink in a stream near the entrance, Doughlas led them into the tunnel. Eleanor turned and looked at the green of the Aemogen woods before she disappeared into the darkness. A fen rider was leading Hegleh and Hastian's horse behind them, for Hastian walked beside Eleanor, carrying a torch, his hand on her arm.

"They will bring it down." He cleared his throat after he said the words.

Eleanor almost didn't recognize his voice, for she never expected to hear it. "I believe they will, if only they can have enough time."

"From what I know of the Aemogen miners, they will do as you have asked," he said.

Eleanor glanced at his face. He was so much younger than she remembered. Perhaps Aedon's age? Or a year or two younger? Being with Hastian was akin to breathing for Eleanor: always there, always sustaining, but when does one ever stop to consider it? She knew his presence far better than his face.

"My father," Hastian continued in an effort to explain, "was a miner at Quickly."

"I did not—" Eleanor began, feeling embarrassed. "I had not remembered that you were from Quickly."

Hastian nodded and spoke no more.

With torches lit, the company moved forward. Fifty feet into the tunnel, a solid reinforced door was built into the stone. Eleanor's father had replaced the door's lock and hinges during his reign. Doughlas had the key and stepped forward, opening it, leading the company into the tunnel.

"It's a fairly even go," Crispin instructed. "There's a little up and a little down, but we've cleared and reinforced the sore spots. Don't leave your mount and don't shout," he added. "In a few hundred yards, there will be more space to ride most of the way through."

Eleanor felt as if it should have taken longer, this journey through the mountain. The stories told of the endless darkness and the waiting, but the day had burned away despite the blackness of the journey. They were making good time, and Doughlas had placed several strips of yellow cloth to mark the path.

"There are ten strips, evenly spaced, along the way," he told them. "Count them as you go, and we'll soon be at Colun Tir."

Gaulter Alden rode without complaint, but Eleanor knew that he was not well. The battle run had taken any reserves his body had carried. He hunched, looking uncomfortable in his saddle, counting the strips of cloth religiously, as if forgetting to take note of even one might send him back to the beginning, when he was so doggedly determined to reach the end.

Halfway through, the company dismounted in one of the larger caverns. Bread and cheese were rationed out, and Eleanor settled herself next to Gaulter Alden, who had managed to find himself a dry place to sit, against the wall. They ate in silence. But after he had eaten a small portion of his meal, he turned his head to Eleanor.

"I have always desired to die in a place where Elaine could find me," he said. Eleanor felt the hairs on the back of her neck stand up, and she placed a hand over his.

"Are you unwell, Pappe?" she asked. It was a nickname she had given him when she was a young child and had thought Gaulter

Alden was her grandfather. His face lit up in recognition of the name, and he moved his other hand to cover hers.

"I am too old to learn a new career," he said. "A war leader who has never killed a man?" He looked up and chuckled. "You must promise me to end this warfare soon enough. I have not the strength to see it through much longer."

"I should have made you stay behind," Eleanor admitted. "But I'm glad to have you with me."

"I am glad you made no such request," he said. "I am not certain if I would have had the courage to say no."

━━◦━◦◉◎◉◦━◦━━

The woods were enveloped in night when they reached the western door of the tunnel. Scouts were sent out into the darkness. They returned within the hour, reporting that all was clear. Eleanor followed Aedon and Doughlas, slipping out a door set inside the mountain crag, where it would remain unseen from the woods. Night air filled her lungs, and she breathed deeply, a relief after the hours in the cave.

Quietly, without torches, they picked their way down to Colun Tir. It was a beautiful fortress, resting but a few miles away from the Aemogen guard post at the mouth of the pass. The soldiers lived in comfortable accommodations below and used Colun Tir as storage more than anything. An old, overgrown road was all that connected the two.

The stables lay near the back, unkempt but usable. Eleanor checked to see that Hegleh was being looked after, and then she entered the fortress. They still did not light any torches, which would have been seen for miles in the Marion valley below. Open windows of hewn stone allowed a sliver of moonlight to guide

Eleanor and her company.

She walked through the main hall—the scuttle of mice underscoring the darkness of the rooms—and went up a set of stairs until she came out onto the large tower on the front of Colun Tir. Doughlas, Aedon, and a few others already stood at the battlements. When Eleanor came up behind them, she gasped.

There, across the valley, settled upon a rise, like glittering ornaments, were hundreds if not thousands of fires. Men could be seen moving about; the faint sounds of horses heard, settling themselves. The metallic rattle gave every indication that a great host was preparing for war. All of the men on the tower turned to look at Eleanor as she pressed her hands against the stone of the battlements.

"This only confirms what we've already known," Eleanor said once she had found her voice, digging into whatever confidence she found there. "The miners won't fail."

She could not see Aedon's face in the darkness, but the way he shifted on his feet was signal enough; he too wanted to believe the miners would see it through.

A messenger was sent down to the guard at the pass, seeking reports of the army that lay far afield. Thousands of cavalry, archers, and well-trained soldiers waited, feeling anxious and, most likely, bored. Eleanor listened without speaking, then watched the far-off fires for hours. The night wore on, and she tried to sleep atop a few blankets and bags of half-used provisions, but any sleep that came was sheared off by vivid dreams, leaving Eleanor sitting up, her heart racing.

She returned to the tower. Hastian roused himself and followed. Fewer fires burned in the silence that now pervaded the valley. Eleanor wrapped her cloak close around her and sat on the cold floor, leaning her head against the crumbled stone on the inside of the embrasure, watching the fires in the distance.

Instead of standing back, like a shadow, Hastian again settled himself near the queen, his back against the wall, looking up into the sky rather than at the Imirillian encampment.

"Tomorrow at this hour, we will know our fate," Eleanor said to the quiet guard. "We will be safe back in Aemogen." She had hoped these words would feel like a prophecy, rolling over her lips. But they didn't settle; they didn't feel certain. Aedon had once explained that an archer could feel the integrity of his arrow when it was released from his bow. She did not feel that surety when she thought of what lay ahead.

"May I ask you a question, Your Majesty?" Hastian's words were almost unintelligible.

"Yes," Eleanor replied, turning her head towards him, staring at the shadows of his face.

"Do you think about Wil Traveler—I mean, the Imirillian prince?" Hastian asked.

Eleanor pulled her arms tighter around her.

"It's only this," Hastian continued. "I can't reconcile the man in my mind. I feel divided about who he truly is."

"Yes," she said. "I've had the same thoughts."

Hastian stood, the moonlight catching the uncertain set of his mouth, and withdrew to the shadow of a nearby archway. Eleanor closed her eyes and focused on her breath leaving her lungs. She did think about Wil. The first thought in her mind, after she had seen the breadth of the Imirillian army, was to wonder where he was.

⸺⊰⊱⊰⊱⸺

All morning, Aedon stood with his head bent and arms crossed, watching his boots. Gaulter Alden sat watching the army organize across the plain. The guard at the pass had been called up, bringing their horses and supplies with them, leaving nothing behind. Eleanor was pacing, alternating between looking west towards the Imirillian army and looking south towards the pass. No sound of explosion had yet been heard.

The soldiers in Eleanor's company stood ready and anxious. Scouts came back from the woods about Colun Tir, reporting no unusual activity. The Imirillians did not know that they were there. Still, Eleanor's lungs tightened every time someone came back up the road. She still wore her white dress but had removed the Battle Crown for the night. It remained with her cloak on a barrel in the storeroom where she'd slept.

"Something must have gone wrong," Gaulter Alden said, at length. "They should have lit the powder by now."

"It has only been light for a few hours," Aedon said. "Give the men time."

"Whatever time we have to give, I'll give gladly," Gaulter Alden replied with an edge. Aedon glanced at the old man but said no more. Eleanor walked past them to the battlements. The preparations of the Imirillian army had begun at first light: men gathering into companies, horses readied, soldiers dressed in black and red. The army stretched wide across the valley floor. But up until this moment, no movement suggesting battle had been seen.

Then the chilling sound of a trumpet split the morning air. It was distinct and clear, and it called forth a dread so strong that Eleanor began to shake. A large rumble of voices came from across the valley and crashed into the mountain. Those at Colun Tir were silent. The Imirillian army was marching.

Aedon exchanged a grim look with Eleanor and shook his head. He sent a soldier to ready the queen's horse. "Only as a precaution," he said firmly, when Eleanor offered him a sour expression.

The army began moving across the plain towards the pass.

"How long will it take them to arrive at the mountain?" Eleanor asked aloud.

"Two hours," Aedon guessed. "Or less. Those miners had better see this through, or all hell will be upon us. What a godless sound it is," he finished, watching the army marching.

As the slow wave of Imirillians advanced, Eleanor and her company waited for the explosion.

It did not come.

The morning shadows shortened, clinging tighter to the rocks and trees, and the heat of the day began to rise. Time was passing faster than Eleanor thought possible.

"We have to stall," Aedon said, his fists clenched.

"Any ideas on how we can do that?" Eleanor asked as she looked around.

"Surrender?" Gaulter Alden replied.

They both twisted, looking back to where Gaulter Alden sat. "If we do not bring down the mountain," he explained. "I can see no other way. If it's not too late—"

"They *will* bring down the mountain!" Aedon said as he rounded on the old man, his face set in anger. "The miners will see it done. Our job is to give them time."

Eleanor reached her hand out, gripping Aedon's arm while her heart jumped. "Let them think we've surrendered." She took a breath and looked Aedon square in the eyes. "We will send a dispatch to plead surrender. They will hold the leaders of the Imirillian army long enough for the miners to bring down the mountain."

"That could work," Aedon said, covering his face with his hands momentarily. He sighed and looked back to Eleanor. "That could work. We must decide what soldiers to send, for they will not make it out alive."

This reality hit Eleanor like a stone. She stared from Aedon to Gaulter Alden.

"I don't—" she said. Eleanor's mouth opened again. "How can I—?"

Gaulter Alden lifted his stiff body, a mournful expression on his face. "I am your war leader, Your Majesty, no matter how deficient. I will select the soldiers." He disappeared into the tower.

Eleanor's heart thudded as she followed him with her mind, down the stairs, into the courtyard. There would be the selection of soldiers, an order to bring their mounts, a somber explanation of what their queen was asking of them.

"What have I done?" she whispered.

"You've thought of a way to save your people," Aedon said. His sharp voice held little comfort.

Eleanor was glad she could not look at the four young men who now mounted their horses and rode away from Colun Tir, for she knew that she could not take the risk of recognizing their faces.

As the sound of the small company's hoofbeats faded over more and more distance, Eleanor rested her hands on the battlement and leaned forward, feeling sick. "The mountain must come down," she repeated, over and over, until she realized she was only muttering, her lips moving, her fingers gripping the stone as she waited for the explosions.

Nothing.

"There they are," Aedon said, and Eleanor's head shot up, her eyes searching over what she could see of the plain. The four soldiers had just broken the edge of the woods, moving towards the Imirillian army. They had hoisted an empty grain sack onto a pole, and Eleanor brought her hand to her mouth, watching as the soldiers rode with full speed towards the army amassed before them.

The morning sun glinted off their armor, their banner flung about in the wind as if it wanted to hurl itself away from the soldiers. The leaders of the Imirillians made a motion and, to Eleanor's dismay, archers began shooting at the Aemogen emissary.

An arrow hit the horse of the lead rider, and it collapsed, throwing the Aemogen soldier to the ground before rolling over him. The soldier lay still, unmoving, as more arrows flew, and two more riders fell to the earth. Another horse went down, then the third. The fourth soldier had turned and was running his horse back towards the pass, when an arrow caught him in the back. He arched, throwing his hands up, as he fell from his horse and crumbled to the ground.

Behind her, Eleanor heard Hastian's sharp intake of breath.

The army began to move forward once more.

Aedon met her eyes and then waited as Eleanor looked away from the soldiers, staring at the vast army on the plain. She tried to ignore all emotion, forcing the valley below to become a chessboard, and Eleanor tallied her pieces, thinking through what she must do, unwilling to sacrifice all of Aemogen because her spine was too caught up in her heart. She had her entire army, just up the pass, and many others waiting, helpless in the fens across

Aemogen.

"We will send another emissary," she said. "If we do not hear an explosion, we will send another emissary and try again."

Aedon nodded.

Time passed, and still no sound came down from the mountain.

"Do the miners have instructions to see it done, regardless of what else happens?" Eleanor asked Aedon.

"They won't stop," Aedon answered. "They'll see it done, unless the Imirillians stop them first."

When the army was past the midpoint of the valley, Eleanor ordered the second emissary, only to watch as they suffered the same results: each soldier killed by an arrow before he could reach the Imirillian line.

"What will make them stop!" Eleanor pounded her fist against the stone. "What can we do, Aedon?"

"I don't know," he said. "Something that will surprise them, catch them off their guard." Aedon began to pace, biting his fingernails. "We have, including the guard from the pass, close to one hundred soldiers. Could we draw the army aside, into the woods?"

"No." Eleanor shook her head. "They would only send a company to kill us all. There must be *something* that would make them pause or make them hesitate." She grabbed Aedon's arm as he walked past. "Wil is down there," she said. "What would make him stop?"

"I—I don't know."

The early afternoon sun had just hit Colun Tir, and Eleanor blinked it away, looking across the valley. She thought of Wil. She thought of the sun. And then, she thought of the moon.

"Seraagh," Eleanor said to herself. "Seraagh! I have it Aedon!"

Eleanor spun and ran into the tower. Hastian followed, then Aedon. "Give the Battle Crown to Edythe," she called over her shoulder. "I have it!"

"What are you talking about?" Aedon demanded. "Eleanor!"

"Don't you see?" Eleanor said, almost giddy as she flew down the stairs and across the dust-filled hall. "*And Seraagh, clothed in white, rode her fair horse above the earth to fulfill every command of the Illuminating God.* Aedon!" she called back. "The scripture says that she reflects his glory, aflame and alight."

Aedon ran past Hastian and caught Eleanor's arm just as they burst into the courtyard. "Eleanor, what are you talking about?" he demanded.

"Aedon." Eleanor was out of breath. "I am riding out to meet them."

"No! No!" Aedon was shouting as Eleanor sprinted towards Hegleh, who, thanks to Aedon's orders, was mounted and waiting for her. "Eleanor, you can't go down there," Aedon said. "They will kill you!"

"They will not expect a woman," Eleanor shouted back at him. "Wil, or Basaal, or whoever he is, will command them not to shoot. I can buy our miners the time they need to bring down the pass!" she explained. "The queen is the most powerful piece on the board. Don't you see?"

"No!" Aedon said, reaching Eleanor and pulling her away from her horse. Hastian was at his heels. Gaulter Alden had also come into the stable yard, as had the other soldiers. Aedon turned Eleanor around by her shoulders. "You can't do this!" he yelled at her face. "You will die. Eleanor, I won't let you!"

"There's no other option!" she screamed back. "It's the best chance we have. If I can send my soldiers to war, I can send myself. They will think I am Seraagh."

"Who is Seraagh?" Aedon shook her. "You have gone completely mad!"

"She's the messenger angel of the Imirillian god. She wears white, she rides a white horse—it's a story they *all* know!" Eleanor broke free of Aedon's grasp and pulled on the ribbon that kept the braid in her hair. "They will not shoot Seraagh."

"I will ride," Aedon said desperately, shaking her shoulders. "I will ride before the army."

"They would kill you, Aedon," Eleanor replied, catching Hegleh's reins from a stunned soldier. "They will not expect me."

Hastian moved past Aedon and stood before Eleanor. "I can't let you go," Hastian said.

"You will," Eleanor flared at Hastian. "That's a direct order, which you have sworn to never disobey. You must help me see this through. It is a way I can defend my people." Hastian looked as if he would cry, but after a moment of his eyes searching hers, he nodded and helped Eleanor mount the large horse.

"Are you a fool?" Aedon shouted, pushing past Hastian, trying to block Eleanor's way. But Hastian pulled Aedon back, tossing him to the ground, and Eleanor cried out, urging Hegleh forward, flying towards the road leading down the mountain to the plain below.

As Eleanor rode, her hair worked itself loose of its braid, whipping around her face. The fabric of her white dress flew wildly behind her, her golden belt flashing in the sun. She had never ridden so fast in her life—her knuckles were white around the reins. Eleanor leaned forward, pulling her face close against Hegleh's neck, shouting the white horse on, the wind ripping at her ears.

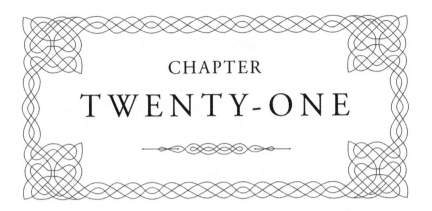

CHAPTER
TWENTY-ONE

Prince Basaal heard screaming in the woods.

He'd left Refigh tethered some distance out and worked his way toward the sound. An old keep came into view, and he could see soldiers moving about the battlements. The screaming stopped, then the sound of a horseman galloping away filled the space. Basaal moved closer as his eyes followed the north wall of the fortress towards higher ground. He could hear more shouting and the sounds of a scuffle. Strange, he thought, for the shouting had sounded like Aedon.

Creeping over a moss-covered crumble of stone, Basaal pressed his back to the wall of the keep itself. He waited, hearing only more arguing. He needed to know what the Aemogens were about, for he wouldn't risk having his soldiers in the pass when they brought down the mountain. So, he had reconnoitered the mouth of the pass and had seen nothing. He hadn't risked going farther and was about to return to his men. Then he had seen a quick shine that caught on his instinct, and, leaving his horse in the woods, he had worked his way toward it, finding the keep. Twice, while moving through the woods, he had heard a company ride out, and both times he had pulled himself into the shadows, curious what Aemogen soldiers would be about in this part of the mountain. Wondering what their actions might be able to tell him.

Now Basaal questioned whether he would be able to learn anything, skulking around the edges of the moss-covered keep. He had waited in watch far longer than he knew to be wise. He didn't even know who was in there. Tapping the wall behind him with his fingers, Basaal decided to leave.

Just as he began to step away from the keep an arm reached around his chest and pulled him back against the wall. Basaal's first reaction was to grab a small dagger from his belt as he spun towards his attacker, only to be smashed in the face with a large rock just after his dagger found its mark.

"Wake up!" someone yelled as he was kicked again in the gut. "Wake up you coward!"

Basaal shook his head and moved from the haze of his thoughts. His hands were bound behind him.

"Get up!" Water came down on Basaal's head, and he flinched from the cold, trying to open his eyes. Basaal's face hurt, and he was dizzy.

Then someone grabbed his shirt and half dragged him until he was forced against a stone wall.

"There she is on the plain!" he heard someone shout. Several people moved towards the battlements, and Basaal blinked a few more times, trying to focus his eyes. Aedon was crouched over him, his face so full of rage, Basaal hardly recognized the councillor. Once their eyes met, Aedon jerked Basaal to his feet and forced him to the battlements.

"You coward!" Aedon yelled at him. "You're not even down there to save her."

"Save who?" Basaal said as he found his words. His lip hurt like the devil, and it was bleeding.

"Eleanor!"

"What?" Basaal asked as he shook his head and looked down the mountain. There, a rider all in white, was racing towards the advancing Imirillian army. He could see her copper hair flying as she raced. His heart jumped, and the fog dropped away from his mind.

"What is she doing!" Basaal demanded as he leaned forward against the battlement. "Is she mad?"

"You shot down our emissaries of peace," Aedon snarled.

"We did?" Basaal cursed. He could see that his archers were again lifting their bows. Aedon tore himself away from the battlement, unable to watch.

"Please, Annan, please. Please, Annan," Basaal muttered to himself under his breath, willing his second in command not to shoot. Gaulter Alden was standing close by, his hands shaking as he leaned against the wall. Hastian was also there, and not himself, his eyes rimmed red, pacing as he watched. Prince Basaal moved his eyes back to Eleanor. Closer and closer she came, a flash of white rushing to meet the endless sea of black and red. The archers were still poised, trained on Eleanor as she raced forward. Basaal's entire chest constricted, and then, he blew his breath out slowly. "They won't shoot," he said. "They would have done so by now."

Eleanor had slowed to a near stop, and a rider on a black horse came out to meet her. "It's Annan," Basaal said, closing his eyes in relief. "He will not kill Eleanor until he speaks with me."

Aedon was sweating. He wiped his arm across his forehead and steadied himself against the wall. After several deep breaths, he opened his eyes and looked at Basaal.

"You have to let me go," Basaal said. "There are men down there who won't hesitate—"

Aedon walked towards him, grabbing his collar, and forcing Basaal backwards, until he was slammed hard against the stone wall of the fortress. Basaal's head cocked back, a flash of pain crossing behind his eyes. He shook his head, trying to see clearly. "Aedon, please—" he said.

"What are you doing here?" Aedon demanded.

"I came up, scouting to see what had become of the guard at the pass, before sending my men through."

"Liar," Aedon said. "Why didn't you, a prince, send out a real scout?"

"Because," Basaal said, spitting blood from his mouth, "if you were still planning on bringing down the mountain, I didn't want my men killed in the act."

"You could have sent anyone to find that out," Aedon pressed.

"Not if I did not want them to know what you were planning to do," Basaal replied hotly.

Aedon took a step back from Basaal and looked toward Gaulter Alden.

"They're taking the queen back towards their camp," Hastian called out. Aedon and Basaal both looked back at the plain to see Eleanor, surrounded by a company of soldiers on black horses, riding west.

"That's Drakta, my father's war leader, and his men," Basaal said, spitting again. "Aedon, you have to let me go. He is a man with no scruples. Eleanor isn't safe with him."

"We will let you go in trade for Eleanor," Aedon said, his jaw working back and forth.

"There's not time for that," Basaal said, and he tried to move his arms, shaking them in frustration when he could not work them loose. "The Imirillian army does not swap hostages," he explained hastily. "It would be a trap. They would not keep their word."

"Surely, your father would agree to—" Aedon began.

"My father is in Zarbadast," Basaal said, his frustrations exacerbated. "I lead this conquest."

Silence hovered around Basaal, and he could feel all of Aemogen's anger against his back.

"Then the price on your head," Aedon disputed, "is all the more valuable."

"I'm not lying, Aedon, when I tell you that they will have their way with Eleanor," Basaal said. "My second in command, Annan, can keep her alive. But Drakta and his men will be speaking with the queen. You must let me go, and I will see her safely home to Aemogen, somehow."

Gaulter Alden pulled Aedon aside and began talking quietly. He motioned several times towards the pass and then back at Basaal.

After a few minutes, Aedon nodded, responding to Gaulter Alden in a harsh tone before he walked over to Basaal, taking him none too gently by the arm. "Come with me," he said. Aedon led Basaal into a room inside the hold and pushed him towards the corner.

"Did I kill him?" Basaal asked, lifting his shoulder, attempting to wipe the blood from his lip. "Who was it?"

"What are you talking about?" Aedon demanded.

"The guard who caught me unawares just now. Did I kill him?"

"No," Aedon scowled. "It was Duncan. You caught his shoulder pretty good though."

Basaal made an effort not to show his relief, but Aedon discerned it.

"What are you about, Wil?" Aedon challenged. "Or Basaal, whoever you are."

Basaal licked the blood from his lip and looked back at Aedon. "I'll tell you honestly, a flat answer, but you have to promise that you will consider releasing me so I can help Eleanor."

"Talk," Aedon said, sounding more like his levelheaded self.

Then a sound, like Basaal had never experienced, shook the mountain: thunder come from earth, rumble after endless rumble. Every other sound of collapse Basaal had ever heard before this now seemed a pathetic tinker compared to the deep baritone of the mountain being rocked.

Basaal stumbled to his knees and looked toward Aedon, whose face had collapsed in relief. The councillor fell the ground, shaking. "They did it," Aedon said as he closed his eyes and repeated the words over and over to himself. "They did it. They did it."

Basaal used his elbow to right himself, hissing at the pain, as he laughed out loud.

—◦◦◦◦◦◦◦—

The sound of the tumbling cliffs still reverberated through Eleanor's tired body. Although the collapse was several hours past, she played it over and over in her head to help her believe that it was indeed true. The Imirillian army would not be marching into Aemogen.

The relief of it was so thick that she didn't feel she cared what happened, until a familiar voice shook her from her private victory. Prince Basaal was just outside the elegant tent, where she had been tied to a chair with a gag placed in her mouth. As his voice continued in low conversation, Eleanor sat up straight, trying to twist her bound wrists into a more comfortable position. It wasn't working.

The tent flap was pulled back, and Prince Basaal entered, a fierce scowl on his face.

"Your Majesty," he growled in Imirillian while walking over to a table and pouring himself a drink. After downing the contents of the cup, he refilled it and turned towards Eleanor. "May I get you something?" The offer held a tinge of relief that did not match his face. His lip was swollen, split through, as if he had been in a fight. There was also a discolored cut beneath his eye. "Well?" Eleanor eyed the food on the table a moment before shaking her head. Seeing him made her too anxious to eat.

"They tell me you've been here for hours," he said. "Which must have been a trial for you, considering no reading material was provided." A mean smile tilted on his face. "Desperation makes fools of us all, doesn't it? Had I known you were so hungry for my company, I could have arranged for it," he added, flippantly.

Eleanor's eyes burned. What astounding arrogance.

"Of all the stupid—" Basaal muttered in the Aemogen language as he slammed his cup on the table, his familiar anger coming through. At least, Eleanor thought, she knew his temper had been authentic. He walked towards her, placing his hands on the arms of her chair, leaning down until his face was right before hers.

"Eleanor, what *foolish* thing have you done?" he whispered. "Do you understand what would have happened to you had I not returned tonight?" He paused, then spoke louder in a mocking tone, looking towards the closed flap of the tent. "Are you quite *comfortable*, Your Majesty?"

Basaal pushed himself away from the chair and ran his fingers through his hair, again speaking just loud enough for her to hear. "Don't you understand they would have ridiculed you, hurt you—had their way with you?"

Eleanor's eyes met his.

"I'm afraid with my father's officers," he continued, "you will not be specially treated or protected, not without my express orders. Monarch or not, you are a woman, and that limits your rights under my father's reign."

She tried to give an angry answer, but the gag firmly held its place.

He looked at her a long while before leaning down towards her again, his lips close to her ear, the scent of cinnamon on his clothes. "Be very careful what you speak, Eleanor. Spies watch me and may hear anything above a whisper. We must be cautious if I am to help you escape."

Eleanor pulled away from his touch and tried to scream, her eyes burning as he dared pair them as allies. He had betrayed her, betrayed them all. Her scream was muffled, but still audible.

Basaal laughed, returning to Imirillian and a normal volume of speaking. "You didn't like that, did you? Well, you will," he said.

Eleanor's eyes widened at the insinuation.

"I will agree to remove your gag if you can converse civilly," he said, still loud enough to be heard by any curious eavesdroppers. "Yell or scream, and you will wish I'd ordered you dead. Do you hear me?" His words stung, even as his expression was apologetic as he came around behind her.

Eleanor glared at Prince Basaal over her shoulder, and he just laughed loudly, cutting the rope from around her arms, then unknotting her gag.

"You swine," Eleanor hissed while he was still close enough to hear her whisper. "How could I ever trust you again?"

Basaal studied her face. "Because I have this," he said quietly, holding up a small piece of paper. "And because I promise to you now that I will never lie to you again." He gave a slightly jaded smile, adding, "unless I'm playing a part."

She took the paper from his hand and stood. It was Aedon's writing, scribbled in Old Aemogen. "His release now in exchange for yours later—only option we had."

"Come," Basaal said as he took the note from her fingers and walked over to a candle, setting it on fire. "Enjoy yourself, Queen Eleanor. You're unbound. Make yourself comfortable."

Eleanor took a step back, feeling the fierce expression of a wounded animal on her face as she turned her eyes warily from his back to the rest of her surroundings. The tent felt more like a royal pavilion, and was certainly made for comfort. It was filled with furnishings of red and blue fabrics lined with gold. Tassels adorned an ornate sofa, piled with cushions, at the opposite end of the tent. Intricately patterned rugs created a makeshift floor. There was an elegant writing table, chairs, several large trunks studded and lined with precious metals and pearl, and more items of luxury set about than Eleanor had in Ainsley Castle—thus traveled the royalty of Imirillia.

The patterns that adorned nearly everything reminded Eleanor of both the mark on Wil's forearm—rather, this Prince Basaal's forearm—and his gift of a pendant that now hung about her neck. Eleanor focused her eyes on his face, and pressed her mouth into a line. He had been watching her as she'd taken in their surroundings, his face showing the dual expressions of impatience mixed with some strange concern.

"Do you approve?" he asked evenly, indicating the comforts of his travel with the slight flick of his wrist. A fierceness rose inside of Eleanor, and she clasped the chain around her neck, yanking hard. It snapped, and Eleanor threw the gold and ruby pendant at his feet.

"Yours, I believe," she said.

Basaal stared at her. When he finally reached down and picked up the pendent, he fingered it carefully.

"This gift was sincerely given," he said, his voice dropping to an intimate tone that, to Eleanor, sounded disingenuous.

"And it was sincerely returned," she replied.

As Basaal pocketed the pendant, his eyes narrowed. "What amazes me, Eleanor, is that you've not bothered to ask I explain myself. Even Aedon gave me that much consideration. Do you really think so little of me as to not wonder at any of this?"

"You, sir," Eleanor said, shaking, "do not stand on any kind of moral high ground. You deceived us for months and came to know my—*our* inner confidences, when you were really *leading* the army that would subjugate us. What more is there to know?" The prince looked at Eleanor with a trace of disdain, and she hated it.

"It was a gamble you were willing to take, in exchange for my services," he replied hotly. "Remember? You took advantage of me, as I did of you." He then regarded her with an impious expression. "There is no moral high ground for either of us to stand on."

"You're nothing but a snake," she said, throwing the words at his face. "And how, with the memory of Common Field, could I *ever* think otherwise?"

His face paled, his split lip pulling tight, and something in his eyes flared. "So be it, Eleanor."

A harsh voice called into the tent, requesting entrance.

"Wait a moment!" Basaal called back in terse reply. He then cursed, turning his glare on Eleanor. "The next few moments might get a little dicey. So, please," he motioned to the chair she'd been tied to all afternoon, "have a seat, and keep quiet." He folded his arms across his chest and leaned back against the long table. When he spoke again, the words were nearly unintelligible. "Let's see how well you can play act, Eleanor," he said. "Our lives could depend on it."

*The world moves and we with it; and I see now
what I did not before I was taken from my place,
and cast upon a stranger's shore.*

—The Third Scroll

Preview of Book Two of Imirillia

The Ruby Prince

CHAPTER

ONE

Eleanor watched as Prince Basaal of Imirillia steeled himself for the interview ahead. "The man who is about to enter this tent is my father's war leader," he said. "He's his own kind of devil, not to be dealt with lightly. I apologize in advance, but I do what I must to keep my head intact—and yours." The prince relaxed his face into a blank mask and called out, "Drakta!"

A man with bird-like eyes and a menacing look entered. Eleanor had seen him before. He was among those who had brought her back to the Imirillian camp. He had threatened her and had spoken low, degrading insults. She'd retaliated as best she could. Now, his very presence made Eleanor ill.

"The scouts are not yet returned from the mountain pass, Your Grace," he growled.

The prince gave a curt nod. "I heard your men almost enjoyed themselves with my queen," Basaal said, offering him a drink and maintaining a steady expression.

Drakta accepted the cup with narrowed eyes. "She's a bit wilder than you would imagine a woman of her kind would be," he answered Basaal gruffly, emptying the cup in one draught.

"Yes, so I gathered myself," Basaal said, rubbing his chin, and Drakta smirked at Eleanor.

Basaal sauntered over to a chair, next to where she sat, and slumped into it. "I want you to make sure," he explained, "that all the men know she is not to be—uh—*touched* in any way. She remains under my protection at all times."

Drakta looked suspiciously at the two of them.

"You see," Basaal continued, not looking in Eleanor's direction. "I intend to make her my first wife."

Eleanor jerked her head up. "What!" she demanded. She was on her feet in an instant.

"Oh—" Basaal looked at her with disinterest. "I forgot you're untied. Drakta? Will you do the honors?"

Drakta reached towards Eleanor, and she panicked, flinging her hands out, her nails catching him along the jaw. A thin line of red appeared. Grunting, Drakta grabbed Eleanor's arm and twisted it behind her. Eleanor's knees gave way under the pain of it.

Turning towards the prince, Drakta muttered something with a harsh laugh.

Basaal's response came evenly. "Yes, I know what I'm doing," He stood up and walked back to the refreshments table, lifting a few grapes in his fingers. "If you think she's beautiful," he said with an expression of pure greed, "wait until you see her country."

Eleanor, breathing hard, lifted her head and stared at Basaal. It was as if two separate people existed in his mind. Where Wil had felt like such a friend, this prince seemed a different creature entirely, someone who would never help her escape. Eleanor tried to pull away from Drakta's grip, but his fingers pushed into the skin of her arms before, with a smirk, he forced her again into the chair.

"I'm not a beast! Don't touch me!" she said as she flung herself against the back of the chair and kicked him as hard as she could.

Eleanor's head jerked to the side as Drakta hit her face, causing a wave of force she had never before experienced. She blinked, and the tears welled up. Opening her eyes, she could see black and gray with small lights moving about in strange patterns. The shadow of Drakta's fist fell across her face, but in two quick steps, Basaal had reached Drakta's side, grabbing his wrist and twisting it with such ferocity that the man dropped to the floor. Basaal was over him in an instant, pinning Drakta's neck down, a murderous expression in his eyes.

"I meant what I said, Drakta." The prince was breathing hard, his words so sharp that they seemed to slice the air. Drakta winced. "She is under *my* protection," Basaal continued. "And you are never to touch her again—ever. Not for any reason, or I'll see you hanged for it. Now, get out until the scouts return from the pass."

Basaal pulled Drakta roughly to his feet and sent him sprawling towards the tent door. Eleanor had never seen such fury as she saw now in Drakta's face when he looked back at Basaal before leaving. Seething, Basaal turned towards Eleanor, but he couldn't bring himself to lift his eyes to hers. His face was tight as he placed the gag in her mouth again. When he moved behind her, carefully binding her hands, he said, "I'm sorry." Eleanor couldn't tell if his voice was breaking from anger or some other emotion.

But to Eleanor, he did not sound sorry. The ringing in her head wouldn't stop. She wiped her nose against her shoulder, for both of Eleanor's eyes were still watering from the blow, and from the humiliation of the entire scene. Why would he think she could ever trust him again? she wondered. And why would Aedon ever ask her to? She felt nothing but disgust for this prince.

The anger Eleanor had felt when she had seen Common Field; the anger that she had felt when Marion had abandoned them; and the anger and hurt she had experienced when Basaal had revealed himself as a traitor—these had all converged, strong and fierce, with a rage like none she had ever experienced. It rose and surged and mounted within her, and she struggled and yelled through the gag.

Finally, after a wave of tears burned down her cheeks, Eleanor gave up struggling. Basaal retreated to the small writing table, covered in reports, sat down, and did not look at her.

He worked for over an hour, in silence, with Eleanor's glare burning into the top of his head. He only shifted his attention when shouts rang through the camp, followed by the sounds of horses.

"Don't make yourself a nuisance," Basaal said, gathering the papers before him as he spoke. "You don't want to catch the attention of these men." He sounded distant and annoyed, but his temper had abated, and the last look that he gave her, before the tent flap was pulled open, seemed to imply a form of encouragement. Eleanor glared at him in return.

A dozen men entered. They looked angry and restless; their war-set eyes, scathing. Eleanor's head was bowed, but her eyes were lifted up, challenging them. Only one, the young man who had ridden out to meet Eleanor on the battlefield, gave her any acknowledgment. He appeared almost apologetic. Eleanor looked away. Hate and anger she could combat, but not pity.

Basaal sat in the chair next to hers as his men formed a semicircle before him. "What is the report?" Basaal asked, quick and authoritative.

The handsome young man stepped forward. "The entire pass has collapsed in on itself. We won't know until the morning, but as of tonight, there appears to be no way in or out."

"How exactly did this happen?" Prince Basaal asked.

"They must have something, some formula, some explosive powerful enough to have brought the mountain down."

"Yes." Basaal was impatient. "You've successfully repeated yourself. How did they have time to bring down the mountain? Were we not marching into the pass?"

"We were," the young man continued. "And then they sent out a small company with a white flag. It was past their allotted time for surrendering," he explained. "So, we shot them down with arrows. Another company came and suffered the same fate."

Eleanor closed her eyes as he spoke, seeing the men—her men—falling under the Imirillian fire as they rode out to stall the army and give her more time. She saw again the sunlight glinting off their helmets, as they rode out to their deaths.

Eleanor remembered the moment when she had the realization, when the battlefield had been laid out before her like a chessboard and she had seen that if she rode out on Basaal's white horse in her white dress like Seraagh, alone, the Imirillians might be swayed, they might stall, and her men would have enough time to reset the damaged lines and bring down the mountain. She thought about how Hegleh had responded, running so fast Eleanor could barely breathe.

"And then she came riding straight at us—" the young man was saying, still telling his story. Eleanor shook herself out of her own thoughts and glanced at Basaal, who sat stone faced and cold. "—blazing white like Seraagh herself. We stopped, and I gave the command to not shoot. She called out, demanding to speak with you, the prince. So, I came forward in your place, and she asked if we could strike a deal: a surrender."

"And none of you questioned this at all?" Basaal asked.

"I thought we should have just killed her and continued our march," an older officer said, appraising Eleanor with disdain. "Annan, in your absence, decided otherwise."

Basaal stood and once again walked to his refreshments table. "I've heard enough for tonight," he said. "We won't know until daylight, regardless, if the mountain is truly impassable. Go. We will meet again come morning."

Drakta balked. "You are just going to leave off—"

"Enough!" the prince roared, and he turned to look at the older man. "I've had enough for one night. You are excused, General, and all your men." Basaal took a deep breath. "Annan, I will detain you a moment longer."

Drakta stalked out, followed by the other officers. Annan stood where he was until the tent had been emptied. When they were again alone, Basaal's face utterly transformed. He seemed tired, even defeated, and in front of Annan, he maintained no display of hierarchy.

"You did well, Annan," Basaal said. "I apologize for that."

"They are restless, Basaal, and disappointed," Annan explained. "I fear that you will have a dangerous group come morning."

"And what was said," Basaal asked, "when I did not come to lead the host across the plain?"

Eleanor watched as the young man, this Annan, shrugged. "At first, nothing was said," he explained. "They know it's not uncommon for your father to send his armies ahead under Drakta's command or to wait until they are in position before riding out himself. But later, when we returned and you were gone, there was talk. Our own spies spread several stories so that there are now too many questions to follow," he reported. "Drakta doesn't know what to make of it, but neither does he know in which direction to place any suspicion. Returning with your face all bruised and battered doesn't help but call attention to your absence, mind."

As Eleanor made a noise of agreement, it was Annan who made eye contact with her. "May I, Your Grace?" he said to her, stepping forward and removing her gag. He then untied the ropes that bound her in the chair. In another thoughtful gesture, he retrieved a cup of water and brought it to her. She thanked him and finished it before he'd even had time to say, "You are most welcome."

Basaal returned to his seat next to Eleanor's and fell into it. "This has been the longest day of my seven lives," he cursed in Imirillian.

Annan settled himself on the rug, reclining on one arm. "Did you know they were going to bring down the mountain, Basaal?" he asked the prince in a near whisper.

"I knew it was a possibility," Basaal responded just as quietly. He cursed again, then turned to Eleanor. "Of all the ridiculous schemes," he said. "You pulled a queen's gambit."

Eleanor was too tired to fight. She sat up straight, rubbing her temples with her hands, feeling the swelling of her cheek beneath her fingertips. "It was the only way to stop the Imirillian army— your army," she added bitterly.

"Yes," Basaal said, leaning forward. "My army, sent down, against my own will, to conquer you."

The trio sat in silence, listening to the movements of the men in the camp. Eleanor was beginning to fall asleep when the sound of Basaal's voice called her back.

"Annan, I must see the queen settled. Will you do what you can to temper Drakta and his scheming? Also, please have men stand watch around my tent—our men, mind you, not my father's."

Annan nodded and lifted himself up slowly before looking from Basaal to Eleanor.

"Sleep well tonight, My Prince," Annan said. "I will ensure your safety. But you must be as sharp as a scimitar come morning." He then bowed to Eleanor and retired from the tent.

Basaal did not move but continued to slump in his chair. Finally, Eleanor stood.

"Tell me where I may sleep," she said. "I am tired."

Getting up slowly, Basaal waved towards the low sofa at the far end of the pavilion. "There," he said. "I will sleep over here." He seemed almost startled when he looked at her again. "Oh, Eleanor, your face—" As if the friendship they'd built had remained intact, he tried to reach out, to touch her cheek, offering an apology, but Eleanor recoiled.

"Do not touch me," she said, lifting her eyes to his. "Ever again."

ACKNOWLEDGEMENTS

There have been so many of you who have given your time, encouragement, and insight. Thank you again for all the hours offered, especially to my beta readers. Each one of you has made a difference.

Thank you: Rose, for all the years of saying we would; Andrea, for being one of the first to wade through the mire; Z, for arguing with me at 1:00 A.M. over a cheap diner breakfast, and for throwing the manuscript across the room in tears; Rob & Jenesse, for running casting calls over Thai Curry; Uncle Brad, for being wise; Aaron, for finding Peter Pan; Angie, for telling me to go for it while we ate end-of-August ice cream.

Thank you to the team who helped get this book off the ground: Phil Jackson, for bringing the ink soul to my pencil maps. Here we are, all these years later, doing what we love. Allysha Unguren, for traversing the desert many, many times, and going to the aid of whomever needed you, whether in Aemogen or Imirillia, or some place in between. It is, after all, what you do. Julie Ogborn, for being such a brilliant finish editor, and having passionate conversations with me about the em dash. Kevin Cantrell, for being an absolute genius and taking the time. The covers are beautiful. Stephanie Winzeler, for the undertaking of bringing my dreams into the physical dimension. I hope you know what it means.

An especial thanks to ALL my siblings, both the natives and the brave souls who married into the tribe. With you lie many of my fiercest affections. Thank you, every one of you. You have been a tremendous support, and been willing to encourage me onward. I love you, and have always been proud to be in this clan.

Thank you, Mom and Dad, for being people of great faith. Mom, you taught me that individuals were complicated, worth seeing, and worth loving. Dad, your passion for words and family has been a polar star in my life. I love you both.

And Kip, I know what it is like to be across the ten thousand miles of the world from you, and I am so glad you are at my side. Thank you for all the evenings you came home and said, "Why don't you write?" I could not have a truer, more supportive husband.

photo by Aaron Thompson

ABOUT THE AUTHOR

Like many of my siblings, I would sneak out of bed, slip into the hallway, and pull my favorite books from the book closet. I read my way through the bottom shelf, then the next shelf up, and the shelf above that, until I could climb to the very top shelf—stacked two layers deep and two layers high—and read the titles of the classics. My desire to create stories grew as I was learning to read them.

Subsequently, I spent my time scribbling in notebooks rather than listening to math lectures at school.

I graduated with a degree in literary studies, and have spent several years working on the novels that keep pounding on the doors of my mind, as none of my characters are very patient to wait their turn. I currently live in Orem, Utah, with my wonderful chemist husband, and books in every room of the house.